# the Murderess of RIDGECLIFFE MANOR

*Donathon Devereaux Upp*

iUniverse, Inc.
Bloomington

# The Murderess of Ridgeclliff Manor

*Copyright © 2011 by Donathon Devereaux Upp*

*All rights reserved. No part of this book may be used or reproduced by any means, graphic, electronic, or mechanical, including photocopying, recording, taping or by any information storage retrieval system without the written permission of the publisher except in the case of brief quotations embodied in critical articles and reviews.*

*This is a work of fiction. All of the characters, names, incidents, organizations, and dialogue in this novel are either the products of the author's imagination or are used fictitiously.*

*iUniverse books may be ordered through booksellers or by contacting:*

*iUniverse*
*1663 Liberty Drive*
*Bloomington, IN 47403*
*www.iuniverse.com*
*1-800-Authors (1-800-288-4677)*

*Because of the dynamic nature of the Internet, any web addresses or links contained in this book may have changed since publication and may no longer be valid. The views expressed in this work are solely those of the author and do not necessarily reflect the views of the publisher, and the publisher hereby disclaims any responsibility for them.*

*Any people depicted in stock imagery provided by Thinkstock are models, and such images are being used for illustrative purposes only.*

*Certain stock imagery © Thinkstock.*

*ISBN: 978-1-4620-6820-3 (sc)*
*ISBN: 978-1-4620-6822-7 (e)*
*ISBN: 978-1-4620-6821-0 (dj)*

*Printed in the United States of America*

*iUniverse rev. date: 12/2/2011*

# Acknowledgements

I sincerely thank you for buying this book and reading it. I hope that you enjoy it as much as I did creating it. I want to give a special shout out to my cover model Michelle. You came in and pulled off exactly what I wanted. Thank you for your time and professionalism and helping to create the perfect cover! I do not think anyone else could have done it better. Thanks to my family and friends for your support and dedication to my work, you guys are a major player in my new career. To my readers… Love the book? Want more? Visit www.ridgecliffemanor.com and find out how you can visit Linda Edwards's mansion and live the book. Ridgecliffe Manor- the murder mystery mansion will open its doors in October 2012. Watch the website for details.

Enjoy,
Donathon

# Contents

| | |
|---|---|
| The Prologue | ix |
| Chapter 1 - The Introduction. | 1 |
| Chapter 2 - Murder in Kansas City | 13 |
| Chapter 3 - Hagan Cove Realty | 23 |
| Chapter 4 - The Closing. | 35 |
| Chapter 5 - Good bye Michael. | 49 |
| Chapter 6 - Welcome to Hagan Cove | 62 |
| Chapter 7 - Dean! | 74 |
| Chapter 8 - Nice to meet you Ray… | 84 |
| Chapter 9 - The battle begins. | 93 |
| Chapter 10 - Searching for answers. | 105 |
| Chapter 11- The first date. | 116 |
| Chapter 12 - Visiting a sick friend | 128 |
| Chapter 13- Dinner and drinks | 138 |
| Chapter 14 - An affair exposed | 151 |
| Chapter 15- The Mayor's dance | 162 |
| Chapter 16 - Paying the consequences. | 175 |
| Chapter 17 - Fighting fire with fire | 189 |
| Chapter 18 - Accusation's fly! | 198 |
| Chapter 19 - Tying up loose ends. | 207 |
| Chapter 20 - Survival of the fittest! | 216 |
| Chapter 21 - Facing the devil herself! | 229 |
| Chapter 22 - Cleaning up the council. | 240 |
| Chapter 23 - Caught in the act! | 251 |
| Chapter 24 - The new Mayor | 260 |
| Chapter 25 - A time to die. | 267 |
| Chapter 26 - Letting go | 280 |
| Chapter 27 - The homecoming. | 290 |
| Chapter 28 - Playing games. | 304 |
| Chapter 29 - Making plans… | 316 |

| | |
|---|---|
| Chapter 30 - Revenge! | 330 |
| Chapter 31 - The final battle. | 343 |
| Chapter 32 - Picking up the pieces. | 351 |
| The Epilogue | 358 |

# The Prologue

"You Idiot!" Samantha screamed at a car that just sped passed her, almost knocking her off the dark, deserted country road.

"He's probably thinking the same thing of you," Valerie scolded as she shook her head in disbelief at her friends' outburst. "If you would concentrate on driving instead of reading directions, maybe then, you could drive the speed limit and people like him wouldn't be passing us and then you wouldn't be so hostile and…"

"Valerie! If you would have read me the directions like I asked you to in the first place, then I wouldn't have to be reading the directions, and then assholes like him wouldn't be passing me, and I wouldn't be yelling at you right now!"

"Hey, it's not my fault that I can't read that chicken scratching that you white people call writing," Valerie said as she pretended that her feelings were hurt. "You wouldn't see a sister write with all those scribbles and loops and crap."

"Valerie," Samantha groaned.

"Hey, I'm just stating the facts," she said smugly. "I think that new shade of red you put on your hair has made you even moodier."

"This is my natural color!" Samantha laughed, pulling her long red hair behind her ear.

"Um hum and I'm a white girl addicted to tanning beds," Valerie shot back laughing as she turned towards the window, looking out into the night.

Samantha let out a chuckle as she tried to refocus on finding the road she needed to turn off on. One of the worst things about being a realtor was showing property at night, especially farmland out in the middle of nowhere. It always made her nervous and tense, but tonight it was worse than usual.

Horrific nightmares had been invading her sleep for about a week, which is one of the reasons she made Valerie, her coworker, come with her. She couldn't really remember a lot of details about the nightmares other than she would awake covered in sweat, shaking like a leaf. She cleared her throat in hopes that doing so would clear her mind as well. It didn't work. Valerie grabbed the paper, turning it to the dome light as she once again tried to read Samantha's scribbled directions.

"I for one would have never agreed to show an old farmhouse out in Snooterville in the middle of the night," Valerie suddenly added, rolling her eyes as she so often did when she became irritated. A look that Samantha had seen numerous times since the day she met her.

"If you're referring to that old television show, I think it was Hooterville," she corrected her. "And Mr. Carroll is a farmer and he had no other available time. He's harvesting all day."

"Samantha honey, how's he going to know what it looks like in the pitch dark?"

"He's already seen the property, tonight he wants to see the house," Samantha informed her as she slowed down, squinting her eyes, trying to read the street sign she was passing. "Valerie, turn off that light. I can't read the signs.

"Fine," she said, flipping the switch. "It sure would be nice if there were streetlights on country roads!"

"Well you know how us white folks are," she said sarcastically to her as she turned on her bright lights, looking for the name on the upcoming street sign. Just as she expected, it was the right road and of course she had passed it.

"You passed it," Valerie said, pointing back to the sign.

Fortunately, there was not another car around as she threw on the brakes, coming to a complete stop. She looked over at Valerie, giving her a 'shut up look' as she put the car into reverse and backed up. A strange screeching noise roared from the engine as it backed up, sending chills up their spine.

"Oh God, what now?" She grumbled to herself.
"What was that?" Valerie asked, concerned.
"It was nothing Valerie."
"Didn't sound like "nothing" to me!"

Car trouble would be the last thing she needed tonight! The car groaned a bit as it continued backing up before she put it in drive and started forward again down the dark road. The headlights dimmed a couple times before the car started running normally again. "We only have five more miles to go. Tomorrow she would take the car in and have it checked out," she thought in an attempt to unsuccessfully comfort herself.

"Samantha, look out!" Valerie screamed
"What?"
"That!" Valerie yelled, pointing.

Samantha turned back, looking out the windshield just in time to see a large deer standing in the middle of the road staring dead at them. She slammed on the brakes, swerving the car to miss the animal, aiming for the shoulder before she realized there was no shoulder on the old country road. She grabbed the wheel and steered it sharply to the left as the car began spinning out of control. Before she knew it, the car double flipped, landing on the side of the road in a pasture.

"Oh my God!" Samantha yelled out, catching her breath and pushing her hair out of her eyes.

"Are we dead?" Valerie asked as she did a mental inventory of her body parts to make sure everything was still intact.

"I don't think so," she replied as she reached for the door and pushed it open. What glass was left in the door fell out around her hand.

"I'm not sure, but I think my leg might be broken!" Valerie cried out as a stabbing pain ripped through her leg as she tried to get out of the car.

Samantha quickly went around to Valerie's side of the car. Her leg didn't look broken, but judging from the screams Valerie gave out as she tried to help her out, she was definitely injured. She reached over her and grabbed her purse, pulling out her cell phone and frantically began dialing for help.

"Damn it!" She yelled out, throwing it into the back seat. "No signal out here, it's dead!"

"Better it than us," Valerie groaned between the pains.

"I'm going to have to go get help," Samantha sighed nervously as she glanced around the darkness, looking for some sign of a house near by. "Are you going to be ok?"

"Go! Just hurry your ass back here; God only knows what's out there in the dark!"

"Thanks Val, that's exactly what I want to hear right before I start walking down a dark deserted country road! Alright, I hear a dog barking, so a house has to be close," Samantha said as she tried to get Valerie as comfortable as she could.

Samantha looked around once again into the darkness before climbing into the back seat and grabbing her cell phone. She checked it once again for a signal before she put it back in her purse, and started on her search for help. The full moon was giving off just enough light so that she could see where she was going, but dark thunder clouds would often cover it, swallowing up what little light was offered. Her high heels clanked on the concrete. Besides an aching head, her feet were going to be killing her tomorrow!

In the far distance she could see lights through a corn field. Relief come over her as she took a deep breath and exited off the road into the field, walking towards the light. On the way she replayed in her mind what had just happened and was amazed by just how calm she really was. The walk to the house seemed to take her forever, but finally the corn stalks cleared. It was too dark to really know where she was or even recognize the house, but it was obvious it was a very large farmhouse.

"Hello!" She called out as she climbed up onto the old porch, twisting the handle on the old doorbell. "Is anyone home?"

Much to her disappointment no one answered the bell and there were no sounds coming from inside the house. Samantha reached into her pocket and out of desperation, tried her cell phone one more time, hoping that just maybe it would work. It didn't.

"Damn it!" She cursed out as she took her fist and banged on the front door. "Hello! Is anyone home? I need help! Please!"

Samantha gave up and turned around, looking off the porch into the dark night. She searched the darkness for another house but saw nothing but flashes of lightning in the distance. She sighed as she turned back around and thought about trying the doorknob. If no one were home, they wouldn't know she was inside. After all, this was an emergency. She'd just use the phone and then get right out.

An eerie feeling of being watched crept over her as she looked to her right at the huge double windows. A piece of peeling paint was ripped off the wood trim by a sudden gust of wind and it rocked back and forth through the air before quietly settling on the rotten boards of the porch. A movement behind the filthy ancient glass caught her eye as the torn lace curtains moved aside as though someone had looked to see who was there, and then let them fall back into place.

"Hello?" Samantha called out, hoping someone was there. "Can you help me? I've had a car accident and my friend is badly injured! I need to use your phone."

Again there was no response other than the rolling thunder in the distance. She sighed, turned back to the front doors and reached for the knob, slowly turning it with her shaking hand. Partly to her relief the knob turned and the door unlatched. She slowly pushed it open, calling out again before she stepped into the hall. The interior of the foyer was barely lit, casting eerie shadows all around her. A sudden breeze blew in through the open doors and swirled through the crystal chandelier, causing it to rock slightly back and forth above her head. She quickly closed the door, shutting out the wind.

"Is anyone here?" She called out into the empty house, listening to her voice echo before her.

Quietly as her shoes would allow her, she moved farther into the foyer, a once magnificent showplace for greeting guests, now just a decayed reminder of what used to be. The massive ornate staircase staked its claim in front of her, running its way up the right side of the foyer to the second floor. At its base stood a massive newel post that held an ornate statue which consisted of a man holding a woman with one hand, and a large lamp with the other. The couple looked shaken, if not scared. She knew how they felt! She looked around the dark stale foyer for any sign of life, preferable human. Despite the decay, the foyer was actually quite beautiful. The walls were capped off with an ornate plaster crown molding that complemented the massive ceiling medallion that surrounded the chandelier. Had it been a different situation, she might have actually enjoyed visiting this place.

"Is anyone home?" She called out once again trying not to breathe in any more of the stale air than she had to.

Directly to her left were two huge ten foot walnut doors, a faint light spilled out from underneath them across the dirty hardwood floors. She took another deep breath, calling out again as she knocked. Again, getting no response, she reached for the doorknob. The doors burst open and slammed into the walls as if she had purposely thrown them open, shaking and cracking the old plaster, exposing a parlor. A large fireplace stood before her with a white marble mantle hanging around it, at each side stood two of the evilest looking lion statues she had ever seen. Their teeth exposed as if they were ready to run across the room and rip her apart at any minute. An unnatural looking fire burned and crackled, putting out a red glowing fog that pushed up and through the flames, covering the wood floor of the large barely furnished room.

"Something is not right about this," she said to herself. "H-e-l-l-o!"

Samantha nervously walked over to the fireplace, ignoring the lions stare and grabbed the fire poker, holding it tightly. She had an overwhelming feeling she needed something for protection. Old wallpaper from several decades ago, flapped loosely, dangling from the walls as a fierce breeze blew through the broken window pane to her left. Stepping quickly, she slipped through the room, trying not to make any noise, afraid of what might be lurking in the shadows.

Ornate woodwork framed the large doorway that led into the dark dining room, which suddenly lit up as she entered, exposing the decayed room with cracked plaster, dangling wallpaper and broken furniture. A rotting corpse of an animal lay spread on the table with rats ripping off its flesh and devouring it, pausing long enough to look at her with hungry eyes, before continuing their feast.

"Oh my God!" She practically screamed as she covered her mouth and nose from the horrible odor.

Samantha reached for the wall, using it as a guide to find her way out, not taking her eyes off the rats, making sure they did not come after her. As if reading her mind, the rats looked up again, staring her in the eyes, before jumping off the table, running towards her. She quickly took off, screaming out as she ran through the closest door, slamming it shut behind her. The plaster cracked and fell from the ceiling, hitting her in the head and then falling to the floor. The house seemed to groan and shift on its foundation as if it were ready to collapse at any given time.

"This was not a good idea!" She said through gritted teeth as she heard the rats hissing behind the closed door.

The room before her seemed to be yet another dining room, but not as elaborately as the other rooms she had passed through. She took a deep breath of stale air and carried forward through the dark room, trying to be careful and not trip over any of the broken furniture. Another doorway, another room.

There was an intense heat in the new room that as her eyes adjusted she realized was the kitchen. It seemed to eat through her skin and burn right into her soul, making the heat that they had endured all summer outside seem like winter in Alaska. A cabinet door fell loose from its hinges and came crashing to the floor as she passed, making her scream. She frantically searched around the room for a phone, digging through piles of trash and God only knew what until she found it! As she picked up the phone, something deep inside her told her she was wasting her time. With the condition of this house, there was no way the telephone was going to work! Much to her surprise, it did!

Samantha dialed 911, quickly giving the dispatcher all the information she knew to tell him. "Thank you God!" She said quietly, hanging up the phone as she began mentally preparing her plans for getting out of the house without being eaten alive by the rats in the other room, who had become suspiciously quiet! Rather than waste any more time trying to find another way out, she decided to exit the way she came in, at least she knew it was a definite way out! She took a deep breath as she prepared to run quickly from the room, but stopped when she thought she heard what appeared to be a faint cry for help.

"Hello?" She called out into the kitchen, looking around in the darkness.

The cry appeared to be coming from the other side of a closed door. Slowly she crossed the room and reached for the doorknob. The door was stuck tight, but with some work, it eventually pulled free. "This is stupid," she silently told herself over and over again. "I should just take off, get the hell out of here and tell the police when I get back to the car."

The now open door exposed a back hallway. The faint cry came again, it was coming from behind a closed door under a back stairway. It didn't take a genius to realize it was coming from the basement. Cursing to herself for being stupid, she opened the door exposing several rickety steps that led to a dark pit below. There was a definite cry for help this time and it was loud and clear! Samantha, with no other options, started her descent downward into the darkness, again reminding herself how stupid she was for going down there.

"Where are you?" She yelled out into the darkness.

Each step creaked loudly as she put her weight down on it; it was if the boards were crying out in pain from her touch. At the base of the stairs she reached around the wall for a light switch. With a click, a single light came on, giving a small amount of light in the large dungy old basement room.

"Help me please, somebody help me!" A male's pleading voice called out from the darkness.

"Where are you?" She asked again, clinching hard to the fire poker. "I can't see you! Hello!"

There was no answer, just a blood curling scream that sent chills up her spine. Something was wrong. It was the voice! It sounded so familiar! She quickly crossed the room to a closed door and tried to push it open, but it was sealed tightly. She could hear the cries on the other side as she pushed and tugged until the door came unlatched.

"Is anyone here?" She asked as the door opened, not really sure she wanted to know.

Samantha carefully stepped into the dark room, its only light came from the small doorway she was standing in. She was about to call out again only to be stopped by an explosion of blinding light that had suddenly swallowed her and the room. Her hands quickly flew up and covered her eyes from the piercing light, letting them slowly slide down as her eyes began to adjust.

The room before her was not just another basement room as she had expected it to be. She gazed around in shock as she stepped into the parlor from upstairs. It was not as she had left it, but had transformed completely into a beautifully redecorated room. The old decayed mess she had left was now replaced with what appeared to be expensive wall coverings and draperies. Antique inspired furniture filled the room, finished off by an enormous crystal chandelier dangling from the ceiling.

"What in the world? How did I get back here?" She asked herself as she glanced around the room, becoming extremely frustrated by the situation. "What happened to this place? What the hell is going on here?"

A huge painting of a woman now hung over the fireplace. She was insanely beautiful, with long blonde curly hair that cascaded over her naked shoulders. She was seated in a seductive Hollywood type pose, draped in a burgundy ball gown that barely covered a body that was decorated with large diamond jewels that hung elegantly from her ears and neck. The painting hypnotized her as it drew her eyes in to it, devouring her stare. Her trance was interrupted quickly by the voice of a woman and a man that seemed to be heading towards her. She looked around quickly for somewhere to hide, settling for behind the oversized drapes.

"You understand that I have to do this, right?" The woman could be heard saying as she entered the room, the man close behind her.

"Yeah, I know, I want you to," came that voice again, the one that sounded so familiar to her.

Samantha carefully pulled the curtain back a bit, trying to see who the guy was as her mind tried feverously to figure out the voice. The guy had knelt down on the floor and was gazing into the fireplace, his back facing her. The woman slid up behind him, kneeling slowly down on the floor, leaning her body against him. She began running her hands softly up his back to his neck and massaging it, moving her lips to his ear and giving him a gentle kiss.

"You have no idea how happy you're making me," the woman whispered excitedly into his ear, smiling as she kissed it again, biting the tip before letting go. He pulled his shirt collar back as she began running her manicured finger up and down his neck. "You're so handsome, so strong. You have so much life running through your veins; I can feel it as I touch you."

Samantha took a deep breath, deciding she had to get out of there! She was still clutching the fire poker as she tried to figure out a plan. How was she going to explain to these people why she was hiding in their living room? Exactly how she got into their living room she wasn't sure! She must have hit her head harder than she thought! She had gotten herself into some messes before, but this one was ranking up there. Something was very wrong here and she could feel it with every fiber of her body!

"You have no idea what it means to me that you came over tonight. What you're willing to do for me. There are not many men out there that would do it," the woman seductively said to the man as she slid around to face him in an almost snake like fashion, slightly smiling as she kissed him.

There was no doubt about it, Samantha could tell from this little scene that the woman totally controlled this man and that he would do anything she wanted. She watched as the woman slid her hands up over his broad chest and started unbuttoning his shirt, sliding it off him as he just sat there in some kind of bizarre trance. She started with kissing his lips before making her way down to his neck. The man moaned, bending his head back, closing his eyes. His profile was very familiar. If only the lighting was better, she might be able to recognize this guy! She felt very uncomfortable, the scene before her was beginning to get a little too steamy, almost pornographic. She decided she better get out now before things got any heavier and embarrassing!

"Excuse me," Samantha said, embarrassed as she looked at the two people. "I'm sorry to interrupt, but could you please help me?"

To her surprise neither of them even bothered to look up at her. The woman's hands just kept massaging up and down the man's back as she kissed on his neck like a vampire looking for that perfect vein.

"Excuse me," Samantha repeated as she moved closer into the room. "I had a car accident and needed a phone. I knocked, but you didn't answer and the door was open. I can't seem to find my way out of here. Hello, can you hear me?"

The closer she got to them the more she realized the woman was the same one as in the painting, but what held her attention was the man. Even though she could not see his face, just looking at the back of his head she could see that there was something familiar about him. The woman's kisses had begun to get more aggressive and passionate. A hungry evil look had come over her beautiful face as her eyes became demented and creature like.

Samantha decided to just get the hell out of there since they weren't even paying attention to her anyway. She turned towards the door, but to her surprise, found it had been shut. She reached for the knob and tried to pull it open, but it was sealed tightly. She pushed again, using all her strength and sighed. She wasn't going to be able to get it open by herself.

"Tonight, I'm going to make you feel things you have never felt before," the woman seductively said to him as she picked up his shirt and threw it into the fire. "Things you only imagined in your dreams."

"Excuse me," Samantha whispered again as she turned back around and faced them; once again becoming mesmerized by the scene going on before her. "I'm sorry to interrupt…"

The woman slowly moved her hand across his bare chest, she appeared to enjoy touching him as much as he was enjoying her touch. He let out another faint moan as her fingers slid through his hair and then down his back. She laughed as she threw back her head, forcing her golden curls to fall back out of her face, as she quickly moved down with her lips and covered his mouth, kissing him passionately. The kiss lasted a couple seconds before she began kissing down over his chin and then back to his lips. He opened his mouth and received her kisses as hungrily as she gave them. Samantha watched at his hands slid up over her slender body, trying to pull her even closer to him.

The kissing continued for what seemed like forever before the woman suddenly stopped, moved her mouth away from his for a brief second and then quickly shot back down. Her teeth clutched shut, breaking the skin of his lips, but the man never moved a muscle. He just knelt there silently and allowed her to do what ever she wanted. The blood dripped from her lips as she ran her tongue over them, savoring the taste as it slipped down her throat. Her lips went back to his, giving him another kiss before moving once again to his neck. His hands slid up her back, holding her tightly against him as she bit into his neck, ripping the skin open. She ran her tongue over her bloody lips as she pulled herself away from him. He tried to stop her from leaving but she broke loose.

"Not yet! We need to slow down a bit," she laughed.

"You people are really gross!" Samantha said in disgust as she watched the scene before her.

As the two continued on, Samantha didn't know what disturbed her most; what had just seen happen between these two, or the fact that she had stood there and watched it! For some unknown reason she couldn't pull herself away. Her eyes were glued to them.

"I think your ready," she said smiling as she reached in and kissed his bloody lips one more time, her hand on his chest. "I need your blood pumping hard through those veins of your beautiful body. I can feel how hard your heart's beating as I touch your chest. Do you want me?"

"Yes!" He whispered as he grabbed on to her, forcing her close. "I will do anything you want!"

"I hope so," she said seriously as she kissed him one last time before pulling free, reaching up to the mantle.

"Would one of you please help me get out of here? The door is stuck and I can't get it open! Then you two can get on with your little sex games," Samantha asked again. The scene these two were performing was starting to get to her.

It didn't matter what she did, they were obviously so engrossed in themselves that they weren't going to help her. They weren't even aware she was in the room with them! They had to be strung out on drugs or something. Especially the guy, he seemed to be under complete mind control of the woman. She couldn't wait anymore, she had to move in closer and get their attention if she was ever going to get out of here. Her mouth dropped open as the man turned around, glanced up at her then looked back at the fire. He had a blank eerie look in his eyes, but it was his familiar face that sent shock waves through her body, almost making her lose her balance. It was Brad!

"Brad!" She managed to whisper in horror. "What is going on here? What are you doing here with this woman?"

Brad had worked with her in the real estate office for a few years and with Valerie, had become one of her best friends. She knew he had messed around with some strange women since she had known him, but she didn't know he was into this kind of stuff! The female figure laughed as she moved away from the mantle, bringing her hand into view, exposing a very large knife. The laugh had now turned into a sadistic smile that crossed over her face. Brad glanced over at the knife and then back at the fire as though he could care less what she did.

"Brad!" Samantha screamed at him, but he didn't seem to hear her. "Get up! She's got a knife! Brad! Are you deaf?"

Brad sat motionless, looking into the fire, waiting patiently for the woman's attack. Samantha rushed towards him to push him out of the way only to pass completely through him and fall forcibly into the piano. Her attempt to save him went unnoticed by both Brad and the woman as she knelt down beside him, her free hand held his back as the knife in her other slid across his neck. A faint sound came out of his mouth and then he fell back, her hand gently lowering him to the floor.

"Brad!" Samantha cried out in disbelief as his green eyes lay wide open, staring at her, no life left in them. "Oh Brad, no!"

The woman started a laugh that began quietly then grew louder until it echoed throughout the large room as she moved away from his body. She placed the bloody knife to her lips and started to lick it, glancing directly over at Samantha. Her eyes had become a piercing red as she glared at her with pure hate, making the hairs on the back of her neck stand straight up.

"Who are you?" Samantha managed to whisper shaking as she pulled herself free from the woman's stare and started standing herself up against the wall, trying to comprehend the scene that had just played out before her. "Why did you do this? Why Brad?"

"Because I wanted him," the woman said motionless. She took her finger and ran it around the knife one last time before placing it to her lips and letting the knife fall to the floor. "And I always get what I want."

"This isn't happening! Brad!" Samantha yelled as she pulled free from the wall, rushing his body, this time managing to pull him into her lap. She held on to him in shock as she looked over at the woman, who had stepped into the shadows. "Why? Why did you do this?"

"Trust me, what he just experienced was the best thing that ever happened to him," the woman laughed as she wiped a blood droplet from her mouth. "Who should we do next? I'm still thirsty."

"You will never get away with this! I'll make sure of that!" She shouted at her, shaking him, trying to get some kind of reaction from his lifeless body.

"You can't save your friends, and you definitely won't be able to save yourself," the woman spoke angrily. "I'm coming soon and I can already tell that you and I, we're going to be the best of friends."

"What?" Samantha asked confused by her words, her brain still adjusting to the horrific scene she had just witnessed.

Darkness suddenly exploded around the room as it began shaking violently, tossing Samantha around the room. The woman suddenly appeared before her, grabbing her by the face and staring deep into her eyes, "See you soon!" She laughed as she let loose of her and disappeared in a burst of dust. Her laughter continued behind her as her voice shook the unstable walls. Boards from the house fell on her, ripping her flesh, blood spilling from her wounds began to run between the cracks in the floor, swallowed by the house.

The house continued to shake as the windows exploded, covering her with fragments of glass and wood. Samantha ducked her head to the floor and covered it with her arms as her surroundings grew chillingly quiet. Darkness devoured her and drew her away from the room and out of that horrible house, known to all as Ridgecliffe Manor!

## Chapter 1 - The Introduction.

The dream had seemed so real last night that Samantha woke panicked and drenched in sweat. Each night for the past week she had this dream and each one was becoming more vivid than the one before. Last night was the first time the mysterious woman had been involved in it. Each dream would reveal a little more to her as if it was trying to tell her, or worse, warn her of something that was about to happen. Why was all this happening now? The answer she did not know. She had never considered herself to be able to predict the future and was not so sure that anyone else could either. But why were these visions getting so elaborate, and why were Brad and Valerie now involved? They had really started to take a toll on her daily life. Since they had begun she had been moody, edgy, and quick to start an argument, which was way out of character for her.

"This has to stop!" She said out loud as she covered her head in her hands.

One thing was for sure, her dreams had something to do with Ridgecliffe Manor, the house she was about to show to a perspective buyer. Out of the three agents that worked in the real estate office, she had to be the one to answer the phone, that dreadful stormy day. Ordinarily she would have loved to show property in this price range, but not this time, and definitely not this house.

Casually she picked up the file and opened it. The photos of the old civil war mansion lie stapled on top of the listing along with some of the historic information. Shivers ran down her spine as she looked at the bare windows. Even the picture managed to bring out the appearance that an evil force hid behind its bricks. Why anyone would want to live there, she could not imagine. The three-story mansion sat back off the main highway about a quarter mile on an old gravel road on seven acres and had been named after the family that had originally built it. When the last living descendant moved into a retirement condo, it was placed with her agency to sell. Normally properties in this price range would go to a Boonville realtor instead of Hagan Cove realtor, especially since the mansion was closer to Boonville. Unfortunately for her, the owner of the office was friends with the family. Two long years it sat there without a single call, no one even asked about it until the agency advertised it nationally. Then one day out of the blue a call came in.

Closing the file, she grabbed her purse and keys in preparation to leave the office. It was now time to do the one thing that she dreaded the most and that was to enter the place she had been dreaming about. She hated to meet the clients at the property. Things just seemed to go smoother if they met at the office, that way she had a chance to talk to them, find out what their interests were and if they were right for that particular house. At the same time, she could spot someone who was just there to gawk and be entertained on a boring day. Unfortunately, this happened quite often, especially with large historic mansions. But not Ridgecliffe Manor. No one had wanted to see it, until now. That place had been the root of her nightmares, and now she would have to face it head on.

The drive was beautiful and scenic on the clear early October afternoon. The leaves were just starting to change, bringing the countryside to life with extreme color. Any other day she would have enjoyed the ride, but today was different. The towering roof was beginning to become visible over the tops of the trees, as if warning her of its presence. In just a matter of minutes she would be in its path. Two large stone pillars with old rust covered iron lanterns greeted her at the entrance of the circular drive. Ivy vines had long since taken over them, their colorful fall leaves distracting the pillar's severity.

"Glad I didn't drive my car!" She said to herself as she headed up the drive, listening to the branches from the overgrown brush sweeping along the side of the company car.

The car came to a quiet stop in front of the mansion. It stood before her tall and strong despite its decay. It appeared to be glaring out at her, just daring her to enter its domain. A slight shiver ran through her body, making her tense up. Without thinking, she reached over and locked the door.

Ridgecliffe Manor had at one time been a pillar in the county's history. During the Civil War, the union troops even raided it and tried to burn it down, but it withstood their fury. Now it stood here before her in all its evil glory waiting for her. The beaming sunlight burst off the filthy windows that sat back in the brick structure, the shutters beside them barely hanging on their hinges. Others had already taken the plunge and landed in their final resting place in the ground below. The iron rails along the roof, all rusted and loose, scraped against each other in the gust of wind that suddenly whipped around the house.

Samantha shivered again as she forced herself to get out of the car and started to straighten her skirt; she hoped it was not too short. Since she was only five foot five, she had heard that showing more leg made you look taller, therefore making it appropriate, but now she was not so sure. Glancing around the property, she saw the matching carriage house and guest house. The buildings like the main house were in bad shape. She could not imagine why anyone would need a guesthouse when the main house had over fifteen rooms, especially since those rooms added up to twelve thousand square feet!

"Come on lady, hurry up!" She said under her breath as she looked at her watch. "I'm not hanging around here all day! This is just a waste of time! There's no way you're going to buy this mess!"

"Bulldozers were the best solution for this dump," she thought out loud with a smile. The problem with tearing it down was that the property had limited use. It was built with the Missouri River sitting directly in front of it and had the grounds flooded several times in the hundred and fifty years it had been standing. A loud crash exploded through the quiet fall day, causing her to jump back against the car as if it could protect her. Dust settled around the remains of the old barn that had just collapsed in the field beside the carriage house. Samantha laughed with relief, trying to slow her rapid heartbeat. Again she straightened her dress as she smoothed her slightly curled red hair.

A roaring engine soared up the drive announcing that her appointment had finally arrived. The bright cherry red sports car came to a screeching halt, throwing up a dusty path from the gravel drive behind it. The car door opened and a meticulously dressed woman stepped out. She was dressed elegantly in a white skirt and silk blouse, which perfectly matched her high heel shoes and purse. She had a diamond and pearl necklace draped around her neck and a massive diamond wedding band that could not be missed on her finger. The woman's long curly blonde hair fell perfectly into place as she ran her long fingernails through it before removing her sunglasses.

Something about this woman was very familiar, but Samantha could not figure out how she could have possibly known her. "This woman would be impossible to forget. Anyone that looked like that had to be made of plastic and silicone, was probably brain dead, spoke with a squeaky voice and most importantly would not be interested in buying a dump like this. Today was obviously going to be a complete waste of her time, she might as well go back to the office," she thought to herself.

"Sorry I'm late, but it's your own fault. Your directions were terrible," the woman said as she walked past her, stopping long enough to give her a disapproving look, then moved closer to the house. She stopped and stared up at it as though it were a priceless gem as Samantha continued looking at her in disbelief.

"My directions were to take the 103 mile marker and turn left, cross the Boonville Bridge and turn right at the first gravel road." Samantha quickly stated, irritated by the tone of her voice. "How could those simple directions be terrible?"

"You forgot to tell me that there were silos and from what I can tell a sand plant at the entrance of the gravel road. Your listing said this place was secluded," The woman growled as she looked around. "I drove three miles out of my way."

"The sand plant has been there for years. As you can see the house is far enough away from them and with all these huge trees you won't even know they're there. You are in a secluded location, therefore the listing is correct." Samantha quickly corrected.

The woman suddenly broke her trance with the house and began walking to the porch. She managed to put off an aura that made all other women in her presence feel inferior to her, even if she wasn't trying to, though she knew with her, it was intentional. "I may not be the most gorgeous woman in the world," Samantha thought to herself, "but I could definitely compete with her!" she gently ran her fingers through her flaming red hair like the other woman had done. The last thing she needed with everything going on was this flake coming here to her town and trying to make her feel like yesterday's news. Somewhere on that body there had to be a scar or zit, she was sure.

"Mrs. Edwards, I presume?" Samantha asked in her best professional voice. This woman was not going to get to her; she would not allow it. She would just give her a dose of her own medicine, even if it did cost her a sell. "My name is Samantha Marshall… I talked to your secretary on the phone."

The woman completely ignored her as she walked up the steps to the front porch. Furious, Samantha rushed up behind her, passing her as she grabbed the door handle and reached for the keys, which she dropped. Her hands started shaking as she looked at the door that brought back all the evil memories of last night. Gathering her strength and the keys, she unlocked the double doors and swung them open. No loud creek as she expected just dead silence and a foul stench that hovered in the air as they entered the foyer.

"I'm Samantha Marshall," she repeated, this time forcing her business card into the woman's manicured hand. She would not ignore her, she would see to that.

"Thank you," the woman said coldly, letting the card drop from her hand and fall to the floor. "If you don't mind, I would like to skip talking about the weather and all the other informalities and just see the house that I drove all this way to see."

"Did she drive a car or fly in on a broom?" Samantha thought to herself as she followed her into the room. In the six years she had been an agent she had never met someone so rude. This woman wasn't brain dead; she was a total bitch! She choked in some stale air and continued on with her sales presentation.

Linda Edwards was obviously ignoring her as she walked around the room, stopping long enough to run her finger gently over the lamp at the base of the steps. She thought she saw the statue of the couple shiver at the woman's touch, if that was possible. The thought sent an icy chill down the back of her neck.

"The mansion has fourteen fireplaces," Samantha began. "Nine of which have Italian marble fronts. You will need them for heat during the winter months, there are two furnaces for the first floor, but they won't heat the second and third floors. I'm sure you're used to that since you currently live in Kansas City. Our weather patterns are pretty much the same."

"Good," Linda said, not paying too much attention to what Samantha was saying as she glanced around the room. "I always loved the winter."

"You're cold blooded?" Samantha asked, not thinking about what just slipped out.

"Cold natured," she corrected sarcastically, giving her an evil look.

"Oh, yeah, sorry, I would definitely get those flues cleaned out," she continued as she watched the woman run her fingers over the mantle. Something about her and that mantle gave Samantha an eerie feeling. "The hand-carved woodwork is beautifully detailed through out the whole house. A good cleaning and I'm sure that it could all be salvaged. Despite the looks of the place, there is no sign of termites or other wood eating bugs."

"Excuse me," Linda interrupted, turning around. "Would you please spare me your little grade school sales pitch? I would greatly appreciate it. I have a busting headache and I just want to see the house, not listen to you ramble on and on."

"I am sorry," Samantha said in a state of shock. "I just assumed you would like some information about the house."

"Well you assumed wrong. I received all the paper work and I have thoroughly gone over it. Besides I know how you people operate," she snarled. "You will say anything to sell a house. Especially when you're dealing with a property like this."

"I think that you seem to take the actions of a very few unprofessional people in the real estate field and believe we're all like that," Samantha said in her defense. "I assure you, everyone that works in our office applies a very strict code of ethics."

'Right," Linda said as she pushed one of the torn drapes aside and looked out the window.

"If you like, you can ask for the drapes in the contract," Samantha said jokingly.

"Is everyone in your agency like you?" Linda asked as she let go of the drapes.

Samantha snickered at her remark but decided it best not to give her the answer that popped up in her head. Sometimes it was better to just remain quiet! Deep down inside it was killing her though. "If you're uncomfortable with our agency, maybe you would like try another one? I can get you a phone book."

"It's not the agency I'm unsure of, it's the agent," Linda said as she left the window and walked off into the dining room.

"I beg your pardon," Samantha said, shocked by the woman's accusation. "You don't even know me, how could you make a statement like that?"

"I don't trust women in general, especially hillbillies, nothing personal," she replied as she continued walking ahead. "Never have, never will."

"Well, I take it personally," Samantha said, trying to stay professional. "And I don't consider myself or anyone in this town a hillbilly."

This woman could not be serious! You don't just come into a town where you don't know a single a person and start insulting everyone! Samantha tried hard to calm down. Despite her clients rudeness she would stay professional and not sink to her level.

"I'm sorry," she replied. "What is the politically correct term you guys use today? Hick?"

"Then why, if you don't trust us, did you set up this appointment with me today?" She asked, dying to hear the woman's reply. "Or even with anyone in this area, after all we are all hillbillies, excuse me hicks in this area."

"Because it was you that unfortunately answered the phone when I called, and it's here again unfortunately where this house is!" She told her, opening the glass doors of the old china hutch that had been left in the house by the previous owner.

"Alright," Samantha said, clearing her throat and trying to hold in her temper. "I'm sorry you feel that way. Maybe you should strongly reconsider your move to our area."

"I can really feel your sympathy and it's overwhelming. Why don't you trot along outside and do some grazing and I'll catch up with you when I'm finished looking at the house. How does that sound?" She asked her as she shut the cabinet doors.

Samantha's mouth dropped open but nothing came out. She could not believe what she had just heard. She watched as the woman glanced around the room one more time before she walked on through into the other room, quickly shutting the door behind her leaving Samantha alone.

"I bet you're very popular back in Kansas City!" She said as she reached out and opened the door and followed her into the next room. Linda Edwards looked up, gave her a disapproving look, and went back to investigating the kitchen.

"This is called a kitchen," Samantha said sarcastically. "Those of us, who live in the real world, would use it to cook in, but for you, it would be a place for your maids to prepare your meals."

"Very funny," Linda said, looking in one of the cabinets she had just opened. "I live in the real world, and I wasn't always rich. I do know how to cook."

"Married into it huh?" Samantha slipped.

"I earned it!"

"What exactly is it that you do Mrs. Edwards, if you don't mind my asking."

"Yes I do mind," she replied over her shoulder as she walked into the back hall. "I hardly feel that we're at a social level to be discussing my personal life."

"Are you embarrassed by what you do?" Samantha asked.

"No, I'm not, frankly it's just none of your business," Linda said through gritted teeth and left the room.

"Probably a high dollar hooker; you sure dress like one," Samantha said under her breath before following her out of the room.

Chills ran through her body as she walked into the dark back hall. The stench of an old decaying house filled her lungs, almost choking her. She hated this house, and that woman! She had to try and pull it together and finish this up and get out of here as soon as possible.

"I thought I asked you for some privacy," Linda said, turning around angrily and staring at her.

"No, you told me to go outside and graze, but I ate before I got here thank you,"

"What was your name again?"

"Samantha. Samantha Marshall," she replied as she handed her another card. This time the woman took it and slipped it into her purse.

"I will be talking to your broker."

"I'll warn him," Samantha shot back as she followed her down the hall. "As you can see here is another set of steps that the servants used back when the original family lived here. This is the only staircase that goes from the basement to the third floor."

"Would you please go outside and give me a moment to look things over privately?" Linda asked angrily.

"I'm sorry, but it is company policy to not leave a potential buyer in a customer's property unattended," Samantha said as she continued to follow the woman.

"What on earth could I possibly take from this place?" She demanded.

"True," Samantha agreed, looking around, wanting to get out of the house anyway. "Alright, I'll wait on the front porch."

"Thank you!" She said, then turned and went on into the other side of the house.

An astonished chuckle slipped from Samantha's lips as she walked back through the house and out through the front doors to the fresh fall air. A definite improvement from what was inside. Secretly she hoped the woman would fall through a floor somewhere and break a fingernail. It was a pleasant thought as she crossed the porch and sat on an old porch chair.

"I didn't want to go through this dump anyway," she mumbled to herself as she started to swing her leg. "That bitch! Go outside and graze! I hate people like her!"

Within minutes of sitting down Samantha heard a creak, then a loud crash, and then her and the chair fell to the floor. After the initial shock, the incident caused her to laugh like she had not laughed in years. All her frustrations instantly slipped away for a brief moment.

"Thank God no one saw that!" Samantha said as she continued to laugh, picked herself up, wiping the dust off her dress. What a day this had been!

"I do hope you know I plan to deduct this mess from your

commission check," Linda demanded as she stepped from the house and gently closed the front doors. She was obviously not amused.

"You mean you want this dump? This house?" Samantha corrected quickly, shocked as she walked through the rubble from the broken chair. "There is no way you could have gone through the entire place in the short amount of time you were in there."

"I don't need to see any more. What I saw was enough. I want you to draw up the papers and have them ready by the twenty-first. I might add that I do not want any delays. So do your job and make sure that there are none. Are you capable of understanding this or do you want to write it down?" Linda asked as she reached into her designer purse and pulled out a check. "Here's my deposit, the remainder will be received at closing."

"I'll need for you to sign the papers, so we can present the owner with a contract," Samantha interrupted as she took the check from her. "If you want to come to the office I could have them ready in about ten minutes."

"I don't have ten minutes. Fax them to me and I'll sign them. My contractors will be getting in touch with you soon. I highly recommend that you cooperate and see to it that they get all the information they need. And make sure you get all this information right. Trust me; you do not want to see me angry! Now clean up this mess," she said as she proceeded down the porch steps and out to her car without waiting for a reply.

"What a witch!" Samantha said a little too loud as she watched her walk away.

"You're lucky I'm not a witch or I'd beat you with my broomstick!" Linda said, smiling over her shoulder and walked on. "Now clean up that mess!"

"I take that back. What a bitch!" She said under her breath.

"What a dim wit!" Linda said as she walked off to her car. "I thought people that dumb only existed in the movies."

Samantha looked at the hundred thousand dollar bank draft as she kicked at a small board from the wreckage. It felt incredible to hold that much money in her hands. She glanced up as Linda Edwards took one last look around, put on her sunglasses, started the engine and roared off down the drive.

"You and your new owner belong together," she said as she locked the front doors. Why she did this she did not know. Nobody around here would set foot on the grounds, let alone go into the house.

Deep inside the house she thought she heard a growl, instantly reminding her that she was here alone. Quickly she stepped off the porch and rushed to her car. Something bad was going to happen, she could feel it, and she had been warned by the nightmares. That was it! The nightmares! A sick feeling rushed through her body as she became dizzy and leaned on the car for support. Linda Edwards was the woman from the dream, that's why she looked so familiar! She was the one that murdered her friend! And now she was really coming to town, and she had just sold her the house!

A loose pane of glass fell from one of the third story windows. Was it just her imagination or was someone standing in the newly formed hole? Was someone looking at her? Not waiting to find out, she grabbed her keys from her purse, jumped in the car, and left Ridgecliffe Manor, telling herself she would never return no matter what happened. Releasing her breath, she turned off the road onto the highway and started the short journey home. The afternoon sun burst through the slight cloud cover, lighting it with beautiful shades of orange and red. The mansion was nowhere in sight.

Tears uncontrollably filled her eyes. This was just the beginning. The beginning of something very bad. She had a feeling deep inside her that nothing in this small town would ever be the same again. Like it or not, Linda Edwards was coming to town.

The tension that was building inside broke loose and she sighed with relief as she passed into the city limits of Hagan Cove. She pulled the car over to the side of the road, rolled down the window, and stuck her head out for some fresh air. She looked back down the road toward the mansion. A terrible sick feeling started building inside her. She could feel it closing in on her, capturing her and squeezing her life away. Samantha quickly pulled her head back into the car, rolled up the window and sped off down the road.

The nightmare was coming true and she was to blame for it. Now everyone she knew, especially Brad, was in great danger. She turned into the real estate office parking lot and tried to pull herself together. She did not know why she had these feelings about that woman, but something deep inside her told her that she was dangerous, and now thanks to her, she was moving here!

# Chapter 2 - Murder in Kansas City

"But why do you want to move so far away; come on Linda, it's practically the other side of the world," Michael asked as he admired the fine curves of his boss's body, showing very nicely under her tight charcoal business suit.

Michael Williams had come on board three years ago when the company was really struggling. He had a vast knowledge of computer software and had definitely earned his fast rise to the executive office. He was a handsome man and an easy puppet for her to control, completely dedicated and would do anything she requested, except leave her alone!

Linda glanced up at him as he sat on the sofa in her office, making himself quite comfortable. She should have never let him get this close; it was becoming more apparent each day. He was entirely too dependent on her and she was really tiring of his love struck puppy routine.

"Helen," Linda ordered into the phone, trying to ignore Michael as she waited for her faithful secretary to answer. "Four things I need you to take care of right away. First, I want you to call Steve Willis down at the police department. Tell him that officer Myers has been following me since I returned and I want him taken care of! Second, I need you to call the broker at Hagan Cove Realty Co. and tell him I don't like the agent I'm working with. I want him to put another one on my deal, preferably a man."

"That doesn't surprise me," Michael said under his breath, smiling at her.

Linda looked over at him and gave him a deadly look. She couldn't understand what he said, but his lips moved so she knew it was something sarcastic! "Then I need you to call the car dealership down there and tell them I definitely want the car, have it gassed and ready for the twenty-first, oh and would you mail them a check please. Last thing, I need for you to get a hold of those contractors you told me about, you know the ones your parents used on their house after that storm destroyed it, I'd like for them to start figuring the cost to remodel the house."

"Is that all?" Michael snickered.

Not waiting for her reply Linda hung up. "What did you say?"

"I just don't understand why you want to up and move so far away from everything, like work... me," he repeated with a sly grin as he played with his tie, not mentioning his last comment.

"I just desperately need change right now, God knows I deserve it. This is the time in my life where I need to put the past behind me and move forward. Don't you think I know all these idiots around here are talking about me? My unfaithful husband and that slut are off somewhere doing God only knows what, leaving me here to take the heat of their gossip!" Linda said as her voice drifted off. "They made me look like a complete fool! I'm a laughing stock around here. It's just more than I want to put up with,"

"But still, it's just so far away. What city was it, Witches Cove?" He asked as he got up from the sofa and sat on top of her desk. The view down the opening of her silk blouse was a very welcoming sight. "God, you are beautiful."

"Hagan Cove," she corrected, ignoring his last remark. "Do you mind not sitting on my desk? Move it Michael!"

"What ever, it hardly sounds like a place for people like us to live. Drive through ok, visit maybe, but not live there. Those people will devour you. Trust me; you will never fit in there in all that polyester and flannel. You think people are talking about you now; you just wait until you move there. Oh and I might add, you'll never get a date," he said, grabbing a mint from her candy dish and popping it into his mouth as he strolled over to the windows.

"What are you talking about now?" Linda asked irritated, coming to the conclusion he obviously wasn't going to leave.

"There is a lot of inbreeding down there. That means they only date people that they can pick up at the family reunion," he said quite seriously.

"I know what it means!" She interrupted angrily. "I just can't believe that you just said that! That is just as bad as saying that people in California think we have cattle and tumble weeds rolling down the streets of Kansas City."

"I read it in some paper somewhere. It's supposed to be a real epidemic. I didn't write it, so don't get pissed off at me,"

Michael loved it when his boss got angry, that was when she was at her best, and she showed no mercy. It didn't matter who you were! Her beautiful blue eyes would slant, turning cold as steel; her body would tense, than look out, hurricane Linda was about to hit shore. She was the most vicious woman he knew; no one on earth was a match for her when she was angry.

"You know, I hate to admit it, but you may be partially right. This dumb ass agent they sent me, Samantha something, I don't remember. Couldn't sell a house if her life depended on it," she laughed, remembering her visit with the realtor. "Actually she was quite funny, not much taller than five foot. She had on these real high heel shoes; probably set her back a whole ten dollars. And this little mini dress. I think she actually thought it would make her look taller. Typical hillbilly, excuse me, hick, as she prefers. Anyway, she had kind of a funny accent. Not like the other people I met while I was there. I doubt it was real. Probably uses it to pick up men at the cattle auction."

"See, you have not even moved yet, and you're already bitching about the people," he commented.

"She is just one person in a town of many. Trust me I can handle her. Besides, the town is beautiful. It actually is right on the Missouri River, just like a cove, guess that's where the name came from, I don't know. Anyway it has all these great old fashioned buildings in their downtown built around a large park. The streets are lined with big trees and lots of flowers. It's just perfect, right out of a movie," she added, the hostility from earlier slipping away.

"Still, if you want my advice,"

"That's just it Michael, I don't want it. Look, as a Vice President, you're the greatest and I really do appreciate you and I depend on you, but you are hardly the person to be giving me any kind of personal advice," Linda said, really wishing once again he would leave.

"Fine, go ahead and cut me down to size, don't appreciate that I love you and care what happens to you, but Linda, don't sell the company! With your husband gone and his family screaming foul play and freezing all your assets, you are going to need the money," he pleaded. "Let's face it you know how to spend some serious money!"

"Only Rick's assets are frozen, not the ones we share together. And I might add, with the money I'm making by selling this place, I'll never have to worry about money again. Personally I don't understand you, from the water cooler gossip I've heard; the new owners offered you my job. I thought you would already have the decorators in here ready to go," she joked, glancing down at her watch. "I guess I better get ready for that meeting with those guys from Houston. They are here right?"

Michael didn't answer, just nodded his head as she opened her drawer and pulled out her cosmetic case and started touching up her makeup. It was amazing that she could make something so simple and ordinary seem so erotic. She was the most beautiful woman he had ever seen and the most ruthless too. Linda knew that she looked good, and she wasn't afraid to use it to get what she wanted. Her looks were a weapon. He knew of no man that could resist her. Women hated her as passionately as the men wanted her. No one ever told her no, especially her husband Rick. That poor bastard never knew what he was in for the day Linda Edwards set her eyes on him.

Hagan Cove was not the place for her. There would be no challenges, nothing for her to do, she would bore of those backwoods hillbillies and want to come back, but there would be nothing to return to. He had to stop the sale, even if he had to stay Vice President for the rest of his life; at least he would be with her. Keeping her here was much more important than any job.

"Michael!" Linda yelled, interrupting his thoughts. "You're staring at me is really getting on my nerves, isn't there something else you could do. I don't know, maybe empty the trash, just do something. Earn all that money I pay you."

"Alright, I'm going, just rethink selling the company, moving away, and about us," he said as he opened the office door and walked out, smiling at her as he closed the door.

"There is no us," Linda said into the empty room. Thank God in just a few weeks she would be rid of him and this stupid company.

"Excuse me, Mrs. Edwards," Helen said as she entered the office with the day's mail. "Here are the faxes from the real estate deal in Hagan Cove that you were expecting. I have fresh coffee in the conference room for you. The gentlemen have already arrived and are setting up."

"Thank you," she said as she took the papers, quickly looking them over for an error. "Did you take care of all those calls?"

"Yes, I did. The carpenter is going down to look the place over on Tuesday. He said he would call and set up an appointment with you when he returned," she said as she watched her boss read and sign the contract.

"Excellent," she said as she handed her the papers, looking up at her. "You can send these back. What about the others?

"I left a message for Captain Willis to call you; he was out of the office. The dealership said no problem and I talked with the broker from the real estate office and said he would personally attend all other meetings between you and the agent from now on. Is there anything else?"

"Nope, I think that covers it. Thanks," Linda said as she watched the secretary leave, shutting the door and finally leaving her alone to collect her thoughts.

Everything was now right on track. Once the sale of the company went through she would pack her bags and start her new life at Ridgecliffe Manor. A whole new world was opening up for her and she planned to embrace it with everything she had. Michael was wrong! She would be able to fit in down there perfectly; she would make sure of that. Helen called her to let her know her conference meeting was ready to begin.

"Yes, I think Hagan Cove will be perfect for me," Linda said to herself as she walked out of the office.

Much to her pleasure the rest of the day went by quickly for Linda as she worked at getting things ready for the sale of the company. The paperwork was overwhelming but would be worth it. There were still a few loose ends she had to tie up before she could move, but it wouldn't take much longer. Grabbing her purse and attaché case, she left the office as she did every night, her head high and her shoulders back. This was her dynasty, and she was the queen.

The limousine pulled up just as she stepped through the front door of Edwards' Enterprises. Soon all this would be gone, she thought as she entered the vehicle. Maybe Michael was right, whether or not Hagan Cove was going to be a smart move, she did not know, only time would tell. One thing was for sure: she had to leave Kansas City. There was no way of getting around that. There was too much pressure here with her husband's so-called disappearance. Cops weren't as easily fooled these days with all the new technology out there. Only she knew the truth about what happened to him, and she intended to keep it that way, no matter what the cost. And this idiot cop, who she noticed was still following her, was going to have to be taken care of.

The car pulled into the drive of the colonial mansion she had called home for the last four years. She used to love this place, but now it reminded her of him, and all the trouble he had caused her. Now she just wanted to be rid of it, but unfortunately it was only in her husband's name, making it impossible for her to sell it. Linda watched the tail lights pull on down the drive, and then covered her eyes as she turned toward the bright light of the car pulling in.

A sigh slipped from her red painted lips as she dropped her hands when the headlights went out on the beat up car that had just parked. Just having it in front of her house had to drop real estate prices in the plush neighborhood. Floyd Myers was the poorest excuse for a human there could be. He was sloppy, dirty, and poor! She actually believed, next to her husband, that he was the second man she hated most, and the first one was already taken care of. It was now time to get rid of this thorn in her side. Because he was a cop, it would make things difficult, but not impossible. All her worries ceased as he got out of the car, staggering and falling. He was drunk!

"Oh Floyd, you make things so easy," she laughed out to herself.

"You think you're real cute, don't you," he said, his words slurring as he picked himself up off the ground and proceeded carefully around the car.

*the Murderess of* RIDGECLIFFE MANOR

"Actually, with the full moon, I think stunning is more appropriate for this evening, don't you?" She asked, laughing at him.

"Mrs. Edwards, You don't want to know what I think of you,"

"Why not, what's wrong Officer Myers? Now that you're not in uniform, the whores don't think you're that attractive? I'm sure you can get one at a costume shop downtown. You know what? I'll even go and buy it for you, have it gift wrapped and send it to you. Now do you feel better?" Linda said to him, trying unsuccessfully to keep from laughing.

Despite the fact that she could not stand the man, she did have to admit to herself she enjoyed tormenting him. He would get so mad his face would turn beat red, his eyes would bulge and his lips would quiver like he was either going to cry or spit. "Go home," she said as she turned to leave.

"You really think you pulled a fast one, getting me suspended don't you? You'll fuck anyone to get what you want. Funny thing is this time, it didn't work. You see, you did me a favor because I have more time to prove you killed your husband without all those other things getting in my way," he said leaning on his car for support. "Here you are doing everyone else, and can't even keep your own man satisfied. Out of curiosity, did you ever join in with him and all those other women?"

"Well, you obviously don't know me as well as you think you do. I fuck for pleasure, I get what I want because I enjoy the game, I play to get it," she started.

"At least you admit you're a game playing whore," Floyd said with his usual snicker.

"You know all you had to do was leave me alone. Everyone knows I'm innocent so it's not my fault you're suspended. You brought it on yourself, and if I remember right, you're not even supposed to be within five hundred feet of me, let alone in front of my house! If I called your captain, which happens to be my very close, personal friend, and told him you were here, you would never see your badge again. I wonder if he would give it to me. I think it would look good on the library wall, in my new house."

"That's right, I heard you were leaving town. Afraid we'll find the bodies and nail your smart ass to the wall? Or maybe you can't stand sleeping in the same bed where your husband fucked those whores while you worked all night," he said, then spat on the ground close to her thousand dollar shoes.

"You're just too smart for me, I give up, but I would like to say that liquor smell on your breath is such an improvement, maybe you should drink more often," Linda retorted as she turned towards the house.

"Did you kill him in that bed too?" He asked, stopping her in her tracks.

"Tell me Officer, do you come up with these crazy stories on your own or do your little crack whore prostitutes help you? I think you should go suck down another bottle of scotch and leave me alone," she said, getting very angry.

"You can laugh and make your jokes, but in the end, I'll be the one that takes you down, hell I bet they even let me pull the switch that fries your ass in the electric chair. Just think, my voice will be the last one you hear before you burn in hell," he drunkenly laughed.

"Hate to burst your bubble, but they don't put people like me in the electric chair. People like me go to a nice hospital for a few months, get better, and then we're released. Then we come back and get the son of a bitch that put us there to begin with. I promise you, if that should that happen, which I seriously doubt, but if it did, when I got out I would come straight to your house and rip your fucking eyes out," she clearly stated staring at him.

"I see that white trash mouth of yours still lurks inside. You sick, fucked up bitch! You're just some dime store whore, all dressed up pretty trying to fit in as a society queen, everyone but you, knows you're not."

"No, what people know is that you're a drunken sorry excuse for a man, let alone a cop," she snarled at him. "You're disgusting."

"If it wasn't for your husband's millions, you would be four feet wide, living in a rundown trailer with six kids, living off the street using your welfare checks to buy your drugs. Shit, I bet you would have an ass so big you could launch a rocket off it. Where is your husband's body at?" He screamed at her.

"So super cop, have you shared your little theory with anyone else?" She asked, her rage calming down as she fought herself to get control over her emotions. "Anyone?"

"You just realized you met your match and now you're scared, I can see it in your eyes. Well, you better be!" he threatened as he turned around to get in his car, losing his balance and dropping the keys.

"You're hardly a match for me," she smiled. "You can barely stand up."

He staggered and picked the keys up, opened the door and got in, slamming it shut. "Your day is coming, you just wait," he stuttered.

"Yes Officer Myers, I am real scared of a dead man," she laughed. "So scared, no, make that terrified."

Linda laughed as she watched him fumble around, trying to get his keys into the ignition. Floyd was an accident waiting to happen sooner or later, and now seemed as good of a time as any. Floyd hung his head out the window to spit just as the rock came crashing down on top of it. He looked up in shock at his attacker's face and watched in paralyzed horror as the rock came down one last time.

---

"Captain Willis, here's that report on Officer Myers' accident," the officer said as he handed him the file, waiting for a reply.

Captain Steve Willis looked down, shaking his head for a moment as the officer stood there, the file in his hand. He stood up and took the file, looking down at the folder with the name 'Floyd Meyers' written across the tab in black marker. The folder felt like a 50 lb weight in his hand.

Silently he opened it, glancing over the first page of many. Several hours had passed since Floyd drove his car off Bennington Canyon Road, yet the shock of it all was still sinking in. The report read that Officer Myers, while on suspension, arrived at the Edwards' home around seven and had a few words with Mrs. Edwards.

"Glad I missed that one!" He said to himself, remembering the countless fights that he had seen between the two, shocked there had never been any bloodshed.

After about twenty minutes of obscenities between the two, he drove off in a fury. Shortly afterward, Linda Edwards called headquarters and reported his drinking and harassment; within thirty minutes later he was found at the bottom of the canyon. The case was shut as quickly as it was opened, but something did not seem right.

"The large gash in the back of his head, do you think it could be foul play?" Steve asked, looking to the officer for a reply.

"Believed to be when the body fell from the car as it crashed off the cliff sir. Do you want a complete autopsy performed?" He asked.

"Probably wouldn't hurt! I know it's pretty obvious what happened, but let's follow standard procedure here. Just try to keep everything under wraps though. The station has already been a bad target for the papers as it is, let's not give them any more. I'll make a press release in the morning" he said, handing the file back to the officer.

Steve ran his hands through his hair as he leaned back in his chair. The loss of any life always drug him down, especially if it was a fellow officer. What a waste. Floyd had his faults, but when you got down to it, he was a hell of a good cop. Lately though, his battle with the bottle had been winning, and Linda Edwards was not helping. That woman could drive anyone to drink. Those two definitely hated each other, why exactly, he did not know. Was it a coincidence that she was the last one to see him alive?

"Could it be possible that she had something to do with his death?" He thought to himself. As quickly as the thought came, he wiped it out. "No way. She would have been no match for him, hell, if she broke a nail it was a catastrophe. No, Floyd knew better than to drive drunk,"

Steve looked over at the phone and thought about calling Linda, but decided he really did not want to hear her complain about them not finding her husband yet. He really could not blame the poor man from hiding from her. She insisted it was foul play, but there was no evidence to prove it.

Rick Edwards was a playboy; he liked his money and loved his women. He still hated himself for ever introducing Linda to him, in a way it was his fault she was so unhappy right now. He knew how bad Rick was. It wasn't long after Linda laid eyes on him that they were making their way down the aisle, a marriage that was a disaster from the beginning. Every week Linda called and cried on his shoulder about something new Rick had done. Sometimes he felt more like their marriage counselor than a friend.

Now five years after their wedding he's missing with his mistress and four million dollars from the company vault. It didn't take a genius to figure this one out. Rick would be back when the money ran out. He just hoped he found him before Linda did. She would kill him!

# Chapter 3 - Hagan Cove Realty

"Here are the faxes from Linda Edwards' office in Kansas City," Valerie said with her heavy southern black accent, smiling as she handed them to Samantha. "You really look tired, why don't you go home and get some rest. I'll cover the office duty today."

"I can't sleep. Have you heard anything from Brad yet?" Samantha asked. She had not seen him since her nightmare three days ago.

"He's supposed to be back today. You two got something going on I need to know about?" Valerie asked joking with her as she quickly rushed to the window to watch a man walk past the building. "Like clockwork."

"Val, you're worse than a school girl,"

Samantha laughed out as she watched her friend ogle the handsome lawyer from the law firm that was upstairs. The real estate office took up the first floor of an old historic Victorian home in the downtown area. The owner had rented the second floor to the law firm. Valerie had been a happy woman ever since her tall dark attorney had moved in.

"God Valerie, why don't you just go talk to the man?" Samantha laughed.

"I ain't going out there, looking like a damn fool. He could be married for all I know."

"Oh ok, just keep on stalking him. That's healthier!"

"Like you haven't asked about Brad fifty times since I walked into the office," Valerie shot back, leaving the window. "Something happen between you two I don't know about?"

"Oh good grief Val! You've got to be kidding me! Brad? He's like my older brother. I'm just worried about him. I told you about the dream I had with him dying and all," she said. Just the thought of the nightmare sent icy shivers down her spine.

"I think you just spend too much time watching those old horror movies and now it's all catching up with you. You know Brad's too damn mean to die. Heaven or hell, either one want him," she said glancing over Samantha's shoulders at the faxes she was reading. "Besides, since his sugar mama died and left him that house and all that money, he's had better things to do than hang around here with us."

"I don't believe this; she now wants to know if we are going to throw her a 'welcome to Hagan Cove' party. She says if we are, please schedule it closer to Thanksgiving," Samantha said, throwing the messages on her messy desk. "Now she wants me to throw her a party!"

"Girl, it sounds like you have yourself a new best friend," Valerie laughed. "You know I wasn't going to say anything, but since you two are so close, Max told me she called him yesterday. She requested another agent, but he told her you already had everything finished so he said he would just sit in on the closing."

"What!" Samantha yelled. "I cannot believe the nerve of her. First she insults the way I look, and then proceeds to tell me that she doesn't trust me, not to mention she told me to quote, unquote, go outside and graze and now this. She struts in like she's God's special gift to the universe. Look at me, I don't think I'm dog meat, I mean, I'm not trying to be conceited here, but come on."

"I don't know, I'd do you," a familiar voice said as he walked in the office door.

"Brad!" Samantha yelled, running to him and hugging him tightly.

"Damn, if I would have known I would get this kind of welcome I would have taken a couple of days off a lot sooner,"

Samantha quickly released him, stepping back. She could not believe she just did that. Now he would never let her live it down. But it would be worth it. It was so good to see him. His handsome face was tan from his hiking trip. She watched as he crossed the room to his desk and picked up his messages. As usual he took off his suit coat and hung it neatly on the hanger, then poured his first cup of coffee. For just a minute, everything seemed back to normal.

"Well stud muffin, how was your hiking trip? What motel did you stay in?" Valerie asked him, crossing the room to her own desk, her heels clanking loudly as she walked across the hardwood floor.

"The purpose of a hiking trip Valerie is to get out and enjoy nature. You don't stay in a motel," he informed her casually as he glanced through all his messages.

"Well then sugar, besides peeing on a tree, what did you do?"

"Kelly and I just walked through the woods, camped out, you know the usual," he added, casually looking up at Samantha, who was deeply involved with a file she held tightly in her hands.

"You took that flake Kelly hiking?" She laughed. "That girl does not know a tree from a shrub."

"She does now," he said, raising his eyebrows and giving her a big smile. "So what did I miss around here? What is so funny?"

"I am sorry, I was just trying to imagine Kelly peeing in the woods," Valerie laughed, trying to compose herself. "Kelly Stevens is the type to call 911 if she got a run in her pantyhose. I'd hardly call her the outdoor type. I think you could have made a better selection. What about that woman from "dial a girl" you were dating? If you can call that dating."

Brad chuckled to himself as he thought back over his little camping trip. It had definitely been an experience with Kelly but he decided to keep it to himself. If he let Valerie know she was right he would never be able to live it down! "I'm so glad you never change Val. So is there anything I need to know before I go see Max?"

"Samantha sold Ridgecliffe Manor," Valerie told him excitedly, then continued to fill him in on all the details.

"Way to go Sammy! Now you can afford to buy me lunch for a change," he joked with her. "So come on, out with it. Who bought it?"

"Samantha's new best friend," Valerie laughed, grinning from ear to ear.

Samantha dropped the file and glared over at Valerie who was really enjoying herself. Brad looked over at her, waiting for her answer. The last person she wanted to talk about today was Linda Edwards! "You would not believe me if I told you,"

"Try me,"

"Some Kansas City big shot with more plastic surgery than a movie star. I mean, fake boobs, bleached hair, the works. Actually, now that I think about it, she's your type of girl. One problem though, she does seem to have a brain," Samantha told him.

"Don't forget attitude," Valerie interrupted laughing, snapping her fingers.

"How could I possibly forget that? She insulted the way I looked, the way I did my job, oh and get this, she told me to graze outside while she looks the house over. Asshole! About five minutes later she came out and bought it," Samantha said as she poured herself her fourth cup of coffee for the morning.

"Graze outside?" Brad repeated.

"You know, like a cow does," Valerie informed him. "And it gets better; she called her a hillbilly too!"

"He gets the message Valerie, thank you," Samantha interrupted before she went on.

"Tell him about the porch chair," Valerie quickly added, knowing that she would skip that part.

"What chair?" Brad asked laughing. "What is she talking about?"

"It was nothing," Samantha glared.

"It was nothing all right, our little princess here sat down on it and it fell. Knocked her on her ass in front of this Edwards chick! I wish I could have been there for that one, I bet it was hilarious!" She laughed, ignoring her glare.

"No way!" He laughed, looking at Samantha. "I would have paid big bucks to see that one."

Despite trying hard not to, she slightly laughed. Everything was getting back to normal again, but she knew it wasn't going to last. "I really think that if you two are done making jokes at my expense that you should get to work. You both have a lot of sales to make to catch up with me this month," she reminded them. Max, their boss, had been getting on to them all lately about not having enough closings, but at least now he would be off her case for a while.

"I want to hear more about this Edwards woman," Brad said, following her to her desk. "She's probably married right?"

"That never stopped you before Brad!" Valerie added from across the room.

"I think so; she had on a huge diamond wedding ring. But now that you mention it, she never said a word about him," Samantha said, puzzled. "Nothing about him coming to see the property, or for that matter anything about him period. Her name is the only one on the contracts."

"I bet she keeps him in chains down in the basement," Valerie added as she rejoined them. Both Samantha and Brad look up at her. "Hey, it happens in my soap opera at least once a month."

"You should have seen this woman. She looked like she belonged in Valerie's soap opera. Her skirt was so tight that if she exhaled it would have ripped open at the seams. I don't know how she walked. And her hair, lets just say it was very blond and perfect, She looked like a high dollar L. A. call girl," Samantha told them.

"Let me get this right, lots of money, bitchy attitude, hot body, and looks like a L. A. prostitute all rolled into one… I think I'm in love," Brad said, holding his hands to his heart. "When can I meet her?"

"I think I'm going to be sick," Samantha said rolling her eyes.

"Well I think you're just jealous of our new neighbor," he added.

"Jealous!" Both women said together.

"There is going to be blood shed now!" Valerie said, crossing back over to her own desk away from the impending war zone.

"You are out of your mind if you think I'm jealous of that candy wrap stupid society ass kissing bitch!" Samantha screamed at him, shoving him back, making him trip over a chair and fall to the floor.

"What in the hell is going on out here!" Maxwell Douglas shouted, throwing open his office door, stepping out.

"Nothing Max, I just tripped," Brad said, trying to contain his smile as he picked himself up off the floor.

Samantha gave him an evil glare as she sat down and started shuffling the papers on her desk. Brad winked at her as he straightened his tie, still laughing as their boss stood in his doorway waiting for more of an explanation than he had already gotten.

"Brad's back," Valerie suddenly said cheerfully.

"So I see. It's about time you get your ass back to work. You're gonna run out of that inheritance the way you keep taking off work and blowing it! Now get out there and sell some of those damn listings you brag about. Sometimes I can't remember if I'm running an office here or a daycare. Where did I find you people?" Max asked, holding his hands up.

"The zoo, and you know you love us sugar, we make your life complete. Now run into your office and make sure you have paid your liability insurance, cause I think Brad's gonna get hurt," Valerie said as she pushed her boss back into his office and shut his door. "Girl, are you crazy?"

"I am not jealous of that woman! I bet it takes her three hours each day just to do her hair and makeup. You want to see a scary thing, go knock on her door at three in the morning. I bet she does not even get up before noon. No way would I want to be anything like her," Samantha said as she paused for a minute to catch her breath. "I could handle some of her money though."

"Well, you better get over that attitude. That 'bitch' as you call her is paying you enough commission off that house to pay your bills for the next few months," Brad said, smiling. It was a lot of fun to get Samantha worked up. It was something he was able to do on a daily basis, and deep down he knew she liked it.

"Yeah, not all of us marry Grandma Grunt, with one foot in the grave," Samantha shot back.

Brad's marriage had only lasted less than six months before Edna had a heart attack and died. While she was alive though she had adored Brad and gave him anything and everything he could possibly want and he ate it up! No one actually believed he had sex with her. Rumor was, she married him so he could get her estate and keep it from going to her kids. Edna didn't like the way her children were living their lives and didn't want them to get their greedy hands on her money. The old woman had decided she'd rather it go to a stranger. Of course the kids contested the will, but it was eventually settled and Brad walked away with all of Edna's money much to her kids' dismay.

"I'll have you know I loved Edna, and I was devastated when she died," Brad said, defending himself, but not really convincingly.

"Until you found out for sure you got all her money," Valerie added.

"I mourned for a long time."

"Brad!" Samantha yelled, "You threw a party the next day!"

"It's called a wake Samantha," he told her.

"With a keg of beer?"

"My mourning process over my deceased wife has nothing to do with the fact that you're insulting the biggest client this office has ever had," he warned.

"I know it's unprofessional, but that woman seems to bring out the worst in me, kind of like you! I just don't trust her. She is nothing but trouble, you just mark my words," Samantha said, sitting back down behind her desk, her anger settling down.

"Well, if you ask me, it sounds like the two of you have a lot in common and you're just marking your territory," Brad laughed, ready for her next blow. "Maybe you're sisters who were separated at birth; it happens on Valerie's soap all the time."

"Well I can see now I'm going to need to get out my Sunday dress cause I'm going to be going to your funeral," Valerie said, picking up the phone and calling her appointment.

"You're going to wish you were on that soap opera if you don't back off," she said with each word getting louder.

"Hey!" Valerie shouted. "I'm on the phone!"

"It's all right, I know that deep down you're just worried that she's going to come into town and move right into your territory," he persisted.

"We're women, not dogs Brad. We don't 'mark our territory', besides, you idiot only male dogs do that! And what exactly do you mean by territory?" She questioned.

"Does the name Dean Richards ring a bell?"

"He's got you there girl," Valerie interrupted, getting back into the conversation now that she was finished with her call.

"Don't you start now," she told Valerie. "What does Dean have to do with anything?"

"Oh man, you have it bad for him and you know it. You won't even date anyone, including him; instead you just keep stringing him along. It's worse than Valerie and that stupid man upstairs!"

"Oh no you didn't! Leave me and my man out of this!" Valerie warned.

"Valerie! You don't even know his name!" Samantha shot back.

"Could be that you're afraid this Edwards woman is going to move in and grab him, leaving you with no other options," Brad told her. "Leaving you high and dry."

"Except for morons like Brad," Valerie added.

"I'm not old enough for Brad!"

"Good thing that I don't offend easily," Brad said, drinking his coffee.

"Honey, Dean is the sweetest guy in town and he sure seems to like you, so I suggest you make your move before it's too late," Valerie said ignoring Brad's statement. "Bad as I hate to I'm going to agree with Brad on this one. Dean will be on the top of her list."

"If I were you, I would pad my bra and shorten my skirt and get ready for one hell of a cat fight," Brad said as he set his coffee cup down and grabbed his coat and keys. "Got to get going, I have a one o'clock. Later my sweet ladies."

"Why do I put up with him?" She asked Valerie. "I don't need to pad my bra!"

"You know you love it. Listen sugar, I would like to continue this conversation, but I promised Max I would go check out this new listing with him in Boonville, you know how he hates to do things alone. God, I'm surprised he doesn't take someone to the bathroom with him to wipe his ass! You going to be okay?"

Samantha nodded and watched Valerie grab her things and exit into Max's office. Brad and Val were right. There was no doubt, even if Linda Edwards was married; she was the type to fool around. Dean would definitely be her target. Every woman in town was after Sheriff Dean Richards. He was the handsomest, sexiest man around. And he looked good in that uniform. Samantha longed to go to him, to allow herself to love him, but it just wasn't conceivable. They could never make it work. She was not strong enough mentally to deal with the pressures. She dug through her drawer and pulled out something for the headache that was forming.

*the Murderess of* RIDGECLIFFE MANOR

Max and Valerie came out of the office, mumbled a few words to her, and left for what they said would be about an hour. She followed them to the door, locking it after they left. Time for a quick nap, no one would ever know, and boy did that old couch by Brad's desk look comfortable. She stretched out on it and closed her eyes. The headache was winning the battle. She yawned and rapidly drifted off to sleep.

Like always, the nightmare moved in fast. As usual it began with dragging her helplessly through the swamps, up the stairs to the porch, and into the house. The horrible feelings of death and decay sweltered around her. The controlling force pulled her through the foyer, but this time took her a different direction into the library. The far wall had an enormous walnut bookcase that took up most of the wall. Some of the shelves had rotted through and were now gone, but those that were still intact were full of old books that started to fall off the shelves as she entered the room. The books crashed onto the dusty floor, sending a dust cloud over them.

The room began shaking like there was an earthquake, but it did not affect her, she had no trouble standing. An exploding crash roared through the noise of the falling books, and if by magic the shaking suddenly stopped. The door on the far wall ripped open, knocking it off its hinges and flying through the room crashing into the windows, shattering glass and sending it everywhere. Samantha turned back to what was left of the doorway just as a figure of a man appeared.

"Brad!" She yelled, running to him, stopping immediately upon seeing it was someone else.

He stood in the doorway, with a large gash in his forehead; blood was running down his face onto his white shirt and down into the fog that covered the floor around him, staining it red. His lips were moving, but she could not make out his pleas. Who was he? Why was he in her nightmare? Was he trying to tell her something? She moved towards him but he vanished into the air, leaving only a puddle of his blood on the floor.

A loud crash in the next room ruptured the eerie silence. The sound of people arguing filled the air as it became louder and louder. They were really fighting. She crossed into the room but found no one, just a decayed master bedroom with a few broken pieces of furniture in it.

She sighed as the yelling started again behind her on the other side of the house.

The doors to the parlor quietly slid open this time, unlike the last time she dreamt, taking her instead to an unfamiliar room. The room was a newer, modern room with nice furniture in it, but though it did have one thing that was familiar: the painting that hung over the fireplace, just like in her dream the other night.

"Where in the hell am I now?" She asked herself looking around in a daze state.

The room obviously wasn't part of the house. It had a huge picture window on one wall, nice bright paint colors and carpet, definitely not like any of the rooms in the old mansion, not to mention it was clean and obviously well cared for. She glanced around for the quickest exit just as the sound of voices came into reach.

"I don't give a damn what you say, Linda!" A male voice yelled. She quickly noticed it was the same man that she had seen earlier as he entered the room. Linda Edwards was close behind.

"Well, you will! That stupid whore is running all over the office telling everyone everything personal about you. It makes us both look like fools and I want it stopped now!" She yelled at him.

"I will talk to Karen, but it isn't going to fix things. I want a divorce. I can't live with you and all this strange shit you do, it's over! I want you to get your stuff and just get out of my house, and my life," he said to her, staring for a moment, breathing heavy before crossing the room and began fixing himself a drink.

"I don't have any intentions of going anywhere; trust me you can't afford for me to leave. And you sure as hell can't afford to divorce me," she informed him.

The man threw the glass across the room, passing through Samantha before she had time to get out of the way, crashing into the wall and covering it with alcohol. He fiercely ran over to Linda and grabbed her around the neck, throwing her against the wall.

"Don't you fucking threaten me you psychotic twisted bitch. I'll rip your head right off your body. I gave you everything you could have ever wanted, and this is the thanks I get?" He let loose of her and she fell to the floor, grabbing her throat where his hands had been earlier. "If you won't leave, then I will! I can't stand to look at you anymore.

Just the sight of you sickens me, you fucking whore! That's exactly what you are, a fucking whore! Just go wrap those legs around some other rich bastard. I'm out of here!"

The man then turned and started for the door, knocking a chair out of his way. Linda stood up and wiped the tears that had formed in her eyes and stormed over to the fireplace. She took a deep breath and grabbed the poker and rushed towards him. Samantha watched in terror, unable to move. Sensing that something was wrong, he turned just in time for the poker to crash into his head. The blow knocked him off his feet and onto the floor. Blood gushed from the wound as his hand rushed to cover the spot as the second deadly blow came sweeping down. This one completed her task. The man was dead.

Linda beat him with the poker twice more before throwing it across the room, hitting a table lamp and knocking it to the floor. Samantha watched in horror as she took his head in her hands and cradled it in her lap. She mumbled something then she bent over and placed her lips over the gaping hole in his head and began drinking the blood.

"Oh my God! You are crazy!" Samantha yelled at her, and then froze when Linda looked up at her. She had heard her yell!

"Do you like what you see?" Linda asked, pushing her husband's body away and standing up, wiping the blood from her lips. "I hope so, because this is just the beginning of our journey."

Samantha pulled loose from the unseen force that held her and ran from the room back into the old mansion that she had entered. Linda's laughter could be heard in the background, she was close behind. She grabbed the front doors, attempting to pull them open, but they held their ground. Pulling back and forth fiercely, she noticed the old lock start to break and collapse with her force. She continued until they pulled open and ran right into Linda, who was waiting for her outside.

"There is no escape here. You've seen too much already. I can't possibly let you leave here alive, besides, I'm still thirsty," Linda said to her, then laughed wickedly.

Samantha jumped up and started to run into the library, but it and all the other doors in the foyer instantly slammed shut and locked, leaving her no escape but upstairs. There was a loud roar in the parlor that sent chills down her spine. It didn't take long for to realize that the lions had came to life in the parlor and they were fighting to get out behind the closed doors. A second later they had ripped through the solid walnut doors, shredding them, sending wood flying as they charged towards her, she screamed out and started up the stairs as fast as her legs would take her. . Behind her, the lions stopped at the bottom of the stairs, gnashing and gnarling at her, almost begging for her to come back down. It seemed the closer to the top she got, the farther away it was! The stairs were growing! Fire had apparently started downstairs as a thick black smoke filled the stairway; it choked her making it impossible to see anything.

A crackling noise erupted around her, shaking the stairs violently. Suddenly as if by magic the smoke slipped into the cracks in the walls and ceiling and disappeared. The plaster shook and split from the wall and started hitting her with the chunks as though someone was throwing them at her, cutting her tender skin. Reaching up, she covered her head with one arm and grabbed the wall with the other, slipping on the slushy wall. She removed her hand and looked down at the blood dripping from it. A terrifying scream soared out of her lips. She glanced over at the wall and stared in disbelief as blood ran down it like a river. Linda's laughter roared up the staircase behind her.

"Need a little help?" Linda asked, directly behind her, a gnarling lion on each side of her, and a shiny ax glowing in her hand.

Samantha twisted back around, losing her balance and fell down the stairs. She tried to jump up but the floor was slippery and she crashed back down painfully on her side. Linda stood directly above her, the raised ax ready to plummet down on her head. Her eyes had flames dancing in them as the ax started to descend down, but stopped when suddenly a terribly loud ringing noise erupted around the house. She threw the ax across the floor and glared at her.

"I have to let you go this time, but next time, and there will be a next time, I'll get you! Why don't you bring a friend along, maybe Brad?" Linda exploded into flames and disappeared. The ringing noise grew louder causing Samantha to cover her ears and scream. Suddenly with a burst of air she woke up. The office telephone was ringing beside her. That was what she heard in that dreadful house! The telephone had saved her life, at least for now.

# Chapter 4 - The Closing.

"What a horrible day! Not only was she going to have to face Linda Edwards, but due to Max's sudden illness, Brad would be joining her at the closing. It was bad enough having Max there watching her every move, but Brad put it all over the edge. She was obviously being punished for something. Dark clouds started to cover the sun. Linda must be close," she thought to herself as she reached to turn off the office television.

"Not yet!" Valerie almost shouted. "Diane Shiane isn't finished."

"Oh come on Val," Samantha groaned. "You've got to be kidding me!" Diane Shiane had to be the worst reporter in the history of reporters. The woman gave the term "dumb blonde" a whole new meaning, but for some reason most of the television viewing state was addicted to her broadcast. They took their dose of Diane Shiane, mouth of the south, very seriously. The name was ridiculous given the fact that to most people, Missouri wasn't even located in the south.

"You have really crossed over!" Samantha said, flipping off the television anyway and going to her desk.

"Umm hum. Do you want me to stay and referee?" Valerie asked her as she finished putting things away on her desk. "I can, you know."

"No, thanks for the offer though. I think I can handle them," Samantha said as she sorted through all the papers for Linda to sign, checking them for accuracy. Everything must be done correctly; there was no way on earth that she would ever admit to Linda Edwards that she had made a mistake!

"I am sure you can. By the way I love the new threads girl, how much that set you back?"

"Five hundred bucks," Samantha told her as she looked in the full view mirror on the back of the closet door. The dark green formfitting business suit looked good on her; it really went well with her auburn hair. Tonight she would show Linda Edwards up. This was her turf, as Brad had stated a few days ago, and she intended on claiming it.

"Holy cow!" Brad said as he walked into the office. "You look great! What happened?"

"Down boy, down!" Valerie ordered him. "Where's Mrs. Ridgecliffe? I thought you were supposed to pick her up or is she riding with her attorney?"

"Nope," Brad smirked. "The courts said she was legal. Can you believe it?"

"Oh Brad! You didn't screw around and forget to pick her up, did you?" Samantha pleaded.

"No! Thank you for your vote of confidence. She insisted on driving herself, she promised she would be on time," Brad told her, looking back over and admiring Samantha.

"You're going to let that woman drive alone all the way over here?" Samantha asked him with a worried look on her face. "Are you crazy?"

"Well I hope you didn't expect me to ride with her. Besides she is only seven blocks away. This Edwards woman must be something else to make you dress like this,"

"I will take that as a compliment coming from you. I thought Mrs. Ridgecliffe lost her license after she made her own drive thru at Steve's Burger Shop?" She asked, changing the subject from her new clothes as she walked over to greet the woman that just entered. "Hi, I am Samantha Marshall, may I help you?"

"Yes, I'm Phyllis Stevens, I'm from title and abstract," the pleasant older woman said with a smile. "I'm here for the Ridgecliffe- Edwards' closing."

"Please come in and have a seat," Samantha said as she showed her to the sofa. "We're just waiting on the other parties, and we'll be ready to go. Thanks for coming out so late, I really appreciate it."

"No problem," she said as she glanced around the office, smiling at the others.

"Well, if the buyer and the seller would get here we could get this dreadful night over with!" Samantha said as she rejoined the others, and looked down at her watch. "It's going to be a scary night out there with both Linda Edwards and Mrs. Ridgecliffe on the road at the same time!"

"I don't know, but if she's on the road, I think I'll just stay put and wait until she gets here," Valerie said jokingly. "That woman can't tell the sun from the moon."

"Comes from years and years of watching Diane Shiane," Samantha joked, trying to cover her nervousness.

"Fine, I'll just go home then since I'm not appreciated around here," Valerie said, acting like her feelings were hurt.

"How about I leave and you take my place? I know Brad's going to show his butt. And Mrs. Ridgecliffe, well, lets just say she's not sure what planet she's on. This night is going to be a disaster," Samantha said once Brad had gone back into the bathroom. "I can already tell!"

"Don't forget the lovely Ms. Edwards will be joining also," he added from the bathroom. "It's going to be a great night. I can't wait to meet her."

"See what I mean! A complete disaster."

"Or one hell of a wild evening. The more I think about it, the more I think I'll stay," Valerie said, putting her purse in her desk and touching up her makeup. She would like to meet this infamous Linda Edwards; she couldn't be as bad as Samantha said. "What's going on here will be better than anything at home."

"I just wish it was anyone other than that woman coming here tonight," Samantha said, sitting in her chair, trying not to wrinkle her skirt.

"Samantha honey, are you sure that you're not being just a little hard on her. I mean, you're not originally from here, so you better than anyone should know what it's like to be new in this town,"

"Valerie!" Samantha interrupted. "I can not believe that you're taking sides with that woman! You haven't even met her yet. Trust me, you'll see. Just wait until she waltzes through that door tonight and starts to insult you. You'll change your mind real fast."

"I'm just saying that if she stands out as bad as you say she does, then you should be able to relate. Come on now, it wasn't that long ago you came here from Australia with your hard to understand accent! We all gave you a chance and now your one of us. I'm not taking sides," she said in her defense. "I'm just saying we should sympathize with her situation."

"I'm from Scotland, not Australia!"

"Close enough," Valerie laughed.

"I'm sorry, I'm just nervous. I promise you will understand once you meet her...," Samantha said, being cut off by a loud crash outside. "What was that?"

"Bet you a dollar Mrs. Ridgecliffe is here," Valerie said as her and Samantha ran outside to see what the noise was.

"I'll give you my dollar later," Samantha said as they looked the car over.

Edith Ridgecliffe carefully stepped from the newly dented car as though nothing happened. She was wearing a large housecoat with big hippos on it, her pink fuzzy slippers, and a large oversized handbag stuffed full at her side.

"Good evening Sabrina. Lovely evening, isn't it?" Edith Ridgecliffe stated as she grabbed Valerie's arm. "Nice tan dear."

"I'm over here Mrs. Ridgecliffe. It's Samantha, not Sabrina, and that's Valerie that you're holding on to, remember Valerie?" Samantha asked taking her other arm.

"Oh yes, she's that colored girl right?" she asked.

"That's right, Mrs. Ridgecliffe, I'm that colored girl with the nice tan," Valerie said, smiling.

Samantha and Valerie looked at each other and held back their laughter as they helped the woman into the building. Brad hung up the phone and gave Samantha a funny look as they entered. The two women slowly escorted the elderly woman into the office as Brad rushed over and pulled out a comfortable chair for her.

"What a sweet man," Mrs. Ridgecliffe smiled up at him.

"Brad!" Valerie said, hitting him in the arm. "Don't hit on the clients."

"Very funny. Samantha, I need to talk with you," Brad said as he motioned for her to come aside.

"Just a minute, can't you see I'm busy?"

"Is everyone alright?" Mrs. Stevens asked as they got settled.

"Yes, everything's fine. Why don't you go ahead and get set up in the closing office while we wait for Mrs. Edwards? It will be much more comfortable in there," Samantha said.

"That would be great," the woman spoke as she gathered her stuff.

Samantha opened the door to the closing office and flipped on the light. She smiled cordially as the woman passed her and sat her stuff on the table. Samantha helped her get things ready and then quickly stepped back in the main office before any other catastrophe happened.

"Mrs. Ridgecliffe, would you like some coffee or a glass of water?" Samantha asked as she returned to see that the woman was finally seated.

"Vodka would be nice dear,"

"I don't think…," she began.

"Samantha, can we talk?" Brad asked again as he pulled her to the side.

"I'll get it," Valerie said as she passed by them on her way to the sink.

"We don't have any vodka in here," Samantha told her.

"I'll give her water. In the state of mind she's in, she'll never know the difference."

"I'm sure she could tell the difference between water and vodka!" Samantha said, following her.

"The woman has on two different house slippers and is wearing her jammies out in public," Valerie said as she started pouring the water. "Trust me sugar, she ain't gonna notice."

"Samantha, I really need to talk to you," Brad said, taking her arm. "Now please!"

Brad led her across the room to his desk out of earshot of the others, giving her a serious look as the stopped. "What Brad! What is it, what do you want?"

"Did you tell Linda Edwards that we would be closing at the house instead of the office?"

"What?" She hissed.

"Did you?"

"Honestly Brad, do you believe for one minute I would set up an appointment out there in the dead of night! For heaven's sake, there isn't even electricity on," she said to him angrily, then suddenly stopped. "Why? Who was on the phone?"

"That was Mrs. Edwards on the phone. She's waiting at the house, not patiently I might add, she said and I quote "you better tell that little bitch to get her ass out here now or the deal is off!" He said to her.

"I'm not going out there; we won't be able to see a damn thing. You told her to meet us here, didn't you?" She asked, trying to contain her anger.

"This was the icing on the cake!" Samantha thought to herself trying to catch her breath. " What moron would go out in the pitch dark to a house that's about to fall down and have a closing! Closings were never done at the property they were either at the title office or at the real estate office! Everyone knew that!"

"She didn't give me a chance," Brad grumbled.

"Well call her back. She's obviously crazier than Mrs. Ridgecliffe if she thinks I'm going out there in the dark. Hell, half the rooms in that dump don't even have floors left! One wrong step and we could end up in the basement!" She said through gritted teeth.

"Give me her cell number and I'll call her back!" He said, getting irritated.

"I don't know what her number is! All I have is her office numbers in Kansas City! You talked to her; don't you know how to take a message?" Samantha yelled at him.

"I assumed, Miss Efficient, that you would have gotten those numbers, but since you didn't, I would suggest that if you want to get your commission and keep your job you better grab your papers, a good flashlight, and head your little ass out there," he said, handing her the file.

Samantha looked around the room and tried to gather her thoughts. "What was she going to do?" She thought. Her first thought was to tell Linda Edwards to shove it up her ass but she knew if this deal fell through she would lose her job. There was only one thing for her to do no matter how badly she hated the idea.

"Fine! Get your coat! I'm not going alone!" She ordered him and hit him over the head with the file.

"Is everything okay?" Valerie asked, not being able to hear anything, but seeing the little scenario between her friends as she stood by Mrs. Ridgecliffe, who was drinking the water she had given her.

"No!" Samantha and Brad said in unison.

"This is good stuff," the old woman said as she finished the water.

Quickly she filled Valerie in on what was going on. The three of them gathered all the flashlights they could find and then helped Mrs. Ridgecliffe and Mrs. Stevens out to the car. "This was quickly becoming one of the worst days of her life!" Samantha thought to herself. "How did all this happen? Linda Edwards knew that the closing was at the office! This was just another one of her deranged games! What was she up to?" In her nervous state, she missed the road to turn off on and had to cross the bridge to Boonville and turn around as Brad continued to remind her about how badly she was messing this sale up. The house was bad enough at day and now she would have to see it at night!

"Told you Mrs. Ridgecliffe should have driven," Brad said quietly so only she could hear.

Samantha glared at him and didn't say a word. There were no streetlights, so she knew he could not see her, but she was sure her silence let him know what she was thinking. There were the stone pillars she noticed as she passed them. Once again she missed her turn off on the driveway and had to stop and turn around in the middle of the road. She didn't think there were any other houses on the road, so where it led she did not know, nor did she want to know.

"Don't you even say a word!" Samantha ordered to Brad as she turned the car around.

"I need to go to the bathroom," Brad said to her with a snicker.

"Me too!" said Valerie from the back seat. Both she and Brad broke up laughing.

"I'm glad you two are having such a good time at my expense. Tell me again, Valerie, why did you come? Oh right! It was for support! Thanks!" Samantha said sarcastically.

"I don't understand what is so funny about going to the bathroom? I could go myself, are we stopping?" Mrs. Ridgecliffe said as they pulled in front of the dark mansion. Samantha rolled her eyes and let out a sigh as Brad and Valerie tried desperately not to laugh. She turned off the ignition and unlocked the doors, grabbed her papers and jumped out, slamming the door not waiting for the others.

Linda Edwards was sitting on the hood of her sports car as they pulled up. She did not look happy. Slowly she slid off the car and walked over to Samantha. She had a snow white leather dress on that seemed to glow in the darkness around her, making her look like a ghost. Samantha could not believe she had stayed out here in the pitch dark all by herself. She was braver than she obviously gave her credit for. She sure wouldn't do it; then again, she would never live here either.

"You're late! Where is Maxwell? He assured me he would be here," she asked impatiently.

"He has the flu," Samantha told her coldly, fighting chills coming from the memory of her last nightmare. "This is real cute! Making us come all the way out here."

"I don't know what you are talking about. I specifically said I wanted the closing to be here. I'm sorry that you have such a short memory."

"Fine! We're here now, lets get this thing going so us normal people can get home," she said, looking at her with a fierce fire in her eyes. She took a deep breath, and then introduced her to the others. Naturally Brad was the only one that she seemed to notice. "We can sign these papers over here on the hood of my car. Here Brad, you hold the flashlight so we can see since there is no electricity!"

"Not so fast! I believe the law allows a walk through before I sign these to make sure that the property is to my liking," Linda said, smiling.

"What!" Samantha yelled. "Are you crazy? We can't go in there in the pitch dark!"

"I think what Samantha is saying is that it is rather dangerous, with none of us other than Mrs. Ridgecliffe being familiar with the lay out to enter at this time of night," Brad said, trying to smooth things out.

"He's right. I'm sure if you would like to see the place again we could reschedule this closing for in the morning," Valerie said politely, not really wanting to go in there at night either.

"I'm sorry, I can't do that. I have to be back in Kansas City tonight. Either we go inside and do the walk through now, or I take my business elsewhere. It's up to you, Ms. Marshall, you are the realtor in charge," Linda said with a glare.

"Come on!" Samantha said through gritted teeth as she aimed her flashlight towards the dark mansion.

The six of them stepped up on the porch and waited as Samantha unlocked the doors. The house was twenty times worse at night than during the day, but was still not as bad as her nightmares. A rat greeted them in the foyer then scattered off into the library's darkness. Everyone seemed uncomfortable, except for Linda Edwards and Mrs. Ridgecliffe. Samantha wondered if that was what Linda would look like when she was seventy.

"I need to sit down," Mrs. Ridgecliffe said. "My hemorrhoids are killing me!"

"Why don't you come over and sit on the steps honey," Valerie said to the woman, trying to hide the nervousness in her voice. "Mrs. Stevens, won't you join us?"

"Um ok," the woman said looking around nervously at the old house.

"Be careful, it's dark," Samantha told them as they escorted the old woman to the steps to sit down, then she turned to Linda Edwards. "You knew that the closing was at the office. This is insane. Somebody is going to get hurt out here."

"You can't blame me for wanting to see the house one last time before I buy it," Linda told her hatefully.

"You had plenty of time to see it the other day, when it was light, or you could have come out earlier today," Samantha told her, trying unsuccessfully to contain her anger.

"I had several meetings today, some of which went over. I couldn't exactly walk out just because I knew my so called realtor was going to screw everything up now could I? I want to see the house now or the deal is off," she repeated.

Samantha took a deep breath and tried to calm her anger and her nerves. The night was going far worse than she had even expected. This had to go down in the real estate hall of fame! Maybe in a few years she would be able to sit back and laugh about it, but she wouldn't be laughing tonight!

"I'm not going through this house with you in the pitch dark. You are completely out of your mind. If you wanted to go through the house, I repeat my past statement; you should have done it the other day when you were here.... Wait a minute; you planned this all along didn't you?" Samantha said, her anger starting to come back.

"I'll take Mrs. Edwards through the house," Brad said, stepping into the conversation.

"That's very sweet of you, but don't you think that Miss Marshall should be the one that does the tour since she's the one making the commission?" Linda asked.

"I don't mind. Samantha can stay down here with the other ladies," Brad said as he smiled widely, showing his perfect white teeth.

"Well, if you insist," Linda smiled back, wrapping her arm in his.

"I really don't think that you two should go off alone in this place," Samantha said as they started off through the house.

"We'll be fine. You just stay here, we won't be gone long," Brad said as he took her flashlight and handed it to Linda so they both could have one.

Linda moved to where only Samantha could see her in the flashlight and gave her a wink. Slowly, she turned and took Brad by the arm again and started through the house. Over by the stairs Valerie and Mrs. Ridgecliffe were talking, their voices echoing loudly through the empty foyer. She started to join them, but remembered the rat that the others did not see and decided to stay by the front doors. Linda Edwards had won again. She obviously underestimated her. This was a good one. She must have sensed the other day that she didn't like this place. Now she was making her suffer.

"How had this evening turned this bad?" She asked herself. She knew that something would go wrong, but not this. She leaned up against the wall and listened to the sounds of Linda Edwards's designer shoes pound off as she walked further and further into the house. An icy chill swept up her body as she started vividly remembering her nightmares, especially the one from the other night with Linda Edwards and Brad. Surely she wouldn't try anything here, would she?

"Wait a minute Brad, I'm coming with you," she said as she went over and took the flashlight they had given Mrs. Ridgecliffe. "Will you be all right?"

"Sure," Valerie smiled. "What else could possible go wrong?"

"Please don't say that," she said as she shown the light off into the dark house.

Samantha followed the light as it guided her through the darkness into the library. The musty smell filled her nose and made her sneeze. In the far distance she could hear Linda and Brad laughing and talking. She gritted her teeth and moved forward. This was almost as bad as dreaming about this place. The smell made her dizzy as she stopped for a minute and leaned against the shelves for support, but the rottenness of them gave way and they crashed to the floor, scaring her half to death.

"Samantha, are you alright?" Valerie yelled from the hallway.

"I'm fine," she yelled back. "Some books fell that's all."

"Well be careful, because I'm not coming after you if you get hurt. My sorry butt isn't going any further than it already has."

"I always knew I could count on you," Samantha said softly to herself as she moved on through the room. "Brad, wait up!"

A rotten board crumbled as her high heel shoe landed on it. If she knew she was going to be doing this she would have worn jeans! The faint sound of someone whispering her name blew into her ears as she passed by an empty dark room. That was all she needed to increase her speed to find them.

"Thank you for waiting," she said sarcastically as she came upon them.

"I thought you were staying back with the others?" He asked, surprised and almost disappointed by her presence.

"Samantha, so you did decide to join us," Linda said through gritted teeth. "I hope you didn't have any trouble finding us."

"Your concern is overwhelming," Samantha said as she moved to the other side of Brad and gave him a dirty look, although she wasn't sure if he saw it or not.

"That about covers everything on the first floor," Brad said as they came to the back of the house.

"We can go ahead and go up the servants steps to the second floor or if you like, we can go through the house and use the main staircase, I'm a little worried about the circular stairs outside the master bedroom, I'm not sure they are usable.."
"I really don't think you need to see the second floor," Samantha added. "Nothing has changed since the other day when you were here, so let's just go and join the others and sign the papers and get out of here."

"Samantha," Brad said, shocked. "If Mrs. Edwards wants to see the second and third floors, then we should show them to her. No one made you join us."

"Brad, may I see you privately for a moment?," she asked, pulling him away from Linda, leaving her alone, and laughing to herself in the dark.

"What has gotten into you?" Brad asked sharply.

"Come on Brad, wake up and smell the coffee. That woman is just putting us on. She's playing games and you know it, so let's just stop all this nonsense and finish up and get the hell out of here."

"It is our job to show her through this place if she wants to go,"

"Is everything alright?" Linda asked from the back staircase. "I do hope I'm not causing you any inconvenience."

"Oh please," Samantha said in anger. "Everything you have done tonight has been an inconvenience and you know it, that's why you're doing it."

"Well, I'm so sorry to put you out. I'll just be on my way," Linda said as she turned from them. "I'll call another agency tomorrow, I'm sure they would be glad to show me a house in this price range anytime I want to see it."

"What about your midnight broom back to Kansas City?" Samantha asked. "I would hate for you to miss it!"

"Mrs. Edwards, please," Brad said, practically running to her, trying to salvage the sell. "Let's go on upstairs. Samantha will wait for us with the others; she's just freaked out about being in this big house in the dark. Isn't that right, Samantha?"

"Right," she said, irritated as she watched them start up the stairs. "You deserve whatever she does to you Brad!"

It was almost an hour before the two came back into the foyer after she had returned. They were laughing, still arm in arm, as they came down the stairs. Samantha felt her stomach turn, but at the same time felt relief that Brad had returned safely.

"Well, I guess we're ready to sign the papers," Linda said, smiling wickedly at her. "Everything is just perfect."

"Are you sure you wouldn't like to walk around the grounds? I'm sure the lagoon area is pleasant this time of night," she stated coldly.

"Funny," Linda laughed. "A realtor with a sense of humor."

*the Murderess of* RIDGECLIFFE MANOR

"Why don't we go into the kitchen and use the counter to sign the papers on," Brad suggested.

"That would be great since we're not at the office where we would normally sign the papers," Samantha said, glaring at him.

The six of them went through the hall into the back dining room and into the kitchen to sign all the papers. Linda pulled out the cashier's check for the rest of the purchase price and handed it to Brad, of course. Then she took her copies as Mrs. Stevens handed them to her and without even saying goodbye, walked out of the room and disappeared into the darkness without a flashlight. A couple minutes later, they heard her car start up and roar off.

"I thought she was pretty nice," Brad said, breaking the silence.

"I thought she was a bitch!" Mrs. Ridgecliffe answered to his reply.

"Thank you, finally someone who agrees with me," Samantha said as she started to help her through the house and out to the car.

"I'm sure that it's a comforting thought to have the only person that agrees with you to be dear sweet out of her mind Mrs. Ridgecliffe, huh?" Brad whispered into her ear as he grabbed the keys, shut the doors and locked them as the two women started down the porch steps with Mrs. Ridgecliffe.

"It's better than having you agree with me!" She said, smiling back at him.

"Would you two just lock the damn doors so we can get out of here?" Valerie called back impatiently.

"Val, what's wrong?" Samantha asked once Mrs. Ridgecliffe and Mrs. Stevens were in the car and Brad was locking the doors.

"I don't know. It's just that house. I felt uncomfortable the whole time I was there, kind of like someone was watching me in the shadows. It's just a scary place. I wish now I had gone home," she said as she got in the car.

"She's all locked up," Brad said, coming up behind them and handing her the keys. "Linda said to give these to her carpenters when they come next week to start working on the house."

"Brad, thanks for tonight, I know I was kind of a bitch. I appreciate you taking her through the house; I don't think I could have done it," she said, opening the passenger door for him.

47

"My pleasure. Let me do one more thing for you, either let me or Mrs. Ridgecliffe drive home; I'd like to get there tonight," he joked.

Samantha gave him the keys and smiled. A howl from a night creature came from the deep woods giving her an uneasy feeling.

"Please God; don't let me come back here again. Not in person or in my dreams," she said quietly where no one could hear… but something told her she would be back.

# Chapter 5 - Goodbye Michael.

Clap. Clap. Clap. Linda loved the noise her shoes made as she walked on the marble floor of her office building. The noise your shoes make lets people know you're coming. The sound should be firm and strong, powerful. Just a couple more days and the company would belong to someone else, no longer Edwards Enterprises, but the new and improved Mezzlemotter Corporation. "What a hideous name," Linda thought every time she said it. This place was doomed, and in a way she hoped it would fail, and then everyone would appreciate her efforts and accomplishments, and realize she did more around here besides just looking good. She was sure she would not be disappointed. Not with Michael running things for the Mezzlemotters.

Exiting the elevator, she noticed the time on the office clock. It was just after eleven p.m. and her plane for once was actually early returning from her brief trip to New York. She continued her trip down the empty lavish hall to her office, where she noticed the lights on and a familiar male voice. She stopped at the doorway, unknown to Michael, and listened to a conversation he was having on the phone. It didn't take long for her to realize he was talking to Captain Willis. "Why would he be talking to him?" She thought to herself. Unable to hear everything, she moved into the office. His back was facing her.

"Yes, okay. I'll tell her you called," Michael said as he hung up and jumped up out of the chair as he turned around and saw Linda. "Linda! My God, you scared the shit out of me!"

"What are you doing in my office this late, and talking on my phone?" She demanded taking his place in her chair behind her desk.

"I forgot some papers. What are you doing here? I did not expect you back until tomorrow," he said in his defense. He was unusually nervous.

"You forgot papers in my office? Who was on the phone?"

"Captain Willis. He wants to talk to you. Listen Linda, I need to tell you something. I know it is going to upset you, but it's not as bad as it seems," he said, his voice starting to quiver a little. "Once you take a look back, I think you will see I did the right thing."

"Captain Willis called this late?"

"He said he was wrapping up some things and was planning to leave you a message. Now don't get mad but…"

"What?" She asked, getting a little nervous herself. "What did you do?"

Linda felt her stomach began to turn into knots as she watched the worried look on Michaels face break out into a sweat. He took a deep breath and cleared his throat, unable to look her in the face. Linda leaned back watching him.

"Like I said, don't get mad, but I managed to get us an extension until February on the sell with Mezzlemotter," he sighed from relief after telling her.

"You did what!" Linda asked, the blood suddenly rushing quickly to her head.

"I felt you were a little confused right now, and needed a little more time to think things over. Besides, they were having a little trouble coming up with the last couple of million. By waiting, they won't have to get a loan. It was no problem really, everything is signed and completed. They don't mind waiting," he pleaded his case.

"How did you legally do this without my signature?" She asked as the news started to settle in.

"You gave me power of attorney, remember, during the original signing. I just initialed it," he answered.

"Of all the stupid, idiotic things that you have done during your time here, this tops it all. You must be out of your mind. You don't know anything about me! How dare you make such a decision that affects me and my life without informing me first! You had my cell number!" She yelled at him, her voice getting louder with each word.

"Just calm down, there's no reason to get this upset. You said yourself the house in Hagan Cove wont be ready before spring. Now you will have something to do until February, and that still gives you a couple of months to move. If you would just calm down and think about this you will see it was the best decision."

"Don't tell me to calm down! How dare you, you son of a bitch! You think you can just waltz in here anytime you want and disrupt my life," Linda screamed at him, jumping up, her chair falling over backwards. In one fast sweep of her hand everything off her desk crashed to the floor. "I want to just grab you by the head and just push until it explodes!"

Linda grabbed her aching head instead and crossed to the windows that lined two walls of her office on the top floor of the downtown high rise building. Outside, the Kansas City skyline shown brightly against the dark night sky. She had to get hold of herself, before she lost control and really killed him. She could not afford the luxury of murdering him.

The room around her seemed extremely hot. He must have turned the heat up as well. Looking over at Michael, she noticed he must be hot too; he had removed his jacket and tie. He glanced at her and looked her in the eyes. She could see that he was scared to death. "Good," she thought. "He should be!"

"Do you think now that you've had your outburst we can discuss this a little further? Like adults?" He asked her quietly.

"You pull a stunt like this, and all you can ask is if I'm done with my outburst?" Linda asked, stunned. "Why is it so hot in here, did you make the decision to turn the heat up as well?"

"No! Something is wrong with the thermostat in here, that's why I was in here. Maintenance just left before you arrived. They are supposed to return tomorrow to fix it," he told her as he sat on the couch. He was getting dizzy. She was right; it was getting very hot in here.

"Well open the damn windows; you know I don't like to sweat!" She ordered.

"What do you want me to do? You know the windows don't open

above the second floor," he told her. After all this time in this office she had to know that. Her commands were really starting to irritate him.

"Then knock them out. I need fresh air!" She shouted. Michael just sat there, shaking his head. "Just forget it, I'll do it!"

"Do what?" He asked, jumping up off the sofa, following her out into the hallway. "What in the hell are you doing?"

Linda stormed down the hall to the elevator and pulled open the firebox door, pulling the ax out and then stomped back to her office. Michael heard the buzzing of the security alarm beeping quietly. "Great, now they will all be up here," he thought to himself as he followed her back to the office. Linda crossed the floor over to the wall of glass. With a one strong swing, she threw the ax into the glass, instantly shattering the large pane, sending fragments exploding out into the night. A few pieces hung jaggedly in the frame as the cold October air instantly filled the office, cooling everything off but Linda's temper.

"Are you crazy? You could kill somebody walking on that sidewalk down there," he yelled at her as he ran to the opening where she was now standing and looked down. Fortunately, the street and sidewalk were empty this late at night.

"Anyone walking the downtown streets at two a.m. deserves whatever happens to them!" She said angrily.

Michael went over to her desk and picked the phone up off the floor, called downstairs to security, and told them to cancel the fire alarm and to get someone outside to clean up the glass off the street and sidewalk. Not answering any other questions, he hung up.

"Linda, you know I would never do anything to hurt you. Okay, I admit maybe I went too far this time, and yes, it was partly selfish, because I can't bare the thought of you being so far away. I need you! Linda, I love you! Can't you see that? We are an incredible team! Don't break us up!" He pleaded to her as she stared out the open window the cold air blowing her long hair.

"Michael, don't start with "us"! There is no "us"! I don't want to hear about how good we are together. I'm the one who does everything; you just follow in my footsteps. I might add when you do something on your own, like you did today, it's all self serving for you, and disastrous to everyone else," Linda said turning away from the window and picking up her desk chair to sit down.

"What do you mean that there was no "us"?" He asked her, "What about those nights we spent together, have you forgotten them?"

"Do you have to bring that up in my face every time we have a fight?" She demanded.

"Obviously, our relationship meant more to me than it did you," he said, no longer able to control his own anger.

"Relationship? What relationship? There's a lot more to it than halfway descent sex! I never loved you! I used you! Did you hear me, I used you! It was nothing more than that. You can't possibly believe for a minute that I was interested in you. Come on Michael, stop visiting earth and land here! You were convenient when I needed someone to get back at Rick with. I would never leave him; you know that, you just happened to be handy. It could have been anyone."

Michael didn't say anything just took a deep breath and looked up at the ceiling. Her words were cutting right through him. She loved him, he knew it. Linda was just too stubborn to admit it. She had to feel like she was the one in control of everything. Someday, hopefully soon, she'll realize she is in love with him and admit it.

"I know you better than that, Linda. You're not that cold hearted. If you were using me, fine! Use away! I can live with that. No commitment, just great sex!" He yelled back.

"It wasn't that great. The pool boy was better," Linda lied to him. She had never slept with him, but Michael didn't know that.

"Very funny. We can work things out, just tell me what you want," he said crossing over to her and kneeling down so he could be eye level with her. "Tell me what you want. I'll do anything for you."

"Anything?" She asked as he shook his head. "Then go jump through that window. Your begging is making me nauseated."

"Can't you be serious for one minute?" He yelled as he stood up and crossed to the open window for some air.

"I thought that I was," she stated coldly.

"Let's just leave here, go get something to eat, maybe go to an after hour bar, just relax," he said as he turned back around and walked over behind her and started rubbing her shoulders. He quietly bent down, lightly kissing her neck.

"Stop it! Don't you touch me again!" She yelled at him, pushing him away. "I am a widow! Do you know how bad it would look if someone walked through that door? They would suspect us for sure."

The rumor of her and Michael having an affair was the last thing she needed right now. The people in the building were already talking enough as it was; she had no desire to fan the fire any especially with Michael!

"A widow?" He repeated, laughing out. "You wish! Come on Linda you can do better than that. We both know he's off somewhere with Karen, living it up. You need to come to terms with it and face it, you got dumped! The divorce papers are probably in the mail now!"

Linda watched angrily as Michael crossed back over to the broken window taking in the fresh air. "He didn't dump me! He's dead. Trust me,"

"How can you be so sure? What did you do, kill him?" He laughed out into the night.

"I bashed his skull in with a fireplace poker," Linda said quietly. "He's not coming back."

"Very funny...," he stated as he turned around, his laughter faded upon seeing she was serious. "My God, you're serious! I can't believe this!"

"I had no choice. He was about to walk out with that whore, and give her everything that is rightfully mine, most of which I worked for while he played around. I couldn't let him do it, so I picked up the poker and hit him with it," she told him, staring him directly into his frightened eyes.

"What about Karen?"

"I called her up and invited her over, stupid bitch came. It was that easy. I had already dragged Rick's body to the incinerator down in the basement. I just added hers to the fire. Nothing left but ashes. Next day, I came to work before everyone else, removed the money from the vault. Later that night I took Rick's favorite clothes and the four million dollars and incinerated it. The ashes are now scattered all over Rick's rose garden. Now as far as everyone is concerned, he just skipped town," she said as a sick grin crossed her face.

"You incinerated four million dollars?" He practically shouted.

"I just confessed to murdering two people and all you're concerned about is that I burned a few bucks?" Linda laughed.

"A few bucks? Four thousand is a few bucks, not four million!" He argued.

"Well, alright so I kept most of it. I couldn't exactly keep all of it, the police are watching my accounts I'm sure. Besides, there's a lot more where that came from, like selling this stupid company that now thanks to you, I can't unload until next year!" She said, her anger refueling.

"And that cop, Floyd Myers?" He asked. "That wasn't an accident either, was it?"

"Maybe," she laughed.

Michael could not believe what she was telling him. This could not be the same woman he had worked with for the last five years! Linda was killing people? He looked over at her as she dug through her desk drawer. She didn't seem fazed a bit about any of it. But still, killing those men? They were full grown men!

"How did you kill Floyd?" He asked, slightly shivering as she smiled excitedly like a kid with a secret.

"That was so easy. The jerk was pretty loaded when he stopped by. I just picked up one of those rocks from around the shrubs and knocked him in the head. It was kind of gross sitting on his lap as I drove to the end of the street, then boom, I just put it into gear and over he went. Of course, he fell out of the damn car!" She said engrossed in her story.

"I can't believe this," Michael managed to mumble

"I know, in rushing to get things done I forgot to put his seat belt on, but that didn't seem to confuse the police too much. The damn medical examiner cost me a small fortune, you know people don't settle for the small amounts of money like they do on those crime shows on television. I have to admit though it would have been much easier for the funeral home, because the car blew up, so he would already have been cremated," Linda spoke as she came up behind him and put her arms around him, giving him a slight kiss, "But no plan is ever perfect."

"I thought you didn't want me?" He asked her after the kiss.

"I don't, it's just that telling this to someone is kind of exciting, don't you think? It's not good to keep things bottled up. And besides, you seem to enjoy hearing about my little escapades," she said, leading him close to the window. "Just think Michael, with your help, what I could do, what we could do. Do you realize we could rule everything out there that you see…"

"What do you mean with my help?" He asked, enjoying her rubbing her hands over his back.

"See the city out there? We could take it over. You and I," she said, moving them up to the ledge.

"How, by killing everybody?" He asked sarcastically, looking out at the skyline below.

"You're right. I guess it wouldn't be possible, I'll just have to get rid of you and do it on my own," she said, pushing on his back, knocking him through the window.

Michael felt his body pushed by her touch. He quickly grabbed the window frame as he passed through it, his hands slipping down the glassy ridges, cutting them deep. He held his grip despite the pain he was enduring before coming to a stop at the bottom of the window. He looked up and saw Linda looking out the opening and down at him.

"Help me, Linda! Please, you have to help me, don't let me die!" He pleaded with her, the cold wind beating his body back and forth against the glass building. He tried to pull himself up, but did not have the strength.

"Give me your hand," Linda shouted suddenly. She reached down for his hand and with the other grabbed on to the support beam close by to keep his weight from pulling her out with him.

"Thank God, she was going to help him!" He thought as he let loose, and with his bloody hand he grabbed hers. Slowly she started to pull him up. "He was going to live!"

"What the hell am I doing?" Linda asked loudly to herself, letting go of Michael's hand.

"No!" He screamed as his body fell quickly down the side of the building before crashing onto the sidewalk the janitor had just cleaned up moments earlier.

A fierce pain ripped through his body. With his last breath, he looked up the building at Linda Edwards who was looking down at him and smiling. Then it was over. The darkness swallowed him.

Linda ran to the phone and with her hand bruised and covered in Michael's blood, dialed 911. Help was on the way, she thought as she ran through the hall to the elevator. She had to get it together! Stay calm and be alert. She could not slip up now. By the time she got to Michael's body, a crowd of maintenance and janitorial crew had already gathered around. His body was half on the sidewalk and half in the street.

A pool of blood covered the entire area under him. Seeing the blood made her hungry. "Not here! Not now!" she ordered herself. Pretending to be upset, she went back into the grand lobby, sat on the long sofa, and waited for the police.

Over the course of the next few hours the police made her go back to her office and show them how the nights events took place. She quickly asked for Captain Steve Willis, and was informed he was on his way. Steve would help her get this mess cleared up. She needed to go home and get some rest! After her flight earlier and now this mess, she was exhausted. In a way she was saddened by Michael's death, but some things were just meant to be.

The police were scattered all over her office, taking pictures and occasionally asking her a question, before going off to a corner and talking among themselves. If only she knew what they were saying? Did they believe her story? Not to worry, it was so convincing that she almost believed it. A little fact, a little fiction, and a lot of drama. Police loved that!

"Mrs. Edwards," the cop said to her. "Captain Willis asked me to drive you home; he said that he would meet you there."

"That will be fine, let me get my things," she told him and gathered her stuff, stopping briefly to talk to security about closing the building and left.

"Thank God!" She thought to herself as they drove away. "It felt good to get away from that death trap." The beady-eyed cop beside her kept glancing over and staring, but never saying a word. It made her sick just wondering what he must be thinking. Finally the car pulled into her drive. Linda quickly said good bye and rushed into the house, she had to hurry. Steve would be there soon and she had a lot of preparation for her grand finale.

Twenty minutes later Linda looked in the full view mirror of her dresser. A wicked smile crossed her beautiful face. There was no way on earth Steve would be able to even think about Michael or what happened tonight. She started at her bare feet, perfect smooth long legs showing from the open slit on her floor length dark green silk nightgown that tightened as it went up her body. It exposed just enough cleavage.

"Always let the imagination wonder a little. Never cross the line. There was sexy and there was sluty. Only tramps crossed the line," she said out loud as she picked at the curls in her hair close to her eyes, before smoothing back the rest of her golden hair that was pinned up. Large diamond studs graced each ear. Just a dab of perfume and she was ready. As if by cue, the doorbell rang downstairs. Linda took one last look, grabbed her matching long robe and descended down the back stairs to the living room. She threw open the French doors and stood facing out. The wind caught the tails of her robe and blew them back. Perfect!

"Come in," she said loudly and waited for him to enter. "I'm in the living room."

Captain Steve Willis stepped into the room and looked at Linda. "Man! This was not going to be easy," he thought to himself. He should have known better than to meet her at home. It was just so late he did not want her to stay at that terrible scene. The roaring flame light from the fireplace danced around the dark room and elegantly lit up her face as she turned around.

"Is everything wrapped up at the office?" Linda asked as she closed the doors before crossing the room to the chair and sat down.

"Yes, your security guards are taking care of locking up. How are you doing?" He asked, standing by the door. He was feeling very uncomfortable.

"I just can't believe what happened tonight, I feel so numb. I don't know. I can't believe that I'll never see him again. That he's really gone. He was just standing there in front of me and the next..."

"It sometimes takes a while to really sink in," he said sympathetically. "I know it's late and you really don't want to talk about it, but I would like to hear what happened from you tonight while it's still fresh on your mind."

"I understand. You can sit down you know," Linda said quietly. "Can I get you something to drink?"

"That won't be necessary. I can't stay long. Let's just start from the beginning," he told her as he sat on the sofa.

"I had just returned from Business in New York. Michael was in my office, talking to you I believe. He told me he had delayed the sell with the Mezzlemotter group until February so I would have time to think about it and his proposal," she told him, looking sadly into his brown eyes.

"What proposal?"

"He wanted me to divorce Rick and marry him. I told him no! And then I screamed at him for messing with my personal business," Linda said, quickly looking away and glancing at the fire. "I was furious with him!"

"Where you two having an affair?" He asked, slightly embarrassed, trying to stay professional.

"No. We pretended that we were to try to make my husband jealous, but it didn't work. Michael just took the charade a little too far. It was really hot in the office, and with us fighting, it was getting hotter. There was no way to open the windows, so I went to the hallway and removed the fire ax and broke out the window. You know how I get sometimes; I just do it and think about it later. I had no idea that in a matter of minutes he would jump from it," she said, still staring into the fire as she forced tears into her eyes, a talent she had learned at a young age.

"He called security shortly after that and told them that their assistance was not needed. Correct?" He asked as he read over the notes that a fellow officer took earlier. Linda nodded. "Why was everything off the top of your desk on the floor?"

"I had a violent rage. I told you I was furious with him. Edwards Enterprises in the current market is worth millions, making me, if I sell it now worth millions, and Michael's little obsession with me just may have cost me the deal. You know how fickle the market is these days," she added. The more she thought about what he did, the madder it made her.

"So your fight was rather violent?" He asked.

"On my side. He just sat quietly, not saying much now that I think about it. Usually he would get right in there and fight with me. That's why I made him vice president. Most people wont stand up to me," Linda told him as she got up from the chair and began fixing herself a drink. "After, I don't know, ten minutes, of my telling him I didn't love him and never would, he went over to the window. I thought he was getting some fresh air. The next thing I knew he was hanging on to the metal window casing. I ran over to help, but he was too heavy."

"That was pretty brave. As heavy as he was, he could have pulled you out with him."

"In a moment like that you don't think about things, you just act on impulse. I tried to save him but he was just too heavy. I couldn't use both hands, I needed one to hold on with," she stopped and wiped away the tears she was managing to squeeze out. This was so easy. She should have been an actor.

"There is just one thing that bothers me that I can't really figure out," he said to her. She turned her eyes away from him and looked back into the fire. "If he was trying to kill himself, then why after he jumped did he try to save himself?"

"I don't know maybe he changed his mind, maybe he didn't intend to really fall. Who knew what he was thinking," she said. Maybe things were not as well as she thought. "He may of just been trying to get my attention, thinking he could pull himself back in, I don't know Steve."

"Maybe he slipped. Or maybe he was pushed," he said directly to her.

"What!" Linda said, turning around and facing him. "Are you telling me you think I pushed him? I can't believe this. I thought we were friends!" Linda said to him, starting to lose her patience with him.

"We are. I was just speaking my mind. I thought we were good enough friends that I could without you getting upset," he said in his defense.

"You're practically accusing me of murder, and expect me not to be upset! I've had a very difficult day, and I really don't need this. Even if I really did kill him, I could get the best lawyer money would buy and walk away. This is America! It's run by criminals," she said angrily.

"Just relax. I know you didn't kill him," he said, trying to calm her down.

"Besides, if I did do it, I sure as hell would not have told you we had a violent fight right before he died. Good lord. I would have just hired someone to get rid of him while I wasn't around. Come on, murder is hardly my style," she said calming back down as she sat on the sofa close to him.

"I know. Besides, before I came here I talked to Michael's cleaning lady. She said that the last few days he had been very depressed lately. She even heard him say he could not live without you. If he had not jumped tonight, he would have probably killed himself some other way. She said he was infatuated with you," he told her, pushing her gently on her shoulder. "Look what you do to us men. You're too damn beautiful, get a scar or something."

Linda sadly smiled at him, and then looked away. Rick Edwards was crazy for leaving this woman. If she were his, he would never let her out of his sight. The sight of her in that nightgown was driving him crazy; he did not know how much more control he could gather.

Linda turned back to him, gently running her hand up the hair on his arm, stopping at his rolled up sleeve. She could tell by the look on his face that he was enjoying it. Slowly she moved over and kissed his lips as her hands began to remove his tie and start unbuttoning his shirt. She bent down and gently kissed his exposed chest with each opened button. He started out tense but before long his hands slid up her back and embraced her. It had been several years since she had left him for Rick. With one kiss all those years seemed to disappear. Linda took his hand and led him through the house to her bedroom.

She had won! Now all she had to do was fix the mess Michael had made. That would not be as easy. Poor Michael, lying in a morgue somewhere. He really should not have stuck his nose where it did not belong. He was always doing it and now he had paid the final price for it. It was time to let go and move on. In Hagan Cove, things would be less complicated. She would not become involved with the people there like she did here. Good bye Michael!

# Chapter 6 - Welcome to Hagan Cove

Samantha slowly opened the car door and looked up at the real estate office and groaned. During the night dark storm clouds had moved into town and decided to linger on into the day. It was almost noon and yet it looked more like midnight! A perfect welcoming for Hagan Cove's newest resident. This was the day Samantha had dreaded for months now. Here it was May already and today was the day Linda Edwards was moving in. It seemed like just yesterday that she was buying the place. Now just a few months later it was time for her to move in.

The last few months had been about as bad as her reoccurring nightmares. At least once a week either Linda called from Kansas City or her carpenters were calling her for some reason or another until last week the final call came in. They must have finished, but there was no way she was going out there to find out. She was there way too much in her nightmares and that was enough!

The last time she had talked to Linda had been a major blow up between the two which ended with Samantha slamming the phone down on her. She had finally had enough of her insults and demands. She had told her that if she had let her show her the house and explain things she would not have all these questions. And that it was her own fault and nobody else's.

Linda of course hit the roof and then proceeded to tell her all about manners and customer relations, as if she knew anything about the subjects. There were very few people in this world that she hated, but Linda Edwards was one of them.

Brad, on the other hand, thought the woman could do no wrong and that she and Valerie were just jealous. "Hardly!" She thought to herself. There was nothing worse than having someone you hate thrown in your face every time you turn around. Just thinking about that woman made Samantha's blood boil. Hopefully Linda's visit would not be permanent. A woman like that would bore easily of a small town like this. She would give her no more than two months if that. Then she would personally drive her out of town herself, she thought with a smile. Now that would be a day to remember.

A loud groan poured out of her mouth and she climbed the stairs and walked up onto the front porch of the Victorian building. She used to love to come to work. Funny how one person can change that! She opened the door and walked in, greeted instantly by Brad.

"Well look who finally decided to come to work," Brad said to Samantha as she sat her stuff down on her desk.

"I'm not that late," she groaned and started for the coffee pot only to find it empty. "And don't start on me today Brad, I'm not in the mood."

"It's past noon you know!"

"When did Max die and make you my boss?"

"You're lucky I'm not your boss! Anyway I thought maybe I would run by Ridgecliffe Manor and see how things are going. Henry at the gas station said at least eight trucks full of furniture has gone by his place today alone, not counting the three that was there yesterday. They say some big shot from New York was in and decorated the place. Might be interesting to see how it looks, do you want to go?" He asked.

Another moving van roared past the office at a very fast speed, rattling the windows as it passed. Hopefully Dean would see him and give the guy a ticket, but she figured working with Linda Edwards was punishment enough.

"How much furniture does that woman have?" Samantha complained as she sat down.

"Probably not enough to fill that house. That place is enormous. So you want to go out there and check it out?"

Samantha glanced over at Brad. He was as excited as a kid at Christmas. He would use any excuse possible to go out there and see Linda Edwards. Just the thought of her name made her skin crawl. What he or anyone saw in her was beyond any thing she could imagine.

"Samantha!" Brad said snapping his fingers in front of her disrupting her thought.

"Stop it!" She demanded smacking his hand away.

"You want to go out there with me, or not?"

"Not hardly, and I don't think you should go either. Every time you're around her you're like a dog in heat. It makes me sick, I'm surprised you haven't humped her leg yet!" She told him as she looked around the quiet office. "Where's Valerie?"

"She called in sick."

"Really? Did she say what's wrong with her?" Samantha asked concerned.

"I don't know Samantha, probably a yeast infection. So what's the real reason you won't go out there?" He asked irritated.

"Brad!" Samantha yelled. "She did not call in with a yeast infection you dork! Where is she? Is she really sick?"

"I don't know ask Max, he's her baby sitter this week, so, we going out there or not?"

"No! I'm not going out there with you or anyone else."

"You know, your little jealousy bit is really getting old. I think you need to lighten up and give her a chance. We have to keep our customers happy. Now would be a good time as any to start. Let's go out, maybe take a plant or something,"

"We could take Poison ivy but it's already growing all over the house," she smarted off. It would be over her cold, dead body before she would purposely go back out to that place.

"Ha ha ha," he laughed. "You're too funny."

"I've already told you a million times, I'm not going out there and neither are you!" She told him sternly.

"No one is going out there today," Max said as he exited his office. "Brad, you said you were going to take Danny Summers to see that Vanderkelling listing at one o'clock. And Sam, you have office duty.

Remember or do I need to write it down and staple it to your forehead? You have skipped out the last three times it was your turn. I want you in here all day! In fact, I'll let you make it up to me for the past times you missed by working the office on Saturday.

"Oh shit!" Brad said, running to the phone and dialing. "I hate taking that guy around. He never buys anything, just wastes my time."

"Saturday!" Samantha yelled out. "It's Brad's weekend. I worked last weekend!"

"I have practice Saturday morning. I'm coaching a baseball team this year," Brad smiled.

"I didn't know Hagan Cove had an old ladies team," Samantha smarted off giving Brad a deadly look. He, just like her would do anything to get out of office duty.

"Ignore her Max, she's just mad because the bitch league was already full," Brad quickly commented.

"You two knock it off. Samantha office duty, Brad go sell a fucking house," Max ordered as he walked off to his office before anyone could make anymore comments.

Samantha rolled her eyes and walked over to the window. She hated office duty! Max was right she had managed to sneak out of it successfully in the past and pawn it off on Valerie. "That was probably the real reason she wasn't here today!" She thought to herself.

Max came back out of his private office with his coat on and glanced around at the two of them and then shook his head as he walked towards the door, stopping next to Samantha. She turned to him with her famous 'what now' look.

"How about you and this Edwards woman make up, huh?" Max said to her while Brad talked on the phone. "She has been a good client at this office, and rumor has it she might buy some commercial property around here. I would like her to buy it from us. Got it?"

"Got it!" Samantha said sarcastically as he left the office.

"Hey Samantha, what do you think about me doing your office duty and you go show this property to Danny?" Brad asked her, holding the file in her face. "Today could be the day he finally buys something!"

"Max would love that! Besides, from what I hear he would rather have you," she told him jokingly. "Got to keep our customers happy, isn't that what you said just a few minutes ago. Just how far would you go to keep the customer happy?"

"Well he married one of them and she was ninety years old so don't be giving him any ideas!" Valerie smarted off as she walked in the office from the back room.

"There she goes again being so funny!" Brad smirked as he walked out of the room.

"I thought you were home sick?" Samantha said surprised to see her.

"Who said that?" She asked sitting her soda down and picking up the mail. "Did this just come in?"

"Yeah, not too long ago. Brad told me you were sick and not going to be here, actually he said you had a yeast infection."

"Brad is a yeast infection," she quickly added. "I ran to the gas station and did some errands. I have to show that old motel outside of Fayette and I was running on empty. You need anything before I go?"

"Nope, I think I'm good. Have fun." Samantha said as she watched Valerie quickly gather all her things for her trip.

"I always have fun, see you sweetie," Valerie said as she walked out the door.

"Ok Sam, I guess I've got everything. If anyone calls for me I'll have my cell phone on," Brad said as he came back into the room.

"I'll alert the media. Why did you tell me Valerie wasn't here?"

"She wasn't," he said smiling.

"She was at the gas station asshole; she wasn't home sick with a yeast infection!" Samantha scolded as she sat down and logged on to the internet. "You better watch that lying, you know it makes your nose grow."

"Thanks for the advice mom. I'm out of here," Brad said as he grabbed his keys and left the office.

"Alone at last!" Samantha thought to herself, closing out her email. Even though summer was around the corner, the office had been quiet. Usually by this time things had already started to pick up from the winter slump. They hadn't even had a new listing in the past month. Three weeks ago Linda Edwards came into the office causing her more trouble and bought another house, of course from Brad. Fortunately for her it was a much smaller two-bedroom bungalow in town and was

*the Murderess of* RIDGECLIFFE MANOR

supposed to be for her housekeeper. She wondered why the housekeeper could not live at the mansion. "It could be that it scared her to death too," Samantha thought to herself. "That was a brave woman to work for Linda Edwards, even braver to live with her."

A bright flash of lightning ripped through the stormy sky just before a loud burst of thunder shook the building. "Linda Edwards must have just driven through town," she thought to herself. Boom! Another burst of thunder and the town plummeted into darkness.

"Alright!" Samantha cried out. "Can't work in the dark, guess I'm going to have to go home!"

Samantha quickly started gathering her stuff up and headed for the door just as the sky opened up and the rain fell down. Rather than getting soaked, she decided to stay put. Suddenly her anger diminished as she burst out laughing. "Wouldn't it be funny if some of Linda Edwards' furniture was outside getting soaked," she thought to herself as she imagined Linda running around screaming at everyone to get it in the house. Her hair drenched, her makeup running, her fancy dress ruined. "What a great thought!"

---

"Make sure you wipe that table off!" Linda yelled at the movers as they moved the furniture in off the last truck. "That piece cost more money than you will ever make in your lifetime!"

Linda heard the men grumble as they walked past her. "Pathetic low lives. Where did Martha, her interior designer, ever find them?" She asked herself as she watched them closely. The morons left half the last truck load of new furniture in the driveway with it pouring down rain, and then looked at her like she should help them bring it in. "No way on earth was she going out there and getting wet! That's what she paid them for!"

"Stella, bring me some tea please!" Linda shouted through the house.

Stella Goold was her new housekeeper and cook; so far it looked like she was going to work out. She had already scared the privacy issues into her. Nothing that happened inside the walls of the mansion was ever to be repeated. After buying the woman a new house followed by a generous salary, she knew that she owned her. The short round woman brought Linda her tea, and then quickly went back to the kitchen to finish unpacking.

Glancing around the grand foyer and the rooms that joined it made Linda smile. The place looked incredible, a blast from the past. Custom draperies complimented the beautiful wall coverings, furnishings, and polished wood floors. It just looked spectacular. Earlier she overheard one of the movers say it looked like a funeral home. Linda warned him not to speak again the rest of the day, and so far as she could tell, his mouth had remained shut. She walked from room to room looking at the gleaming chandeliers.

The house seemed to be alive, except for the outside; all the work had been done inside, so it still looked rough, but not for long. The movers finished hanging the painting over the fireplace in the library as the others were putting the books on the shelves. Smiling Linda walked through the library to her bedroom, like the rest of the house it too was elegantly decorated in rich vibrant colors. Her favorite! Most of the bedroom suite had been unpacked except for her personal items, which, according to her contract, she was responsible for unpacking. Like she wanted those greasy bums going through her private things.

"Mrs. Edwards," Stella said, knocking on the door. "The movers are going to lunch, now that it has stopped raining. Shall I make you something?"

"You know what, I think I'll eat downtown, I need to run a couple errands. Thank you," Linda told her then watched her leave.

After checking her hair and makeup, she took her purse and left her mansion. The sun was breaking through the dark clouds, making a dramatic appearance in the sky. The Porsche's engine roared all the way to town. The cute little restaurant that she had seen earlier was only open for breakfast and dinner, so she went to the next place she could find. It looked like it could clog your arteries by just walking through the door.

The outside of Lilly's Café looked like a large train caboose that had seen better days. "Obviously the health department had not been to Hagan Cove lately," Linda grumbled as she pulled the car into the small lot and parked. Running along the front of the building were decorative shrubs growing in tires that had been cut in half. She really did not understand the décor, but it was the group of rugged men sitting

*the Murderess of RIDGECLIFFE MANOR*

on the patio tables that concerned her. This she had seen time and time again and it never proved to be a good thing.

The men looked as though they were trying to copy a sixties bike group from a bad teen movie with a touch of modern day sleaze. Old jeans, white tee shirts, black leather jackets, unshaven faces, greasy hair.

Just as she expected, she heard the usual hooting and hollering. Typical pigs, she thought as she passed them and waited for one of the hoodlums to open the door. Catching the hint, one of them finally jumped off the table and opened the door.

"Madam," he said as he opened it, then spit a wad of tobacco out on the ground and licked his lips. "Umm baby! Gotta have me sum of that!"

"Oh I can see that happening!" Linda said sarcastically under her breath as she entered. The door slammed behind her.

"Good afternoon. How many in your party?" The bubbly waitress asked, chomping on her gum.

"How many do you see?" Linda asked as the waitress gave her a dumbfounded look. This was obviously a challenging question for her and math was not her strongest subject. "One and I want a booth in non-smoking, if that's possible."

The waitress smiled and quickly turned as she wiggled to a booth by the front windows, handed her a menu, then wiggled off. This place was unreal! It needed a paint job five years ago; the floor was so sticky Linda was afraid to look down. She took her napkin and wiped a piece of hamburger off the table that she hoped was from the people that sat there before her and not from yesterday.

The waitress started toward her table, and then passed it. Linda hated to wait! That little wiggle she walked with could not be real. No woman ever walked like that for real. God was not that mean to women. Hopefully it wasn't to pick up guys. If that's what it took around here she would have to give up dating!

"Ooh baby! God has answered my prayers and sent me an angel!" One of the greasy men from outside said as he sat down beside her, tossing his jacket into the seat across from them. He was wearing skintight faded blue jeans and a tee shirt with the phrase "Bikers do it best." The sleeves were ripped out to expose his tattooed arms. She recognized him as being the same one that opened the door.

"I doubt that it was God that answered your prayers, and darling trust me, I'm not an angel," Linda said to him as she moved close to the wall away from him.

"Now that's what I like, a bitch with a sense of humor. Hand me an ashtray babe!" He demanded as he lit a cigarette.

"She would need more than a sense of humor to be with you, and this is a non-smoking table moron," Linda told him sternly.

"Hey Debbie, Yo!" He called out to the waitress as she passed by. "Get me an ashtray, and bring me and my old lady a cold one."

"That's it!" Linda thought to herself. "No one calls me their old lady. She could put up with a lot, but not that. This guy was going to pay! Big time!"

Linda looked at him. Maybe if he was bathed in bleach water and put into some nice clothes he could be worth a glance or two. In his spare time of table sitting, smoking and God knows what else, he apparently worked out some. With the right guidance he could definitely be an entertaining evening.

Debbie, the waitress brought him his ashtray and quickly walked off before Linda could remind her she had not taken her order. The Neanderthal next to her puffed on his cigarette as he turned towards her smiling. Linda restrained herself from laughing in his face. Surely the women of Hagan Cove didn't find this attractive!

"So sexy, have you got a name?" She asked him, turning to him, but not getting too close. "You know that name that people call you around here?"

"Girlfriends call me hourly, everyone else calls me Duke. But babe, you can call me anything or anytime you want," he said, enjoying her sudden attention.

"Duke huh?" Linda repeated as she took her hand and with one quick swoop, knocked the ash tray off the table, sending it and the cigarette butts to the floor. "Duke, this is a non smoking table."

"I will smoke where I want. I don't think there is anyone here that will argue with me," he said as he bent over to pick it up.

Linda rolled her eyes as his torn underwear band was exposed before he straightened up and tossed the ashtray back on the table and blew smoke out into the air. He smiled and whistled loudly to the waitress before turning back to Linda.

"Fucking waitresses in this dump can't give head or wait tables,"

"I'll try to keep that in mind," Linda said sarcastically and looked out the window, debating how much longer she was going to put up with him.

"Here you go," Debbie, the waitress said setting down two beer bottles as she popped a big bubble with her gum. "Anything else?"

"Yeah, get me a cheeseburger with everything on it, and meet me out back later. You still owe me from last time."

"Ok," she said with a huge smile. "But we have to go somewhere else. Lilly gets so pissed when we mess around back."

"Excuse me," Linda interrupted. "Do you mind taking my order, or is all this more than you can absorb with one visit?"

"Well, I'm waiting? What do you want?" The waitress asked.

"Forget it; just bring me a bottled water, unopened. Anything else and I'll probably need my stomach pumped."

"Gotcha," Debbie said with as she winked and quickly walked off as Duke smacked her butt. She turned back around and giggled, blew him a kiss and rushed off.

"Well, I have my afternoon full, but I still have sometime for you right now," he said smiling at her. "Want to head off to the restroom for a quickie?"

"As tempting as that is, I'm going to have to pass on that," Linda quickly stated. Just the thought of having sex with him sickened her.

"I thought so. You're not one of those kinda girls that don't like it fast you want it all night, over and over. I could come by your place after eleven."

"I'll keep that in mind," Linda said as the waitress came over with her water, she looked up into her young face grinning ear to ear with that goofy smile of hers. "You can go ahead and take your brother out back. I'm done with him."

"He's not my brother," Debbie laughed. "That would be just gross!"

"Go on and get my fucking burger," Duke said getting irritated that Linda wasn't accepting his advances. "So what are you a dyke?"

"Are you serious?" Linda laughed, her voice getting loud. "You think because I'm not interested in you that I must be a lesbian? Did it ever occur to you that I think you smell bad, you have enough oil in your hair to drive my car to Dallas. Your breath smells like an ashtray and I can tell by that tootsie roll size bulge in your pants that a pencil could give me more pleasure than your penis. So I'm sorry Duke, I don't want to go into the restroom with you, or see you later tonight. I'm going to swing by Wal-mart later and get me a whole pack of pencils, so I should be good for the summer."

"Excuse me!" An elderly lady said turning around in the next booth. "I don't like that kind of language."

Linda glared over at the old woman who quickly turned around and went back to eating. The waitress brought Duke's cheeseburger and sat it down. He motioned for her to leave as he looked down at his cheeseburger. Linda could tell by the look on his face she had hurt his pride. She almost felt sorry for him.

"I knew you were a lesbian," he said after he had taken a bite of his cheeseburger.

"Duke," she said softly, moving closer to him. One hand went down and started massaging his leg, the other played with one of the frayed strings of his shirt. "I didn't mean to hurt your feelings. Is Duke your real name?"

"Yeah," he said looking over at her, surprised by her sudden interest.

"That's a sweet name, I used to have a dog named Duke," she said seductively.

"Honey, I ain't a dog, but if you rub a little higher on my leg, I promise I'll do a trick,"

"I killed that dog!" She said and with a swift motion, grabbed the fork and stabbed him with it. "Screw with me again, and I promise, I'll aim higher."

"You fucking bitch!" He yelled as he jumped up from the table, knocking it over into the other seat.

Linda got up from the bench, blew him a kiss, and headed for the ladies room. It, like the rest of the place, was filthy. Loud yelling had erupted out in the café. She smiled and reapplied her lipstick. There was no way she was going to eat here, she decided. She exited the restroom, gave the waitress twenty bucks, and left.

Duke was back outside with his buddies by the time she got out there rubbing his injured leg. They snickered at her as she passed by making her smile. She had to admit, she had enjoyed playing with him today. She would have to have more fun with him later, she thought to herself, and then stopped dead in her tracks as she reached her car. Someone had taken a sharp object and scratched the paint down the side of it. It did not take a genius to figure it out who did it. They were all laughing behind her. Maybe they would play a lot sooner than she had planned.

"So you want to play dirty!" Linda said to herself as she got into the car, slamming the door.

Within an instant, the engine roared and she backed out, facing them head on. Stepping on the gas, she aimed the sports car directly at the guys, sending them scattering and falling as she crashed through their bikes, throwing them on top of her car and all around. She stopped the car in the middle of the road, opened the door, and stepped out.

"When you grow up little boy and learn how to play like a man, then come see me. I'm sure you're smart enough to be able to find me. Prick!" She yelled out to Duke before getting back in her car and roaring off. Duke and the others ran after the car screaming revenge. This was just the beginning with him. There would be a lot more fun, she was sure of it. Duke would probably be her first guest at her new home. Linda laughed suddenly, stopping as she noticed the car lot. She now, thanks to Duke, needed a new car.

# Chapter 7 - Dean!

It had been a long day for Linda. After reordering her car, she drove the damaged one back home and watched as the movers finished unpacking the house and leave for the day. Stella had already cleared the dinner dishes and the sound of the dishwasher could be heard throughout the quiet, lonely first floor of the house. For the first time in her life she was really alone. It felt strange. She straightened the painting of herself in the parlor and picked up the phone. She decided she would call Brad, but before she could dial, she heard a car pulling into the drive. It was too dark to see who it was, as she waited anxiously for the doorbell to ring.

The entry hall Chandelier burst with light as she flipped the switch and crossed through to the front doors. She turned on the outside lights and opened the door. For the first time in her life, she was speechless. The most handsome man she had ever seen was standing before her. He was over six feet tall, had short light brown, almost blond hair and a fine chiseled face. He was wearing the standard sheriff's uniform; the shirt had a couple buttons open exposing a gleaming white tee shirt stretched tight across his chest underneath, the short sleeves barely large enough to go over his large biceps. The shiny badge across his broad chest glistened in all the light illuminating his handsome face.

"Can I help you?" She managed to say, trying to keep her voice steady.

"Good evening," he said in a firm masculine voice. "I'm looking for a Linda Edwards."

"I'm Linda Edwards, please come in," she said as she moved aside and let him in.

"I'm Sheriff Dean Richards with the Hagan County Sheriffs Department. I'm sorry but I'm going to need a few moments of your time," he stated, his dark brown eyes not leaving hers.

"You can have all night," Linda said under her breath as she led him into the parlor.

Dean looked around at the renovated mansion as he followed her into the other room. Brad had said she was beautiful, but that was an understatement. He admired the view as he followed her; she was definitely a welcoming sight to these parts. He sat on the sofa and watched as she sat beside him. The room was very nicely decorated but kind of dark, even though there was a large chandelier in the room. The white slacks and silk blouse she wore made her look like an angel among the darkness of the room's decor. She turned to face him, pulling her leg up under her and leaned back, resting her elbow across the back of the sofa, her hand playing with the large diamond in her ear.

"So am I in some kind of trouble?" She asked, as he began to speak. "Sorry, go ahead."

"I'm sorry," he repeated, slightly laughing. "I was about to say how great the old place looks."

"Thank you, it has definitely been a challenge, but I think it's worth it. Would you like a drink or something?"

"No, thank you. I am actually here on official business," he said sitting back in the sofa as she moved a little closer to him.

Linda pulled one of her loose curls behind her ear as she looked in awe at the handsome man sitting beside her. This was the kinda of man that she would fantasize about, one that would sweep her off her feet and make love to her all night long, then hold her in the morning. A man that would appreciate and understand a woman like her. She watched as he looked around the room and then looked back at her. His eyes were the most beautiful color of brown she had ever seen.

"Ms. Edwards, I'm sorry to take up your time, I know you're busy."

"It's ok, I wasn't doing anything. I have to ask this, are you really the Sheriff or is this a joke?" Linda asked, still looking into his eyes.

"I'm sorry, I'm not sure I'm following you," he said, confused.

"You look more like a male dancer than a Sheriff," she said, slightly flirting with him. Her initial nervousness was now gone.

"No, I'm the Sheriff, trust me. What I'm here for is about a little altercation that happened down at Lilly's Café earlier today. I understand that there was some property damage…"

"Duke sent you here?" She interrupted laughing. She would have to thank him for this.

"Not exactly, the owner's of the Café filed the report. I talked with Duke, he does not want to press charges, and the café said they wouldn't either as long as both of you agreed to stay away and not cause any more trouble," he said.

"That won't be a problem," she told him as she slid even closer. She was able to smell a slight scent of cologne.

"I'm sure that Duke instigated this, knowing him as well as I do. Do you wish to press any charges against him?" He asked, starting to get a little uncomfortable with her closeness.

"No, I don't want to. I can handle guys like him, trust me. So you're really a cop? I mean Sheriff? I've had the pleasure of seeing some beautiful men before, but let me say you definitely put them to shame," she told him glancing over his broad chest. "You could be a model and make a fortune."

"Thank you," he said uncomfortably as he stood up and started to make his way to the foyer. "I had better get going."

"So you're not going to take off your clothes and dance for me, are you?" She joked wickedly.

"No, I'm sorry, not tonight," he said as he turned from her and headed for the door. It was locked.

"You know men in uniform have always been my weakness, I guess it's just their power, their demanding attitude, I don't know," she whispered to him as she stepped up and kissed him on the lips.

Dean stood paralyzed by her kiss. Tender, yet passionate. Her touch took his breath away and sent his head spinning, making his knees weak. Her hands slid up his back to his neck as she pulled slightly away. She stared at him with her blue penetrating eyes, and then moved her lips back to his and kissed him again, his hands quickly moved around her waist, pulling her to him as her soft fingers crossed his freshly shaven face and once again she pulled away, this time stepping back.

"You don't kiss like a cop either," she winked as she unlocked the doors. "It was nice to meet you Sheriff.

"I will uh... I've got to go," he said as he headed through the doors. "Here is my card if you change your mind or have any more problems with Duke."

"Thanks, I'll keep that in mind," Linda said taking the card and smiling.

"You're welcome."

"Come back sometime Sheriff, I would like to get to know you better," she said to him as he quickly walked to his car, almost tripping over a rock.

"You already know me better than my dentist," he said to himself once inside the car.

Dean drove back to town quickly. His brain was dazed and confused. He really did not know how to take this woman. He had met aggressive women before, but never anyone like Linda Edwards! It was like she had mind control over him and all he could do was stand there and let her do whatever she wanted. One thing was for sure, she definitely knew how to kiss! He spotted Brad's car in the café parking lot and made a quick turn, parking next to Brad's.

"Evening Dean," the waitress greeted him as he entered.

"Hey Doris, how's it going this evening?" He asked, wiping his feet on the dirty floor mat.

"Going good sweetie, you want your usual tonight?"

"Yeah, cheeseburger and fries," he said and gave her a friendly wink. "I'll be down here at dumb butts table."

"Red's definitely your color," Brad told him as he plopped down in the padded bench across from him.

"What?" Dean questioned, grabbing Brad's water glass and taking a drink.

"You have lip stick all over your mouth," he laughed as he watched Dean wipe it off with a napkin. "So are you going to tell me who she is or do I have to guess?"

"Nothing to talk about," he told him, quickly looking away.

Dean looked around at the nearly empty restaurant then down at the napkin he had just used, looking at the smudged lipstick. He was embarrassed. It was a good thing he didn't have any calls between

Linda's place and here! He glanced over at the kitchen wishing they would hurry with his order.

"It wasn't that drunken drag queen running around the town square again was it, oh what the hell was his name? Head a Cabbage?" He asked with a big smile on his face.

"You're very funny. His name was Head a Lettuce, and no it wasn't. I don't know why you don't give up real estate and open a comedy club! You're just so fuckin funny," he commented as the waitress brought out his order. "Thanks."

"You guys need anything else?" The waitress asked.

"No, I think this should take care of it," Dean said smiling.

"You boys yell if want something," Doris said as she picked up the napkin and winked at Dean. "She's a lucky girl."

'Yeah, but is it really a girl, when it's a man dressed up like one?" Brad asked smirking as the waitress gave him a funny look and decided not to ask anything else as she turned and walked off.

"Brad!" Dean groaned giving him a warning look.

"Comedy club huh? Interesting idea, I'll have to keep that in mind," Brad said as he stole one of Dean's french fries. "So what really happened then? Collide with a cosmetic truck during a high speed chase?"

"High speed chase in this town? John Deer doesn't make a tractor that can out run my trust worthy 1952 police cruiser," Dean joked, his mood lightening. "What do you know about Linda Edwards?" He asked.

"What?" Brad asked practically choking on the fries.

"The lady you guys sold Ridgecliffe Manor to," Dean added.

"Holy shit! Tell me it wasn't Linda Edwards that kissed you? Damn it! How do you get every woman in town before me? I'm a lot better looking, I dress better, and I'm a hell of a lot funnier. Must be the badge!" He said, grabbing another hand full of fries.

"I'm sure it's the badge. Now what do you know about her?" He asked as he slid the plate of fries over to his side of the table as if bribing him with the food.

"Kind of bitchy, Samantha hates her guts! Lots of money! Body to die for, supposed to be a husband somewhere, but I think they are divorced or he's dead, she doesn't talk about him. So did you two get it on tonight or what?"

"I don't know what happened. One minute we're talking about her and Duke fighting here this afternoon and the next thing I know she had her tongue down my throat," Dean said, his face turning slightly red as he recalled tonight's events.

"Do you have an extra uniform for me? I'm not doing anything tonight. Kelly's raggin and went home early, that's why I'm eating here tonight. Hell I'll even let you deputize me."

"With that attitude, I'm sure it's not the only reason you're eating here alone tonight."

"Oh lighten up, it was just a kiss. No big deal," he said laughing.

"It's not funny Brad! She took me off guard, she could have been an attacker and grabbed my gun and shot me!" Dean informed him throwing the hamburger down on the plate. It was way too greasy!

"Come on Dean, this is Hagan Cove, not Los Angeles. The only gun you have to worry about women around here grabbing isn't in your holster," he told him, picking up the cheeseburger and finishing it off.

"Thank you, Mr. Pervert, for that thoughtful overview," Dean said, slightly embarrassed by Brad's remark. "I'm just not used to women being that aggressive."

"That's because women in this city are stuck in a time warp! If some chick like Linda Edwards made a pass like that at me, I sure as hell would not be here talking to you about it. Buddy, I would be in the throws of passion, probably for the third time tonight!"

"Whatever," Dean laughed. "You need to take some of that money your grandma left you and buy some morals."

"She wasn't my grandma, she was my wife!" He smiled looking out the window. "Oh God!"

"In your case about the same thing," he said, sipping on his soda and glancing around to the window. "What is it?"

Dean glanced out the window into the dark parking lot and smiled as Valerie climbed out of her car, grabbing her jacket and put it on over her sweat clothes. She had apparently just come from the gym. "Only Valerie would go work out and then come eat a cheeseburger," he thought to himself with a chuckle.

"Good Lord in Heaven," Valerie yelled out as she entered the dinner. "Don't you boys ever eat at home?"

"Hey Val," Dean said smiling as she sat down beside him. "What are you up to tonight?"

"I just finished exercise class. I always need a little grease after twenty on the treadmill."

"Kinda defeats the purpose doesn't it?" Brad quickly added as he stole some more french fries.

"Did I push the button on your back that makes your lips move?" Valerie asked as Brad laughed. "I didn't think so."

"Here you go Valerie," the waitress said as she handed Valerie her food all sacked up.

"Thanks Doris," Valerie said taking the bag. "So what are you boys up to tonight?"

"This and that," Brad said reaching out for her sack of food.

"You better just keep your greasy little hands on that side of the table before I grab that knife over there and cut them off and end your sex life,"

"My hands are better than that battery operated thing you call a man," Brad quickly added.

"Wow. That was just too much information from you two!" Dean laughed

"Boy needs to learn some manners," Valerie commented, clutching her sack of food. "And honey, I don't need a battery operated machine. I can get me a man anytime I want."

"You know I love you Val!" Brad laughed

"On that note, I need to get my sore ass home, I taped Springer today, and it was a special episode. Pregnant hoes and the circus freaks that love them." Valerie said standing up. "I could have saved the tape I guess and just went to Brad's family reunion. 'Night Dean."

"What, no goodnight for me?" Brad asked pretending to be bothered by her exclusion.

Valerie gave him a dirty look and held her hand up and walked off towards the door as Dean and Brad laughed. She stopped for a moment before suddenly walking back. She stood over Brad, reaching down and grabbed his crotch hard.

"By the way, you ever tell anyone again that I have a yeast infection, baby your balls aren't going to be the only thing permanently dangling. You catch my drift sugar?" Valerie said not letting go.

"Yes," Brad managed to say, his face draining of color.

"Fool probably doesn't even know what a yeast infection is," Valerie mumbled to herself as she let go, smacked him upside the head, and walked off towards the door. "You boys have a good night."

Dean watched as Valerie got into her car, blew them a kiss and pulled out of the parking lot. He looked back over at Brad who was starting to get the color back in his face. He cleared his throat and sat up as the waitress came back over and asked them if they wanted anything else. Brad ordered another glass of water and sat quietly.

"You ok?" Dean asked after a moment of silence.

"Um hum,"

"What was that all about?"

"Little office humor," Brad said as the waitress brought him his water.

"Looks kinda dangerous,"

"Naw, the girls love it. Valerie would be bored as shit if she didn't have me around to pick on. I guess I better be heading out."

"Going to see Val?" Dean said smirked.

"Careful there, I would hate to tell Samantha about your little affair tonight," Brad quickly commented as he got up from the table. "Now there's a woman on the edge! She's having all those crazy dreams again like she did back in high school."

"What?" Dean asked grabbing Brad's arm and pulling him back down to the bench. "What's wrong with Samantha, and why am I just now hearing about this?"

"I don't think it's anything to worry about, she's just having some crazy dreams. I shouldn't have brought it up. She'd have my other nut if she knew I told you." Brad said shifting himself, still sore from how hard Valerie had grabbed him.

"The last time she had those dreams her father was killed in that hostage hold up at the factory," Dean said concerned, remembering how hard she had taken her father's death.

"I'm keeping an eye on her, I don't think it's anything, but I will let you know if I think you need to get involved. She's just having dreams about Ridgecliffe Manor. Nothing like before. Brad said as he started back up again.

"Why is she dreaming about that place?" Dean asked confused.

"Hell if I know," he said smiling maybe she's the one with the yeast infection.

"You know I'm going to have to tell her that one," Dean joked trying not to laugh.

"Go ahead and I'll have to tell her about your affair.' Brad said as he held out his hand. "Spot me a ten, I forgot my wallet."

"What affair?" Dean asked as he reached into his pocket and pulled out the money and handed it to him as he sighed.

"Head of Radish, I forgot what his, her name was," he laughed as he walked over to the register.

"It's Cabbage, and there is no affair with anyone!" Dean called out.

"You know that, and I know that, but she won't. Thanks," he said and walked out the door.

"Keep the change," he said as Brad left, ignoring him.

One thing you could always count on was Brad not having any money! The guy had a small fortune in the bank and still walked around with empty pockets. Dean got up, dropped five dollars on the table and went over to the counter to pay his bill.

"Want some pie to go?" The waitress asked him.

Dean smiled and answered "No Thanks," he paid the bill and walked out to the patrol car. This was going to be a long night, he thought to himself as he drove off. As much as he tried, he could not shake the memory of Linda Edwards and their kiss. She did not realize how serious this thing with Duke was. He usually was not dangerous, he just liked to talk big, but he had been embarrassed in front of his friends, so who knew what he might do. Dean had no doubt that Linda could take care of herself, but Duke could be more than she bargained for; next time a fork might not stop him.

---

Linda threw the last of the boxes she had unpacked down to the basement, and then went down to pile them with the ones she had thrown down earlier neatly in the corner. The basement itself was as large as the first floor. It was full of junk left over from years piling, not to mention dark and dirty. All the outside rooms were made of stone, but the inside walls that broke the basement into six rooms were made of brick.

Lonely light bulbs, hung from cord switches were all that lit it up, barely giving off enough light to see. She stacked the boxes in the corner, and then investigated each of the rooms. The last and farthest room was a meat locker room, where the Ridgecliffe's used to butcher their meat. A large freezer was built along the far wall where the meat used to be stored when the mansion was in its prime.

A quiet purr filled the room as she plugged the freezer in. She opened the door and stared in. It would be perfect for what she needed it for. The room made her thirsty. It started with her feet then soared through all her veins to her head. Tonight was the night she would start feeding again. There was no way around it, and she would start it now. She turned off the lights downstairs and went up to get dressed. She was going out to get some real food.

# Chapter 8 - Nice to meet you Ray...

Linda stuffed the last blonde curl under the long red wig. She hated this wig, it reminded her of Samantha, but if she was going to do this it meant sacrificing. The blood red dress fit her snugly as she ran her hands over her body.

"Even in this horrible wig, they won't able to resist me," she said to her image as she took off her wedding rings and glanced back in the mirror to apply another layer of dark red lipstick to her lips.

The lipstick was the finishing touches on her evening look. She knew she was going to stand out in the bar like a sore thumb, which is exactly what she wanted. She wanted to attract them all. Attention was better than any drug. Plus the more she attracted the better her selection would be.

"Look out guys, here I come," Linda said out loud, smiling as she exited the house.

The red sports car quickly backed out of the garage, sending the gravel rock flying and blowing up a cloud of smoke into the dark night. The taste for blood was overwhelming her, she wasn't sure she would be able to make it to the club. It had been several weeks since she had fed and she could tell it in her complexion.

Columbia, Missouri was about twenty miles east of the mansion and had a larger population than Hagan Cove, thanks in part to the universities in town, so it was the perfect spot. Linda pulled the Porsche through Rocheport, a small town between the two cities where she had rented a storage building. Quickly she pulled around the building and pushed the button that opened the double garage doors and turned on the lights. Without hesitation she pulled the car in beside a black Eclipse. Her heels clapped on the concrete floor as she went around the car and got into the other. It sure was nice of Michael's estate to sell his car to her after he committed suicide. She smiled as the doors closed and she pulled back out on the highway. "God, I love it here," she thought to herself as she listened to the relaxing orchestra music coming from the radio.

The dance club on the outer edge of town was lit up like a Christmas tree. The parking lot was already packed and what spots that were empty, were filing up fast. This was the perfect spot. "So many people around too many opinions of what she looked like," she thought as she pulled the car into a space that another car had just pulled out of. With a crowd that large police would get a million different descriptions when they questioned them about the soon to be missing man.

Inside the bar, the latest dance hits blared through the sound system as bright lights flashed to the pulsating beats. The sound was about twenty notches louder than it should be for her liking. "Half the people here would be deaf tomorrow," she thought as she passed her way through the drunks and drunken wannabes and made herself available at the bar.

The rum and coke she ordered was a little strong, so she took small sips. She had to keep a clear mind, she remembered as she glanced around the club. Several men there fit the right profile. Her rules were that they had to be nice looking if possible, definitely clean, and married. Being married took precedence over the other two, it was the most important. Cheating husbands had to be stopped! She needed something that they had, so this way she killed two birds with one stone.

After completely surveying the building, she found her target. He was a nice looking blond about thirty-three, clean, and had some tramp on his lap. They were joined at the lips. She turned her stool around, facing him, her skirt riding up, exposing more of her long legs. She stared at him for a couple of minutes before he caught her stare and smiled back. She winked and turned back around so she was facing the bar, keeping a close eye on him through the mirror behind the bar. He would be over soon, they always did. A man slid into the seat next to her and tried to buy her a drink, but she gave him a dirty look that said "get lost" and he did.

"This seat taken?" He asked smoothly, sitting beside her, not waiting for an answer. He looked her body up and down, smiling as he did.

"It's open; the last guy didn't measure up. He was looking for a commitment," she said sexily, slowly taking a slip from her drink, watching him closely from the corner of her eye.

"And you're not?"

"I'm looking for a one night stand! No questions, no answers. You interested?" She asked seductively, looking him directly in the eyes.

"I'm still here. Name's Ray. What's yours?" He asked as he ordered them another drink.

"Call me…Samantha," Linda said. The name just seemed to run off her lips naturally.

"Well Samantha, is it just me or can you feel the electricity between us?"

"Oh I feel something, but I don't think its electricity," she said as she guided his hand away as it started to slip under her dress. "What happened to your girlfriend? You two looked like Siamese twins joined at the lips."

"Just a friend," he quietly stated as he quickly gulped down his drink.

"You treat all your friends that way?" She laughed as she took another small sip of her drink.

"Only the female ones," he said as he started to slide his hand under her dress again.

"What does your wife think of your… friends?" She asked. His hand slipped completely away from her this time and wrapped around his drink as his body stiffened. She could tell he was contemplating leaving.

"She's not exactly here now is she," he said, starting to get up.

"Relax sugar; I don't want her here either. What she doesn't know won't hurt her, will it?" She asked as she grabbed his hand and put it back on her leg, keeping it covered with her own as she leaned in closer to him. "It's a little crowded in here what you think about taking a ride? I could use a little fresh air."

Linda had to say no more. He grabbed her hand and started pushing his way through the crowd to the front door. She had him. She knew from the start today was going to be perfect. She watched his body move quickly as he pulled her through the crowd. She desperately needed his blood. She just hoped she could wait.

"My truck is just over here," he said, leading her that way.

"That's not exactly my style, why don't we go to my place. It's not far," she said, dragging him to her car. He started to protest, but she kissed him and gave him a preview of what was to come. He shut up and did as he was commanded.

"You live in a storage warehouse?" Ray questioned nervously as they pulled up to the dark building.

"No," Linda laughed as she pushed the button and opened the doors. "I just keep my car here."

"Whose car are we in?" He asked looking around the dark surroundings. Thoughts of a recent horror film he had just seen on television started rushing into his brain.

"It belongs to a friend of mine. There's my car," she said as she drove up beside the Porsche and stopped the car. "I don't like driving it to the clubs. Drunks tend to do things to it."

"Like what?" He asked as he got out of the car and started admiring the Porsche. "What a fucking hot car!"

"Yes, well it was. Some asshole keyed down the whole drivers side and then I got hit by a bike at a club last week, so I stopped driving it when I decide to go out and, well slut around," Linda said taking his hand. So you want to drive?" Ray about wet his pants with excitement as she handed him the keys. She became a little irritated with him for not opening the door for her; he just rushed over to the driver side and jumped in. Linda sighed heavily as she opened her door and climbed in. Maybe letting him drive the car was not as good of an idea as she thought, but it did instantly relax him, she could tell he was starting to have doubts about being with her.

Linda continued giving him directions as he drove the sports car at top speed, truly enjoying himself and getting them to the mansion at record breaking time. This was an advantage, because she didn't know how much longer she could take his tasteless jokes and sexual advances.

"This is where you live?" He asked as he reluctantly stepped from the car, and looked up at the mansion standing before him.

"I know it's small, but I kind of like it. Are you coming in?" She asked as she stepped up on the porch and unlocked the front doors. "Please don't keep me waiting."

"This isn't going to cost me anything is it, I've only got about fifty bucks on me," he asked as he followed her into the house.

It took every ounce of strength she had to keep from killing him right then and there. How dare he confuse her with a hooker. He would pay dearly for that remark. A hooker could not even afford the shoes she was wearing.

"Now Ray darling, do I look like that kind of girl?" She asked, trying to hide the anger in her voice.

"No, not really. I just wanted to make sure, that's all. You don't have an old man coming home soon, do you?" He asked nervously.

"No, I'm a widow, so you can relax," she said as she kissed him and started unbuttoning his shirt. "We have the whole house to ourselves. Come on, let's go upstairs."

"Never seen that color of red before," he remarked about the color of the walls in the library.

"And you probably won't again. It was specially made just for me. I stuck a needle in my finger and spilled my blood on the paper smeared it around and told them to match it. I think they did a good job, don't you?" She asked. "I painted the dining room the same color. Now are you here to discuss my decorating or do you want to go upstairs and have some fun?"

Ray didn't answer, just smiled as he followed closely behind her, smacking her butt once they got to the top of the stairs. She turned around fast like she was going to hit him, but suddenly smiled and kissed him again. She led him down the hallway to the guest bedroom.

Once they had completely entered the room he was all over her. She definitely had a live one tonight. She pulled his shirt off and ran her fingers over his chest. He threw his head back and moaned as her nails gently dug into his skin. "He was in for the time of his life, one that he would have never forgotten, providing he would have been given the opportunity to live through it." Linda thought as she watched him.

"Get undressed," she ordered as she kicked off her shoes, slipped out of her dress and crossed around the bed to the night table in just her silk slip.

Linda waited patiently as he finished undressing and pulled back the covers of the bed, climbing in. She pulled open the drawer, taking out several pairs of nylon stockings. She smiled and placed them on the bed beside him, blowing him a kiss. He never said a word, just watched her closely. She took his hand, first massaging it and running her fingers through his before bringing it to her lips, kissing the back of his hand gently. She smiled to him as she moved it over to the solid wood post, tying it up with nylon. It was a little tight, but when she climbed on top of him and started kissing him on the mouth he soon forgot about it, as she moved over to the other hand.

After both hands were tied up, she ripped the covers off him, dragging them across the room, exposing him to the chilly air of the central air. She let out a small laugh as she watched him shiver. Goose bumps had completely covered his body.

"It's kind of chilly in here," he said to her, starting to get uncomfortable with the situation. "Can you turn the air off?"

"Don't worry, I plan to warm you up," she said as she went over and lit the gas fireplace.

Linda waited for the fire to take off before she turned off the lights. Shadows danced across the walls like large demons gathering for a sacrifice. She slithered back to the bed, grabbing the other nylons and tied his feet to the foot boards post.

"Are you enjoying yourself yet?" She asked as she stuffed the last nylon deep into his mouth. "Now you can be as loud as you want, and you won't give me a headache."

Linda kissed the side of his face and then down across his neck, over his shoulders and down his arm. He let out a groan through the gag. She glanced back at him, looked him right in the eyes and smiled, then went back to kissing his arm all the way down to his wrist. Suddenly, without warning, she bit into his wrist, cutting into the tender skin.

The blood trickled into her open lips filling her with the desire for more. She reached under the pillow, grabbing the small pocket knife she had placed there earlier and sliced his wrist open before he even had time to register what had just happened. The blood rushed into her mouth so quickly she could not swallow it as fast, sending it pouring out the side of her mouth. He jerked and twisted, desperately trying to break free.

"Stop squirming, you can't get loose. If you would have stayed home with your wife like you should have, this would not have happened to you!" She yelled at him through bloody teeth as she slid across the bed and sliced into his other wrist.

The blood tasted sweet as it gushed down her throat, filling her with its warmth. It had been a long time since she had drank human blood. Her husband had let her cut him a couple times while they made love, but it was never as fulfilling as this. She crossed the room to the closet and pulled out the empty jars. Holding the jars under his wrist, she squeezed out what blood she could, waiting patiently for the jars to fill before she sealed them and put them on the night table.

"I just want to tell you Ray, I really enjoyed our evening tonight. I guess you see now why I'm only into one night stands," she told him as she reached into the night table drawer and pulled out a larger knife. "One night with me and there just isn't much left for another."

Ray's eyes grew wide as she brought the knife to her lips and kissed it. He tried to break free one last time, but moving just dug the nylons deep into the wounds in his wrist, making the pain even more excruciating. Linda slowly bent over and kissed his neck several times. She could feel his heart beating in his neck. In one swift motion the knife cut deep into his throat ending his struggling battle to be free and his life. Linda's lips found their way to his throat and she fed.

After drinking all the blood her body could hold, she took the gray tape and covered the wounds in his wrist and throat to prevent leakage, before taping over his eyes and mouth. She untied the nylons, released the body, and let it drop to the floor. Stripping off all the sheets and grabbing his clothes, she threw them into a basket; she would incinerate them shortly.

Ray's body slid nicely on the polished wood floors to the back staircase where she rolled it down the stairs. She then drug him through the back hall to the basement door, where once again, she threw his body down the stairs. Getting him this far had been a lot easier than she had planned. Originally it had been her idea to carpet the house stairs, but thank God she had listened to her decorator and refinished them instead.

Linda dragged the corpse through the basement rooms and laid him on the floor in the back of the freezer. As long as Stella did not come down here, everything would be fine. But as scared of the dark as that woman was, she did not think that would be a problem. This part might take a little more planning, she thought as she broke out the light bulbs overhead in rooms that came before the meat locker, making the basement pitch dark. She glanced through the dark smiling as she went back upstairs to clean up the mess.

"Too bad Stella couldn't clean this mess up!" Linda grunted out loud as she washed the plastic mattress cover and made the bed up with fresh linens.

After finishing with the bed, she mopped the floor and glanced around the room. She smiled to herself, no one could not tell that anyone had even been in this room tonight, let alone died here. She turned out the light and shut the door.

"It's so good to be drinking blood again," she said as she headed back to the main floor to her bedroom.

Linda pulled the wig off and let her blond hair fall down around her shoulders. "It felt so good to have that hot thing off," she thought to herself as she turned on the water in the shower and let the blood stained slip fall to the floor, she would have to incinerate it after she was done bathing.

Softly stepping from the shower, her feet sunk into the plush carpet as she crossed the bathroom to her new whirlpool tub and slid in. This was the life, she thought to herself as the bubbly water boiled around her. She felt so relaxed, so calm. No more Rick yelling at her, hitting her, and then running off to that slut. No more Michael Williams always nagging her with business. No more Floyd Myers following her, breathing his bad breath down her neck.

"Fuck all you guys!" Linda said evilly as she smiled.

All those things seemed like years ago. She did miss Steve though. It had been nice waking up beside him these past few weeks in the morning, holding on to him at night; it made her feel so lonely to sleep alone. She had started to invite Steve to move to Ridgecliffe Manor with her, but knew that obviously would not be a good idea. He was furious with her when she broke it off, but she was sure he would survive; besides, he was starting to ask her too many questions all the time. No, it was best that she ended that relationship before she had to kill him too.

Now there was Sheriff Dean Richards in her life. Just the thought of him made her body tingle all over. She wanted him more than she ever wanted any man before and she intended to have him! She picked up her glass and drank another sip of Ray's blood. She wondered what Dean's blood tasted like as she licked her lips.

"Stop it!" She yelled out to herself. She had to stop thinking about him or she would explode! She would give just about anything if he was here right now.

Linda closed her eyes and imagined Dean walking into the bathroom, slowly removing his clothes and climbing into the tub to make love to her. She could almost feel his hard muscled body against her. In the middle of their passionate lovemaking he would bite into his wrist and offer his blood to her. How sweet it would taste. But for now she would have to settle for Ray's.

"Thank you Ray," she said out loud and laughed. "It was very nice to meet you, or as the English would say, bloody nice to meet you. Soon Dean, you and I will be together. Soon it will be your blood," she took another drink and let it run down her throat as she laughed out loud.

# Chapter 9 - The battle begins.

Sheriff Dean Richards made his nightly rounds through the downtown square where most of the stores in town held up shop. It was a nice quiet, friendly area, filled with rich elegant mid eighteen hundreds architecture. Most of the buildings still had their old charm, but were showing signs of deterioration. The town mayor had started a campaign to restore the square, but so far not much money had been raised. As he slowly turned the cruiser around the corner and started off into the residential areas, his mind slid back to the memories of that evening.

Linda Edwards was definitely some lady. He had encountered aggressive women before, especially when he was writing them tickets, their offers ranging from intimate back rubs to sexual favors. But Linda was in her own category way above the others. She definitely was a great kisser, he thought with a smile. She had only been in town a day and already there was trouble, but just how much trouble was yet to be seen.

Duke Etherton was one man that you don't mess with, especially his ego, and Linda had managed within five minutes to do both! There would be another confrontation and he would have to be ready for it. But still he had to admire her; most women would have never stood up to Duke. Dean wondered if all the women in Kansas City were like her, if they were, he was definitely going there on his next vacation.

After driving the car back through the neighborhood once again, he proceeded to cross to the other side of town, in the historic district where cities most influential lived. Turning the corner, he noticed the lights on inside the Hagan Cove Realty office and Samantha's car parked by the door. Instantly he stopped and pulled the vehicle in the lot beside hers. It had been a few days since he had seen her, and usually Brad was there, so he thought it would be nice to talk to her alone. Samantha peeked through the closed blinds and then unlocked the door, throwing it open and greeting him with a friendly smile.

"Dean, I didn't expect you out tonight, I figured you would be out busting all the local bad guys," she joked with him as she let him in, closing and locking the door behind him.

"All rounded up and sleeping like babies," he replied.

"And now after all that hard work you suddenly got the urge to buy a new house, right?" She asked as she finished gathering up the papers on her desk.

"Yeah right, not on my salary, if you will please remember, it was you tight wad voters vetoed out my raise for this year! Remember?" He joked with her as he looked at the pictures of the houses for sale around town.

"Now why would I vote that down knowing that you would use that extra twenty bucks a year to buy a house? There's a nice three bedroom by your left hand that is just two blocks from your office, so you could go home and see the little rug rats on your lunch hour," she said as she pointed to a nice little brick ranch by his hand.

"How can I have rug rats when I can't even get you to go out with me?" He asked her seriously, looking from the picture over to her.

"Well there is always adoption. I hear being a single father these days is the in thing. Women claim that it is really sexy."

"What are you talking about?" He asked, confused.

"Just something I read somewhere, just forget it," she said, stepping back away from him and suddenly feeling very uncomfortable.

"Listen, not to change this suddenly strange subject. I uh, what I really wanted to ask you is that the mayor has got this city fund raiser started for the downtown remodeling project and the first big event is a dance, and as a city official, I need to be there and I figured that you would want to make an appearance for possible contacts. This is really something that you need a date for, someone real charming, and I really don't know any charming women and so I kind of hoped maybe you would go with me," he joked shyly.

"Thank you, now I really know why you're thirty and still single."

"You know I'm just kidding, but I would like for you to be my date," he asked again.

"I'm sorry Dean; with summer here we have been so busy. I just don't see how I would ever be able to stop long enough to go. I have enough paper work to last me a year! I wish I could, but…,"

"It's all right, I'm sure I can find someone out there desperate enough to go with me," he joked, cutting her off and looking back at the pictures.

"Brad's pretty desperate," she said and relaxed when she saw him smile.

"I will keep that in mind," he said as he glanced over the photos and stopped at the last one that had big red letters saying "sold" across the glossy photo. "Linda Edwards paid that much for that place?"

"Hard to believe isn't it, but one better, she paid it in cash!" She replied, coming up behind him. "It's a morbid evil place, and it fits her perfectly!"

"I take it that you two don't get along?" He asked.

"That's an understatement! I just don't like people who think they are better than everyone else. That woman thinks she's the queen bee of the world and the rest of us are here just to please her," Samantha said with a hint of anger in her voice. "Since you know her name, I assume that you have had the displeasure of meeting her, or has Brad filled you in on her low cut bust line and short skirts?"

"I met her actually," he smiled as he thought back to their kiss, hoping he wasn't blushing. "Her and Duke Etherton had a little altercation this afternoon at Lilly's Café."

"An altercation? Really, what happened?" She asked, listening with sudden eagerness.

"Well according to the café, she and Duke were having lunch and got into an argument and she stabbed him with her fork in the upper thigh. A little higher and he could have sang soprano in the church choir next Sunday, providing he could find the church," he said, trying not to laugh.

"Linda Edwards and Duke were having lunch together! Come on Dean, he's hardly her type!" Samantha said in disbelief.

"Well the waitress said he called her his old lady and she assumed they had a lovers spat," he told her of what he knew about the case. "That's not the best of it. Apparently after the incident inside she went out and drove her car through their bikes and told him when he became a real man to call her."

Both of them laughed uncontrollably at the days' mishaps until they had tears in their eyes. This was one of the things he liked about Samantha; times like this when he could just be himself, when they just talked about things and let loose. If only she would go out with him. He had asked her now for years and she always had an excuse, but he kept trying just in case she let down one day and said yes.

"I'm sorry I missed that one. Was he hurt?" She asked as she calmed down.

"Not really, just mainly drew blood, ruined his filthy jeans," he laughed.

"Did you arrest her?" She asked curiously.

"No, neither Duke nor the Café would press charges, so I gave both of them a warning, but I don't think either one of them paid much attention to me. They're probably plotting each others murder right now as we speak," he said as he looked at his watch and noticed the hour. "Listen, I better run and let you get home, it's getting pretty late. Are you sure about the dance?"

"Sorry, I really can't make it, Max is on my case now as it is," she repeated as she walked him to the door, locking it as he exited.

Samantha watched as Dean drove off. It took every ounce of her being to not burst through that door and run after him, but she couldn't. Every time she saw him in his uniform it would bring back the memories of her childhood and that terrible night that the deputies knocked on their door and told her and her mother that her father, the sheriff, had been shot and killed in the line of duty. She remembered the way it tore her family apart. She would never let herself get in a position like that again no matter what, not for Dean, not for anyone.

The telephone suddenly rang behind her making her jump, as it brought her back into reality. It was after ten, who would be calling this late? At first she wasn't going to answer it, but something told her to. She knew as she picked up the receiver and spoke that she would later regret it.

"Samantha, thank God! I have tried everywhere to reach you. Aren't you ever home?" A terrified woman's voice she recognized as Mary Pullman, Duke's girlfriend.

"Mary, calm down, what's wrong?" Samantha asked her.

"It's Ray, I think he's in trouble! He left me and ran off with some strange woman he saw at the bar! That was over two hours ago! His truck is in the lot, but he's no where to be found! I've looked everywhere. I don't know what to do! He's vanished!" She cried.

"I think you need to go home and forget him. Let his wife mess with him. Besides, Duke told you he would kill you if he caught you with Ray again. I really don't understand you. You know someone is going to tell him that you were out with another man, you know how people talk around this town!" She told the person who had attached herself to Samantha two years ago and now thought they were best friends.

"I can't just leave! Something has happened to him, he would have never left his truck! You should have seen this woman. She was unbelievable! No woman really looks like that!" Mary continued.

"Did she have long blonde hair?" Samantha asked her curiously off the top of her head.

"No, it was long, but red, kind of like yours. She had on a tight dress, acted like one of those high society bitches you see on television. She definitely was not from around here!"

"I really don't know what you want me to do about it?" Samantha asked her. Surely it wasn't Linda Edwards with him? But, then again, she was with Duke earlier today.

"I don't know. You're just so smart I knew that you would know what to do. Please, you have to help me!" She pleaded. "Something terrible has happened to him, I can just feel it. You know how I sense these things!"

"You better get home before Duke does and beats the crap out of you like he did the last time. Just get some sleep and I'm sure Ray will be back in the morning," she told her and listened as Mary hung up.

Mary Pullman was the type of woman who got herself in one problem after another and then went and cried to everybody for help. At the beginning of Duke's and her relationship she had tried to help Mary get out and make a new start, but she kept running back, so Samantha more or less wrote her off then. Still, at least once a month she would call her with a new problem, and it was usually about Ray or Duke or even some other guy she had met!

Duke was insanely jealous of Mary and would constantly beat her every time she even looked at another man, yet she still ran off and started having an affair. Her latest was Ray Thompson, who wasn't a bad guy, except for the fact that he had been married for the last eight years. Every once in a while Mary would call her and fill her in on all the gory details of their sex life, if you called what those two did sex, sometimes just barely finishing up as Duke came home from his nightly escapades with other women. Those three made her life dull and boring in comparison, which she gladly accepted.

One thing bothered her about the woman Mary had described. She fit all the details of Linda Edwards except for the hair, which could be a wig, but what would she want with Ray? But she was with Duke earlier today. What was she up to? Samantha thought as she went though her file and found Linda's phone number. There was an easy way to find out if Linda had been with Ray, she thought as she dialed Linda's number.

"What!" Linda shouted into the phone after several rings.

"I need to talk to Ray Thompson," Samantha told her not using her real voice.

"You idiot, you have the wrong number. I suggest you check the listing before you call this late again," she yelled at her.

"I saw him with you earlier tonight and he went home with you didn't he?" She baited her.

"Well you're mistaken Samantha, I don't run around with married men!" Linda yelled, and then slammed the phone down.

Samantha's hand dropped the receiver and she stood motionless. Her heart beat rapidly as she realized Linda knew it was her! How could she have known it was her? She had blocked the call, but most importantly how did she know Ray was married? She caught a hold of herself and put the receiver back and grabbed her things. She had to get out of here!

Within five minutes she was pulling her car into her driveway and searching unsuccessfully for the garage door opener. Giving up, she grabbed her things and got out. The summer winds were blowing her neighbor's trash that the dogs had gotten into across her yard. She decided she was going to buy them a trash can!

The full moon lit up her one and a half story contemporary house. It, like the others in the area, had lots of glass that gave the rooms a bright open feeling during the day but at night allowed everyone to see in. Some like her had vertical blinds over the large windows, but others like her neighbor's left them open, giving the world an inside look at their private lives. Their own reality show! Samantha smiled as she walked up her sidewalk and looked into the house next door. The family of four was playing cards together. It gave her a sudden feeling of loneliness and a desire for a family of her own.

The house next door shown brightly with warmth and family, but glancing into the open blinds in her living room showed nothing but emptiness. The moon was brightly lighting up the room through the three large skylights in the roof, perfectly silhouetting each piece of furniture and picture on the wall. She was grateful the house was clean.

Suddenly she froze in her tracks; tiny shivers started from her head and poured through her body. A dark figure had just run through the living room! Her heart beat rapidly as she moved closer to the door. Her first instinct was to run next door and call Dean, but since all these nightmares lately she had learned not to trust her eyes. She would have to go in there alone. Most likely she had just imagined it. Her hands were sweaty as she unlocked the door and opened it. A blast of heat hit her the minute she walked through the door.

Forgetting about the mysterious figure, she turned on the lights, rushing into the hall to the thermostat. It read ninety degrees! She turned the heat off, then started running around downstairs, opening windows and letting in the fresh evening air. Before she could start upstairs, she was stopped by the ringing of the telephone.

"Hello," she answered, but there was no one there, only dead silence. It must be off the hook upstairs. Someone was upstairs!

Samantha reached into the hall closet and grabbed a baseball bat and started upstairs. Step by step she proceeded. Her heart was beating hard as though it was about to pound out of her chest. She crossed the balcony overlooking the living room below and came upon the closed master bedroom door. The doorknob, despite the heat in the house, was cold and clammy. The door creaked open. She reached for the bedroom light, but nothing came on. Slowly she walked across the room to her dresser and flipped on the lamp, instantly lighting the room.

A scream ripped from her throat as she looked in the mirror and then turned around. Linda Edwards was standing in front of the window, holding an ax at her side. Blood dripped from its sharp edge.

"You just could not mind your own business, could you? You just have to stick your nose in where it doesn't belong!" Linda said to her, her breathing became rapid as she raised the ax.

Samantha ran across the room to the door. Behind her she could feel the ax whipping in the wind. There was a splintering crash as it ripped into the door trim beside her, just barely missing her head.

"You can't run from me, I'm everywhere! I'll find you!" Linda screamed at her as she ran from the room.

Running as fast as she could she reached the stairs, but before she could start down them Linda grabbed the back of her long hair and painfully stopped her. She was jerked around and forced to look her attacker straight in the eye. An evil smile spread across Linda's face and flames appeared in her eyes as she glared at her; pure hate had consumed her. Then with one push she threw Samantha through the rail of the balcony and watched as she crashed to the floor below. Looking up from the floor, she could see Linda laughing at her. The room started spinning and suddenly everything grew pitch dark!

Samantha awoke still in the darkness. Hissing noises were coming from all around her, giving her goose bumps. Was she dead? She thought to herself. She felt around the floor, finally reaching a wall and stood up. Using it as a guide she walked slowly around until she came upon a door. Quickly she turned the knob and opened it. Light flooded around her as she stepped through the door and into the hallway. The walls around her were blood red. The trophies of animals' heads were hanging on the walls, their stuffed heads moving and screeching at her as she passed them. Blood poured from their mouths as if they had just been beheaded. Every bone in her body felt as though it had broken.

The horrible smell of rotting corpses covered the air around her, making her gag. Something was oozing around her feet, making it difficult to walk, but she dared not look down. A large door was all that was left now of the hall and she had no option left but to enter it. She had died and this was her personal hell! Reaching out, she opened the door and stepped in. White neon tube lights came on overhead as she entered. The door behind her slammed shut! As she looked around, she realized she was in what appeared to be a meat locker.

She crossed the room to the large freezer at the far end. Her shoes stuck like glue to the blood covered floor. Reaching down, she pulled her feet out of her shoes and moved forward. Something was in that freezer that she needed to see! The freezer door opened with a clank and the light came on as she stepped in. Her bare feet instantly stuck to the floor. Her skin ripped off and stuck to the frozen floor as she pulled them free. With an intense pain, she continued moving toward the large bag hanging from the hook at the end of the freezer. She shivered from the cold air and moved toward the bag.

Fresh blood was dripping out of the bottom of the zipper. Reaching out with her hand she touched the cold zipper and pulled it down, opening the bag. Ray Thompson's mutilated body stared out at her. Blood dripped from his empty eye sockets. She turned to run and slipped, falling on her face and causing it to stick to the frozen floor. As Samantha ripped her face away from the floor, pain exploded through her body, but all she could think about was getting out of there! Blood poured out from the fresh muscle and tissue now exposed. Her hand reaching up, she screamed as tears filled her eyes as she touched what was left of her face.

"Help me!" She heard Ray's body say behind her just before he fell on her. Throwing the body off her, she jumped up off the floor with renewed strength. A loud laughter was coming from all directions around her. There was no doubt about it, it was Linda Edwards! She ran to the door and forced herself back out into the locker.

"I don't mess with married men, Samantha!" Linda laughed behind her.

The laugh echoed throughout her brain, making her feel like it was going to explode! Turning to face Linda, she noticed she had slipped from the room and the door was starting to close behind her. Running as fast as she could go, she barely managed to get through just before it slammed shut. She was back into the bloody hallway. The animal trophies had apparently died, for all their heads were hanging low and they had quit making all that noise. At the end of the hall she could see a man staring back at her. It was Brad! She started to run towards him, but stopped as she came upon him. Something was not right. He was stripped from the waist up and had a dead look in his eyes like he was in a trance. He suddenly knelt before her and stayed on his knees.

"Welcome to my little party, I'm so glad you could make it," Linda said as she stepped from the darkness. A large knife was in her right hand.

She walked up behind him and knelt down. Slowly she kissed his ear and then licked down across his throat. Samantha stood paralyzed as she watched her. Brad smiled and kissed Linda on the lips, their kisses becoming more and more passionate. Linda stopped and brought the knife to his throat and made a small incision. Blood streamed from it and Linda's lips immediately covered the fresh wound. Brad's hand reached up and pushed Linda's head closer. "He was enjoying it!" Samantha thought to herself.

"You really should try this," Linda said to her, then took the knife and ripped through his throat.

"Brad!" She screamed as she ran to his slumped over body.

Linda smiled at her and licked the blood off her lips. A flaming glare erupted in her eyes as she slowly walked down the hall, not looking back at Samantha and Brad. Her hand reached up and touched one of the cows' heads. It awoke and screeched in pain just before it exploded. Linda's evil laughter shook the hall as she disappeared.

"Brad!" Samantha cried as she held his body close. "I'm so sorry Brad."

Suddenly something grabbed her and shook her. The hallway started to crack and rip apart. All the animal heads all came back to life, howling in pain as the walls burst into flames. Samantha covered her face and screamed. A bright light blinded her.

"Samantha, can you hear me!" A strange man asked lightly shaking her.

"Brad!" She screamed as she jumped to alertness.

"I'm right here!" He said as he ran to her bedside. "I'm right here."

"Where am I?" She asked, quickly looking around the room, then facing him. "Thank God you're alive!"

"It's more like thank God you're alive, after that fall off the balcony.

You're in the emergency room! Your neighbors called me. They heard you screaming and yelling. When they got in your house you were lying on the floor. They thought you were dead! But don't worry, the doctor says after you get some rest you 'll be all right," he said, stroking her hair.

Suddenly everything came back to her. The phone call, the dark shadow running across the living room, and Linda Edwards! She had been in her house and had tried to kill her! And Ray Thompson! She started screaming and tried to get up from the bed. Pain burst through every inch of her body as Brad and the doctor forced her back down. A nurse rushed over and gave her a shot.

"Don't do this to me! Don't make me go back to sleep, she'll make me go back to that horrible place!" She cried. "Linda was in my house, she tried to kill me Brad! She was there and she wants to kill you too!"

"Just calm down. No one can get you now. I'm here and Dean's just down the hall. It's going to be okay!" She heard Brad say as she drifted off to sleep.

"Is she going to be all right?" Dean asked Brad as he came from the room.

"Physically yes, Doctor says nothing's broken. She's going to be real sore for a few days, but other than that she is fine. It's mentally that I'm worried about," he told him as he sat down in the chair and ran his fingers through his hair.

"What do you mean by that?"

"She's just really out there, could be the drugs the doctor gave her," Brad said, suddenly realizing how tired he was and not really wanting to discus this any more.

"Did she give you any idea how she fell?" Dean asked as he sat in the chair beside him.

"She said Linda Edwards pushed her," he replied.

"Linda Edwards?" Dean said shocked. "How could she? The neighbors reported not seeing anyone around the house but her. There were no signs of forced entry."

"I don't know. She was pretty upset. You need to talk to Valerie about it. She told me Samantha's been having some pretty bad nightmares about Linda and some bad things about that old house. I told you what

I knew earlier I don't know what else to tell you Dean, maybe she's now seeing them while she's awake," he said, getting up. "I need to get going; I have to get up in four hours to get ready for an appointment. Call me tomorrow with what you find out, okay?"

"I'll call your cell," Dean said, then watched Brad wave and get in the elevator.

He quietly walked into Samantha's room and watched her sleeping. Could it be possible that Linda was there? It just seemed hard to believe that the same woman that just a few hours ago had her tongue down his throat just pushed Samantha off a balcony. Silently he turned and walked down the hallway. Thankfully he would be off work in another hour, he desperately needed some sleep as well.

# Chapter 10 - Searching for answers.

Linda, after only one week in town, had already found herself bored. She was used to the hustle of the corporate life and now was all alone out in the sticks with nothing to do. "Could Michael have been right?" She thought to herself. "Is she going to regret giving up her job and moving here?" Quickly Linda let that thought pass from her mind.

There were lots of things to do; she just had to discover them. This was a whole new world for her. She decided it was time to go out and get a good look at the new city she called home. She got dressed and drove downtown to do a little shopping, when it came to shopping, she definitely missed the Kansas City stores! She turned the corner past the little grocery store and came to a dead stop in the middle of the street.

"Things are definitely looking up now," she said smiling to herself.

The sheriff's car was in the parking lot. Linda quickly turned her car around, pulling in beside the patrol car. She made her attack plans as she checked her hair and makeup, jumped out of the car and entered the store. Her high heels clapped loudly on the tile floor, causing everyone she passed to stop and look, but she paid no attention. She had one mission in this place and that was to find Sheriff Dean Richards!

The inside of the store was larger than it looked from the outside. Finding him was going to be harder than she thought. She grabbed a cart and started down the isle, casually throwing things in. Not really paying attention to what she was buying, she focused her attention on her mission. Several isles later she found him in the produce department. She smiled and headed right for him.

"Well imagine seeing you here, I figured all you did was give tickets and rescue damsels in distress?" She said smiling as she stood beside him.

"That's only when I'm working, now that I'm off duty I like to stake out grocery stores. Make sure the vegetables are fresh," he said with a smile. "How are you doing Mrs. Edwards? Are you enjoying life in the small town?"

"Please call me Linda. Mrs. Edwards makes me sound like an old woman,"

"Okay, Linda, you wouldn't by any chance know how to cook this do you?" He asked, holding up a strange looking vegetable.

"I'm not even sure what it is; let alone how to cook it. I really hate to admit it, but I don't know much about things like that. The last time I tried to cook they had to call the fire department."

"I figured you would be a gourmet cook," he said grinning as he put it back on the shelf.

"If I can be honest with you, I still have not figured out what all those buttons are on the stove. I mean, I know how to turn the burners on. The problem is all the other things. I swear my kitchen appliances have more buttons on them than my computer. I think that they are starting to make things too complicated in hopes of simplifying our lives."

"That's why I stick to buying used appliances, you're lucky if it has all the burner knobs," he said laughing.

Linda watched his face as his smile took it over. He was the kind of guy that when he smiled, his whole face lit up. It was a genuine smile. "I'll keep that in mind." she said as she grabbed some bananas and carelessly tossed them into the cart. "It's really sad, I can run a multi million dollar company, but put me in the kitchen and it is a recipe for disaster!"

"That's why God created TV dinners and sandwiches. Well anyway, it was good seeing you, I better get going; I have to pick up a friend of mine that is getting out of the hospital today. I hope to see you later," he said as he started pushing his cart down the isle.

"Sheriff!" Linda said, stopping him. "About last night, when you were at my house. I really need to apologize for the way I acted, I don't normally come on to guys like that, especially kiss them, it was completely out of character. I really don't know what came over me," she apologized as her words rambled on.

"I have to admit it was a little awkward, but it was kind of nice also. A little unusual, but a nice surprise," he said shyly, stumbling through his own words. His face turned a little red as he remembered how much he actually enjoyed it. "By the way, you can call me Dean."

"Please Dean, don't think I'm always like that, actually I'm a little shy, but I don't know what it was about you that just made me go temporarily crazy. I hope that you will let me make it up to you," she asked. "I'm sure you're used to women going bananas over you."

"That's really not necessary," he told her, wondering silently what she had in mind.

"Why don't you come over to my house for dinner tonight so I can show you that I really am a lady, and not just some cop junkie," she said, looking him directly in the eyes.

"I would like that, but you really don't have to prove anything to me," he said, then suddenly remembered he was on call tonight. "I am on call; I might have to leave if an emergency comes up."

"Not a problem. I'll have Stella make you a meal you will never forget, is six all right?"

"Six would be great, I'll be there," he said as he turned and walked on. He could feel her watching him.

"See you later Dean," Linda smiled to herself at her newly finished mission.

Linda Edwards was definitely a unique woman. He really didn't know what to make of her. Or better yet, if he could trust her. After their first encounter he had no idea what to expect from tonight, but he would take his chances. He put the few groceries he had picked up on the check out counter and paid his bill, then walked out to his car. He smiled as he looked over her Porsche. Man, he would like to have a car like that!

"Ok Dean, enough dreaming; time to get back to reality!" He told himself as he got into his car and started toward the hospital.

Despite it still being the beginning of summer, the temperature was feeling more like August. "Definitely a sign that it was going to be another hot summer in Missouri!" Dean thought to himself as he pulled into the hospital parking lot. He felt his excitement over his upcoming date with Linda fade to somberness as he entered the hospital and waited patiently for Samantha to be discharged. He pulled the car up to the main doors as the nurse helped her out. She smiled lightly at him as he closed the door and walked around to the driver's side.

"Have a good one sheriff," the nurse replied before turning back into the building.

"You too," he said and climbed into the car.

Samantha still looked pale, he noticed as he casually glanced over to her during their ride home. She said nothing, just mainly looked out the window and watched the world pass by. Obviously she was still medicated or she would have already been talking his leg off or trying to sell him a house. She lived and breathed real estate and took very little time away from it, always trying to make that next sell. Dean pulled the car into her drive and parked next to her car.

"Sam, I know you don't want to do this, but I would like to go over what happened last night. Do you feel like having a little talk?" He asked her.

"Yeah, come on in, I really don't want to be alone right now anyway," she told him as she stepped from the car and dug out her keys to the front door. "Don't forget my bag in the back seat."

Dean grabbed her overnight bag and followed her into the house. He could see her stiffen as she walked through the door. It was really tough for her to come back here. Setting the bag down, he then followed her into the kitchen and sat at the table.

"If you want me to, I would be glad to clean up that mess for you," he told her as he looked through the kitchen door into the living room at the broken coffee table that she landed on from her fall.

"No, that's all right. I'll get it later. I'm taking a few days off work and I'm sure in the next day or two I'll be climbing the walls looking for something to do. Thank you anyway," she said in a light daze.

"If you find yourself too bored you can always come down to the station and do some filing, clean out a couple jail cells. That would definitely take your mind off things."

"I'll keep that in mind," she said with a slight laugh.

"Are you sure you don't want me to help clean up? You are looking really tired," he asked as he looked into her face.

"Come on Dean; just ask what you're dying to ask. You know as well as I do you don't want to clean that mess up, you're just scared to start the conversation."

"I just know you're tired and need some rest. I don't want to push you, but I need some answers."

"I'm fine; they gave me some pretty good drugs, told me not to operate any big farm machinery. Since I can't plow the field, we might as well get into it and get it over with," Samantha said as she slowly sat down at the kitchen table beside him.

"Now that's more like the Sam we all know and love," he said, watching her smile. "I know you have already filed a report, but I would like to really break it down and try to figure out what happened now that you've had time to think about it."

"My story isn't going to change any now that a few hours have passed. I have already gone through it a million times, and like I told you all those times before, I came home and Linda was here in my house and she tried to kill me! I want you to arrest her Dean!" She told him, getting up from the table, grabbing a glass from the dishwasher. "Frankly I'm surprised you haven't even questioned her."

Samantha glanced over at him as he sighed and caught her glance. She quickly looked away, turning on the faucet, pouring her a glass of water. She could already tell Dean wasn't going to be much help she thought as she took a handful of pills to help ease the pain that seemed to cover every inch of her body, especially when she thought about Linda Edwards!

"Why would she want to kill you?" He asked cautiously.

"I don't know. Who knows why that woman does anything she does. I suppose because she hates me and wants me out of the way. All I know is she looked me straight in the eye and pushed me over the balcony. What about Ray? Have you found his body? It's in a freezer somewhere, I suspect in her house. Have you searched it yet?" She asked, carefully sitting back down at the table.

"No, we haven't. Samantha, you know we can't just burst into her home and search it without probable cause, and your dream does not qualify. It's too early for Ray's wife to file a report, but she said it's not unlike him to stay out overnight. I interviewed his girlfriend, but she hasn't been able to give us a very good description of the woman he left with. I know you will find this surprising but she had been drinking quite a bit last night. We questioned several others, but keep getting a mixed profile. About the only thing people have agreed on is she had red hair and had a red dress. You know it's kind of funny, if I hadn't been talking with you at your office I might have had to question you about your whereabouts."

Samantha gave him a dirty look but didn't say anything. Dean decided he would leave humor out of the rest of the questioning, but ironically the description he had been able to get from the bar patrons sounded exactly like Samantha! "Are you sure that you're not leaving anything out?"

"Dean!" She said, starting to get angry. "I told you Mary called the office right after you left, I called Linda, and then I came straight home and she was here! She tried to kill me! What part of all of this can't you understand?"

"Ok, now wait a minute. Let's calm down and break this all down. You said Mary called and then you called Linda from your office right after I left?" He questioned her. "How long was your conversation with Mary?"

"Five minutes tops."

"You called Linda directly after that and then went straight home. Didn't go to the bathroom, get a drink, nothing? Just locked the door, talked to Mary, called Linda, on her home phone or cell phone?"

"Home phone, I don't have her cell number," Samantha sighed.

Dean was really starting to get on her nerves. She sighed deeply trying to remain calm as she watched him read over his notes on the small note pad. She yawned and waited for the next question to be asked, already knowing what it was going to be.

"So you called her home number, and then went straight home, correct?"

"Yes Dean!"

"Remind me again why it was that you called Linda?"

"I called her after some of the things Mary described about the woman sounded like Linda to me."

"Nothing about the description she gave me sounds anything like Ms. Edwards," he quickly stated.

"Dean!" Samantha gripped.

"Don't get mad, I'm just trying to put things together here. I don't see how you got her out of that description. Help me here Samantha."

"They do make wigs you know, don't be so naive Dean. Her body type, her actions, it just sounded like her to me."

Dean wasn't that stupid! Any woman could easily change her appearance with a wig and make up. He was purposely choosing to ignore it and she wanted to know why! This was very unlike him to be so one sided with his thoughts. That was one of the things she liked about him was how he would always look at all options before making a decision.

"Alright, fine. So let's recap. You thought it sounded like Linda Edwards so you decided to what, play a little phone prank on her?"

"I know it sounds stupid now, but at the time it sounded like something to do. You had just told me about her fight with Duke and now this thing with Ray, well I thought it might be kind of fun to shake her up a bit. The woman is always so cool. I'd like to see her sweat." Samantha said standing up and stretching. The pills were starting to make her sleepy.

"And you thought a phone prank would make her do that?"

"Stop talking to me like I'm a child," she said, glaring down at him.

"Don't act like one."

"You know Dean, I think I've had about all the fun with you today I can handle..." she said, her voice getting louder with each word.

Samantha could not believe he was talking to her like that! It was as if he was changing right before her eyes. She shook her head in disgust and picked up her glass and took a big drink. So much for coming home and not getting worked up like her doctor had warned!

"Just calm down Sam, you called her, what happened next?"

"I disguised my voice but she still recognized me. She said that she didn't mess with married men! How did she know he was married if she wasn't with him? She had to have been there with him last night!" She said, sitting back down.

"You came straight home, didn't stop anywhere in between?"

"Yes for the thousand time. I came straight home, didn't stop and pee or spray paint graffiti on the side of a building. I came straight home!" She interrupted. "Why?"

"Samantha, there's no possible way Linda could have been here. She lives ten miles on the other side of town. If you came straight home she would have had to pass you! Driving at record speed," he told her.

"She was here Dean, I swear it!" She argued.

"Are you sure you called the home phone not her cell number?"

"Her home number Dean! For the last time I don't have her cell number!"

Dean sighed this time as he glanced over his notes. She just wasn't making sense. If she would just stop and think she would realize it herself. "If she was home when you called then you could have walked home and beat her here even if she was driving a hundred miles an hour."

"I don't know, maybe she flew on a rocket powered broom stick! But I do know I looked into her eyes right here in my house! And I can prove it! She threw an ax at me in my bedroom; the marks are by the door where it hit! Come on!" She demanded as she jumped up from the table and ran upstairs, Dean following close behind.

"Sam, slow down. Remember the doctor said take it easy," Dean reminded as he followed her upstairs.

"Look right here in the doorway!" She said, running into the room, pointing to the doorway and gasped. "Where did they go? I know they were here!"

Dean looked at the doorway for any sign of marks as Samantha went over and sat on the bed. Tears formed in her eyes no matter how much she tried to stop them. There was no evidence of an ax crashing into the wall or that anyone was even in the room. Her head was aching and she was so confused.

"She changed the wood casing while I was in the hospital. She's trying to drive me crazy!" She said from the bed.

"It's impossible, there's no way she could have got in here without your neighbors seeing her, let alone replace and stain the wood work.

Come on Samantha, you were spooked. Are you sure you didn't just imagine she was here?" He asked her, glancing over the woodwork again.

"I told you she was here! I would bet my life on it!" She yelled at him. "I'm not imagining it Dean! Trust me; my imagination is not that good!"

"Samantha, you know I have to ask this," Dean said with a heavy sigh. "Is history repeating itself?"

"No," She said looking away. She wouldn't admit it, but it was just like the events before her father died. She had horrible nightmares and visions of what was going to happen. The killers even invaded her dreams, terrorizing her for weeks before the robbery that led to her father's death and she had never met them before. The whole event sent her to the hospital for six weeks for mental rest they had told her.

"You would tell me if it was wouldn't you?" He asked sincerely. She knew he wanted to help, but she also knew deep down she could no longer trust him. Linda had already crossed him over to her side.

"Yes, I would tell, but it's not like that. This time I'm not dreaming, she was here!" She told him.

"Samantha, I know you do not want to hear this, but it sounds to me like you had a little scare with the telephone and when you got home you let your imagination get the best of you. I can't tell you how many times at work I've had something strange happen and when I get home it messes with me," he told her as he came over to her, sitting beside her on the bed and putting his arm around her.

"Don't treat me like a two year old. I know what I saw. That woman is a mastermind at deception. I don't know how she does the things that she does, but I'm going to get her. I'll prove to you she was here, just wait!" She told him as she jumped up and left the room.

"All right, prove it! Give me some shred of evidence that she was here the other night and I'll personally go get her, take her in and question her!" He yelled after her, following her out of the room. "There is no way she could have been here and you know it! She would have had to pass you to get here. Did any cars pass you on your way home?"

Samantha stopped at the balcony where she was pushed. Chills covered her as visions of that night raced before he eyes. She was not imagining things she had seen Linda Edwards, felt her touch her as she grabbed her and pushed her over the balcony.

"Well?"

"What?" She asked coming out of her daze.

"I asked you if any cars passed you on your way home."

"No! You know Dean, you're right, I'm wrong, just like always. I must really be loosing my mind. No woman that beautiful could possibly try to hurt someone, is that it?" She screamed at him.

"It sure seems funny to me that every time you mention anything to do with Linda Edwards it has to do with her looks. Listen Samantha, I think that there is definitely a problem here and I don't think that it has to do with anything that Linda Edwards is doing. It seems to me that you have some issues with the fact that she is a very pretty woman. You have nothing to worry about because I happen to think that you are equally as beautiful."

"Oh my God! I can not believe I'm hearing this out of your mouth too!" Samantha yelled.

"What?"

"Once again, you and Brad are right. I'm just insanely jealous of her, so I invent her trying to kill me. Thank God you're the town sheriff. You sure cleared that one up. Don't you think that it's time for you to leave?" She said to him as she went over and threw the door open.

"You need to calm down and think before you start running all over town blaming people for things that they couldn't have possibly done!" He told her, not leaving.

"I don't know how she did it, but she did. I'm going to prove that she was here and that she killed Ray Thompson if it's the last thing I do!" She yelled at him. "Now go, and don't let the door hit you in the butt as you leave!"

There was nothing left to say to him. He was wrapped under Linda Edwards spell just like Brad was. She would have to deal with this on her own and forget about any help from her friends. She tried hard to keep herself from crying again. She had to be strong but the uneasy feeling of being completely alone in this was overwhelming.

"Sam, listen to me," he said, gently grabbing her by the shoulders and looking her in the eyes. "I don't know what you are planning up there in that thick head of yours, but remember this. I don't know Linda very well, but I do know that she has a lot of money and probably one hell of a lawyer. So in other words as your friend, I do not recommend you run all over town saying she tried to kill you. Let me look into it and see what I can come up with. Do you understand?"

"I know. Thanks Dean," she said, calming down and sighing as she gave him a hug. For a brief minute she felt so safe in his strong grip. "I just wish I could make you believe me."

"Samantha, I never said I didn't believe you. I just need to find some evidence that's all. Just think real hard about everything that happened and if you remember something else contact me. Don't tell anyone but me ok?"

"Ok," she said into his shoulder, still trying not to cry.

"I better run, you going to be all right?" He asked, stepping away from her.

"Yes, thanks for everything, I'll try to be careful, you're right about her, she would probably love to see me in jail for harassment," she said as she walked him to his car. If anything was clear it was that she was going to have to trap Linda on her own. Dean would not be any help. "Good bye Dean."

"You get some rest, call me if you need anything," he yelled from his window as he pulled out of her drive and started home. It wouldn't be long before he had dinner with Linda Edwards. He was starting to believe that maybe that was not such a good idea.

Dean turned the car onto the main road and sighed. He knew she had lied to him about the dreams. Brad had told him last night that she was having the nightmares again. They had been in the eighth grade when it all happened. He remembered the way Samantha had suddenly started changing. She wasn't her usual self, before long her personality had become unrecognizable. She was saying all these crazy things about men stalking her and chasing her, she was sleep walking and hurting herself, saying the men were doing it.

He remembered his father telling his mother one night when he didn't know Dean was listening that several people believed it was Samantha's fault her father got killed. She had him and her mother so stressed out that he couldn't think or do his job right. No one could actually prove that her dreams came true that day, but Samantha swore it was exactly how her dreams had said it would be. The strange thing was after her father died, the nightmares stopped, never to return until now.

# Chapter 11 - The first date.

Dean pulled into city hall and quickly finished up so he could hurry up and get home. Samantha was right; he really should look for a house, he had lived in this little one bedroom apartment since he graduated and moved from his parent's house. He checked his messages as he grabbed a beer from the refrigerator and started getting out of his uniform. He had just enough time for a quick nap.

The so-called quick nap lasted about an hour longer than planned. He scolded himself for not setting the alarm as he jumped out of the shower and started to shave. He hated to keep people waiting. Especially women, because it irritated him when they did it to him. He finished dressing, continuously chewing himself out as he rushed out the door.

"I should have left twenty minutes ago," he said loudly to himself, glancing down at his watch for the thousandth time as he left the flower shop.

The closer he got to Linda's house, the more nervous he became. He really could not understand why he was feeling this way. It hadn't happened before, not that he dated that much. His job kept him quite busy, especially since the city council decided to eliminate two off his deputy's jobs due to budget cuts.

He turned down the gravel road that led to Ridgecliffe Manor. The brush was getting so thick that the place was no longer viewable from the road. The mansion was now straight in front of him. It seemed like every time he was here the place got larger. Why would a single woman want to be out here in this large old place that needed so much work? He picked up the roses and jumped out of the jeep and stepped up on the rickety steps to the porch.

Scaffoldings had been set up down the front of the house. Work was about to start on the outside, and judging from the way the front porch was leaning, it wasn't a moment too soon. Dean took his nervous hand and twisted the ringer next to the door. He could hear Linda walking in the hall towards the front doors. It was too late to back out now, he thought to himself, hoping he wasn't making a mistake. What if she did have something to do with attacking Samantha? The thought seemed impossible, just like he had told her.

"I was afraid that you were going to change your mind," Linda said as she opened the doors.

Dean was practically speechless as he looked at her. She was wearing a floor length black satin evening gown. There was a low cut front exposing her soft white neck that was draped with a diamond necklace that would blind you if she stood in the direct sunlight. Her long hair was pulled up on her head with a few twisting curls dangling down in just the right places, allowing the massive diamond earrings to glisten.

"Is everything all right?" She asked, a little worried by the shocked look in his eyes.

"I am sorry you just completely caught me off guard. I feel a little underdressed," he said referring to his jeans, shirt and tie.

"Oh, please forgive me; it's just that I have not had an occasion to get dressed up for a while. I could change into something less formal if it would make you more comfortable," she said, taking the flowers from him and smelling them.

"No, please don't, you look incredible!" He told her, following her into the parlor while watching her every move as she led him into the room.

"Thank you, make yourself at home. I'll go put these in water and check on dinner. There's a liquor cabinet in the corner," she called back as she passed through the dining room and into the kitchen.

Dean sat on the sofa and looked around the beautiful room filled with fine furnishings. But it was the huge painting that definitely captured his eye just like the last time he was in this room. It looked so real, like she was about to step out of it and come into the room. Getting up from the sofa, he moved to the painting and looked at some of the other pictures on the fireplace mantel. One was a picture of Linda and another man. It was apparently her wedding picture.

"That's my husband Rick," Linda said as she entered the room. "He left me last summer for a nineteen year old bean pole in receiving. Please forgive my sarcasm but it's still difficult to deal with. Having someone you love trade you in for a newer, younger model. I have filed for divorce, but who knows how long it will take. No one seems to be able to find him. I keep the picture out to remind me to never get myself in that position again."

"I'm sorry, I assumed your husband was dead," he replied, putting the picture back down.

"He will too, once the divorce is final, that is if he ever shows back up," Linda said as she poured herself a drink.

"He's missing then?" Dean asked.

"No, not missing, just roaming the world with his girlfriend and four million dollars of Edwards Enterprise's money," she told him bitterly as she smiled at him.

Stella entered the dining room and started bringing in all the food. Instantly the room filled with the delicious scents of a fine meal, making Dean's stomach growl. He suddenly remembered he had forgotten to eat lunch.

"I hope you're hungry," Linda said, taking his arm and leading him over to the table. "I really wasn't sure what you liked, so I picked one of my favorites."

"I'll eat just about anything," he commented as he pulled her chair out for her and then sat down himself. "Your house looks great, did you decorate it yourself?"

"Not hardly," she laughed. "I put some things in a drawer and that was about it. I'm not gifted enough to do things like that; I leave it to the professionals. "

All through dinner Dean was amazed about the places she had been and all the people she met. Her life made his seem dull in comparison. It was fun to learn of things that happen in the outside world. Often in a small town you get wrapped up in the low profile and forget that life even goes on out there. Linda made him laugh; she was actually quite funny with her jokes and stories. She was a lot different than he had expected. Stella came and took away their plates as they finished. It had been a very interesting dinner

"Come on, let's go outside I want to show you something," Linda told him as she took his hand and pulled him up from the table. She led him into the servant's hall and out the back door.

"It's amazing," was all Dean could say as they walked out onto the back porch.

The full moon lit up the old gardens with a beautiful silver shine. The darkness was far more forgiving of the dilapidated trellises and overgrown vines than in the daylight. It had a haunting beauty about it, just like its owner.

"I love nights like this," she said as she stepped down from the porch and walked on the old brick sidewalk down into the gardens, stopping by a bench that sat next to newly installed fountain.

"I remember back when old man Ridgecliffe was still alive, these gardens were so beautiful. He had the most incredible roses. I remember everyone in town used to talk about them," he said as he looked around at the weed covered areas.

Time felt like it had just passed over night. It seemed like yesterday! He glanced back at Linda, who was smiling at him, eating up every word he said. She was so beautiful in the moonlight, so sweet and innocent; nothing like the monster Samantha was making her out to be.

"Well soon they will be beautiful again. I've hired some landscapers to bring them back to life. My designer plans to add dramatic lighting to the trellises and as you can see I already have my new fountain. I plan to put in tons of flowers and plants," she told him, coming up behind him and taking his hand in hers.

"The Ridgecliffe's I'm sure would be glad to hear that," he told her, squeezing her hand as they walked down the brick sidewalk that weaved through the old gardens.

"How did he die?" Linda asked.

Dean started in with the story, the best he knew of how the Ridgecliffe's used to raise their own cattle, butchered them at the estate." One day as the story went, the old man had a heart attack and died, it was said he fell into the meat grinder."

"Oh my God," Linda gasped. "How horrible."

"There are so many stories about this place," he continued. "I heard

Mrs. Ridgecliffe came home and found him dead, not sure if that's true or not but I do know she kind of lost it then. Finally after a few years of shutting herself up here she surprisingly put it up for sale. She's quite a character. Can't drive worth a damn. Remember that dinner where you met Duke? Well, she drove her car through it about a year ago. Lost her license," he laughed.

"Yes, I met her at the closing. Interesting woman. She seemed nice, I really liked her," Linda lied, vaguely remembering the crazy lady in her bathrobe.

"I remember as a kid, we would hear all kinds of scary things about this place, and as you told someone else about it you would have to add things to make it worse. I bet you half the people in town are still scared to death of this place," he said to her. She was hanging on his every word. "I'm sorry I just keep rambling on."

"You don't need to apologize, I love listening to you with that sexy southern draw in your voice not to mention that I love a good ghost story, I find them and you very fascinating," she said, reaching up to gently kiss him on the lips.

Dean felt his breath slip away as their lips touched. He could not believe the power this woman had over him! He reluctantly pulled away and smiled. "I can't believe that. I must sound like a dumb red neck compared to all the other men you have met."

"Most men go out of their way to try to impress me to get me into bed, but you're so real and down to earth, and I find it incredibly sexy," she told him.

"You must be really bored to find me fascinating," he said, smiling as he gently squeezed her hand.

"Don't underestimate yourself. You have dedicated your life to protecting and saving others. You risk your life everyday for people, who I'm sure if the tables were turned, would not do the same for you." she told him as she pulled away. It was almost ironic to her that he saved lives and she took them.

"Please don't make me a hero yet. The most dangerous thing that I've done lately is try to rescue a cat from a tree," he joked.

"I still have great respect for you," she joked back. "Someone has to save the town cats!"

A light fog was slowly making its rise up from the neighboring cornfield, giving the distant yard of the estate an eerie feeling. Dean glanced back over to Linda who was watching him closely smiling. He blushed and looked away. He felt like he was back in high school again.

"What?" She asked smiling.

"Tell me something, why are you sitting here with a simple small town guy like me when you could be out with some big time stock broker?" He asked, slightly laughing,

"I don't know. I still haven't figured out if you're really the sheriff or a male stripper."

"Well if you ever saw me dance, you would immediately know the answer to that one."

"Well, trust me, it's not the dancing that I would be watching," she said to him as she wrapped her arms around him, holding on tightly and enjoying the warmth of his body.

"Just a country raised farm boy Sheriff here," he whispered in her ear as he hugged her back.

"Well you know, with this cute butt of yours, you could go far," she told him as she grabbed his butt and watched his face turn beat red.

"Okay, if you have had your fun now, I want to ask you a serious question," he said, pulling away from her. "Tell me about yourself. What were you like as a child?"

Linda stiffened as the conversation moved to her and her past. She wasn't the kind of woman who wanted to talk about herself, especially her past! She quickly scanned through her head deciding just how much she would tell him.

"Well?" He asked.

"Now that's a really interesting thing to talk about," she joked.

"It is to me, I'm serious."

"There's nothing really to tell, I was born on earth, where I still reside…"

"All right, I can see you don't want to talk about it," he interrupted.

"It's just not very interesting, I'd rather you tell me about you," she said, sitting on the bench.

"Well, I was actually born in Kansas, My father moved us here when I was a small child. He landed a job in Columbia at the University. My mother hated the big city and moved us here, where she taught second grade over in Boonville. Dad got the distinct pleasure of traveling back and forth, but it worked... I imagine like them, I will die here, but wouldn't have it any other way," he told her.

"Any brothers, sisters, illegitimate children," she laughed.

"One brother, I haven't seen him since our parents died in a car accident a few years back. We never really got along. There you have it. Now you know all about me, I seriously want to know about you," he said sitting beside her. "At least give me a little something to go on."

"You know, I think you are the first man to ever actually ask about me and mean it. Well, let's see, where do I start? I was born in Kansas City. My parents had to get married; they never loved each other, or me. My mother was a little off the wall; Daddy used to beat her every time she said something he didn't agree with. One day she had enough and murdered him, and then killed herself," Linda said with a sigh.

"Oh my God. I'm sorry, I had no idea it was that bad," he said putting his arm around her.

Linda tried to wipe the memories of her family life away from her brain but they haunted her, and probably always would. This was the first time she had ever opened up to anyone about it. She almost felt like a large burden was being released from her.

"I lived with my aunt until college, where I met my husband. He was rich, handsome, and treated me halfway descent, so I married him. For a wedding gift he bought me a company out of bankruptcy, and while I was bringing it around he took all the credit for it. Then one night, I came home and his clothes were gone," she told him, still staring off into the darkness.

"He hasn't been in touch with you since then?" He asked.

"No and I doubt he will until he gets tired of his new flame. He likes to trade women like most men do cars. I finally got tired of everyone talking behind my back, so I sold the company and moved here, and now I sit here with you, and I don't have a single regret," she said softly, looking into his eyes.

"Mrs. Edwards," Stella called out suddenly from the porch, breaking the trance she was in. "Everything is cleaned up. I'll be on my way unless you need something else."

"No thanks Stella, everything is fine. Why don't you wait and come in around two tomorrow," Linda said, getting up from the bench, smiling at the woman.

"Thank you for dinner, it was great," Dean added, standing beside her.

"Thank you Sheriff. Good night," she said politely and then turned and walked on down the porch to her car and drove off.

"It must be really nice having your own maid to clean up after you," Dean said as he walked to the edge of the gardens, looking off into the field.

"She's not a maid, she's a housekeeper," Linda laughed, walking up beside him and taking his hand.

"What's the difference," he asked.

"Maids live with you, housekeepers don't. I would hate to see this place without Stella. She has been a godsend. I can't do much around the house. It's just not my nature," she said looking at his fine chiseled features in the moonlight.

"I have a difficult time believing that a woman, who can run a multi-million dollar company, can not run a sweeper and do her own dishes."

"I have very sensitive hands," she told him as she ran her soft fingertips around his face. "See?"

Before Dean could say anything, she was kissing him again, the longer the kiss lasted, the more passionate it became. It had been a long time since he felt this way as much as he tried to stop; he couldn't, so he returned her kisses. Her hands slipped down and pulled his tie off. She started unbuttoning his shirt, slipping her hand inside, running it over his broad, smooth chest. The heat coming from his body instantly took away the chill she was beginning to feel in the unusually cool evening.

"Linda, I think that we're moving a little fast. Don't you?" He asked as he pulled away from her slightly.

"If it was anyone other than you, I would say yes. But we are meant to be together, can't you feel it?" She asked, looking at him with her penetrating blue eyes.

"I just don't want either of us regretting our hasty decision in the morning," he told her softly, not really wanting to stop.

"You're not a prisoner, you can leave at any time," she said as she wrapped her arms around him, pulling him tightly to her.

"I really don't have any other plans," he said with a smile as he brought his lips back down on hers.

"That's good. I plan to keep you," she told him, taking his hand and leading him back into the house.

---

Dean was suddenly awakened by the bad odor of something burning. He jumped with a start and looked around, trying to remember where he was. Linda waltzed into the room radiantly, her long nightgown flowing behind her. She was carrying a tray of food and placed it on the bed.

"Good morning," she said as she kissed him. "I thought you were going to sleep all day."

"What time is it?" He asked sleepily.

"Ten thirty, I made you breakfast. You should feel lucky, I haven't cooked anything in ages, you were my inspiration," she told him proudly.

"It's ten thirty," he repeated. "Oh man, I promised Samantha I would stop by this morning and check on her."

Dean sighed as he leaned back, the covers slipping down and exposing his finely chiseled body. Linda smiled as she looked him over enjoying the site of him a lot. He rubbed his eyes and yawned.

"Well, aren't you going to eat your breakfast?" She asked as he got out of bed and started getting dressed.

"Can you bag it for me and I'll eat it on my way home?" He asked looking down at the burnt toast and something else that he thought might be an egg.

"I wouldn't know where to look for one. Just leave it, I'll eat it, but at least drink your juice," she told him as she bit into the piece of toast. "It is kind of strong, isn't it?"

"Yeah a little," he said as he swallowed the very strong mixture of her juice.

"I know, I don't plan to let Stella buy that kind again, you would think that you would be able to get more than one glass from those cans," she told him.

"I'll tell you something I learned. If you mix water with it you can usually get a whole pitcher instead of one glass," he told her and kissed her again.

Linda managed a fake smile as she held on to him for a second then let him go so he could finish getting dressed. "Dean, why are you going to Samantha's house? Are you dating her?"

"No, nothing like that, we're just good friends. She had a little accident the other night and fell off the balcony at her house," he told her as he put on his shoes.

"Was she hurt?" she asked, not really concerned but managing to sound like it anyway. She slipped in behind him and started rubbing his shoulders.

"She's really sore, ooh man, that feels great! She was shaken up pretty badly," he turned around and looked into her face. "When was the last time you saw her?"

Linda thought hard trying to remember when the last time she had seen Samantha was. For all the trouble she was causing her and her life, she really hadn't even seen the little bitch that much since she had moved to town!

"Gosh, I don't know, I don't think I've seen her since I moved in. She did call me a couple nights ago in the middle of the night. I think she was drunk, kind of sounded funny, why?" She asked innocently as she started massaging him again.

"She seems to think you're the one that pushed her off the balcony," he told her.

"Me!" Linda laughed, suddenly stopping the massage and moving around so she could face him. "You have to be kidding me. Why on earth would I do that? I mean, I'm the first to admit I really don't care much for her, but that's hardly enough grounds to push her off a balcony, is it?"

Deep inside Linda was dying laughing but holding it in. She didn't want Dean to think she was insensitive. She had thought about doing something to Samantha, but pushing her off the balcony was not it, but it was a good idea.

"She says you did it because she knew about your encounter with a married man at a bar who is now missing."

"Who's missing?" Linda asked. "And how could she know anything about what has happened in Kansas City?"

"It didn't happen in Kansas City. She said it was in Columbia at Dave Evert's Bar," he told her as he finished tying his shoes.

"Where is that? I've never heard of that place," Linda lied.

"It's on the other side of town towards St. Louis."

"Well, I don't have a clue as to what you're talking about. I don't go to bars, especially not to pick up men. It's hardly my style. I prefer grocery stores," she said and kissed him before pausing a minute. "You know, now that I think about it, the night she called she asked for somebody named Ray, or something like that. Is that the guy that's missing?"

"Yes, he disappeared with a mysterious woman at the club. I told her there was no way you could have gotten to her house before she did, but I don't think she's convinced. You might watch out for her, and don't pay any attention to anything she says, she's a little out of it right now with all the pain killers she's on," he said, quickly kissing her again. "I've got to go."

"If you think it would help I could call her today, maybe go check on her later," Linda said, following him out of the room. The idea of messing with her drugged up head sounded like a very entertaining afternoon.

"I really don't think that would be a good idea right now. She's not thinking real clearly," he said, trying not to even think about what would happen if Linda showed up at Samantha's house.

"I never thought she did anyway. You should have seen how she handled the sale of this place. If it hadn't been for Brad, I probably would have taken my business elsewhere. She's kind of a scatter brain."

"Now I know it would not be a good idea to call her," he said as he finished dressing.

"Will I see you tonight?" Linda asked as they got to the front doors.

"I'm working tonight. But listen, there's this little town social this Saturday night at city hall to raise money to remodel the buildings downtown, and I would really like for you to go with me, you might even get to see me dance," he said to her, shaking his hips.

"I don't know, will I get to dress up?" Linda joked as she held on to him tightly, not wanting to ever let go.

"You can wear a crown if you want," he said holding her close and kissing her.

"Well than Sheriff, I would be honored,"

Linda watched as he drove down the drive. That Samantha bitch was becoming a pain in the ass. Where did she get off telling people she was in her house trying to kill her? She didn't even know where she lived. Maybe she should teach her a lesson in minding her own business. And this thing with Ray Thompson, how did she put together that it was her that was there with him? She wasn't even at the club, or maybe she was and she just didn't notice her. It was pretty crowded in there. She would have to be much more careful in the future, especially now that she was involved with Dean!

Instantly forgetting the news about Samantha, she smiled and went back into the house. Last night had been the best night of her life. Dean was incredible! He made her feel special. He was now hers and she would never let him go. Samantha could try anything she wanted. One thing was now for sure, she definitely wasn't bored anymore!

# Chapter 12 - Visiting a sick friend

"May I help you?" An overly chipper clerk asked as Linda walked through the door of the downtown floral shop.

"I hope so," she replied, managing a fake smile. "Do you have any nearly dead house plants?"

"Excuse me?" The clerk asked, giving her a confused smile.

"I'm looking for a plant that looks sickly, you know one that you would just throw away because it looks too bad to sell to a customer," Linda said as she glanced around the shop. It had so many craft like items in it she wasn't sure that they should be allowed to call it a flower shop. It looked more like a flea market to her.

"No I'm sorry we don't, we try not to let our plants get into that condition."

"Alright," she sighed. "Just give me that one over there."

The clerk gave her an odd look as she took the house plant from the shelf and walked over to the counter. She started looking for a bright bow for the front but Linda told her not to bother. She managed a smile as she wrung up the purchase watching Linda dig through her purse and pull out her card.

"Will that be all for you?" The cashier asked as she took the credit card. "We have a great collection of assorted candies on sale."

"No, I don't think so," she said looking around the flower shop one last time. "She's on the chunky side and I really don't think I should encourage her to get any bigger."

"Oh, ok," the cashier managed to smile as she handed her card back. She finished the sale and gave the potted plant to Linda.

"Thank you," she said and quickly, grabbing the plant and leaving the store before the woman tried to sell her anything else. Linda walked out into the bright sunshine smiling, trying to imagine the surprised look that will be on Samantha's face when she would open the door and see her! It definitely would be worth a few minutes of entertainment today. Now she needed to find out exactly where Samantha lived. This shouldn't prove to be too big of deal, with Hagan Cove being a small town. Linda pulled the car into the one place she knew could give her the exact information she desired. The real estate office! She knew Valerie would never tell her, but Brad would with the right amount of sweetness, and she knew how to be very sweet!

"Brad it is," she said to herself, climbing out of the car and grabbing the plant.

"You've got to be kidding me!" Valerie groaned as she glanced out the window, watching Linda Edwards come up to the front door with a plant.

"Good morning," Linda greeted as she walked in. "Is Samantha working today by any chance?"

"No, I'm sorry she is not," Valerie managed to say nicely as she walked over and reached for the plant. "She's going to be out of the office for a couple more days. I will let her know you came by and brought a plant."

"Oh," Linda said, not handing her the plant. "Maybe I should go by and see her at home then. I'm sure she would probably like some company."

"I'm not real sure she is up for any company. She hasn't been feeling very well," she informed her. Linda would be the last person Samantha would ever want to see would be her.

"All the more reason for me to go and see her. I'm sure it would cheer her up to have…"

"Valerie," Brad called out interrupting her as he entered from the back room. "Did you say my appointment for this afternoon called and rescheduled?"

"Yes," she said and turned back to Linda.

"Oh, good morning," Brad said, instantly grinning from ear to ear.

Linda said good morning as she gave Valerie an evil look and walked over to Brad. She went into detail about how bad she felt for Samantha and thought she should bring a plant to her. Brad absorbed her story in, clinging to every word. Valerie watched and tried to listen to what they were saying but they were talking too quietly for her to hear.

"Good Lord," Valerie said giving up, shaking her head as she walked over to her desk. "He better not give that woman her address."

"Thanks Brad," Linda said smiling at him as she turned and walked towards the door. "Have a good day Valerie."

A faint scent of Linda's perfume followed her like a shadow as she walked past Valerie's desk to the front door. She said goodbye once again just before the door closed. Valerie quickly shot around and gave Brad a look that could kill.

"Brad! You didn't give her Samantha's address did you?" Valerie yelled out as soon as she heard the door completely shut.

"She was concerned and wanted to take her a plant. Maybe this will help the two of them patch things up and become friends."

"You're an idiot!" Valerie yelled across the room to him. "Samantha can't stand her! For God's sake you moron, she thinks Linda tried to kill her! She is not going to want to see her, trust me!"

Linda laughed out to herself as she heard Valerie yelling at Brad. One thing she could always count on was a man doing what ever she wanted. She followed the directions Brad had given to her and in a matter of minutes she was turning the corner and pulling up to the driveway of Samantha's house. Dean had asked her not to call her, but he didn't say not to come see her, so she wasn't exactly going against his wishes.

Linda glanced over at the shiny rubber tree she had bought. She really wished she had found one that wasn't so nice. Quickly reaching over, she yanked off most of the leaves. "Much better," she said as she rolled down the window and tossed them out into the drive.

There was nothing she liked better than rubbing salt into a fresh wound. Samantha was obviously trying to play the victim to get Dean to come running to her. She had to be desperate to throw herself off a

*the Murderess of RIDGECLIFFE MANOR*

balcony! "He's mine now, and there will be no way in hell that he will come running back to you no matter what you do!" Linda said to herself as she checked her look in the car mirror one last time before grabbing the potted plant and heading for the front door. Trying to hold back her laughter, she rang the bell. It caught her by surprise that Samantha lived in such a nice house, so modern and nice even though it was small. She expected a typical three bedroom two bath ranch from her, something you might see in public housing.

"Hell...o," Samantha muttered in shock as she opened the door and saw Linda.

"Oh my God, Samantha, you look like you have been in a train wreck!" Linda said as she looked her up and down. "I'm so embarrassed for you."

"How kind of you," Samantha mumbled, her shock turning quickly to anger. "What are you doing here?"

"I heard you had fallen ill and I thought I should stop by. I hate to hear when my friends are sick. Is there anything I can do?" She asked as she walked past her, entering Samantha's house, setting the plant on the television. "You have a lovely home."

"Oh please, do come in," Samantha sighed, closing the door. "It's not like you don't know your way around my house."

Linda giggled to herself as she looked around Samantha's nicely decorated modern home for something she could pick at her about, but couldn't really find anything. A small part of her looked at Samantha and her home, her career, her friends, and she was envious. Samantha had a blessed life, and she didn't even appreciate it.

"I actually thought Valerie would have called you and told you I was on my way over," Linda said turning back around and facing her.

"Valerie knew you were coming over?"

"Yeah, her and Brad gave me directions."

"I'll make sure to thank them later," Samantha said as the phone rang. "Excuse me."

"Samantha, I just have a second but I wanted to warn you, dumb ass gave Linda Edwards your address, she should be pulling up any second," Valerie quickly muttered into the phone.

"Yes, she's in my living room, thanks for the advanced warning."

"I tried to call earlier but your phone was busy."

"I'll talk with you later," Samantha said, hanging up before she had another chance to speak. She looked back over at Linda, who was making herself at home.

"Are you planning to offer me a drink?" Linda asked, glancing up at her and smiling.

"If you're referring to water or soda, no," she replied as she sat in the chair. "If you want alcohol, you'll have to hit the bar up the street but it's not open this early."

"You know Samantha; you really should work on your hostess skills. They leave much to be desired. I do believe they have classes that can help you with your social graces."

"Well thanks for the advice, I'll rush right out and sign up."

"Oh well, that's alright, I'm not really here to judge your manners, or house keeping skills obviously. I just decided I would go and do some charity work, visit sick friends, check on the needy, oh and of course visit the elderly. I decided I could wrap all four up with one visit by coming here," Linda said as she smiled innocently.

"You're just too generous," Samantha smarted back. She thought about arguing back but decided it wasn't worth it.

"Well you know me, I do try," Linda said, almost mocking her, and then sniffed into the air. "Do you have pets? I smell a faint odor in here."

"No," she smarted back. "The only odor in here is the over abundance of your perfume. You know really most of the women that wear that brand usually wait to put it on at night just before they go to work."

"Ohhhh, good come back," Linda snickered. "Trust me though; I doubt seriously there is a whore or even a realtor out there that could afford my perfume."

"Well that is nice to know. Since I obviously can't afford your perfume and I doubt seriously you plan to give me another gift, seeing you have already given me that beautiful, but broken plant, why don't you tell me why you're really here," she replied, ignoring her insult. "Because in the short amount of time I've known you, I've quickly discovered you don't have a charitable bone in your body that doesn't have something in return for you."

Linda slightly laughed at her and then glanced around the room and then back at Samantha, who was shaking her leg nervously back and forth. Linda could tell that just by her being here was driving her insane and making her a nervous wreck.

"So?" She repeated interrupting her thoughts. "Why are you really here?"

Samantha doubted seriously that Linda would ever tell her the truth even if she attempted to beat it out of her, but that was a fun thought. It was obvious to her that she was here to see what she remembered and if she had told the police anything.

"I've come to the conclusion that we should at least try to be friends, I mean, after all, our paths do cross quite frequently. I know I can be difficult at times and a little hard to deal with, but it's only because people don't understand me. I'm a complicated person."

"Is that what you like to call it?" Samantha squeezed in before Linda got on with her speech. "I've heard so many descriptions of you lately; I wasn't exactly sure which one you would prefer. I know I have my favorites."

Linda managed a fake laugh. "I'd like to take the opportunity to get to know you a little better, that's all. Does that make me a bad person?"

This whole episode was obviously a joke and Linda wasn't even really trying to hide it. Her whole personality was a joke since she walked through the door with the damaged house plant. Samantha looked over at her as she continued talking to her like nothing had ever happened between them.

"Ok, fine, I'd love to have the opportunity to ask you a few questions myself," Samantha answered. She was so nervous and scared, but she tried to hide it. This woman was far too clever and to get her, she would have to play along with her game. Deep down she wanted to ask about Ray, but decided it was in her best interest not to.

Linda Edwards was sitting in her living room acting like she had never been here before and imposing that they could actually be friends? Just a couple days ago she was here trying to kill her and now she acts like nothing happened! What was she up to? There was no way this woman was here trying to be her friend, she was definitely up to something!

"Good. See, I think we can put the past behind us and be great friends. Who knows, maybe even go shopping together, though I have to warn you I don't care to shop at Good Will," Linda smiled, then after a few seconds she started again. "So, tell me about some of your other friends."

"You've met them, nothing to really tell," she replied, studying her closely. This woman was probably the most diabolical person to ever walk the earth and here she was talking with her in her own house! "I can't imagine telling you anything you don't already know."

"Well, are you just friends with Brad and Dean or do you all date or....?"

"What are you implying?" Samantha asked, starting to get upset. "That the three of us are having sex?"

"Well," Linda laughed. "I didn't mean at the same time. I can see Brad maybe doing that, but not Dean, and definitely not you!"

Linda's mind quickly flew to the image of Dean and Brad having sex with her at the same time! She felt herself slightly blush at the steamy images floating in her head and Samantha's voice started getting louder, interrupting her erotic day dream.

"Are you so bored that all you have to do is concern yourself with other people's sex life?" Samantha continued but Linda only heard the last of it.

"I just asked you a simple question, I didn't mean to upset you," Linda slightly laughed, pushing all her dirty thoughts aside. "So, I can take it your not having sex with either of them?"

"No!" she shot back. "Dean, Brad and I are just friends! That's it. Nothing more. I can't believe your sitting here and asking me this crap."

"So you're not intimate with either one of them?" she continued despite her protest.

"I do not have sex with my friends!" she said, almost loosing her temper. Why did she care?

"So you and Dean never...."

"Wait a minute! So that's what this is all about!" Samantha said, figuring out what exactly she was doing. "You're after Dean!"

Finally! The whole charade was making sense to her now! Linda had come over here today to fish information out about Dean. She wasn't here trying to find out what she remembered about the other night as she had originally thought.

"I don't know what you're talking about," she replied innocently. "I'm just asking general questions, trying to get to know you better."

"Well you can just forget it. Dean has better sense than to hang around with the likes of you. He wouldn't even give you the time of day, so don't even bother trying. I'm sure if you look hard enough around town you can find some guy that will stoop to your level, sorry, date you."

"Umm humm," was all Linda said, debating whether of not to tell her that Dean was giving her the time of day and a lot more.

"What is that supposed to mean?" Samantha asked, irritated.

"Nothing at all," she simply answered. "So you've never been with Dean?"

"No!" Samantha yelled.

"Then you and Valerie?"

Linda loved watching Samantha get all worked up. This visit had definitely done her some good today. It was obvious that Samantha and Dean were just friends, but it was apparent that she was in love with him judging from her emotionally outburst to her simple questions. Dean obviously must have refused to date her! The thought made Linda smile.

"No! I am not dating Valerie either! In fact since your obviously so interested in my sex life, the last time I had sex was about six months ago and that was with Andrew Fischer. He lives in a trailer over on South Street. We had went bowling that night and had a little too much to drink. One thing lead to another, you know how it is," Samantha smarted off. "Why don't you stop asking all these stupid questions and just come out with what you really want know?"

"Well I thought asking these questions would be a good way of learning more about each other, I had no idea you really were the virgin ice princess that everyone around town calls you."

"I find virgin ice princess a far better term than what I'm hearing people around town calling you," Samantha said standing up from her chair. "Didn't you say you had someplace to go?"

"No, not really," Linda said not getting up. "I set aside the whole afternoon just for you. I mean how are we going to become friends if we don't spend any time together?"

Samantha had tolerated about all from this woman as she could handle. If she didn't get her out of here soon she was probably going to do something drastic! She sighed and looked over at Linda, who was obviously enjoying herself way too much.

"Well, my friends help out when they come over and since you're in such a charitable mood, why don't you help me," Samantha said trying to hide her anger.

"And just what would I be doing?" Linda asked, amused.

"Well the bathroom needs to be cleaned. Are you good at toilets?"

"Funny," Linda snickered.

"I thought so," Samantha said getting up and walking over to the door. "Listen, I know you must have a lot of stuff to do, so I don't want to keep you."

"You're not keeping me," Linda said, still not getting up. "I don't think we have exactly finished our conversation."

"No," Samantha said, getting a little nervous because the woman wasn't leaving. "I think it's time for you to go."

"Why don't you just sit down and relax a bit and let us finish our little morning talk," Linda said in a bossy tone of voice.

Samantha quickly glanced outside the open door as her legs started to shake. It was the late morning and everyone was at school or work. If she screamed it was doubtful anyone would hear her. She felt her heart racing as she turned back towards Linda. She had to get a grip on herself and not let Linda see her fear!

"I don't feel we have anything to talk about," Samantha said, letting her fear change over to anger. "Now get out before I call the police."

"I have one more question I have to ask you," Linda said slowly standing up. "Do you remember that old story about the little boy that cried wolf all the time? Remember how he kept getting the townsfolk in an uproar over an imaginary wolf. He cried it so many times that the town people eventually stopped listening to him. Then one day the wolf really did show up, the poor boy yelled out and no one helped him. He was eaten by the wolf. Ripped to shreds. Must have been a sad sight."

"Your point?" She asked standing by the open door. "Because I'm sure you think you have one."

"My point is that if you keep calling police with your wild crazy stories and they have to keep coming out here to your rescue, they are going to get tired of it, just like the town folk and that little boy. And then, when the day comes that I do come after you," Linda paused. "The cops, like the towns people won't respond and I will devour you."

"Get out!" Samantha screamed.

"Samantha, you need to really calm down!" Linda laughed, walking slowly to her and the door. "At your age, you could have a heart attack."

"I said get the hell out of my house now!" She screamed, breathing heavily.

"Okay, okay, I'm going," Linda said, walking by the television, knocking the plant off, causing dirt to spill on the floor. "Oops. Oh well, the carpet needed a good cleaning; now you have a full day of work ahead of you."

"Just get out of here!" She yelled, sighing with relief as she watched as Linda passed her. "Don't you ever come back to my house again!"

Linda laughed as she walked down the sidewalk to her car, listening to Samantha slam the door behind her. An instant later the door flew back open and she rushed out with the plant.

"You forgot your plant!" She yelled as she threw it at her, barely missing her and smashing the pot all over the drive.

"Better clean that up before you pull out of the garage. I'd hate for you to run over that and get a flat tire," Linda laughed as she climbed into her car.

"Don't you ever come to my house again or I will kill you!" She yelled out to her.

"I'll call you later and check on you," Linda laughed and rolled up the car window.

Samantha didn't say anything to her as she watched her start the car up and pull out of the driveway. She looked around the neighborhood at a couple of people walking down the sidewalk across the street staring at her. She was almost shaking; she was so nervous and angry. She groaned out to herself as she slammed the door shut.

"That's it Samantha, keep up the grand standing," Linda laughed, glancing back in the mirror as she drove off.

Linda needed Samantha to keep showing public displays of craziness if she was going to win Dean over to her side and have him stand against Samantha. She wasn't sure about this so called attempt to kill her that she claimed happened the other night, but it was definitely giving her some ideas!

# Chapter 13 - Dinner and drinks

"Yes baby! Poppa loves ya!" Brad yelled out as he made his third basket in a row. "Now that's how it's done! I can feel the NBA calling!'"

Dean pushed him away as he tried to body slam him. He should have went home and took a nap before work instead he was talked into coming down to the gym and shooting hoops with Brad, which was proving to be a big mistake considering he was getting smeared!

"Your shot," Brad said as he tossed the ball to Dean.

"I'm done man, we'll just call this one your lucky day," Dean said as he tossed the ball back and started for the locker room.

"Oh yeah, I see how it is." Brad called out as he followed. You win and its skill, but I win and it's just luck? I don't think so."

Dean stopped by the fountain and started filling up his water bottle. Brad was right he was acting like a little bitch, but he had a lot on his mind and right now basketball wasn't one of them. He was really confused about his feelings for Linda and how fast they had hit him.

"So," Brad said as he sat on the bench. "You going to tell me what's going on or am I going to have to guess?"

"It's nothing," He said then took a big drink, drinking over half the bottle. He sighed and filled it back up.

"Bull shit," Brad laughed. "You know you can't keep anything from me so tell me before I go around making things up."

"It's Linda," he started, not looking at him. "I slept with her last night"

"Holy mother of all…" Brad almost shouted jumping up. "You and Linda Edwards? You?"

Valerie dropped her gym bag down in shock as the door to the ladies locker room shut. She leaned against the wall that divided her and two men talking. She listened carefully waiting to hear what was probably going to be the biggest piece of gossip to hit the town in weeks!

"Yeah me," Dean responded almost offended. Usually he could take Brad's put downs but today wasn't one of those days. "She happens to be into me, you know there are quite a few others as well. I'm not some dateless nerd sitting at home playing video games and jacking off to Megan Fox videos."

"Come on man, I'm just teasing you, God don't get your panties in a knot." Brad said smiling as he lightly punched him on the arm. "Must have been a long night because usually you have a sense of humor."

"It was a long night alright," Dean said suddenly smiling as he started to blush. "Oh my God, that woman is incredible! Just when I thought, ok now we're going to go to sleep, she would get me going again. Honest to God, I've never had that much sex in one night."

"How many times did you two do it?" Brad asked, getting a serious look on his face.

"Five times."

"What!" Brad shot out louder than he expected. "Man, I'm lucky if Kelly even lets me finish round one. She's all 'Ewe you know I don't like that nasty stuff all over me, go finish in the bathroom!' I swear one of these days she's gonna be saying that and I'm going to bust a nut right in her big mouth."

Valerie almost burst out as she tried to contain her laughter. She wasn't sure which was better, the gossip about Dean and Linda or Brad's sex life! She had the urge to call Samantha right away and fill her in on all the details, but she decided she wasn't brave enough to be the one to tell her about Dean and Linda. She was going to explode over that one.

"If it's that bad why do you stay?" Dean asked as he finished laughing.

"Come on Dean you drive around town, it's nothing but oinks and moos, and I'm not talking about the animals. I can't believe it. A hot piece of ass comes to town and you beat me to it! I told you I needed a uniform!"

"Man, don't talk that way about Linda, she's different. I don't see this as being a one night stand. In fact I'm taking her to the Mayor's little shindig on Saturday," Dean said as he sat on the bench beside Brad.

"Samantha's going to love that," Brad laughed out as a bunch of teenagers rushed out loudly to the basket ball court and began bouncing the balls.

"She doesn't have a whole lot to say about it now does she?" Dean said as he got up and started for the locker room.

"You think that will stop her?" Brad asked as he followed him in.

"Well hell!" Valerie grumbled as she heard them go into the men's locker room. There would be no way for her to hear the rest of the conversation even if the noise of the basket balls wasn't vibrating off the walls.

Dean relaxed as he slid under the hot water of the shower. He felt all the stress of his life slip away as the water ran down his body. He didn't understand how something so simple could be so relaxing, but it was. That is until Brad climbed into the shower stall beside him and started singing the chorus of Lady Gaga's Poker face.

"Dude!" Dean called out over the shower wall. "What are you singing?"

"My audition song for American Idol! The judges are gonna love it." Brad joked and then continued on with his bad singing.

"Yeah, I can see you making it at least to the finals," Dean shot back, proud of his quick comeback.

"So, what are you going to do?" Brad asked, ignoring his comment.

"About?"

"Ah little redhead who's madly in love with you and thinks you're going to wait around for her to come around."

"I asked her first, she said no, so I guess she will just have to deal with it."

"Hah!" Brad laughed out, jumping up the wall and holding on, looking down at Dean. "She will rip your balls off and feed them to Valerie's cats! She fucking hates that woman!"

"Get off the wall pervert!" Dean said as he threw a bar of soap at him, hitting him in the forehead.

"Shit," Brad yelled out as he landed back down on the floor. "That hurt."

Dean continued on with his shower as did Brad with his singing. After a couple more minutes he gave up turned off the water and started drying off. Brad was right; Samantha was going to be very difficult. He needed to find a way to get those two to be friends.

"I have an idea," Dean said as Brad finally finished his song and came out of the shower.

"You want me to take Linda out?"

"Kind of," Dean said, stopping Brad from drying off and giving him his full attention. "I want us to all get together tomorrow night. You, me, Samantha, Valerie, and Linda. We'll go have dinner and drinks. What do you think?"

"Samantha won't go, Kelly will have a bitch fit because she's not invited and Valerie will insult us all night. That's what I think," Brad said as he started getting dressed. I think you stand a better chance of having dinner with the president and first lady than Samantha and Linda."

"That's where you come in and help. You get Samantha to show up and I'll work on Linda."

"I bet you will," he said with a big smile. "Alright, I'll get Val to help, but I have to bring Kelly or no deal."

"Fine, but I don't want this to feel like a date night. Just a friendly dinner, then I'll tell her about my seeing Linda."

"Yeah, make sure I'm around for that one!" Brad said as he hung up his wet towel.

Dean and Brad finished making their plans for the big night out and headed out of the gym. Valerie watched from the corner as the two men exited the building and quickly walked over to the men's locker room and waited patiently by the door.

"Well," She asked as the teenage boy walked out of the locker room. "What did you hear?"

"Where's my forty bucks?" He quickly asked.

Valerie quickly pulled out the two twenties and held them up. He reached for them but she pulled them out of his reach. "I need info first, and then you get the money."

"Wasn't much going on lady, the dark haired dude is trying out for American Idol and the other dude is planning a dinner party."

"A dinner party?" Valerie asked disbelieving.

"Yeah, now where's my money," he asked.

"That's it?" She asked as she started her hand towards him with the money, but quickly shot back. "You sure there is nothing else?"

"All they talked about was getting these two women that hate each other together so they might become friends and then one of them won't be so mad that the other ones fucking her boyfriend. That's it."

"So when are they planning the dinner party?" Valerie asked handing him the money.

"Tomorrow night, now can I get back to my game?" He asked impatiently.

"Go, and watch your fucking language," she said disappointed. She was hoping for more gossip not singing and dinner.

Valerie continued to process the new gossip and information through out the day and into the next morning on the way to work, worrying about whether or not she should tell Samantha about Linda and Dean. She was her best friend and she owed it to her, but at the same time Dean was planning on telling her so maybe she should just stay out of it. She had picked up the phone a dozen times to call her but always backed down before she finished dialing.

"Morning Valerie," Samantha said as entered the office. "Unusual for you to get here after me, have a big night?"

"I wish," Valerie said with a big smile. "Is dufus here yet?"

"Yes, he's in Max's office bitching about tomorrow," Samantha said as she followed her over to her desk.

"What's up for tomorrow? Max making him work the office?" Valerie asked as she grabbed her coffee cup. "I know how he hates to work on Saturdays.

"He wants all of us here since they're having the downtown revitalization ribbon cutting ceremony. He thinks all four people that go to it are going to leave there and come right over and buy a house.

## the Murderess of RIDGECLIFFE MANOR

"Yeah he told me yesterday before I left, how you feeling honey?" Valerie asked noticing how tired she looked as she followed her over to the sofa and they sat down.

"I'm tired, but doing pretty good. Brad wants us all to get together tonight and go have dinner and drinks. Are you going to go?" She asked.

"I guess I will," Valerie said acting surprised. There was no way she would miss that dinner, even if she had to hide! "Are you?"

"Yeah, I told him I would. It seems like forever since we all got together, could be fun. I can't drink with the meds I'm on but I can eat."

"Who's going?" Valerie asked casually.

"Just us, oh and I think he said Kelly was going."

"Us?" Valerie asked.

"Yeah, you and me, Dean, Brad and Kelly. Why who else did you think would be there, Linda Edwards?" Samantha said smartly as she got up from the couch as Valerie almost choked on her coffee.

"Wouldn't that be fun?" Valerie managed a laugh as she wiped the spilt coffee off her jacket.

"Like a funeral!" Samantha shot back as Brad came out of Max's office.

"I can't believe he's making us work tomorrow, that sucks. I had plans." He groaned as he sat down behind his desk pouting.

"Oh don't worry about it sweetie you can get your rocks off later, your computer porn will still be there when you get off work." Valerie teased with a big smile. "So Sam says we're all going out tomorrow night, that true?"

"Yes, and I need to talk to you about that," he said quietly where Samantha couldn't hear.

"What about?" She asked innocently, knowing exactly what he was going to say.

"I need you to help me get Samantha there," he said glancing over making sure she didn't hear.

"That won't be a problem; she already said she was going."

"She's going to change her mind real fast. You just play along and help me out."

Samantha looked out of the side of her eye and saw the two of them talking quietly together. It was a scary site to her because it was a signal something was wrong. Those two never carried on a private conversation. Either someone was dying or they were plotting something and she was betting they were going to stick her with Saturday office duty by herself!

"Hey Sam," Brad said suddenly as he started towards he desk. "You know how tomorrow night is a little welcome back to work party and all."

"Yes."

"Well wouldn't it be more fun if we invited some others to come along?" He asked trying a little too hard. She knew now he was up to something.

"Like who?"

"Linda?"

"Are you out of your mind?" She screamed out. "I'd rather poke my eyes out than have dinner with that woman!"

"Dean and Val and I just thought that maybe it would be nice if we could all get together and try to bring all these problems to a close."

"Hold up there cowboy, you leave "Valerie" out of it. I don't have anything to do with this, I just found out myself Samantha," Valerie quickly shot back.

"Thanks for the help Val," Brad shot over to her sarcastically then turned back to Samantha. "I just think that if the two of you ever just sat down and talked maybe you might find that you like each other."

"First off Brad, the woman broke into my house and tried to kill me," Samantha said trying hard to hold back her anger. "I know you both don't believe that so let's move on to yesterday morning when she stopped by trying to be a 'friend' as she called it, which ended in her insulting and threatening me. So I'm sorry but no, I don't want to have dinner with her or the rest of you if she's there."

"Val," Brad said, motioning for her to step in and help him convince her to go.

"What?" Val asked acting dumb. "You can't make her go if she doesn't want to go. Personally myself, I'd go because I'd be afraid that they would all end up liking her better than me and the next thing I know I wouldn't have any friends."

"Yeah baby!" Brad motioned excitedly to Valerie where Samantha couldn't see. He knew he could count on Valerie to bring it home.

"What?" Samantha asked, suddenly irritated at her. "You think I should go?"

"I'm not telling you what to do, but I've seen it happen before. One girl doesn't like the other and starts sticking to herself, the next thing you know she's out of the group and the other girl's taken her place. If it was me, I'd go and make sure that the group doesn't accept her in."

Samantha glared at them. So this is what they were up to. They wanted to make sure she went tonight to eat with them so they decided to play this dirty little trick. She would deal with Valerie later. How stupid did they think she was? Unfortunately Valerie was right. If she didn't go and Linda did, it would give her the evening to manipulate her friends against her. As bad as she hated it, she was going to have to go.

The day continued on slowly without much said between the friends. Samantha spent most of it trying to find away to cancel tonight without being obvious, but couldn't come up with anything. She showed a few houses later in the afternoon which helped take her mind of things and try to get back to a normal routine but no matter how hard she tried she couldn't get out of her mind that she was about to sit down to dinner with a cold blooded killer, one who had even made an attempt on her own life!

"Ok, you can do this," Samantha told herself as she climbed out of her car and started towards the restaurant. She saw Dean and Brad's car but she couldn't find Linda's. That was good news; maybe she wasn't going to come.

"Samantha," Valarie said, startling her as she came around the building.

"God Val, you almost gave me a heart attack!" Samantha practically screamed as she tried to calm her nerves.

"Sorry, I just wanted to talk with you for a second before you went in," she said taking her by the hands and facing her. "I want you to know I have your back in there."

"Like you did this morning?" Samantha smirked.

"You needed to be here and you knew it, I just helped give you that push."

"Remind me to stay clear of bridges."

"Are we done with the pissing contest so I can tell you what I want to tell you so we can get inside? It may be early summer but it's hotter than hell out here!" Valerie groaned.

"What?" She demanded. "What is so important?"

"It's just some friendly advice that's all. Watch yourself tonight," she told her sternly. "You need to come off as the person who tried. We both know Linda is going to sash shay in here and be her usually self, which means you need to be your usual sweet lovable self. I'm telling you if you don't you will regret it."

Samantha looked at Valerie. She was obviously trying to tell her something without actually being the one to tell her. Since Brad had Kelly here tonight it was Dean. Linda was obviously making a move on Dean and Valerie wanted to make sure she didn't push him any further into her arms. Samantha smiled. She wasn't as dumb as her and Brad thought. "I got it Val, thanks for the advice."

"No problem, now take it and behave yourself tonight," Valerie warned. "Nice top by the way. Girl you been getting all kinds of new clothes, I may have to go raid your closet."

The restaurant was the typical chain store bar and grill. They made their way through to the back corner table where Dean and Brad sat drinking a beer. Kelly came up behind them and gave each of the girls a hug and they all took a seat. The waitress came and got their drink orders and quickly left them to their little party.

Samantha looked around the table at all her friends and smiled. It really did feel great to have the whole gang together again. It had been a long time since they had all got together and done anything. Someone was always busy or working. Now if only Linda wouldn't show up, the evening would be perfect.

"Are you guys ready to order or are you still waiting for someone?" The waitress asked as she sat the girl's drinks down.

"One more," Dean said smiling as he looked over at Samantha whose body tightened up at the mere mention of Linda.

"So where is our other guest?" Samantha managed to ask politely.

"I don't know," Dean answered. "How are you doing? You look good. Very nice actually."

"Thanks, I feel good. Glad I came out tonight. I needed this." She said with a smile, deep down she was lying, she would rather have a tooth pulled than be here.

"Sorry to keep you waiting," came a familiar voice that made Samantha cringe. She didn't need to hear her to know she had walked in the room. The looks on the guy's faces told her that Linda had arrived.

"That's ok," Dean said standing up and pulling out a chair for her. "We haven't ordered yet. What would you like to drink; I'll let the waitress know."

"Jack Daniels on the rocks to get me started and a coke for dinner, thanks Dean." Linda said as she glanced around the table at everyone. "Hello everyone."

"I hope she means the soft drink," Valerie whispered to Samantha making her smile as everyone around the table said hello.

Samantha slowly turned around to see the woman of her nightmares, her eyes quickly froze. It was if she had transformed into another person. Gone were the designer tight dresses and golden curls. They had been replaced with jeans and designer shirt, her hair had been straightened and she was stripped of the jewels she usually wore except for the very large diamond stud earrings. She actually looked a lot younger without her normal over the top diva look, but still a beautiful woman.

Dean came back to the table followed by the waitress with Linda's drink. One by one they gave their food orders until everyone had ordered and the waitress left. Samantha was actually surprised; so far Linda had been actually pleasant to everyone, except her which she hadn't even spoken to.

"So how's Ridgecliffe Manor coming along, are you finished with it yet?" Brad asked casually as Kelly looked Linda over closely.

"Very well thanks, the inside is complete and the work has now begun on the outside restoration. It's going to be a long summer full of work, but my carpenters have assured me that it will be done by fall." Linda said and took a large drink.

Samantha could tell by the way she was sucking down the alcohol that she did not want to be there either. Maybe the evening wasn't going to be as bad as she thought. It would be nice to let Linda be the one that 'lost it' tonight instead of her, but she could feel all eyes watching her except Kelly, who obviously didn't like all the attention Brad was paying to Linda.

"So Linda," Samantha finally spoke to her as everyone became silent to see if the war was about to begin. "You look very nice tonight. Is this look something you're trying or a look you plan to keep?"

"Thank you Samantha, I just like to experiment with my looks from time to time," Linda said with a smile that Samantha knew was fake.

"I agree," Brad spoke up quickly. "You always look fantastic!"

"You need to lay off the liquor," Kelly suddenly spoke up. "So Linda is it, where is your husband? I assume you have one since I've heard you called Mrs. Edwards."

"Among other things," Valerie joked quietly to where only Samantha could hear. "Whore, bitch, the list goes on."

Samantha almost choked on her breadstick. She tried not to laugh as she listened to Kelly's questions over Val's jokes. She had never really heard what happened to her husband and was always curious herself. She waited as Linda finished her drink and looked over at the woman.

"We are in the process of getting divorced," Linda said as she signaled for the waitress to bring her another drink. "Hopefully everything will be finalized very soon. I would like to get on with my life."

"Well I hope you didn't come here looking for a man, because all the good ones here are taken or gay," Kelly said emphasizing taken very clearly.

"I'll keep that in mind," Linda told her just as her drink was delivered. "Where is our food? It seems like we ordered it an hour ago."

"I'll go check on that and be right back," the waitress said and quickly left the table.

Brad quietly whispered something to Kelly as the rest of the table carried on their own conversations. Samantha caught Linda glaring at her a couple times. It was funny; Linda was trying very hard to control herself. She was really laying out all the stops, putting on a great show for Dean. She planed to make sure Linda failed.

"If you will excuse me I'm going to the ladies room," Linda said getting up.

"That's a good idea, our food should be here soon," Samantha said getting up herself. She could see the sudden tension in her friends faces. "It's alright. Here Linda, I'll show you where the rest rooms are."

"Thank you," she said and followed her through the restaurant.

"You're choking out there," Samantha said once they had entered the restrooms, beaming.

"Hardly," Linda said as she walked over to the vanity and sat her purse down. "You're awfully calm this evening. Valium?"

"No, I'm just having a nice quiet evening with friends and you unfortunately."

"I was surprised when I saw you here. I thought there would be no way in hell that you would show up for this," Linda said as she started refreshing her lipstick.

"Listen here you fucking little bitch," Kelly yelled out as she entered the ladies room, startling both Linda and Samantha.

"Excuse me," Linda snickered back at her.

"I don't know what kind of game you're playing here, but it ends now. You may be the big shit up in Kansas City but you're nobody here. You got it?" She practically yelled pushing Linda into a near by stall.

Samantha quickly stepped back out of the way and leaned against the wall. This was absolutely the best thing that had ever happened to her in her life! Linda was about to get her ass kicked in the ladies room right in front of her!

"You stay the fuck away from Brad, and this is your only warning," she continued. "The next time I won't be so nice."

Linda watched in fury as Kelly turned around and started out. She grabbed a hold of the back of the toilet lid and smashed it in half. As Kelly turned around she took what was left of it and quickly pinned the woman to the wall, the jagged edges of the lid against her throat as Samantha looked on in shock.

"Listen to me you little hillbilly slut, you may talk to other people that way, but you will not talk like that to me. I will date or fuck any man I want rather he's 'taken or gay' and you and the others will just deal with it," she said with anger in her voice, slightly releasing her grip on the woman, glancing quickly over at Samantha, then back at Kelly. "Next time you push or talk to me that way I'll slit your throat so deep it will sever your spinal cord. Do you understand me?"

"Yes," Kelly managed to say still in a state of shock.

"Good," Linda said as she managed a smile and went back to the counter. She looked up in the mirror at Samantha looking at her then over to Kelly who quickly walked out of the restroom. "That goes for you and your delusions as well."

"What?" Samantha managed to say as she was still trying to figure out what had just happened.

"I've tried to be nice to you and you just keep stirring things up. Well no more. You want to bitch fight, then you just bring it on. I've had it up to here with all you crazy Hagan Cove bitches. I should put all of you out of your misery."

"You started all this when you moved here, you never gave any of us a chance so don't give me this line of crap that we're ganging up on you," Samantha yelled at her. "You could have killed her with that thing."

"And she would have deserved it," Linda quickly shot back as she started towards the door. "You should see what I have in store for you."

Samantha stayed against the wall as Linda gave her one last glare and walked out of the restroom. She took a second to catch her breath and walked out the door. By the time she got back to the table all hell had broke loose. Kelly was yelling at Brad, who in his drunken state was yelling back, while the manager and Dean were over trying to quiet everyone down. If she hadn't just been threatened it would have been a funny site.

One thing that was missing from the scene was Linda. Samantha looked around the restaurant finally catching a glimpse of her at the bar. She had ordered another drink and quickly drank it down. In a rush Kelly stormed by with Brad close behind.

"There you are," Valerie said as she came upon her. "You should have been out here. Kelly has completely lost the last brain cell and flipped out. The manager made her and Brad leave, Dean's on the phone with a police call, I don't know where in the hell Linda is, so I guess the party is over."

"Oh yeah," Samantha sighed. "But the battle is just beginning. I'm going home; tell Dean I'll talk with him later."

"Ok," Valerie managed to get out as Samantha walked away. She turned back to the table to find it empty. "Oh hell no! Hope you dumb asses don't think I'm paying for all this."

# Chapter 14 - An affair exposed

Samantha pulled her car into the real estate office parking lot and shut off the ignition, basking in the warm rays of morning sun that poured through her windshield. The penetrating heat felt so good on her skin. She took a deep breath and held it, then counted to ten and released it.

She had to find someway to prove to everybody that Linda Edwards was up to no good! The sooner the better. The woman was sinking her claws into everyone in town! They thought she could do no wrong. The longer she waited, the harder it was going to be to convince people that she killed Ray and God knows who else! The fact that she came to her house and acted like nothing ever happened proved her capable of anything!

She shut the car door quietly as she pulled her files close to her chest and walked towards the building. Why was she so nervous? There was no reason to be! Her stomach was in knots, a feeling she had not experienced since coming back to high school after a long summer break.

"Girl, are you out of your mind?" Valerie asked as Samantha came through the front door of the real estate office, not giving her a chance to even shut the door.

"Why? What did I do now?" She asked, putting her things on her desk. She hadn't talked to Valerie since last night so unless Kelly had told her, she couldn't have been talking about what happened in the ladies room.

"Well. For starters you owe me twelve dollars and ninety eight cents for your dinner last night and second, you're going to be Brad's date at the dance tonight? Brad? Even you could do better than that!" She said following her. "You must have hit your head harder than we thought!"

"Thank you so much. I'm glad that you think that even I could do better!"

"You know what I mean!" Valerie said, ignoring her sarcasm. "Come on, let's face it, we're talking about Brad! Just about every woman in town has been out with him! He's like Chinese take out. Everybody tries it, but few go back for more!

"That was a good one!" She laughed, giving her a high five. Brad's extra curricular activities were often the butt of many office jokes. "You know Valerie, I was not aware that Brad was your concern. Did you want to go with him? I'll gladly step aside and let you."

"Oh honey, I don't think so! But don't you think Dean will be a little pissed at you when you show up with his best friend after turning him down?" Valerie asked as she poured her and Samantha a cup of coffee. "What are you trying to do, start a war?"

"I seriously doubt I'll start a war between them just because I went to a dance with one and not the other!" Samantha informed her as she joined her by the coffeepot. "Besides it's not like there's anything romantically going on between us for heaven's sake!"

"Great nations have fallen for much less!"

"What did…," she sighed. "What did he do come here first thing this morning and blab to everyone about it?"

Samantha made a quick mental note to beat Brad upside the head next time she saw him. She only agreed to go with him after Maxwell had practically made it mandatory for her to go. She figured it would be better to be seen with him than sitting by herself!

"Sugar, you know Brad, he probably announced it on the morning news on his way to ordering the wedding announcements," she joked. "Can I be in the wedding, I still have that God awful dress I wore at my brother's wedding. I could save you some money and wear it if you like?"

"You kept that ugly dress?" Samantha asked, shaking her head.

"Um hum," she groaned. "Even the trash man wouldn't take that thing! Now back to Brad!"

"It's nothing really. Kelly's still pissed about last night and won't go with him and he really needed to be there, you know how he likes to smooze! He called last night and cried this sob story about how he had to go and that he didn't want to go alone, Besides Max told me I had to go, so after a couple of pain killers, twenty dollars, and an hour of his begging I finally broke down."

"Twenty bucks?" Valerie screamed, almost dropping the coffeepot. "He's paying you! Girl, even the hookers are getting at least sixty these days! More if it's with Brad!"

"Very funny," she managed to fake a laugh. "I'm not even going to ask how you know that."

"Well, one thing to remember, get your money up front!" She informed her as she grabbed the box of sugar. "I know sure as the sun will set tonight that Brad never has any money on him! The little fart inherited a fortune from that old lady he was doin and still walks around with empty pockets, expecting us to pay for everything."

"What? You want to be my pimp? Oh Valerie, don't put all that sugar in my coffee, I'll be bouncing off the walls by night," she told her, grabbing her coffee cup.

"Well I would have held out for more than twenty bucks. If he was as desperate as you say, you might have been able to get fifty," she said as she cleaned up the sugar she spilt when Samantha grabbed the cup. "What are you going to say to Dean when you see him?"

"I don't know, I'll worry about that when it happens," she told her as she started going through some of the leasing contracts to be signed on her desk. "Maybe he won't show up."

Valerie sighed as she turned around and faced her. They both knew he wasn't going to be too happy about it. Dean being the gentleman he was would keep quiet, but inside it would tear him and their friendship apart. "Well I wouldn't count on that. If what I heard was true, you are going to have something else to deal with,"

"What now?" She asked, looking up. "I must caution you, I'm not a well woman and can be very dangerous at times!"

"Brad also accidentally let it slip out that Dean is bringing a date with him as well."

"Really," Samantha said not looking up, acting like it was no big deal, but inside her heart just stopped beating. "Who it is? I didn't know he was seeing anyone."

"Yeah, trust me there are a lot of things you don't know about sweetie," she said, slowly moving away from her before she told her who it was.

"Well?" She asked looking up, getting irritated. "Who is it?"

"Linda Edwards, and before you loose it, I have also heard from a very good source that it's getting pretty hot between those two," she told her, waiting anxiously for her reply. "Actually, his words were steamier than a hot Missouri summer."

"Very funny Val, I expected far better from you," she said laughing with relief. There was no way on earth Dean would ever go out with her!

"Actually that's not a joke," Valerie said clearing her throat and sitting on the corner of her desk.

"No way! I don't believe you. Dean could see right through a woman like that," she said, becoming irritated at even the thought of those two together, though now Linda Edwards visit and all her questions were making even more sense now. "He would never go out with her. You will have to come up with a better one than that and try to be a little more original this time!"

"I'm serious kiddo!" She defended.

"They have nothing in common! Face it, she wouldn't even give him the time of day and he wouldn't go near the likes of her unless he had to!"

"Well, what I heard from Brad was that he did go near the likes of her. Really near, if you get my drift! They went at it on the first date! And he bragged to Brad that it lasted it all night, and was the best sex he ever had!" She told her. "He didn't even get home until noon the next day."

"Spare me your locker room gossip!" Samantha said, barely able to hide her anger and going back to her pile of papers.

"I'm just trying to prepare you by giving you the facts before you hear a much distorted version from someone else!" Valerie politely informed her. "I'm telling you this because I'm your friend. Besides, you know how this town likes to gossip!"

"Yes, I know how you like to gossip!"

Deep down she knew what Valerie was saying was true but she hoped if she kept denying it, it would all go away. Just the thought of Linda touching Dean made her skin crawl. She had to give Linda credit; she didn't waste anytime moving in for the big kill!

"Fine," Valerie said after a deep sigh, pretending to be hurt by her comment. "It must be pretty serious if he stayed all night, so you better prepare yourself for the worst!"

"How would Brad know what time he got in?" Samantha asked hatefully.

"Brad did not tell me that! Kathy, you know that new dispatcher down at the station, well she kept trying to get a hold of him and he did not call till after twelve the next day. So you do the math and figure it out. It's the big story all over town."

"Oh come on, Valerie! Dean's not like that, He would never sleep with a stranger, especially someone like her on the first date! He's terrified of getting diseases. I've known him for years, we both have, and we both know he's not that easy. He doesn't just jump into bed with anyone, I mean come on, he and I are really close and we've never slept together," she said in his defense.

"From what I've heard he tried and you're the one that's not easy!" Valerie laughed.

"Who told you that?" Samantha asked shocked. She was getting really tired of hearing people tell her that.

"You!"

"I never told you such a thing!" Samantha argued.

"Samantha! You did too… 'Oh Valerie, I don't know what to do! I'm so scared to get involved with him; after all… my father was a sheriff…' Need I go on?" Valerie said sarcastically as she imitated Samantha.

"No!" She said, turning away from her. "Just because I wouldn't sleep with him doesn't mean he would run off and sleep with the first woman he ran into."

"Samantha!" Valerie called out in shock. "You have been turning him down since high school! You don't think he's been waiting around for you to thaw out, do you?"

"What is that supposed to mean?" She asked, sitting on the corner of her desk and folding her arms across her chest.

"You mean to tell me you actually believe he has waited all this time for you? I mean this is a small town, you had to have heard."

"No, I don't think that," she smirked, becoming furious then suddenly hearing her last comment again inside her head. "Heard what?"

Valerie almost burst out laughing. Samantha Marshall was one of the smartest people she knew and yet one of the dumbest! Dean got around just like the other single guys in town; he was just more discrete about it. Samantha no matter how much she denied it knew he wasn't just hanging on to her strings!

"Heard what Valerie?" She repeated.

"About the other women. Get your head out of your butt and look around. Dean is gorgeous and boy does he look good in that uniform. Women are throwing themselves at him all the time. And as sweet as he is, he is a man and he's been around the block a few times, if you know what I mean," she said as she sat at her desk, trying to avoid Samantha's stares. "Don't make me name names."

"I don't believe you," she said, not moving.

"Samantha please. You're kidding right? You couldn't possible think he's been saving himself for you. As cute as you are sweetie, even you're not that cute. A man has needs! Remind me again how many times have you turned him down?"

"That's none of your business, and hardly relevant to this conversation," Samantha defended.

"Not relevant?" Valerie burst out laughing. "Are we engaged in the same conversation here? It was only a matter of time before he found himself a woman that said yes. I'm sorry to be the one to break it to you sweetheart, but you really need to come face to face with reality here and get on with your own life, cause Dean definitely has!"

"Alright fine, so he's dated, but not her! She's not his type!"

"His type? What's his type? You?" She asked, as she moved on. "All I know is what I heard. He's a man, what do you expect. It's been awhile since he dated; maybe he could not control himself…"

"I'm not even going to dignify that with an answer. I can't believe Brad told you this, when did you two get so close?" she asked, angrily cutting her off.

"He didn't tell me exactly, I overheard it when Dean was telling him on the phone. Don't you dare tell Brad I know," she warned.

Now Samantha was really about to explode! The information she was sharing wasn't coming from the town gossips it was coming directly from Dean! "Now you're eavesdropping? What's next, bugging the restroom? I don't believe you!"

"Don't believe what?" Brad asked as he entered the office. "What's going on?

"Don't worry about it," Valerie said before Samantha could say anything.

"Are you expecting something from Kansas City?" Brad asked Samantha as he carried a large envelope and handed it to her.

"Where did you get that?" She asked, grabbing it from him and starring at it.

"Well, good to see you too Sam. I signed for it outside, what is it?" He asked.

Samantha stared nervously at the large envelope she held in her hands. She could feel her breath becoming short and her head starting to spin. Inside this envelope could be the information she desperately needed to expose Linda Edwards, or just another dead end!

"Well, aren't you going to open it?" Valerie asked, getting impatient.

"Don't you two have something to do? I don't know maybe work?" She asked them, bringing her thoughts back into the room. "This is private. Brad, can I see you."

"Sure," he said, staying. "What's up?"

"I can't believe you came running in here and shouting to the world that I'm going to the dance with you tonight like were back in high school! Did you manage to get a billboard while you were out?" She said, smacking him upside the head with the envelope.

"Ouch! The only one I told was Valerie!" He said, looking over at her and giving her a death look. "Which I see now was a mistake!"

"I'm only doing this as a friend! Let's get that straight right now!" She warned, smacking him again with the envelope. "Don't expect anything out of this and don't even think about trying anything! Got it! I'm out of your league and age bracket!"

The very thought of everyone in town thinking she was with Brad was turning her stomach. She wasn't exactly sure why. Brad was good looking but always seemed desperate despite his looks, money and abundance of women.

"Got it," he repeated and started to head to the back room, safely away from her and her mysterious envelope.

"Wait," she said, stopping him. "Have you seen Dean lately?"

"Yeah," he said, turning to leave again. The last thing he wanted to talk about in her current mood was Dean!

"Anything I should know about?"

"No, not really," he said, getting closer to the safety of the back door.

"Is he still going to be at the dance tonight?"

"I'm not sure. He talked about it. Why?"

"Just curious," she said, glancing over at Valerie, who was pretending to be busy.

"Ok," Brad quietly said and exited through the door, quickly shutting it.

Samantha watched as Valerie went about her business acting like nothing was wrong, but she could feel her watching her. She looked back down at the envelope she was holding as she sat down in her chair. She had just called the Kansas City newspaper a couple of days ago, she had no idea they would send this to her so fast.

Slowly she opened the envelope, almost afraid of what she was going to find out. The contents dumped out and fell upon her desk. Nervously she picked up the photo copies of the news clippings and glanced over them. Most of them were about the massive rise to power Linda had made with her company, others were about her public disputes and the turmoil's in her marriage. One picture on the bottom of the pile caught her attention. The man looked very familiar to her. She quickly read the story of his disappearance and the missing money. That was it! It was Linda's husband. Suddenly everything came into place, sending shivers down her spine.

"Oh my God!" Samantha cried out.

"What?" Valerie asked, looking up. "Break a nail?"

The nightmares that she had been having were involving this man! He had been trying to tell her something, and now she had figured it out! Linda Edwards had killed her husband and probably the girlfriend too. That must mean that the other dreams involving Brad were going to come true also. Dean! If what Valerie said was true, Dean was in more danger right now than Brad. She grabbed the phone and dialed his number, but got no response. Quickly she scooped up all the stuff on her desk and grabbed her bag to leave.

"I've got to go," she told her as she headed for the door, digging out her keys as she did. "Val, tell Max I wasn't feeling well and have Brad pick me up at six, and whatever you do, don't go near Linda Edwards, don't even talk to her!"

Samantha rushed through the door, not giving her a chance to say anything. Valerie jumped up and followed her to the door, watching her race off down the street as Brad came back in from the back room.

"Is she alright?" Brad asked coming up behind her.

"Girl needs to lay off the caffeine!" Valerie said as she turned around and started back to her desk.

"I wonder what was in that envelope that was so important?" he asked, following her. "Did you see how she was looking at it?"

"Yes I did, question is did you see where it came from?"

"Kansas City," he suspiciously replied. "The local newspaper actually."

"Why would she receive something from them?" She asked looking at him, but she deep down already knew the answer.

"I'll give you one guess. One thing for sure, it's not a real estate listing," he sighed as he crossed the room and went back to the window, watching the dust settle from the parking spot she had quickly pulled out of. "Oh Sam, what are you up to?"

"My guess is that since it came from Kansas City and Linda Edwards is from Kansas City and she warned us to stay away from her, it involves her," Valerie said, looking at him.

"That is pretty much what I'm thinking as well."

Brad sighed, trying not to worry about what in God's name she was up to. He had known her for quite awhile and he learned along time ago to expect the unexpected from her, but she had never been this bad! Once she set her mind on something there was no changing it and she was dead set that Linda Edwards was a bad person. God help her if she was!

"By the way Brad, why didn't you tell her that Dean was going to the dance tonight with Linda?"

"How did you know about that?" He asked surprised that she knew.

"Small town, news travels fast."

"I just decided that it wasn't my place to tell her," he said, still looking out the window.

"That's a crock and you know it!" She laughed. "You were scared to tell her, weren't you?"

"Drop it Val."

"You know she's going to flip when she sees them tonight!" She informed him. "She's already strung out; this is going to send her over the edge!"

"Yes I know, but it wasn't me that informed her, so she won't be mad at me. You ever hear of that old saying about not killing the messenger?"

"You big baby!" She laughed. "All hell is going to break loose at that dance tonight!"

Valerie chuckled with the thought of what could and would most likely go down tonight. If Dean and Samantha weren't her best friends she would really enjoy the fireworks that were surely going to happen. Part of her told her to try and talk Samantha out of going tonight, the other part said stay out of it! "You know I think I probably should go tonight."

"Yeah, you probably should. Too bad you don't have a date," Brad smirked as he passed by her desk.

"Oh I have a date," she proudly informed him.

"You do?" He asked in surprise, stopping at her desk. "The stud puppy from upstairs?"

"No," she smiled. "You're taking me."

"Me!" He said in shock. "I can't take you, I'm going with Samantha."

"Now you have two dates!" She informed him. "Just think about it. You are going to the hottest event of the year with the two most beautiful women in the state. Samantha said pick her up at six, so pick me up first."

Valerie watched him shake his head, walk over to the coat closet, take off his jacket, and sit down. He glanced over at her once again before getting into his work. Something was going on between Samantha and Dean and this Linda Edwards woman. What exactly he didn't know, but obviously by Samantha's actions she was on to something, and deep inside his gut he could feel that it wasn't good!

# Chapter 15 - The Mayor's dance

Linda ran her palms back over the sides of her hair, making sure the pins were tight. It was all pulled up to the back and clipped with diamond studded combs with several loose curls dangling down in back. She smiled to herself as she thought about spending another evening in Dean arms. This past week had been torturous with not being able to see Dean. Talking to him on the phone just didn't satisfy her. She yearned to be with him so badly, to feel his touch.

She finished off the last of the blood from the glass and started down the stairs. She wasn't crazy about the taste of day old blood, but it was not that easy to get. She couldn't just run to the super market and grab a man and slit his throat. Already this week she had made another kill, and she desperately needed another, but she had to be careful not to take too many at first, especially with Samantha Marshall on the loose.

How did she know about Ray? She just could not stop thinking about it. There was no way she could have known it was her? Even worse was the stories she was telling everyone that she tried to kill her! The woman was going crazy. She was definitely a thorn in her side that needed to be removed.

The ringing doorbell brought her attention back to the present. Anxiously she walked to the doors and opened them, smiling at the handsome man that awaited her.

*the Murderess of* RIDGECLIFFE MANOR

"You look like a prince," Linda told him as she rushed into his arms and kissed him deeply.

"And you… that dress," he said stepping back, and looking at her gown. It was a black see through lace that just barely covered enough to make it decent.

"You don't think it's too much, do you?" She asked with a sexy smile.

"If there was any less, I'd have to arrest you for being naked in a public place," he joked as he tugged on his tie.

Linda laughed as she grabbed her purse. She felt like a queen with her king beside her, she thought as they stepped off the porch and started towards his jeep.

"You look very handsome," she told him as they reached the jeep and he dug in his pockets for his keys.

"I feel like a clown in this suit. When I bought it and tried it on yesterday I realized I have not worn one since my parent's funeral," he told her as he unlocked the door.

"Can I ask you a question?"

"Sure, what?" He asked as she hesitated to get into the vehicle.

"Why did you lock your doors out here? I don't think anyone will steel your car," she laughed.

"I don't know, I guess it's just a habit. Are you going to get in?" He asked.

"No, I have a better idea. Here," she said, handing him her keys. "Take my new car."

"You have a new car? What happened to the other one?" He asked as he rushed over to the car parked by the garage, grinning like a kid in a toy store as he looked the new bright red Porsche over.

"It's in the garage for now. I think the dealership may have a buyer for it. They're just not the same once they have been wrecked," she told him as he opened her door for her.

Dean loved the way the car drove as he sped off down the deserted country road. He could definitely get used to driving this car, no doubt about it. Linda's hand moved over and rested on top of his on the gearshift.

"Why are you so quiet?" She asked him, after a few minutes of silence.

"Just thinking how easily I could get used to driving a car like this all the time. Do you think that the sheriff's department would get me one if I asked?" He joked.

"Something tells me it's more than that," Linda said, not really knowing how far she should push to get it out of him.

"Oh just work, unlike a nine to five job, it's hard to let it go when you come home," he said managing a smile.

"What's going on? Can you talk about it?"

"It's not like it's top secret or anything, just another missing persons report filed, and the situation is real similar to the one we had earlier, with Ray Thompson," he told her, watching the dark road ahead.

"Another one here?" She asked concerned.

"Boone County, next County over…"

"I didn't realize that you got involved in other County's work. Don't you have a certain precinct to stay in?" She asked, interrupting him.

"I think you mean jurisdiction," he corrected. "If two cases have similar details we work together. We always share information with each other, and besides Ray disappeared over there, but he lived here in Hagan Cove."

Linda's smile faded as she turned away from him and looked out the window. For just a few minutes it seemed like they had a normal life. A life she longed for but would never have. She cleared her throat and turned back to face him. "So now there are two? God, do you think they're dead?"

"Honestly, I think they are, but you never really know till you find them," he replied as he pulled the car into city limits.

"So it kind of sounds like there might be a serial killer on the loose. Great thing to have in my new town," she told him pretending to be concerned.

"I don't know if I would go as far as to say that. And for pete's sake, don't tell anyone else that. That would be all I need, everyone in town panicking over that," he told her.

"My lips are sealed," she said to him as they pulled into the parking lot of the city hall.

"And what beautiful lips they are," he said as he reached over and kissed her gently. "I really missed you this week."

"Well you have me tonight," she said to the empty car as she watched him walk around and open her door for her.

They laughed as they held each other tightly, making their way into the building and down the long hall to the noise that flowed up from the basement ballroom below. He glanced over at Linda and smiled. He would be the envy of every man in the building tonight. Suddenly he felt her stiffen as they came upon the doors leading to the basement ballroom. He looked away from her and saw why. Samantha and Brad were standing just inside the door, talking to some other people.

"You know, maybe this was not a good idea. We could go catch a movie or something," he told her.

"Don't be silly, I can't go to a movie dressed like this, come on, how bad could it be?" She asked, leading him into the room and intentionally bumping into Samantha. "Oh, excuse me. Oh well hello Samantha, Brad."

"Linda," Samantha mumbled as she glared over at Dean. "Dean, nice to see you."

"Samantha, Hey Brad," he said surprised to see her with him as he shook Brad's hand. "We better get a table, it looks pretty packed in here."

"See you around," Linda said, smirking as Dean quickly drug her away from them.

"You bumped into her on purpose, didn't you?" He laughed once they were out of earshot as Linda smiled. "You are so bad!"

"Why Sheriff, you wouldn't be trying to get me backed up in a dark corner so you could take advantage of me now, would you?" She asked as he directed her to a table in a dark corner.

"Just trying to protect you from all those men out there undressing you with their eyes," he joked as he pulled her chair out for her.

"Well they wouldn't have much to take off now, would they?" Samantha said, coming up behind him, wrapping her arm around his waist as Valerie following closely behind. "Is material really getting that scarce? Or did you run out of money remodeling your house?"

"Samantha, please don't start anything here," he said, to where only she could hear. "I thought you couldn't make it."

The night was going so well and the last thing Dean wanted was another blow up between the women. It seemed each fight was getting worse and worse. He looked over at Linda, she was smiling wickedly. There was no doubt an argument was going to break out between them and she was ready. He sighed and turned back to Samantha.

"I wasn't planning on coming but Max insisted everyone from the office attend, so we all came together," she said as she turned and faced Linda. "I see you found a date. If you were that desperate Dean, I wish you had told me. I'm sure I could have found you somebody, anyone."

"I see that the second hand store had a sale. Don't you look darling; I personally myself, I never really thought styles from the seventies were very flattering. I remember why now. And Valene, how nice to see you again," Linda snarled at her.

"Its Valerie, Lydia," she corrected.

"This dress is not from a second hand store and has no influence of the seventies at all and even if it was I would prefer it over something that looked like it got chopped up by the garbage disposal." Samantha quickly shot back.

"You know Samantha, not to be mean but you could be so much more attractive if you could lose some weight, especially in the butt area," Linda said with an evil smile.

"Linda!" Dean chuckled nervously. "Samantha doesn't need to lose weight. If the wind picked up she would blow away."

Linda smiled evily as she leaned back in her seat. Samantha glared at her and then looked over at Dean, who was obviously very nervous about all of them being together. "Lying to her will never help her deal with reality Dean. I'm simply trying to help her. That's all. Sometimes the truth can be brutal."

"It's all right Dean. All that silicone and bleach has affected her brain, and now she's just obnoxious, you can't blame her. That's what happens when scientists experiment on humans," Samantha replied as she sat down.

"This is my natural hair color! And no doctor has ever laid a hand on me!" Linda replied quickly, getting upset.

"Maybe the doctors' hands haven't, but I'd sure make a high bet that everyone else's has," Samantha said, enjoying Linda's glares. Score one for her!

"Has anyone seen Brad?" Valerie asked, getting very uncomfortable with the direction that the conversation had taken.

"Is there something that you want?" Linda asked Samantha. "I'm sure Maxwell wouldn't want us taking up all your time, after all, this is a working event for you isn't it?"

"Actually, I came to see if you would like to dance," she asked, standing back up, giving him the look that told him it was not a question but an order. "That is if your date doesn't mind."

"I don't mind," Linda said to him. "But first would you mind getting me a drink?"

"I'm not sure it's safe to leave you two alone," he said, clearing his throat.

"It's a public place, what could happen," Linda said to him as he got up from his chair.

"World war three maybe," Valerie said with a slight smile.

"That's what I'm afraid of. Val, try to help keep the peace while I'm away," Dean said to her as he turned and disappeared into the crowd.

Samantha watched Dean walk off as the music changed to a faster beat. If the evening wasn't so tense it would be fun to sit back and watch the locals out on the dance floor dancing. Most hadn't been dancing in years, and it was obvious.

"Great evening isn't" Linda suddenly spoke up, breaking the silence between them.

"Just what exactly are you up to now?" Samantha asked her sternly as soon as she was sure Dean was out of sight.

"Nothing really. A hot guy asked me out and I said yes. I see you are recovering nicely from the nut house," Linda smiled to her. "I must say you looked like hell the other day when I visited. It's nice you fixed your hair; it helps take away the attention from the bruises on your face."

"There are no bruises on my face!" Samantha said through her gritted teeth.

"Oh my God!" Linda acted like she was shocked. "I'm sorry; I didn't realize that was your make-up! Was it your keen fashion sense that sent you over the edge and into the hospital? I never really heard why you were there."

"Oh God," Valerie said out loud as she glanced around the crowded room for Brad. "Brad, where in the hell are you?"

"I was in the hospital because you pushed me off a balcony and you know it," she yelled at her. "And I know a lot of other things about you, and if you don't let Dean go and leave us all alone, I'm going to tell everyone everything about that cop in Kansas City. All about your business partner, and let's not forget your missing husband, but he really isn't missing now, is he?"

"I think you have popped one too many painkillers. Who do you think they will believe? You the crazy ding-a-ling who sees me in her house trying to kill her, floating through walls when there is no possible way I could be there, or me, the nice lady who just donated one hundred thousand dollars to rebuild their downtown. It doesn't take a genius to figure that one out," Linda said, laughing at her.

"You gave away a hundred thousand dollars to this city? Girl, are you nuts?" Valerie asked, stunned.

Samantha groaned out at Valerie. It was just like her to do that. You could be talking about one thing and she'll focus on something else that was off the subject needing to be discussed. "Valerie! Would you please just drop it! She only did it to buy everybody off. Just tell me this, how did you get in my house? It was amazing how you were able to replace the woodwork. I have to give you credit. You're very good. I have never met a better schemer than you."

"For the last time, I was never in your house; the other day was the first time! And I don't have a clue what you mean about this woodwork thing you're talking about. You're completely crazy!" Linda said, getting really tired of her.

"You're the one that's crazy! A hundred thousand dollars! You could have bought them fools off for far less than that," Valerie told Linda.

"That's enough Valerie! Linda, I swear I don't know how you did it, but I'll find out. And make damn sure you pay for it!" Samantha said as she started to get up.

"Listen to me, you little neurotic bitch! You are so infatuated with me that you're having delusions. I suggest you leave me alone, because if you don't, I'll make damn sure you go to the mental home. Permanently. Oh and by the way I think that you should know Dean is incredible in bed. He's very satisfying, and I do mean satisfying in every sense of the word. I thought you might want to know since you will never get the chance to find out. I bet now you wish you hadn't kept those chubby little legs crossed. Don't you?" Linda said, watching Samantha's face turn red with anger.

Valerie's mouth dropped open as Samantha started to go for Linda's throat, but she stopped as she saw Dean making his way through the crowd. A large victory smile crept upon Linda's face as she quietly smirked.

"Well I see you two survived round one," Dean said, handing Linda her drink and setting his on the table.

"How about that dance," Samantha said, grabbing his arm and pulling him out on the floor as the music changed to a ballad, getting him as far from Linda as she could get without giving him a chance to object.

"Slow down Sam, you're about to pull my arm out of socket," he told her making her stop.

"Are you out of your mind? I can't believe you brought that slut here!" She shouted at him over the music.

"You know, I really don't appreciate you talking that way about her. And, I might add, I asked you first, which you declined, saying you were too busy and now you're here with my best friend," he told her calmly as they slow danced.

"Is that why you brought her, to get revenge on me for not going out with you?" She asked.

"No! You know me better than that. I happen to enjoy her company, if it's any of your business. We are really hitting it off."

"Yes, so I've heard, actually every body here tonight has heard. You two are the talk of the party. You must be so proud. You know you can get diseases screwing women like her. I mean, come on, anyone who would dress like she does obviously gets around. You just happen to be this week's boy toy. I hope it's worth it in the end," Samantha said to him, hoping he would wake up and come to his senses. "Because you look like a fool!"

"If all you're going to do is stand here and tear us both down, I'm going to leave," he warned her.

"Nice suit. Ms. Money bags buy you that for services rendered," she asked after a moment of silence.

"I'm glad you're feeling better," he answered.

"You must be a pretty good lay. This suit looks expensive," she cracked, pulling at the lapel. "What's next, a new car? I hear that's quite high on boy toy lists."

"I don't know what has got into you, but friend or not, you are not going to talk that way about someone I happen to be in love with," he said before he realized what he said. "I happen to have a little bit of money saved up myself! Linda has not given nor will I take a dime from her!"

"Love!" She screamed. "You have only known her at the most three or four weeks! How the hell could you be in love with her? Trust me Dean, it doesn't happen that fast! Just because you have sex with her every night doesn't make it love! It's called lust!"

"What we do is none of your damn business. I gave you every chance to try to get together now for years, so I think it's a little late to be jealous," Dean said, stopping and starting to walk away from her.

"That woman doesn't know the first thing about love! All she knows is how to destroy people! Everybody she comes in contact with dies, Dean!" She yelled after him.

"Have you completely lost your mind?" He yelled, turning back around and facing her. "I can't believe the way you're talking tonight! I think you need to grow up!"

"Well I think you need to stop thinking with that thing in your pants and start thinking with your head!" She screamed.

People around them had stopped dancing and were listening to them fight. Dean's words were ripping through her brain as she tried to absorb it. How could he possibly be in love with her? He didn't even know her. She felt herself getting sick!

"I've had enough of this," Dean said as he started to move through the crowd of on lookers.

"I have a bunch of things you need to see, things I got from the Kansas City paper," she said, rushing up behind him, grabbing his arm.

"What are you talking about now?" He demanded.

Dean had known Samantha for as long as he could remember. She was always a passionate and sometimes went too far, but this was the worst she had ever been. A part of him knew she wouldn't be getting this worked up if she wasn't positive there was something wrong. The other part told him it was just good old fashioned jealousy.

"Ask her about her husband, how he just conveniently disappeared. And the cop who was investigating it, how he just drove off a cliff one night, and let's not forget the guy that took a nosedive out her office window. Come on Dean, wake up! She is a cold blooded killer. She just keeps killing while you guys sit around with your thumbs up your butt talking about her beauty!"

"That's enough!" He shouted at her. "I don't want to hear anymore! Do you understand? You need help! A lot more than I thought."

"You know Dean, I thought you were smarter than the others were, but I guess I was wrong. You just couldn't wait to jump in bed with her, could you? Well I hope it was worth it because fucking her has a price, and you can't afford it! It's in all the newspapers up there in black and white! Just open your eyes before it's too late!" She yelled at him again.

"You listen to me, and listen good! I do not want you anywhere near her! Don't you call her or say anything else about her! You don't have a clue what's going on out here in the real world, and I'm sick to death of hearing how badly this woman has treated you! Get over it and leave us alone! Or I promise you that you will be sorry!" He threatened before once again walking off.

"What kind of flowers should I send to your funeral?" She yelled after him. "She kills everyone she comes in contact with and you're next!"

Dean, not turning around this time, stormed through the crowd of observers over to their table, grabbed Linda's purse and helped her up. He didn't say a word to anyone as he started making his way through the crowd as Linda held onto his arm tightly. People starred but quickly stepped aside to let them through.

"Are you all right?" Linda asked concerned once they got outside.

"I'm sorry about the scene I caused in there. She just made me so God damn mad! I shouldn't have let her get to me like that," he said, trying to calm down.

"Thank you," Linda said quietly to him, and then looked away.

"For what, embarrassing the hell out of you?" He asked as he sat on the brick wall, trying desperately to calm down. He couldn't remember the last time he had been so angry at anyone.

"You could never embarrass me. What you did in there was defend me. And no one has ever defended me before," she started to say more but stopped as her eyes filled with tears.

"I would do anything for you," he told her managing a smile.

His heart saddened as he noticed she was serious by the tears forming in her eyes. He gently took his fingers and wiped them away, pulling her into his arms. He knew she didn't let just anyone see this side of her. Tonight was a breaking point in their relationship. They weren't just dating anymore.

"Dean," she said pulling away from him. "It scares me the way you make me feel. Nobody has ever had control over me like you do. I'm afraid you're going to make me into one of those mushy women who want nothing but to please her man."

"I don't think that would be so bad," he laughed, breaking the tension as he pulled her close to him and kissed her again.

Samantha stood at the top of the stairs, looking down at Dean and Linda kissing. She sighed as she watched them walk off into the darkness towards the parking lot. Nothing she had told him mattered. Linda Edwards had him completely under her spell. She just hoped it wasn't too late to break it.

"Are you okay?" Valerie asked, coming up behind her. "That was some fight in there."

"Yes, I'm fine, it's just Dean that I'm worried about. She's going to hurt him and I have to figure out how to stop her," Samantha said, staring off into the darkness.

"I think you need to let yourself accept the way you really feel about him, and then go tell him. Come on Sam, everybody knows by the way you two look at each other that there's something there, but you're just too stupid to let it happen. The only reason he's with that tart is because you told him no! And besides, did you see that dress? She looked like she got attacked with a weed whacker!" She joked hoping to lighten the mood a bit.

"That was a strange dress," Samantha managed a laughed. "I don't know Valerie; things are just not that easy."

"Sweetie, you're the only one making it difficult," Valerie quickly added.

"I just can't deal with the pressures his job would put on me. I went through that with my father, I couldn't do it again," Samantha said, trying to stop the tears that were starting to form.

"I just have one more thing to say and I want you to listen. Honey, the chances of something happening to him in a town like this are close to zero. Let's face it, you're already emotionally attached to him, so if something should happen to him, God forbid, you would feel all those emotions anyway. So why deprive yourself of his love now?" She asked her quietly. "It's not too late. Make your move now before it is!"

"There you two are!" Brad said, coming out the doors. "Wow that was some fight! Everybody insides talking about it. Boy Sam, Max is going to shit a brick tomorrow when he hears how badly you messed this up."

"Drop it Brad! We don't need any of your jokes right now," Valerie warned.

"That wasn't a joke actually." Brad said as he turned to Samantha. "Can I give you some advice?"

"This should be good," Valerie interrupted.

"I'm serious. Dean has talked a lot about her lately, and I think their relationship is all physical. If you just stay out of it and leave them alone it will be over in a couple weeks, but if you keep interfering like you did tonight you're just going to draw them closer. Trust me!"

"I can't just sit back and watch her treat him like she does everyone else. I'm sorry, I just care too much about him," she said in her defense.

"Care or love?" Brad asked.

"Brad!" Valerie said, glaring at him.

"Oh great, now you sound like Dr. Valerie here. Just both of you stop it, I can't deal with this right now," she said as she grabbed Brad's keys and started down the steps. "Are you two coming or are you going to take a cab? It's obvious Brad's had too much to drink to drive."

"Well here's something else to think about. If Linda Edwards killed all those people in Kansas City and had something to do with those guys disappearing here, then I wouldn't want to be you!" he said, following close behind.

"What the hell are you talking about now?" Valerie asked, running to catch up with them.

"Just think about it. Samantha here just announced to the whole city that Linda killed off half of Kansas City and now she's doing the same thing here! I'd say you pissed her off and she's going to nail your ass to the wall. I don't know her very well, but judging from what I've seen, I'd say she knows how to play dirty. Maybe you should leave town for awhile?" He warned, seeing the sudden fear in her eyes.

Samantha let all her fears come back and grab her. For a little while she had managed to get over being afraid of Linda and actually feeling like she could take her on. One of her many character flaws was anger! When she got mad, she got stupid and reality took a back seat.

"Maybe you should leave town for awhile," Valerie repeated to Brad, going over and wrapping her arms around Samantha. "You're scaring her half to death, you jerk."

"I'm just telling her to be careful!" He told Valerie, being quite serious. "This isn't a game. She has royally pissed her off. Don't tell me you honestly think that she is going to just sit back and not do something?"

"He's right! What am I going to do?" Samantha asked, her voice shaking.

"Just stay away from her," Brad said rubbing her shoulders. "Let all this craziness blow over."

"I think you better be careful what you say about her and like Brad said, avoid her if you can! Sooner or later Dean and the others will figure her out. People like her eventually slip up. And you have to give Dean credit. He isn't that dumb. He'll catch her," Valerie told her, trying to comfort her.

"It's her game Sam, we have to play by her rules or she will win! She can't keep doing this and get away with it; she'll slip up. Just wait. Let her nail herself," Brad added. "If you don't she's going to make your life a living hell!"

"You're right, Dean is so hooked in her that he wouldn't believe anything anyone told him. He's going to have to see it with his own eyes. I just hope he does before it's too late," Samantha said as she unlocked the car. "How did you two suddenly get so smart?"

"From Valerie's soaps!" Brad joked.

"Get in the car Brad!" Valerie ordered, and then slammed his door shut.

## Chapter 16 - Paying the consequences.

"If Samantha sent you here, you might as well save your breath and turn back around and leave," Dean warned Brad as he entered his office. "I don't have time for this bull shit today."

"Hey! Calm down man. Can't a friend just stop by and say hello with out getting his head bit off?" Brad asked as he pulled over a chair and plopped down, not waiting for an answer.

"Have a seat," Dean said sarcastically after he had already sat down.

"It has been awhile since we talked and I was just wondering how things are going with you and Ms. Moneybags?" He asked as he made himself comfortable by putting his feet up on Dean's desk.

"Her name Is Linda and I thought you didn't come to talk about that?" Dean asked, pushing Brad's feet off his desk, giving him a look that told him not to put them back.

"No, I told you Sam did not send me here to talk about it. Careful what you ask. I have to say that was some fight the other night."

Dean groaned out as he laid his head back against his chair. The argument between him and Samantha may not have made front page news but had been number one gossip all around town. Everyone was talking about it and it was driving him nuts.

"People just can't stop talking about it."

"If you don't mind I would rather not be reminded, thank you," Dean told him sternly. "People need to learn to mind their own business."

"Kinda hard to do when you put it out there for everyone to see," Brad reminded.

"If you recall, I was not the one that 'put it out there' so save your lectures for someone else. I have a lot of things going on around here and really don't have time to shoot the shit with you."

"Well how about after work we shoot hoops instead?" Brad asked excitedly. "We haven't done that in ages, maybe get the girls together and hit the movie theatre?"

"I'd sooner pluck my eye ball out with this pen," Dean said as he stopped filling out the paperwork and tossed the pen across his desk. "Ok, maybe shoot some baskets later, I'll have to call you and let you know. Let's see how the afternoon goes."

It would fell good to get out and play some basketball with Brad again, it seemed like ages since they had done that, but getting the girls together meant Val and Samantha and not Linda. He wouldn't even consider going with out her and he sure couldn't take her with Samantha going. There would be more drama in the isle than on the screen and that was the last thing he wanted or needed right now.

"Don't you want to know how she is?" Brad questioned after a moment of silence.

"Do I have a choice?"

"Not really. Listen Dean, I know you don't want to hear this, but she really does like you and it's tearing her up that you won't talk to her anymore. Are things so serious between you and Linda that you would put it over what you and Sam have together?" He asked him.

"You know Brad; you're the only one that seems to think that there's something going on with Sam and me. All I can remember is me asking her out and her telling me no! Time after time after time. Frankly, I'm sick of being rejected. What was I supposed to do just keep asking till one of us dropped dead?" He asked as he wadded up the papers on his desk and threw them away. "I can't help it that I moved on and found someone who actually said yes when I asked her out."

"So then are things really getting serious between you two?" Brad persisted.

Dean sighed and tried hard not to smile as he thought about his

*the Murderess of* RIDGECLIFFE MANOR

whirlwind romance with Linda. He had to be careful what he said because he knew Brad was going to go back and tell the girls everything. He used to think Brad was in his court but now he trusted no one but Linda.

"Well?"

"Unlike you, yes I have found someone that I like better than myself," he quickly answered.

"You're very funny. By the way, your eyes shine when you talk about her. I'd say you have either been bitten by the love bug or you have a bottle of happy juice stashed in a drawer in your desk," Brad said as he moved his fingers back and forth in front of Dean's eyes.

"Would you stop it! "Dean said smacking his hands away from his face. I've never really felt like this before, well at least felt like this about someone that feels the same way back. It's kinda scary."

"Could be the flu. That's going around you know."

"Brad!" Dean groaned. "That's why I can't talk to you about anything; you always have to make a joke."

"Alright, I'm just not used to you being such a girl that's all. I don't think you should give up on Samantha just yet," he defended.

"I don't really care what you think. Samantha has put me off for the last time. You and Valerie keep telling me that she is in love with me, but I fail to see it. I have finally found someone who feels the same way I do. Sam's just going to have to deal with it. Don't you have some house to show or something?"

"I just think that you two fell in love awfully fast. Maybe you should slow it down a notch or two, don't you think?" Brad said as he reached into the candy jar on Dean's desk and grabbed a handful.

"I know what I'm doing, I'm a big boy now dad. Isn't it time for you to go before you start telling me the facts of life?" Dean asked, as he grabbed the candy jar and put it out of reach. "I can only imagine what your version would be like!"

Knowing Brad's track record with women, Dean was sure it would be a fascinating story. The only problem with Brad's version is it would be about fifty percent accurate. He had been best friends with Brad for several years and he loved him like a brother but he knew not to believe half of what he said.

"Afraid it's too late for the birds and the bees after what you told me the other day," Brad joked then backed off after the look Dean gave him. "Okay! Okay! But before I go I think that there is something you should know. Samantha would kill me if she knew I was here…"

"Just get on with it Brad, I am at work, remember!" Dean interrupted.

"Alright! Just know that Samantha is on a mission to prove Linda killed those guys that are missing. Val and I both have talked to her, but you know how stubborn she can be. She really believes Linda is some kind of sadistic killer who she claims killed a bunch of people in Kansas City and now she's doing it here. She got some things from the newspaper up there, but she never let me see what it was," Brad said with concern in his voice.

What little enjoyment Dean had started to have for the day quickly vanished as reality came quickly crashing back in. It was really difficult to be in love with someone and want to share them with your friends and have your friends hate them. It was really difficult to be happy anymore anywhere but in Linda's embrace.

"I know," Dean sighed. "She was screaming it to me at the dance. If you listen to her stories and break them down you'll realize it is impossible! There was no way Linda could have beaten her home the other night and knocked her off that balcony. You know that and I know that!"

"But the problem is she doesn't know that! And that makes her about as dangerous as she thinks Linda is!" Brad added.

"Don't you think if Linda did kill these men here, which I might add there are no bodies, she would have done something to Duke Etherton? I mean, come on, there is definitely no love loss there!" Dean told him.

"Excuse me Sheriff," a woman in uniform said as she entered his office.

"Yes Kathy, what is it?" Dean asked the dispatcher.

"I just got off the phone with the National Weather Service and they have placed us and all the surrounding counties under a tornado watch until midnight. They said that we were definitely going to get hit by some major storms tonight, and judging by the dark clouds moving in, I don't think it will be long. Should I send out the weather spotters?" She asked.

"Yeah, go ahead, I'll be through here in a minute, thank you," Dean said as they watched her leave, her long dark ponytail swaying behind her.

"Who was that?" Brad asked of the dispatcher.

"She's new in town. Name's Kathy Pembroke. She just started here the other day. Came from the Boone County office lives in Huntsville I think. She seems nice, and I think she's single," Dean hinted thinking if Brad found a date maybe he would leave him alone.

"Yeah?" Brad answered. "Well I better get rolling if a storm's coming, I just thought I should warn you about Samantha, and what she's up to," Brad told him as he got up from the chair, concentrating on the woman talking on her phone outside Dean's office..

"I appreciate it. Listen, let me know if she starts planning something," Dean told him as he left. He watched as Brad stopped by the new dispatcher's desk and started talking to her.

If there was one thing you could count on it was Brad making friends with every available woman in town. Then again, that may be why he is so successful in his job. Brad finally stopped talking and looked back at Dean standing in the doorway. He smiled brightly and waved good bye. As Brad left Deputy Harris walked in. The dismal frown on his face let Dean know it wasn't good news.

"Here's the latest missing persons report. This one is from Morgan County. That now makes four in less than a month," Deputy Harris told him as he handed him the latest fax report he had just received.

"Another one! I can't believe this! What in the hell is going on?" Dean said, getting frustrated because he had no leads.

"I don't know, but it's starting to get people restless. All around us. Just about every paper in the state has called this morning. They just seem to be vanishing into thin air!" He said thinking out loud.

"Yeah I know. The problem is there's no real connection. So far only the first one, Ray Thompson was seen with this mystery lady," Dean reminded him.

"I guess you can say the only real connection is that they have all four seemed to just vanish in thin air. I don't think we should rule out this mystery woman though Dean, she might have gotten smarter and found a different way of picking them up..."

"Or they're just not connected," Dean added again, knowing where he was leading.

Deputy Allan Harris had been with the force for two years now and had been a handful for Dean. He was a good deputy; he was just a little quick to jump to conclusions, especially about anyone new in town. He was always running the plates of out of town visitors, suspecting the worse. Needless to say he had been suspicious of Linda before she ever moved to town.

"You know Dean, I hate to have to be the one to tell you this, but there are some people out there who are starting to question some of the things that Samantha brought up at the Mayor's dance the other night," the deputy informed him.

"Samantha Marshall has an over active and heavily medicated imagination. That I might add is working on overtime! I don't know what to do about her and I'm getting sick of hearing about it," Dean yelled. "It's like the old witch trials. Someone new comes to town that's a little different and the town's ready to burn her at the stake. I'll personally deal with Ms. Marshall," Dean said just before the first burst of thunder ripped through the sky above, rattling the windows in his office.

Deputy Harris decided it was in his best interest to say no more and left the office, leaving Dean alone. Dean felt bad about his outburst; it was not something that he did much until lately. It was just getting to him how everyone was turning against Linda. What on earth would she be doing with these guys? They hardly fit into her social standing. But then again neither did he. But she had never tried anything out of the ordinary with him. No, Linda had nothing to do with it. He hated himself for even thinking about it. There was no possible way Linda had anything to do with those men disappearing, or worse their deaths.

---

Rod looked up as a lightning bolted ripped through the dark stormy sky. Any minute now those dark clouds were going to burst open, drowning them. The weatherman on the radio had warned them of severe weather and for once it looked like he was going to be right. The wind began to pick up as they moved the vehicle slowly through the cornfield behind Ridgecliffe Manor. Silently to himself he hoped Duke knew where he was going, one wrong turn and they would easily drive off into the river.

"Are you sure you really want to do this?" Rod asked, looking at Duke.

"Damn right! You saw what that bitch did to our bikes. She deserves a lot worse than we're gonna give her!" He cursed, turning his head and spitting a mouthful of chew out the window.

"Couldn't we pick some other night? This storm looks like it's gonna be a big one!" Rod said just as another loud clasp of thunder roared through the silent night.

"Come on man! Don't be a dick, this storm is just gonna make things easier for us. That bitch is probably sittin in that old house just a shaken. Hell, I bet she might even be glad to see us!" Duke said, then smiled a wicked smile just thinking about what he had planned for her tonight.

Duke pulled the car forward slowly then shut the engine off. Warning Rod to stay put, he grabbed his flashlight and got out of the car. After five minutes he returned and started the engine up and proceeded forward, this time leaving the headlights off.

"What did you do?" Rod asked.

"The house is just ahead, had to check for farm equipment. Can't exactly drive up there with the headlights on now, could we? You ever use that head of yours?" He asked him.

"I just don't see why we couldn't have parked on the highway and walked up here," he complained.

"Just shut the fuck up and come on!" Duke said as he got out of the car.

Why did he bring Rod along? Duke wondered to himself. The asshole's idea of scaring someone was running up to them and saying boo! They stopped by the large bushes in the gardens and looked up at the brick mansion. Lightning flashed through the sky, lighting up the old place with a sinister glow. Linda Edwards was in for the night of her life! Revenge was going to be so sweet!

Another clasp of thunder and the rain let loose, instantly drowning them as they ran up to the mansion. Behind them the storm started in full force. The mansions' bricks, despite the earlier heat, felt like ice to their exposed skin as they leaned against the house for shelter.

"What if we have a tornado?" Rod asked as they reached the back porch.

"Would you shut the fuck up? Do you want her to hear us? Damn! There isn't gonna be a fuckin tornado!" He whispered angrily at him as they moved closer to the back porch that wrapped across the back end of the house.

Another bright flash of lightning along with an intense blast of thunder sent the mansion into complete darkness. The wind suddenly whipped around them, knocking them into the wall just as the sky opened up and began tossing small pebbles of hail down hard against the ground.

"Hot damn! It just gets easier and easier. Now the bitch doesn't have any lights. Shit Rod, even you might look good to her in the dark!" Duke joked.

"Real fuckin funny!" Rod blasted him.

Duke reached out and tried the back door, surprised that it was locked. She must be scared! Hardly anyone around here locked their doors. Reaching into his pants pocket, he pulled out his switchblade and went to the window, slicing through the old screen, and then pulled the rest loose. Using both hands, he lifted the window open.

"One thing you can count on in these old houses is the latches being broken," he said as he climbed through the now open window. "Come on! Hurry up!"

Both men jumped as another burst of thunder roared outside, shaking the whole house and making the windows rattle. Upstairs they could hear Linda cursing in the dark, and then a loud crash as something fell down the stairs.

"My God, did she fall down the stairs?" Rod asked as he started through the room.

Duke grabbed him and forced him against the wall as they followed the noise through the kitchen and into the back hall. Lightning flashed through the windows, allowing them brief moments to see through the countless rooms as they made their way to the front of the house into what appeared to be a library.

The house was surrounded by an eerie stillness despite the raging storm outside. There was a bad feeling that something was very wrong here and both men could feel it. Linda Edwards could still be heard shuffling around in the hallway just on the other side of the wall. Strange shapes danced along the walls by the oil lamps' shadows. Duke peeked out the door and around the corner, and then quickly snapped his head back. It was dark, but Rod could feel something was wrong by the way he was breathing.

"There's a fucking dead man in the hallway! I can't believe it! This crazy bitch just killed a man!" Duke whispered to his friend.

"We gotta get out of here before we're next!" Rod whispered to Duke

"Come on, follow me!" Duke told him, holding the switchblade in front of him as he rushed into the hallway.

"Are you crazy? Let's get out of here!" Rod pleaded as he followed him.

Duke grabbed his arm and pulled him close behind as they walked quietly around the body of the man. They looked at him but could not tell who he was. There was tape over his eyes, mouth and his throat. Blood had stained his naked body. Linda was nowhere to be found.

"She must have gone this way," Duke said as he led them into the dark parlor.

The storm continued to rage outside, sounding as if it was going to rip through the house at any given moment. Lightning lit the dining room up as they passed through into the kitchen door. Rod could feel his heart beating fast against his chest. There was a loud crack, followed by a severe sharp pain in his head as he fell to the floor and passed out.

"Damn it Rod! I thought I told you to be quiet!" Duke said as he stopped, quickly turned around. He looked to see what Rod had knocked over just as another lightning flashed through the room, lighting up Linda Edwards' smiling face and Rod's bloody body slumped over on the floor at her feet.

"It was very nice of you to stop by and check on me with this storm, I just wish you would have called first, and especially told me you were bringing a friend," Linda said as she pointed the gun she was holding to Duke's face.

"You're a fuckin lunatic!" he screamed at her.

"That's probably the nicest thing you ever said to me. I'm touched.

Now pick up your friend and let's go have a party in the basement," she ordered.

"I'm not going anywhere with you, you sick bitch!" Duke yelled back at her.

"Oh I think you will, now grab your friend and move!" She yelled as she cocked the gun.

Duke picked up Rod's body and did as he was told; all the way to the basement he plotted his next move and how he was going to get out of there. They crossed through one room after another till they got to the back of the basement. Linda lit the doorknob up with the flashlight she was holding and ordered him to open the door.

"What the fuck is this place?" He asked as he entered the room.

"Isn't it great? It's an old butcher room where the former owners used to butcher their own meat. I like to think of it as my private torture chamber," Linda said, then laughed loudly sending shivers through his body. "Do you like it?"

"You will never get away with this! They will find my car! You're gonna get your ass nailed to the fucking wall! You fucked up bitch," he yelled at her as he dropped his friend's body on the floor.

"Pick him up and put him on that table!" Linda ordered, lighting the table up as Duke followed her instructions. "Hurry up, I don't have all night!"

"I'll get even, you just wait," he said, looking her directly in the eyes.

"Give it up! You're not going to do anything unless I tell you to! Knowing you, you're probably getting off on this. Now shut up and move over to that corner by the sewer pipe," she ordered.

"You know, Dean will find my car when he stops by for his nightly fuck!" He repeated to her.

"I'll take care of Dean, and your beat up car," she smiled at him.

"You don't know where it's at," he yelled at her.

"Oh come on, Duke! I could hear that old muffler of yours as you pulled in behind the house. I knew you were here the minute you got here! I mean, come on! I believe you must have the mental capacity of a five-year-old. I'm sure even they could find much more intelligent ways to sneak up on people. Here put these on," she ordered as she pulled out some handcuffs from her pocket.

"You sick bitch!" Duke said as he reluctantly did as he was told.

Linda then pulled out another set and fastened the cuffs he had on to the sewer pipe. All those visits to Dean's office paid off, she thought to herself as she pulled off Duke's filthy boots and fastened the last set around his ankles. She blew him a kiss, and then left the room. Duke started yelling obscenities that she could hear all the way into the kitchen.

The man's body still lay at the foot of the stairs where she had left it. Too bad she hadn't thought to have Duke bring it down before she cuffed him, she thought to herself, dragging the body through the dark house and down into the basement. She then carefully placed him in the freezer next to the others, listening to Duke shout more obscenities at her as she passed.

"I sure hope the lights are not off very long or those bodies are going to start stinking," she said to Duke as she went over to him. "I sure wouldn't want to be you left down here with that horrible stench. I hear it's pretty bad."

"I'm gonna get loose and break every bone in your fuckin body!" Duke yelled at her as he tried to break free.

"You better be careful those cuffs are sharp. You might cut you hands off," she said to him, laughing at his bloody wrist. The sight of the fresh blood made her hungry again even though she had just fed.

"You're gonna wish you never laid eyes on me!" Duke screamed at her.

"You have me shaking in my heels," Linda said to him as she crossed the room to the table and looked at Rod's body.

Linda walked over to a drawer and pulled out a large knife then grabbed a couple of jars and some tape, placing them beside Rod's body. Duke watched in horror as she sliced his wrist open and drained the blood into the jars. After she had filled both jars she taped up the wounds, and then covered his mouth and eyes with tape, knocking the body over onto the floor and dragging him to the freezer with the others.

"What a productive night... what's this?" She asked herself out loud as she flashed the light down to the dark object on the floor.

As she picked it up she realized it was Rod's wallet. Casually she opened it and started searching through it, stopping to pull out a condom. Linda started laughing. "I always wondered if guys really carried these things around in their wallet, now I know it's true. Nice drivers license picture."

"I'm gonna get you bitch! I swear it!" He yelled at her, but she ignored him.

"You know a nice girl like me could see a thing like this in a guy's wallet and get the wrong idea about you Mid Missouri boys," Linda said as she threw the condom at him. "God only knows what's in your wallet."

"Fuck you!" Duke screamed.

"You know I'm getting real tired of your nasty mouth," Linda said as she took a piece of tape and put it over his mouth. "I think most of the storm is over now, so I better go upstairs and clean that mess up just in case Dean does stop by. Boy, I'm glad you decided to come and see me, I have such great plans for you!"

Duke moaned through the tape as she closed the door to the room and went through the basement and back upstairs. Everything was going to work out perfectly. She did not know why she had not thought of this plan before. There was now enough blood to last her for awhile, so she could let things settle down. It was time to start in a new area before people caught on. Thanks to Samantha Marshall, it was happening a lot sooner than planned, but it wouldn't be long before she would be out of the picture.

Quickly Linda finished cleaning, burned the bed linens and the man's clothes and headed back to the kitchen just as the lights came back on. Things were definitely looking up! She thought to herself as she put the blood in the refrigerator.

"Damn it!" Linda said out loud as she remembered that she had left those two jars of blood downstairs.

She sighed as she flipped on the basement lights and went back down. Duke was still locked up to the pipe, but had a large gash in his forehead where he had hit it against the wall.

"You really should stop throwing those little tantrums before you hurt yourself!" Linda smiled as she picked up the jars.

Duke was muttering something to her, so she put down the jars and removed the tape from his mouth.

## the Murderess of RIDGECLIFFE MANOR

"What are you doing with that blood?" Duke asked as he licked his dry lips.

"Not that it's any of your business, but I drink it. Blood keeps me alive, healthy, and beautiful," she said as she turned away from him and went back to the table.

"Not that blood!" Duke said then, started laughing, a sick glare in his eyes.

"What do you mean?" Linda asked.

"You don't want to drink that blood," he replied.

"Why not?" She asked, picking up a jar and holding it up to the light.

"Remember that rubber you found in his wallet?" He asked.

"Yes, so?" Linda said, glaring at him.

"He uses it to protect his whores from his disease," he laughed.

"What disease?" she asked suddenly getting irritated. "What disease?"

"AIDS you stupid bitch. The fucker had AIDS!"

"You're a liar! Come on Duke, I figure even you can come up with a better one than that," Linda said as she put the jar down and looked at him.

"Go ahead. Drink it, see if I care. I don't give a shit what happens to you, but you are fucking Dean, and he's a pretty cool guy…"

"Shut up!" Linda screamed as she picked up the jar and threw it at the brick wall beside Duke, covering him in his friend's blood. "Just shut up!"

Linda picked up the other jar and angrily threw it across the room, sending blood and glass everywhere. After a couple of deep breaths she managed to calm herself down. She turned back around and glanced over at Duke, who was watching her every move in fear.

"This is just brilliant!" she said through gritted teeth, glaring at him. "Now it looks like I'll just have to get some more! Any ideas as to where I might get it?"

Linda, not waiting for his answer, grabbed the knife from the table and slowly walked over to Duke, her smile getting bigger the closer she got. He squirmed and yelled some more as she came upon him and stopped. She laughed out as she took the knife and sliced Duke's forearm open, and then took the blood that spilled all over him and smeared it in with his own.

"Guess you better hope he doesn't have aids, huh Duke?" She said laughing as she reached down and pulled one of his socks off, stuffing it into his mouth before covering it with tape. She grabbed his shoulder, pushing him forward so she could reach behind him and get his keys off the chain attached to his jeans. She looked back at him as she crossed the room to turn off the light, almost feeling sorry for him. A few minutes later she was back in the kitchen. Things had now taken a turn. She would have to kill again before she took a break. But tonight she had other things and people to take care of. It was time that Samantha got what was coming to her. Linda laughed out loud as she started planning what she was going to do. Her laughter echoed throughout the house.

# Chapter 17 - Fighting fire with fire

Samantha sat nervously in her dark living room watching the storm through the large open windows. A strong gust of wind had knocked down a large branch in her front yard, just one of many around the neighborhood. With all the damage the winds were causing, it was hard to tell how long it would be before the electricity comes back on. Deep inside she wanted to go upstairs and just go to sleep, but here lately, storms scared her, so sleeping was out of the question. The wind was whistling so noisily through the gaps in the old windows that she doubted she would be able to sleep anyway.

"How much longer is this going to last?" She asked herself as she rubbed her arms, trying to shake her uneasy feeling.

The stormy season was definitely here. A time of year that she used to look forward to. The thunder, lightning, and strong winds. Something about a good thunderstorm always seemed to fill her with excitement. She thought back to the movie nights they used to have when it stormed. There was nothing like watching a scary movie with a bad storm happening in the background. Not anymore! Not since Linda Edwards moved to town!

Lightning suddenly flashed lighting up a shiny red car that had just drove past her house slowly; it seemed to almost stop, but had vanished before the next flash of lightning. It gave her chills as it reminded her that Linda Edwards could be close by, even possibly in that car! Watching her, waiting for her.

Something was going to have to be done about her; she could not allow her to keep doing the things she had been doing. She was making her life a living nightmare! Samantha tried to wipe her from her mind as she went into the kitchen and grabbed the little pill bottle, pulling out tonight's selection of sedative and pain killer cocktail. She swallowed the last pill and set the glass in the sink. It seemed strange to her that with all the pills she was taking, none calmed her nerves.

Despite the late hour she picked up her cell phone to call Valerie. She really needed someone to talk to and Valerie told her that she could call her anytime she wanted. But to her dismay, there was no answer. Where on earth could she be this late at night? She listened to it ring and ring. Just as she started to hang up, she heard a quiet noise forming over the ringing, getting louder and louder until finally it was distinguished enough that she could figure it out. It was Linda Edwards' voice!

"I don't mess with married men, Samantha," she said, managing a laugh at the end. "But I'll mess with you!"

"No!" She screamed, without thinking she threw it across the room. "Just brilliant! That will cost a fortune to replace."

Samantha continued to scold herself as she went over and picked up the phone and all its many pieces and sat it down on the table. She quietly cursed as she bent over and looked at the small hole she had just made in the wall. "It's all in my head!" she told herself over and over, trying to settle her nerves. "That was not Linda Edwards on the phone. The storm is just making me edgy!"

Lightning flashed across the sky, lighting up the house. With it came another round of the fierce winds that had been calming down. The storm must be returning, she thought as she got up off the couch and went into the kitchen to pour herself another cup of coffee. She checked the house line phone, but it was dead.

"Maybe I didn't even get a dial tone when I called Valerie," she sighed to herself. She was on a lot of medication tonight and could have just imagined that she had heard a bell tone. She sat at the kitchen table and took a sip of the now cold coffee. With the lights out she could not warm the coffee up, but at this point she would do anything to calm her nerves. Usually coffee would do the trick, even if it was cold and full of caffeine.

Another lightning bolt flashed and the thunder burst, shaking her house and causing Samantha to jump, knocking her coffee cup off the table and crashing down to the floor. It wasn't the thunder that made her gasp and drop the coffee; staring at her from outside the kitchen window was Linda Edwards. She was soaking wet and glared at her with her demonic eyes. In another flash and she was gone.

"She was not really there, I'm just seeing things," she told herself as she carefully moved closer to the window.

Another sudden flash brought her evil face back to the window directly in front of her. She jumped back and turned to run just as the glass window crashed open into the room, knocking her to the floor, covering her with glass and brush from a tree branch that Linda had apparently thrown through the window. The gusty wind now blew through the house, blowing everything in the kitchen all around the room so fiercely that they almost became weapons.

Quickly she picked herself up off the floor and knocked the glass off of her. "What was she going to do? Linda was out there waiting for her," she thought to herself as she collected her thoughts. She ran into the living room checking to make sure the front door was locked, her hands shaking as she reached over and closed the blinds, blocking out the outside world. Still not feeling safe enough, she moved the large sofa in front of the door before she started lighting the other oil lanterns she had set out earlier, lighting up the room. After checking the other doors around the house, she went back to the kitchen to make sure Linda was not in there. The window would be too high for her to crawl into, so as long as the doors were locked she could not get in, or could she? She thought as she glanced around the rain soaked kitchen.

Samantha tiredly climbed the stairs, rubbing her aching temples as she stepped into the bathroom and opened the medicine cabinet. She jumped back just in time before most of the contents fell out into the sink and floor. Cursing, she started picking up the bottles and replaced them. She grabbed the aspirins and headed down the hall to her bedroom. There was a strange scratching noise coming from behind the closed door. She slowly opened the door and walked in, the light from the lantern bathed the room in an eerie orange light, but it showed nothing out of the ordinary. Slowly she dragged her tired body to her dressing table and looked at herself in the mirror.

"God you look terrible!" She told the image that stared out at her.

She picked up the hairbrush and started brushing her hair, but after realizing it wasn't going to help her appearance she put the brush back down. As she looked at her reflection, she noticed a small shiny object in the corner of the mirror move by itself. Its form was hard to make out until it got larger and then she was able to realize that it was a large kitchen knife. She tried to turn and run but the knife quickly flew up and slit open her throat! She tried to scream but nothing would come out as she lifted her hands up to the gashing wound. Blood poured through her fingers, soaking her with the warm substance. She fell over onto the floor, the room floating in circles all around her.

"Thought you said I couldn't get you!" Linda laughed as she stood over her.

"I can't breathe!" she managed to squeeze out as she choked on her own blood.

"Tastes pretty good, doesn't it?" Linda asked as she stuck her finger down and rolled it around in Samantha's blood, then brought it to her lips. "Little low in fiber though. Really Samantha, at your age you really should take better care of yourself."

Suddenly the room shook and the ceiling exploded outward into the night, causing Linda to jump back away from her. Both women looked into the large hole that had filled up with a bright light. It covered Samantha's body, bathing her with a warm comforting feeling. Despite the brightness, she could see clearly. Its warmth brought a peace to her entire body that she had never experienced before.

"No!" Linda screamed into the light. "You can't take her; I'm not done with her yet!"

Samantha felt her body slowly start floating off into the light, she relaxed and welcomed it! Just as she was about to pass over into the light she felt pressure on her ankles, grabbing tightly, pulling her back down and away from the light. She glanced down to see that Linda had a hold of her and was pulling her toward a fiery pit, laughing hysterically at her. She screamed frantically, trying to escape, then suddenly woke up finding herself on the bedroom floor with her hands wrapped around her throat, squeezing tightly.

She jumped up from the floor and looked in the mirror and discovered she had no wounds. It had been a dream! She took a deep breath and sighed with relief, she must have overdosed on the painkillers!

"That was one hell of a dream!" She told her reflection. "I've got to get off this stuff!"

A sudden knock on her bedroom window brought her back to reality. Carefully she crossed the room and pulled open the drapes. Linda crashed through the window, knocking her to the floor, as she grabbed Samantha's throat, tightening as she beat her head against the floor viciously. She tried to break free but Linda's grip was too strong. With her free hand she reached for the lamp cord on the dresser and pulled on it, knocking it to the floor. Quickly she grabbed it and hit her upside the head so hard that she let loose and fell off her.

Samantha crawled over to the dresser and pulled herself up. In the mirror she could see Linda lying unconscious on the floor, blood pouring from the gapping wound in her forehead. She glanced at herself in the mirror. Her face was covered with scratches from the broken glass and there were hand impressions on her throat. The mirror started swaying back and forth slightly, as a strange scratching noise erupted from the sudden silence. She soon realized that it was not scratching; the mirror was breaking into little lines and those lines were forming letters. As quick as it started the breaking stopped and the mirror quit shaking. Icy chills covered her body as she read it out loud.

"I don't mess with married men, I kill them!" She read.

Samantha screamed as she picked up her hairbrush and threw it at the mirror, shattering it. Linda suddenly awoke and grabbed her feet, knocking her to the floor. She kicked and screamed until she was free and ran from the room, slamming the door shut behind her.

Quickly Samantha grabbed the large old table she had in the hall and pushed it in front of the bedroom door. She could tell by the loud crashing noises that Linda was moving around in the bedroom. She took a deep breath and ran for the hall closet, forcing it open, she searched frantically and sighed with relief at the jug of lantern oil that sat on the floor at the back of the closet. With shaking hands she grabbed the large jug and rushed back down the hall, dousing everything, especially the table and bedroom door.

"Samantha!" Linda laughed through the closed door.

"Burn in hell, you bitch!" Samantha screamed reached into her pocket and pulled out the lighter. With a flick the flame appeared. She smiled as she threw the lighter onto the table and watched it explode in flames.

"Come on Samantha, you could do better than that!" Linda yelled through the burning door.

Once again she heard Linda's laughter, but this time it wasn't coming from the bedroom, she was somehow downstairs in the kitchen. No! It can't be. How did she get out? Samantha rushed down the stairs, through the house so fast she didn't take time to think about what she was doing. She had one thing on her mind and that was killing Linda Edwards tonight! She ran into the garage frantically looking for something that would help her finish the job. Her eyes stopped instantly on the can of gasoline.

"You're not getting away from me Linda, not this time!" she screamed as she slung the gas all over the first floor rooms. "I'll burn down the whole damn house if I have to!"

She opened the desk drawer and grabbed the lighter, holding it tightly; she went from one smoke filled room to another. The fire from the second floor balcony was already swooping down the sloped ceiling into the living room brightly lighting it. The smoke alarms blaring, but she tuned them out, looking around at the house for Linda.

The thick dark smoke was making the air hard to breath. She stepped into the downstairs bathroom, pulled the hand towel off the rack, soaked it with water and put it over her mouth and nose to protect her. She quickly turned around to the sound of Linda laughing in the kitchen as her heart started beating even faster. It was time to kill her! She ran into the kitchen looking around the smoky room but could not see her; all she could do is hear her laughter. She moved further into the room before realizing Linda was not in the kitchen, but standing outside the house in the storm.

"Son of a bitch!" Samantha screamed out as she raced to the dinning rooms sliding glass doors. She quickly reached up, ripping the curtains from the rods and threw them in the floor. There she was standing in the pouring rain laughing at her, mocking her.

"No!" Samantha yelled as she tried unsuccessfully to unlock the doors. Angrily she picked up the chair and threw it through the glass doors. The strong winds from the storm instantly blew most of the glass into the room, covering her with chills and glass. Once the glass settled she straightened up and rushed outside in the rain, but Linda was nowhere to be found.

"What the hell is going on…," Mr. Martin her neighbor yelled as he rushed out his back door and saw Samantha standing in the pouring rain, as the fire poured out the second floor windows of the house. "Marsha call the fire department! Samantha's house is on fire!"

"If you want me you better come get me before it's too late!" Linda said as she stood in the doorway that she had just broke out, directing Samantha's attention back into the house.

"Mr. Martin, Stay over there! It's too dangerous she's still here!" She ordered as she watched her neighbor start to come over to her yard. "Call Dean at the sheriff's office and tell him I need his help!"

"Who is still there?" He questioned. "What are you talking about? Is someone in the house?"

"Yes!" She yelled. "Linda Edwards attacked me tonight and is trying to kill me! Call Dean and tell him to get here now!"

"Alright!" He yelled back as he turned and rushed back into his house.

"Better tell him to hurry up, time is running out! If they don't get here soon I'll be gone and they will think you had another neurotic episode!" Linda laughed from inside the house.

"You're not going to get away this time!" Samantha yelled back at her. "I'm going to make sure of that!"

Samantha turned around and ran into the house, stopping in the middle of the dining room, looking at Linda standing in the kitchen door. They stood there staring at each other. Samantha started mumbling something but Linda could not understand. Samantha suddenly smiled as she quickly pulled open the cabinet, grabbed another bottle of lantern oil and threw it all over Linda. She grabbed a match off the counter, lit it and threw it at her but nothing happened.

"Come on, you can do better than that you stupid little twit!" Linda hissed at her, starting to move closer to her then suddenly stopped.

"Get away from me!" she screamed at her.

"You're the one that called me remember?" Linda laughed not even the least bit taken in by her threat of the fire.

Samantha quickly lit another match, this time it caught and the flames roared up between the two women and caught Linda on fire. The flames consumed everything around her but didn't make a mark on her. The fire didn't concern her as she started moving towards Samantha spreading the fire around until it took a hold of some of the gas she had poured and in the matter of a second the entire first floor of the house went up in flames.

"No!" Samantha screamed as she turned and ran through the dining room and out the broken door into the stormy night.

"There's no place you can run to. I'll always be with you," Linda said walking up to the door but not out into the rain as the fire roared all around her, but not so much as singeing a single hair on her head.

Samantha fought fiercely to clear her head and try to think as the rain beat hard against her. She could tell from the reflections around her that the house was burning out of control as Linda's laughter could be still be heard from behind. It seemed to be getting lower and lower. She obviously wasn't following her.

"Help me!" She continued screaming out into the darkness as she moved forward.

The rain and hail beat hard against her but nothing could stop her, but she was determined to keep moving as long as her legs would carry her. Linda Edwards was not going to kill her! She turned and looked back at her house, losing her balance and slipping on the wet grass. Flames roared from all the windows and were pouring onto the roof despite the heavy rain. She picked herself back up and turned away running as fast as she could, through the open field of waist high grass. It felt like her strength was renewing and she was moving faster and faster. Ahead of her she could see a building with lots of lights on.

"Thank God!" She said loudly and ran to the building.

The closer she got the better she felt. She was going to be safe. Linda would never try to get her there. She thought as she ran faster. Mud had started to build up on her shoes weighing her down and making each step more difficult but she persisted. The lights in the building where shining brightly now before her.

"Help me!" She yelled out at the building before her. "Someone please help me! She's trying to kill me!"

A bolt of lightning opened up the dark sky and lit up the building before her. Samantha screamed at the sight. She was at Ridgecliffe Manor! She tried to turn and run, but her body gave out and she fell to the ground. Linda opened the front door and walked out onto the covered porch that was sheltering her from the rain.

"Why Samantha," She smiled wickedly. "How nice of you to stop by."

"Stay away from me!" She screamed unable to get up.

"How can I stay away from you when you keep calling me and stopping by? Really Samantha, I wish you would please make up your mind!" Linda teased.

"No! This can't be happening! It's a dream!" Samantha kept mumbling over to herself. "You're not really here!"

"That's it, just keep telling yourself that." she laughed.

Samantha screamed out in frustration as she let the rest of her body collapse to the ground. Her deep breathing seemed to be getting louder but even that could not block out the laughter of the woman standing on the porch was the last thing she heard before she passed out.

# Chapter 18 - Accusation's fly!

"Would you two stop looking at me like that?" Dean told Valerie and Brad as they waited in the emergency room waiting area.

"This is all your fault!" Valerie said quietly to Dean.

"My fault!" He said, getting angry. "I don't see how Samantha going delusional and torching her house could be my fault!"

"Don't play Mr. Innocent. The only reason you're seeing that Edwards woman is to make her jealous and you know it! Well I hope it's worth it because tonight you almost killed her!" Valerie said loudly, getting up from her chair and looking out at the dark sky. "You almost got her killed Dean!"

"Okay Valerie. We're all tired and I don't think…"

"Shut up!" Valerie ordered Brad.

"Valerie, you need to calm down!" Brad stated, ignoring her.

Valerie glared at Brad as he started to speak, but quickly decided it was in his best interest to not go on. She watched at he shook his head and walked across the room away from her. Right now she was so angry she would take on anyone, even her best friends.

"I'm not seeing Linda to make her jealous. I am getting really sick of everyone making the accusation! I would never use another person like that!" Dean said quietly after a few more seconds of eerie silence.

"So what you're saying is that you're tapping that shit for real? You're sicker than I thought," Valerie snapped.

"That's uncalled for," Dean came back. "You don't even know

her, you shouldn't be judging her. There's no proof she has ever done anything to Samantha."

"Well wake up, your little girlfriend is sick! It doesn't take a genius to see what she is doing. She's intentionally trying to drive Samantha crazy, and you just sit back and let it happen!" Valerie said her voice getting louder. The Nurse looked up from her desk.

"Can you please quiet down a bit," the nurse asked nicely.

"I'm sorry," Brad apologized to her for them all. "Would you two chill out!"

The nurse sighed and slowly closed the glass window over her desk. She watched them closely through the glass for a moment and then went back to work. It wasn't much longer and they were back at it again. She could already tell she was going to have to call security tonight.

"Stop blaming Linda for this! The doctor already told us that she had severely overdosed on the medication that she was supposed to have already stopped taking last week. Sam was bombed out of her mind!" Dean reminded her, trying to calm down and remain professional. "I'm shocked she didn't see flying elephants!"

"I'd like to knock you upside the head with an elephant, maybe it would knock some sense into you," Valerie quickly added.

"Okay guys, lets just calm down, it's three in the morning there are sick people in here trying to sleep," Brad said, trying to remind them once again to be quiet before they all got kicked out of the hospital.

"How do you know Linda was not in her house? You weren't there with her!" Valerie asked, ignoring Brad. "Did you talk to her tonight when this was all going on?"

"Linda is not a suspect; she does not have to report to me every five minutes!" Dean said, going over to the soda machine and getting a can.

"Oh come on! If that were anyone else out there but her, you would be ripping the town apart! Do your damn job Dean! Stop letting your personal life get in the way or step down. I have to be honest with you; I no longer like the idea of you being the Sheriff."

"Would you two stop it?" Brad yelled louder then the other two. "We have a real serious problem here, and whether or not Linda Edwards is the cause of that problem is not the concern right now! Our friend is in trouble, we need to focus on this right now. We have to help her."

The nurse looked up from her paperwork at the arguing adults outside in the waiting room. She had just about lost her patience with them! She slid the window back open and glared at them. "I'm sorry, but if you guys don't keep it down, I'm going to have to ask you to leave."

"You can ask, but don't count on us going anywhere as long as our friend is in this dump, so get your white ass out of my face!" Valerie warned back.

"Valerie!" Brad said distinctively.

"She's getting on my last nerve," Valerie shot back.

"I'm really sorry, we'll keep it down, I promise," Brad said, apologizing again to the desk nurse as she closed the window, glaring at Valerie.

Dean took a drink of his soda and sat in a chair on the opposite side of the room. Maybe Valerie was right. Could he still do his job effectively where Linda was involved? Stop it! He thought to himself. Linda was not responsible. But still one thing did bother him. He had tried to call her earlier, but there was no answer. But then again the lines could be down; after all there had been a storm tonight, not just the one brewing in here between him and Valerie.

This was a small town, suddenly struck with big city violence! He had to face the fact that he was losing control of his town. He looked across the room at Brad comforting Valerie. She was really upset; he had never heard her yell like this tonight.

"Sheriff, Doctor Coleman said that you may see Ms. Marshall now as long as you don't upset her. The rest of you will have to wait," the nurse told the others, giving Valerie another disapproving look as they tried to follow Dean down the hall.

He slowly walked into her room, it was barely lit but he could see she was wide awake. Her pretty face was covered with scratches and bruises. She looked so small and fragile in that bed.

"I don't know why you bothered coming here. You don't believe anything I tell you," she said quietly. "You never do. Saying anything to you is a waste of breath!"

"So you want me to believe Linda was in your house and did this to you?" He asked quietly as he leaned against the sink in her room.

"She was there tonight Dean. I'm not seeing things. I admit I have been hallucinating lately but tonight I felt her hot breath, I pulled her hair. She was there," she told him, her voice shaking.

"Samantha," he paused and rethought his words. "How did she get in?"

"She came through the master bedroom window," she said softly.

"The second floor window?" He questioned knowing it was impossible for her to get that high up without a ladder and all the neighbors seeing her.

"Dean, I hit her in the head with a lamp! Go see her and look at her forehead. No, never mind, it's probably already healed," her voice drifted off.

Samantha turned her head away from him and looked out the large window beside her bed. There was a flash of lightning off in the far distance, sending shivers through her body, a small reminder of the storm they had earlier. If only Linda would go away like the thunder storm did.

"Samantha," Dean said, disrupting her thoughts.

"What?" She asked as she slowly turned her aching head to him.

"What do you mean healed?" He asked, moving closer to her bed. "That would be humanly impossible!"

"That's just it Dean, she's not human. I literally set her on fire tonight and she walked through it! I tried to get away, I ran outside, but before I knew it I was at her house!" She said as she started to cry.

"Sam, you were nowhere near her house. When you were found, you were at the courthouse lawn in the middle of downtown screaming bloody murder! And you know Linda is human, what else could she be?" He asked, trying very hard to remain calm and professional.

"I don't know! She kills people and drinks their blood. Maybe she's a vampire!" She said, looking him in the eyes.

"A vampire?" Dean lightly laughed. "Trust me, I know Linda pretty well. I think by now I would know if something like this if it were true!"

Dean quickly cut of his laugh. Of everything Samantha had said lately this took the cake! Now she thought Linda was a vampire? If it had come from anyone else he would still be laughing, but Samantha was one of the most level headed people he knew. Well, at least she was.

"I saw her drink human blood! If that doesn't make her a vampire then what would you call it?" She asked.

"Come on Samantha, let's be serious here. You know that there is no such thing as a vampire, what on earth makes you think this?" He asked as he sat on the edge of the bed.

"I saw her in my dreams. She murdered her husband and drank his blood! And I would bet my life that she has done the same things with those other guys that are missing!" She said, grabbing his hand. "Please for God's sake get away from her before it's too late!"

"Even if I believed in vampires, I've been practically living with her; I think I would have noticed by now. All right, let's think this through. One... she comes out in daylight. Two, she has a reflection in the mirror, she practically lives in front of one, three, she doesn't sleep in a coffin, I happen to know for a fact. Four..."

"Stop it!" She screamed. "I'm not a child, so stop treating me like one. That woman is trying to kill me because I know too much about her. Just forget it! You can just leave, get out of here. Nothing I tell you is going to make a difference, so just go. Get out of here!"

Samantha sighed and closed her eyes. She wished desperately she was home snuggled up in her own bed about to wake up from all this to have it be another one of her nightmares. She heard Dean take a deep breath and pull up the chair beside her bed and sit down.

"I can't exactly just leave right now. Things are a little more complicated. From what I have read in the scene reports and what the doctors have said, it looks like you tried to kill yourself tonight," he said quietly.

"I did not try to kill myself and I resent the fact that you would believe otherwise!" She said glaring at him. "I'm not that stupid!"

"Then what would you call it?" He asked back, taking a deep breath.

"Attempted murder sounds good!" She informed him. "I want you to press charges against her."

"I need some shred of evidence before I can do that. Right now all I have is your testimony to go on and I'm going to be honest with you, that's not much in the line of evidence!"

"What? Does she have to kill me before you doing anything?" She asked, quite upset.

"Sam!"

"Dean!"

"This is a very serious situation here! You need help! You are talking completely crazy. You may be right about her messing with your head. I'll give you that. It would be just like Linda to be playing games with you, you have definitely given her enough ammunition! But then you bounce off the walls with blood sucking fire walking zombies. Do you honestly believe that I or anyone else is going to believe you?" He said, getting loud again.

"Just get out!" She screamed. "Get out! Doctor! Get him out of here!"

"First you overdosed on drugs that you should have stopped taking last week, then you burned your house down! I can't just walk away and pretend it didn't happen," he yelled over her screaming.

"I don't care what you believe anymore! Go ahead and run back to her, but just remember what I told you as she slits your throat!" She yelled back.

"I think it's time you leave Sheriff," Dr. Coleman said as he rushed into the room.

Dean stepped back and let the doctor attend to Samantha as he continued letting her words soak into his head. In all his years in the sheriffs department this was one of the craziest stories he had ever heard. He watched as the doctor got Samantha calmed down. He turned around, taking a deep breath and looked down the empty hall.

"My story is not going to change! Dean, you better wake up before it's too late. Just like I have told you before, it's a matter of time before you discover something or see something that you shouldn't. Trust me she will eventually slip up and you will see what I'm talking about and you will be dead! Just like the others!" she yelled as he left the doorway.

"Feisty one, isn't she?" Dr. Coleman said as he caught up with Dean in the hallway.

"You can say that again," Dean said to him as they walked to the door. "Do you see any signs on her that another person might have attacked her?"

"Not that I could tell. All her wounds looked self induced, I would rule this one as a psychotic episode, brought on most likely by an overdose of prescription drugs and an overactive imagination," the doctor said. "Where there any signs of a struggle at her home that would make you think that someone else was involved?" "I'm going to have a look through it tomorrow. Best I could tell the house was destroyed. It was so dark and still very dangerous that it was hard to really tell," he told him. "Would you please keep me posted on her condition and your findings?"

"Absolutely," the doctor said as he shook the Sheriff's hand. "I'll be in touch in the next couple of days."

Dean thanked him and watched as the doctor walked on down the hall without him. His mind racing back and forth over what Samantha had told him and what logic had to say. There just didn't seem to be a happy medium. He took a deep breath, pushed the lobby doors open and started through to his friends.

"How is she?" Brad and Valerie asked as he entered the waiting room.

"Well you two don't want to hear this, but she's taken it all a step farther this time. Now she's talking about flying women and vampires," he told them as he sat in the chair and ran his hands through his hair.

"Vampires!" Valerie repeated.

"Flying women?" Brad asked.

"I don't know what to think anymore. You guys are probably right, I'm sure Linda's provoking her, but Sam says she flew up to her bedroom window, came through the glass and tried to kill her, she then set her on fire and she walked through it! Oh, and she drinks blood. Now tell me, does this sound like a normal healthy person to you?" he asked them.

"No, and it doesn't sound like Samantha either," Brad said. "What's wrong with her Dean?"

"I don't know. Hopefully the doctors can figure it out. Doctor Coleman said they were going to keep her for a while. She's really out there with this story. Listen guys, I still have some things to do at the office; it's been a real crazy night. I'll get with you all tomorrow and we can try to figure out what to do," he told them as he got up to leave.

"Dean," Valerie said, running up to him and hugging him with tears in her eyes. "I'm sorry about yelling at you, I didn't mean it. It's just that Sam's got me so scared. I don't know what to do for her. I feel so helpless."

"Don't think anymore about it," he smiled as he wiped the tears from her eyes. "I'm sorry too, but you were right. I've got to get a better perspective on this and look at both sides. Thank you for reminding me."

"We have to stick together if we're going to help Sam through this," Brad said as he came up behind them. "We better get going. Sam's sleeping now, we can come back tomorrow. I'll call you Dean."

"Thanks Brad. I'll be in the office late tomorrow afternoon," he said then turned and went out into the parking lot. There was a faint hint that the morning sun was about to break free.

Dean pulled the patrol car out of the parking lot and down the street to city hall to his office. It was much quieter than it was when he was here before, he thought as he entered his office and started in on the things he needed to do before he went home. The phone rang an hour later as he was about to leave and go home. Reluctantly he answered it.

"Sheriff," came the female's voice. "This is Mary Pullman, I know I should not be calling, but I'm really scared."

"What can I do for you?" He asked, noticing the terror in her voice.

"It's Duke. Him and that crazy friend Rod. They were planning something, to get somebody I think. I don't know. I'm not real sure. I didn't hear everything they were saying," she stuttered. "If he knew I was calling, he would kill me!"

"It's all right, just calm down and tell me what they were going to do?" He asked.

"He said he was going to kill someone! Just like he did Ray! Oh God no!" The woman screamed and the line went dead.

"I need assistance at the Pullman house now!" Dean yelled out into the main office as he grabbed his car keys and rushed out.

Linda smiled as she hung the receiver up and looked down at Mary's dead body. Stupid woman should have known she was going to kill her after she made the call. It was too bad she had to be involved with a creep like Duke, she should have known better Linda thought as she left through the back door of the messy little house and went down the alley to her car and quickly left.

"Okay Samantha, I'm ready for you next," Linda laughed to herself as she drove home.

Deceiving Dean was her only regret, but she had to admit this had to be her best plan yet. In just one more day she would tie up all the loose ends and wrap it all up by finishing off Samantha Marshall. She drove fast to get back home as soon as possible. The sky was beginning to change from dark to beautiful colorful shades of red and orange as the morning sun started to break free. Linda smiled as she pulled into the drive, parked the car and got out. Quickly she rushed in, checked the house over for anything that might have been left behind and went to bed.

It had been three hours since Mary Pullman had been found dead. A full manhunt was now posted for Duke Etherton and his friend Rod Dunkin. "This has been the craziest night ever!" Dean thought as he pulled his jeep up the circle drive in front of Linda's house. Everything here seemed so peaceful. He started to turn around and go to his own apartment but he desperately needed to be with her and to feel her body next to his. He quietly entered the mansion, through the library and in to the master bedroom where she was sleeping.

Linda looked so beautiful as she slept, so peaceful. He thought as he took off his clothes and crawled into bed beside her. He moved in close, sliding his hand up to her head, carefully moving her hair away from her forehead. He smiled with relief after not finding any marks as Samantha had warned him earlier. He moved closer and put his arm around her. God it felt good to be next to her. All the events with the storm and Samantha's attack and the new murder slipped away as he quickly fell asleep. Down in the basement Duke continued trying to get free, only embedding the handcuffs deeper into his flesh. He tried to scream, but his attempts went unheard as the sock and tape over his mouth quieted his cries.

# Chapter 19 – Tying up loose ends.

Linda smiled brightly as she entered the kitchen. Stella had already started making breakfast and its delicious smell filled the house. The kitchen was the only room in the house that had a welcoming feeling to it; the rest of the place just screamed to be looked at but not touched. Maybe that was why she liked this room so much. She glanced at her reflection in the mirror behind the back door and smiled. It amazed her what fresh blood did for her complexion. She took one more glance at her reflection before heading to the refrigerator for another glass of cold blood. The sweet taste awoke the remaining sleepy joints in her body.

Stella did not say a word as Linda drank the glass of 'red juice" as she continued to make breakfast. She valued this good paying job too much to ask questions. The blood Linda drank was as addictive to her as alcohol was to alcoholics. It made her feel alive and free. She remembered back to the very first time she drank blood, the truth was similar to what she had told Dean, but of course she had left out a few little details. It was a very bad stormy night and her parents were arguing and hitting each other as they usually did. She may have only been six, but things like that you don't ever forget.

This fight had been about their daughter and her consistent urge to cut herself and kill small animals. Her father had screamed at her mother, blaming their daughter's craziness from her side of the family. Linda had been hiding in the hallway closet hanging on to each word as her parents yelled about how evil and horrible their no good for nothing daughter was. She remembered standing in that dark little space crying.

After about twenty minutes of fighting and hitting, her mother ran from the room to her bedroom crying. Her father just sat down in the chair and put his large hands over his face and shook his head. She really did not quite understand what sending her away for help was supposed to mean, but she had seen enough movies on television to know it was not good. Her parents no longer wanted her here and they were going to throw her away just like they did the garbage.

Without making a sound she slipped from the closet and went into the kitchen, pulled out the knife drawer and grabbed the largest she could find. She didn't really remember what was going on in her mind at the time but she remembered that she wanted her father dead! Dead like the animals she had been killing. She could still feel the excitement she had felt back then as she plunged the knife into the back of his neck. She remembered pulling it out and repeated several times. Blood had splattered everywhere, including her face, into her open mouth. Her tongue slipped out and explored the great new taste on her lips. Before she knew what she was doing, she bent over her father's neck and licked the oozing blood. She had never tasted anything so good before. It instantly made her feel better and stronger.

It was at this time her mother came up behind her, knocking her out of the way as she screamed hysterically. "What have you done?" Her mother had asked as she pulled the knife out of his back. She started babbling incoherently about things that Linda did not understand. She screamed at her a few more times before grabbing the car keys and stormed from the house. That was the last time she ever saw her mother. She crashed into a large truck in her hurry to get away and died. All the papers blamed her mother for killing her father and then committing suicide as they had called it.

"Bet you never thought your crazy daughter would do so well for herself, did you daddy?" Linda said smiling to herself where only she could hear.

"What are you smiling about?" Dean asked as he sleepily walked into the kitchen, wrapping his bare arms around her and kissing the back of her neck.

"You're up awfully early for as late as you got in," Linda said, turning around and returning his kiss.

"I couldn't help it, I smelled this great breakfast!" He replied as he looked down at the glass she was holding. "Yuck! What is that? It looks nasty!"

"It's a Swedish health drink. It helps me keep my figure," she told him as she sat it down on the table and pulled him close, pressing her body against him as she whispered in his ear. "I thought I asked you not to run around half naked in front of Stella. She's too old to get that excited."

"Sorry," Dean blushed as he slipped his tee shirt he was carrying with him on. "I have my jeans on."

"I don't care if you run around completely naked as long as the help isn't around," she smiled at him.

"I'll try to contain my sexiness," he joked as he poured himself some orange juice.

"I figured you would have stayed in town last night with the storm and all," Linda said as she got up to answer the ringing phone.

Dean shrugged as he opened the refrigerator to get some butter for the fresh bread that Stella had just pulled out of the oven. All across the back was quart jars full of the same stuff Linda was drinking. He reached in to get one, but she pulled him back and forced him into the chair. She grabbed the butter and put it on the table as she screamed into the phone.

"I don't care about your mother's ailing health! You told me last night that you could get my hole dug and I want it dug this morning. No! Listen here, you idiot. Your mother could be Queen of England for all I care, but that will not get my hole dug. I have a very expensive tree coming tomorrow and I plan for them to plant it without delay! No, I will not wait for you to plant it; you morons wouldn't have the first clue how to plant such a delicate tree! Now get here, and get it dug this morning or you will never have a job in landscaping again. I promise!" She screamed and slammed the phone down.

"Remind me never to work for you," he joked. "I didn't know you were planting a tree. Don't you have enough around here already?"

"This is a special flowering tree," she told him as she went over to pick up the ringing phone again. She answered it and handed it to Dean. "It's your office. I don't care much for this flake you have working there!"

"Be nice," Dean said as he took the phone and listened to Kathy remind him of an appointment. "Okay, I should be there shortly. Thanks for calling."

"Why is she calling you here?" Linda asked. "Doesn't she have your cell number?"

"Guess the battery is dead she said it went to messages. I told her to try here only if it was an emergency."

"No big deal. But I do charge for taking messages. So what's going on?" Linda asked as she sat down and started eating breakfast.

"This place has about as much action as a major city lately, and most of the action last night was not from the storm," he replied.

"Maybe I brought it with me," she joked.

"Now you sound like Samantha," Dean said, but wished he hadn't after seeing the look on her face. "I have to meet the insurance man at her house in an hour."

The name Samantha sent chills down her spine. Never in all her life had she felt such hatred for someone like she did that woman! She took a deep breath and tried to calm the rage that was building inside her. She was not going to let her ruin her breakfast.

"For a stupid broken rail, and why do you have to go over there? Can't she do it herself? I know she's mentally ill, but I thought she could at least do some things for herself," Linda asked getting irritated.

"No as a matter of fact, she can't. She's in the hospital again," he told her.

"Great, what does the neurotic bitch claim I did this time?" Linda sasked sarcastically.

"The same as before, that you tried to strangle her, and I don't know; now there's something about drinking blood. She probably saw you drinking that crap your drinking. She set her house on fire thinking she had you trapped in it and burnt the place to the ground," he told her, expecting her to have an outburst.

"This just gets better and better," Linda said and started laughing hysterically.

"That's not exactly how I expected you to take it," Dean told her, surprised by her actions.

"It's so ridiculous that I can't help but laugh. You saw that storm last night; I don't know how I could have possibly driven in that mess. You don't believe her, do you?" She asked as her laughter quieted.

"No, not all of it, but I know you and I'm sure you are probably messing with her mind. Have you been calling her?" He asked as he ate a piece of bread.

"No. I don't even have her home number. The only time I ever talked to her on the phone was the other night when she called me and I don't appreciate your allegations! You don't think she's getting dangerous, do you?" She asked, suddenly getting serious. "She could try to attack me thinking it's in self defense."

"I think judging from the way you just handled that guy on the phone that you can take care of yourself. I can't believe the way you just threatened that poor man just a minute ago," he told her, giving her the same stern voice she had just used on him.

"Please! That idiot was faking. They bitch and moan about wanting to work, so you let them and then they cry because they have to. Now don't you think you better go get ready if you're going to meet that man at ding bat's house?" Linda asked, taking his plate away and putting it in the sink. "Wash this Stella, Dean's done!"

"Something else I need to tell you about," he said, following her from the kitchen into the parlor.

"Well I have to warn you that I was too busy trying to kill Samantha last night that I didn't have any free time left to bother anyone else," she told him as he grabbed her arm.

Linda laughed at him as she grabbed him and pulled him to her. Her hands slipped behind his head as she pulled his face to hers and kissed him. She was falling so much in love with him that she was getting scared. Dean pulled back giving her a serious look.

"Linda, this is serious. Duke, that man you stabbed at the café the other day, is a suspect in a murder last night and he's at large. I don't think he will come around here but if you want me to I'll put a man here to watch over things," he said seriously.

"That's sweet," Linda said and kissed him. "I think Samantha is far more of a danger than he is. You don't need to do that. I'm fine, he doesn't bother me."

"He's probably skipped town, but just in case you should see him, call me fast!" He told her and kissed her back. "Do not mess with him, he is very dangerous."

"I promise, I won't mess with him, now you better go and get ready," she told him as he kissed her again and then started upstairs to take a shower.

Linda quickly got wrapped into her thoughts as she thought back to what Dean had told her. How in the world could Samantha know she was drinking blood? What the hell she was doing, calling one of those psychic hot lines advertised on television a thousand times a day? To make things worse, she was now in the damn hospital. That really screwed up everything, or did it?

Linda mentally rearranged her plans for the day as she waited for Dean. Dean came down the steps with a quick foot, stopping long enough to kiss her good bye. She watched as he got in his jeep and drove off. Already she missed him, but she had more important things to do and killing Samantha was now her top priority. Pulling up the drive as Dean was leaving was her gardener. She knew he would show up. She showed him where to dig the hole and went inside, saying nothing more to the man.

———

"I'm surprised to see you alive," Samantha told Dean as he entered her room. "Do I need to check your neck?"

"You never let up, do you?" He asked her as he sat the fresh flowers he had brought her on the night table beside her.

"Did you look at her head?" She asked him as he sat on the end of her bed.

"Are you sure that maybe you did not see a man dressed like Linda Edwards?" He asked her.

"I like to think I'm smart enough to be able to tell the difference," she said coldly.

"It's just that I had a woman call and tell me that she overheard Duke saying he was going to play a joke on somebody last night. And well under the circumstances, I put the two together."

"It wasn't Duke! It was her!" She insisted.

Samantha sat back in the bed and sighed. She had hoped that maybe Dean had started thinking clearly during the night but it was painfully obvious that it was only wishful thinking. She took a couple of deep breaths trying to remain calm. Her doctor warned her about getting so upset and how bad it was for her health, especially right now.

"It's just that I could believe Duke was able to get into your second story window, but not Linda. Besides, our witness was a pretty good source," he told her.

"What do you mean… was?" She asked as she sat back up in bed.

"She was murdered before she finished the call. Duke has not been seen since early yesterday evening before the storm," he replied.

"It was Mary, wasn't it?" She asked him as he nodded. "Oh my God!"

"We're out searching for Duke now, but so far no leads. I don't think that he would come here, but just in case he does…"

"It could be Linda. She is so good at manipulating. This could all be her doing! Oh sorry, just forget I mentioned your precious one," she told him after seeing him shake his head. "I forgot you could care less what I say, you already have the papers signed to get me locked up in the nut house."

Dean closed his eyes and tried counting to five before saying anything else. "Come on Sam, you know I have to look at this from all directions! Your situation wasn't the only mishap last night, and judging from the call, it sounded like it was already happening. I hadn't been gone from here very long, so it would have given Duke plenty of time to get home and catch Mary on the phone with me and kill her."

"If you're looking at all directions, then why don't you look at my directions and investigate what I tell you?" She shouted.

"I'm trying to, but you don't stop yelling long enough to talk about it," he said, trying to calm her down.

"I'm tired of talking about it now. I just had a big fight with my insurance company guy that you just left. I don't even know why I bothered even having it for all the good it's doing," she said, calming down.

"Do you have a place to stay after you get released?" Dean asked.

"I'm going to stay with Brad. His house is huge, and Valerie's apartment is so small that I could not stay with her, but Brad's been so sweet about everything. It's nice to have some true friends to be there when you need them. He's even letting her move in for a couple of weeks to stay with me," she said, smiling. It was the first time he had seen her smile for a long time.

"That should be interesting, the three of you living together. The neighbors will have me out there all the time breaking up your cat fights," he joked.

"We're not that bad," she laughed, despite the pain it caused.

"We'll see, I better get going. I'll catch you later," he said as he left the room.

"Thanks for coming by," she said to the empty room. She jumped as the phone beside her rang.

"Well, I'm glad to see you're feeling better," Linda said over the phone. "I hear we had quite a night last night, didn't we?"

"What do you want?" Samantha asked angrily.

"I think you and I need to settle this once and for all so we can both get on with our lives."

"Fine! Where?" She asked.

"My house in five hours. I'll send a cab to pick you up," Linda told her.

"I'm not coming to your house, you come here!" She informed her.

"I don't think so. We could hardly talk openly there and I have a lot to say! And we can't exactly meet in the airy openness of your place, now can we?" Linda laughed. "You can escape, can't you?"

"Fine! You better have the cab here," Samantha said and slammed the phone down.

Linda Edwards finished dressing and put her other clothes in the hamper. It would not be much longer before Samantha arrived and she now had everything ready for her. Earlier she had met with a nurse in Wentzville that got her the little party favors for tonight's little event. Thank God for male nurses and money, she thought to herself as she went downstairs. The man digging the hole had left a couple hours ago.

She wondered if he had any idea that he was really digging a grave. Samantha's grave!

The phone rang a couple of times before the Linda answered it, listening to the woman on the line as she nervously informed her that Samantha had just left. Perfect, she was on her way. Tonight would be a night to tie up all the loose ends.

Samantha tried to relax as the cab got closer to Ridgecliffe Manor. The same house she swore she would never set foot in again. Getting out of the hospital was easier than she thought, she just stashed the clothes that the hospital had cleaned for her and told the nurse she was going to the game room, and out she went. She promised the cab driver an extra twenty bucks if he stopped by her office where she pulled out the hidden key that Max hid and stole the loaded gun he kept in his desk.

Samantha was ready to meet the devil head on, and tonight she planned to put an end to Linda Edwards' terrorizing no matter what. Even spending the next thirty years in prison sounded good. It would be worth it to see those evil eyes close forever and send that bitch to hell were she belonged. She felt in her lab jacket that she stole from the hospital and checked to make sure it was still there. She could not wait to see Linda!

The sun was beginning to set and a light breeze had begun to stir around. It was the same breeze that would bring in the high humidity that would stay with them throughout the summer and part of the fall. But the humidity was the furthest thing from her mind as the roof of the large structure became visible through the trees that tried to shield it. She didn't know what was worse that horrible house or the monster that owned it! Her hand rested nervously on the gun as they turned on the county road. In a matter of seconds the battle would begin!

# Chapter 20 - Survival of the fittest!

"Why are you stopping here?" Samantha questioned the cab driver as he stopped at the gravel roads entrance.

"This is where the lady said to let you off, that you would enjoy the walk to the house," the driver told her.

"If you want to get paid you will have to go up to the house, I don't have any money on me!" She told him angrily.

"It's already taken care of," he said from the front seat as he rested his arm across the seat and looked over his shoulder.

"It's at least half a mile up to the damn house!" She screamed. "Oh, just forget it, jerk!"

Samantha stormed out of the car and watched the cab turn around and leave. The drivers smirk burned into her memory. Angrily she started up the long drive, mumbling to herself. This was just like Linda Edwards to pull a stunt like this. She was probably watching her with binoculars right now. Darkness had just about finished setting in by the time she finally reached the house. There was no way she was walking down that drive to go back. Either that cab would come all the way or she would take Linda's car!

"Well, this is it!" She told herself as she stepped up on the porch and twisted the bell in the door. She could hear Linda's heels clapping on the hardwood floors.

"Well, what do you know, you did show up. I was beginning to think you had changed your mind," Linda said as Samantha entered.

"The little cab joke you just pulled was about as funny as the one where you made us come out here in the pitch dark to sign papers," she told her as she entered the foyer, glancing into the library and looked at the blood red walls. "My God Linda, it looks like your walls are bleeding!"

"I'm glad you like it! Come on into the parlor. May I get you a drink? Drain cleaner maybe?" Linda asked politely. "I thought the walk might help you with your weight problem."

"Plain water. I don't trust you, and I do not have a weight problem!" Samantha told her and watched her leave for the kitchen. "Bitch!"

As she glanced around the greeting parlor and the dining room she had to admit that with the exception of the library and dining rooms red walls, the house looked pretty nice. She looked up at the huge painting that had haunted her dreams for months. It gave her cold chills to see it in reality.

"Here you go, water just like you asked," Linda said as she came back into the room. "You look awful, what did you do to your face this time?"

"Your concern is as fake as your smile. I think you know exactly what happened and I want to know how you got out of that fire," she demanded, quickly drinking the water.

"There's more water in the wine cabinet," Linda told her, not offering to get her more.

"I don't want anymore water; let's just get on with it. How did you get out of that fire!" she repeated sternly.

"Fine! First of all, I was nowhere near your house last night. It was the drugs you were taking. I paid your pharmacist a little bonus to help you through your painful experience. I guess last night you took the magical pill. I wanted you to have a bottle full, but he would only put in one. I hope you enjoyed it; I was just trying to help with your pain. That's what friends are for. Now the first time dummy, you did that one completely on your own," Linda told her smiling.

Linda had to admit to herself that this was fun! Earlier she hadn't been sure if she should go through with it but now she was positive that she had made the right decision. It felt good letting Samantha know she actually was delusional and that tonight was going to be the first and last time she messed with her.

"You are not, nor will you ever be, my friend!" She growled. "I don't believe you. I saw you with my own eyes!"

"You just think you saw me. Trust me; I had my hands full with Duke and what was her name. Oh, Mary, that was it," Linda told her. "But it sounds like your little party was a lot more fun than mine."

"No!" Samantha said and stood up, but slipped back down dizzily.

"Samantha, as much as I would like to take credit for being the cause of your previous torture, I just can't. I have to give credit for that one solely to you. Are you feeling all right?" Linda asked, pretending to be concerned. "What's wrong? Is it the water?"

"What did you put in my water?" She yelled.

"Oh that, it's a little pill that will make you sleep for about twenty minutes or so while I take care of business," she told her as she got up from her chair.

"You're not the only one with a trick up your sleeve," Samantha said as she pulled out the gun and fired. Her aim was way off as she fell over and quickly went to sleep.

"Samantha!" Linda screamed. "Are you nuts? You could hurt someone with that thing! Give me that!"

Linda grabbed the gun and placed it in the drawer of the liquor cabinet. She angrily walked over to look at the fresh bullet hole on the wall. How on earth would she hide that from Dean! "Just great," she thought to herself. "Wouldn't you know that she would have to do something to mess things up." She quickly went to the pantry and took out the hammer and nails and rearranged some pictures on the wall to cover the new bullet hole for now.

The basement steps creaked as she went down them, stopping at the bottom long enough to turn on the flashlight so she could get through the dark rooms to the meat locker. Duke was slumped over against the wall; his head all bloody where he had beat it against the wall. Linda laughed as she went over to the drawer and pulled it open, getting the keys and her gun. She snickered at him as she walked over and released the cuffs, holding the gun to his head.

"Put your shoes and socks on and hurry up! Time is running out," Linda ordered.

"Fuck you! I'm not moving. You're going to kill me, so just do it now. I'm sick of this shit!" He said dryly, in desperate need of a drink.

"That's where you're wrong. Don't you think if I was going to kill you I would have already done it and not taken the chance of your being discovered? I have one more little thing for you to do, and then you can leave," she said as she went over and poured him a drink while he put on his shoes.

"You're crazy. There's no way you're going to let me go and we both know it!" He said as he grabbed the glass and quickly drank the water. "I'm going to rip you to pieces when I get loose."

"Stop it Duke, you're scaring me!" She laughed as she placed the bloody cuffs back on his hands and ordered him to the door. "Besides, when I set you free you will be so glad to get out of here that you will run faster than you ever thought possible. As long as you disappear, you will be safe, from me anyway. I suggest California. It's pleasant this time of year."

Duke, still not believing she would ever let him live through this, slowly started out of the room. He stumbled back, barely able to walk after being cuffed in the same place for so long. His stomach growled loudly, reminding him that he was starving for something to eat. Carefully he walked up the stairs and through the rooms as ordered into the parlor where he saw Samantha Marshall laying perfectly still on the sofa.

"You kill her too?" He asked dryly, puffing for breath.

"Not yet. But I did do you a favor and took care of that little tramp of a girlfriend of yours! She won't be bothering you again, I promise. See, now you owe me," Linda said, and then ordered him to sit on the floor by Samantha.

"I need another drink," he said as he coughed.

"Too bad! You should have thought about that last night. Just what were you planning to do? Rob me? Scare me? Or maybe rape me? You don't deserve another drink. You're lucky I'm going to let you live. Oh my, would you look at that Samantha. Your friend Duke here was so excited to see you that he wet himself," Linda laughed as she noticed the wet spot in his dirty jeans.

"Fuck you! What was I suppose to do, you chained me to the fuckin pipe!" he yelled at her.

"Just shut up! I don't care a thing about you or your little problems," Linda said as she took Samantha's hand and drug her nails deeply across Dukes face, drawing blood as she held the gun to his head to make sure he did not move.

"Shit!" he screamed in pain, pulling away. "What the hell did you do that for, you stupid bitch!"

"For the last time. If you want to live to see tomorrow I suggest you shut up and stand up!" she ordered.

Duke slowly tried to stand up, but he lost his balance and fell to the floor. Linda stood back and laughed at him as he tried to get up again. Before she had time to react, he quickly grabbed her leg and knocked her to the floor. He tried desperately to get the gun away from her, but was unsuccessful as she brought the end of it hard against the back of his head. He let loose and grabbed his bleeding head with his hands.

"Damn you! Look what you did! You made me break two nails! Damn it! You son of a bitch!" she yelled as she kicked him hard in the groin and then again in the stomach.

Duke lay on the floor gasping for breath and holding his crotch, waiting for the pain to stop. Large amounts of saliva poured from his mouth as he fought back the tears. Linda took a few minutes to catch her breath, then went over to a drawer in the liquor cabinet and pulled out a syringe and gave it to Samantha in the arm. She ordered Duke up on his feet and warned him not to try anything funny as she reached down under the cabinet and grabbed a brown bag and handed it to Duke.

"I have a special gift for you Duke. I like you and for most of it you have been a pretty good sport, so here you go," Linda said as she reached in the bag he was holding, pulled out a long curly blonde wig, and told him to put it on. "Doesn't he just look beautiful, Samantha? Well, you're still asleep, but I'm sure Duke that she would agree. Blonde is definitely your color."

Linda ordered him to get up, waiting impatiently as he slowly stood up with difficulty. She motioned with the gun and a smile for him to start walking. He tried to talk to her, but she would not listen as she gave him directions through the house.

"Listen man, if all you want is to get rid of that bitch in there, I'd be glad to do it for you, just let me go!" He begged.

"Now why on earth would I let you have all the fun!" Linda laughed at his pleading. "I've wanted to kill that bitch for weeks now!"

"Come on! Don't do this!"

"Can't you move faster, I don't have all night!" Linda ordered, making him walk to his car, which had been moved away from the house, closer to the river.

Duke stood silently beside his car, breathing fast as he looked around in the dark trying to figure out an escape plan. There was no way this broad was going to be the death of him. He would not die quietly!

"Tell me Duke; has your life flashed before your eyes yet? You know everyone says it does and I always wondered," she asked. "Have you repented?"

"Fuck you!" He spat at her.

"Now Duke! That is not a very nice word and I do not like to hear it! But don't worry; I won't hold it against you. After all you grew up out here in the sticks. I bet they don't teach manners around here like they did where I grew up. So I forgive you," she said as she smiled at him and cocked the pistol.

"That's a fucking relief!" He said to her.

"You know it's funny; the crazy thing is I really do like you for some strange reason. Despite your filthy mouth and clothes, I really like you. We have a lot in common, so that's why I've decided to let you live. But I warn you, if you ever come back here I'll kill you without blinking an eye. So I suggest you quickly leave town, after all, the cops are looking for you. So just get out of town and never come back!"

"Yeah, right. You expect me to believe you're going to let me just drive out of here, just like that?" He smirked.

"No, really I am. Just get in your car and leave. Oh, by the way, I wouldn't open the trunk if I was you, I had to dispose of my friends and naturally since you were leaving I didn't think you would mind taking them along."

"Ah shit man, you put those bodies in my car?" He yelled.

"I figured it was the least you could do since I took care of your girlfriend," she said with a big smile. "So if I were you I would be careful and not get pulled over."

"Is that it?" He asked. "I can just leave?"

"Sure, but you will need to drive carefully. After all, I had to knock out your headlights, so I suggest you use extreme caution, remember you are in the bottom lands and the river is flooding. One wrong turn and you could drive right off into the river," she said as she blew him a kiss. "Now go and be free!"

Linda laughed as Duke jumped into the car and sped off into the dark night through the bottom lands. She watched as the taillights got lighter and lighter the further away he got, then suddenly stopping. Just as predicted, he took a wrong turn and that old clunker was sinking fast.

"I love this area," she said as she headed back into the mansion. Duke's blood curling screams could be heard far off then suddenly stopped. "Oh well, I gave him a chance. One down, one to go!"

Linda rushed back to the house, anxious to get rid of her last guest. This one was going to be even more fun! As she reached the back door, her heart skipped a beat as she heard the phone ringing. Quickly she rushed in and answered it.

"Linda! Where in the world have you been? I've been letting it ring for the last five minutes. I was about to run out there," Dean yelled into the phone.

"I'm sorry. I was outside on the porch waiting for Samantha and did not hear the phone ringing. I rushed in as soon as I heard it. What did you want?" She asked trying to hide the irritation out of her voice.

"Samantha is coming there?" He asked

"Well, she called two hours ago, so I guess she's not coming. I thought maybe it was her calling. Why, what's up?" She asked

"Just great! I knew she walked out of the hospital, but I never dreamed she would actually come out there. Listen, just sit tight and I'll be right there," he told her.

"I don't. I don't think you need to come out here!" Linda said quickly. She sure did not need him here! "Is there some place else she might go?"

"I don't know. I'll look around a few places here and get a hold of Brad, he can help too. For God's sake Linda, if she comes out there don't provoke her, just call me on my cell number."

*the Murderess of* RIDGECLIFFE MANOR

"Ok, you call me if you find her. I'm sure what ever she's up to she's planning to get me in the middle of it!" Linda said angrily.

"Let's just find her and deal with it then, okay? I love you," he told her.

"I love you too," Linda said as she hung the phone up.

Samantha woke with a start but was unable to move a single bone in her body, not even her lips. She started to panic, trying with every ounce of strength to move from the couch, but all it did was completely exhaust her.

"Well sleepy head, you finally woke up. Can't move, can you. I can tell because you mouth isn't running like it usually does. I know you're wondering what I gave you. Well along with making friends with your pharmacist, I also met a nurse who could get me all these neat little drugs, like the one I gave you. This little dandy is called succinylcholine chloride. It completely numbs the entire body! Isn't that great! Oh but don't worry, you can still feel pain. See!" Linda said as she smacked her hard across the face, bringing tears to her eyes.

Linda smiled as she went to refill her drink, all this action tonight was making her thirsty. "This was going to be so much fun!" She thought to herself as she went back over to Samantha and bent over her.

"Don't worry, it doesn't last forever. But I must warn you it can cause severe persistent respiratory depression. I know you're wondering what that means, but don't you worry about it! You will be dead by the time it wears off. And Samantha, you're not dreaming this one!" She laughed as she left the room to get her gloves.

Samantha still lay slouched over on the sofa, perfectly still. She tried to imagine what must have been going on in her little pathetic mind. She almost felt sorry for her as she glanced up at the clock. There was only about twenty more minutes of the drug left, and who knew if Dean was on his way or not! She quickly picked her up and drug her through the hall and out the front door to the side of the house by the garage, where she dumped her into the hole.

Killing her was better than taking any kind of drug. The emotional high it was giving her was incredible, she thought as she climbed into the hole and arranged her body so it would be face up before climbing back out and grabbing a shovel.

"I bet you're thinking right now that you wish that you never sold me this house, aren't you? Yes, I bet that's what is running through your pathetic little mind. Well I promise you every time I pass this garage and look at the pretty tree that is going to be on top of you, I will stop and remember that you made it all possible. Sleep tight, Bitch!" Linda yelled at her as she began covering the hole, watching as her eyes widen with horror.

Samantha's chest was moving rapidly as she gasped for breath as the dirt covered her lower body. Large clumps fell down her chest and rolled beside her head. If only she could move, but it was impossible. No matter how hard she tried, her body just laid still. In a matter of seconds, her upper body, with the exception of her face, was now covered. Samantha looked at the face of her murderer. The once beautiful face was all sinister and twisted, violently ugly as she smiled her demonic smile and threw another load of dirt on her face. She quickly closed her eyes as it hit, filling her with a heavy weight on her face that kept getting heavier. She gasped for breath, but there was no air to breathe. Her chest started heaving, her heartbeat so hard she thought it was going to explode. Linda had won! Samantha took in her last breath.

"I hope you rot in hell!" Linda yelled at the hole that used to be six feet deep but was now just four.

Linda patted the ground firmly with the shovel making it secure. No one would ever know she was there. The stupid gardener that dug the hole would not be back until next week, so he would never know that the hole wasn't as deep as he had originally dug, and by then the new tree would be in place. Linda's little party suddenly ended and her heart stopped as Dean's patrol car with its lights flashing pulled in the drive way beside her. He got out and rushed over to her.

"Linda, what the hell are you doing out here?" Dean yelled as he walked up to her. "I've been trying to call you, but when you didn't answer I rushed out here. What's going on?"

Linda's breathing became rapid as she gripped the shovel so tight she thought it was going to break. This could not be happening! Dean was not supposed to be here! He promised. A battleground erupted in her mind as she tried to figure out what to do. The only thing was to kill him! She gripped the shovel tight, then suddenly released it and threw it at him.

"Start digging!" She yelled as she reached over and grabbed the other one leaning on the garage wall.

"What are we digging for?" Dean asked as he started scooping dirt out of the hole.

"I'm not sure, I saw some silver colored hot rod drive up the drive, I grabbed my binoculars and watched them mess with something over here, and then they took off. I ran out here and saw that this hole was not as deep as it was originally dug, so I was about to start digging and you showed up," she said, out of breath as she kept digging.

"Sounds like Duke's car!" He told her as he dug faster. "You say they headed towards the river?"

"Yes they went that direction," Linda said as she pointed in the direction where she had seen Duke's car sink.

"Oh my God!" Dean yelled as he threw his shovel out of the hole and started pawing with his hands throwing dirt everywhere. "Oh God, no!"

"What is it?" Linda asked.

"Get in the house and call 911, now!" He shouted at her as he pulled Samantha's limp body out of the grave.

"Oh my God!" She shouted acting surprised at his findings.

Linda jumped out and ran to the house, stopping as she got on the porch to watch as Dean tried to bring her back with CPR. Once she got into the house Linda leaned on the wall for support. She had to be dead! The room around her started spinning. She had to be dead! "Damn it, Dean! Why did you have to show up now! If only you had waited ten more minutes!" Linda thought as she picked up a vase and threw it across the hall.

"Calm down! Calm down! Calm down! They can't prove anything. I saw Duke rush off into the bottom lands, even if they could dig the car out, providing they found it. He had a wig on and Samantha has his hair and skin tissues under her nails. Remember, you covered all the options," Linda said to herself as she smiled and calmed down and went to the phone in the parlor. She looked at her watch and waited another minute, then picked up the phone and dialed.

Quickly she gave the dispatcher all the information and hung up. Please be dead! She thought to herself as she got herself worked up so she could put on the performance of a lifetime. Quickly her eyes clouded over with tears and she ran back outside to Dean, and hopefully, a dead body in his arms.

The next half hour rushed by as her driveway filled with rescue vehicles. She watched as the ambulance headed down the drive carrying a recovering Samantha Marshall. How could she be alive! "Good God, the woman had more lives than a cat!" Linda thought to herself, quickly containing the rage that built up in her as Dean came over and put his arms around her.

"I've got to head off to the hospital, so I can be there when she wakes up. I want you to go and pack a suit case and come stay with me at my apartment until we find Duke," he told her as she clutched on to him tightly.

"No," she said, pulling slightly away from him. "I'm not letting that maniac run me out of my house."

"Alright then, I'm going to leave Deputy Rodgers here to stay with you just in case Duke comes back around, and I don't want to hear anymore about it. I'll call you in the morning, try to get some sleep," he told her, and then kissed her.

"Is she going to be all right?" Linda asked, managing to add sincerity to her voice.

"I don't know, I just thank God you saw the car out here and came out or she would definitely be dead. You're a hero. You saved her life. I've got to go. It's going to be okay now," he said as he started to pull away.

"I love you," she said as he walked off back over to his car and pulled away, leaving her alone with all the cops.

Linda went into the house after watching the last cop leave. She showed Deputy Rodgers around and got him settled in and went into the master bedroom to take a shower, making sure the door was locked. She hated having a stranger in the house. She undressed and stepped into the shower, washing all the dirt away. If only getting rid of Samantha had been that easy. Quickly she jumped from the shower and answered the phone that had interrupted her thoughts.

"Samantha's going to be fine, I figured you wanted to know," Dean told her over the phone.

"Thank God! Did she tell you what happened?" She asked, dripping water all over the carpet.

"No, they won't let me in. When she came to, she was totally out of it. The doctor said she did not remember anything about it. He said that it's not uncommon for this sort of thing to happen after such a traumatic experience like this," he said tiredly.

"Have you heard anything on Duke yet?" Linda said smiling.

"No, I doubt that we will if he went off into the bottom lands, The dumb ass was probably drunk and drove off into the river, they are searching for him. I don't want you to worry about it, just try to get some sleep and I'll talk to you tomorrow. I love you," he said and hung up.

"I may not have gotten you yet Samantha, but I will," she said quietly into the empty room. "That is a promise."

Dean shut the door to his office and sat back in his chair, enjoying the silence. There had never been this much action in three years that he had been sheriff. It was as if everyone, including him, was going crazy.

"Let me know if there is any report on Duke. I mean anything!" He said to the dispatcher through the intercom.

He had known Duke Etherton almost his whole life. They all even went to school together. He was always a troublemaker, but never a murderer, at least until now. He picked up the murder investigation on Mary Pullman and read it through, stopping to think about tonight's events. There were so many questions. The brutal murder of Mary, the attack on Samantha, and if what his latest murder victim had said was true before she was murdered. Duke was definitely involved with the disappearance of Ray Thompson, which made sense. After all, Mary was having an affair with him. Duke definitely had a motive.

Still one thing bothered him. No matter what happened, Linda Edwards's name was always mentioned. He tried not to think about it, but he had to admit that everything in town was pretty quiet until she moved here. Samantha was happy and healthy and dodging his advances, there were no missing men, and Duke was semi behaving. Could Linda be connected with all this?

A cold shiver ran down his spine as he had an uncontrollable urge to turn around. It felt like someone was behind him. He quickly turned around and relaxed at the sight of the empty office. A slight breeze from the opened window blew a bunch of papers off his desk and onto the floor. He bent over to pick them up and froze.

On the front page of the paper were Linda, the City Administrator, and the Mayor altogether. She was presenting them with a hundred thousand dollar check for the city. Maybe he did not know her as well as he thought. What other secrets did she have?

"What in the world are you up to, Linda?" Dean asked himself as he grabbed the paper and got in his jeep and drove towards Ridgecliffe Manor.

## Chapter 21 – Facing the devil herself!

Linda Edwards stood by the open window allowing the fresh air to blow around her. The breeze caught her long nightgown, making it flap in the wind. She imagined herself as a ghost just floating around, with nothing to worry about. Nobody could hurt her or get in her way, like Samantha Marshall!

"Good Morning," Dean said as he wrapped his arms and the blanket he was covered with around her, resting his head on her shoulders.

"Could have been better," she whispered. She was giving up any hope that Samantha was going to die.

"I don't see how. You're here, I'm here. What else do we need?" He asked, snuggling closer.

She loved it when he wrapped himself around her; she had never felt so secure and safe. Just the touch of his body beside hers excited her like no other man ever had. She turned around and kissed him softly on the lips.

"I thought you were going to sleep all day," she said, smiling at him and watching him with her penetrating blue eyes.

"I didn't get here till sunrise. And unfortunately, you were asleep," he told her as he started kissing her soft neck.

"That's not my fault. If you would keep normal hours I would wait up," she said, stepping away from him. "I have a bath ready. I was going to invite the mailman to join me, but since you're awake now."

"If you hurry you might be able to get the paper boy," he joked.

"I think I'll settle for the sheriff," she told him as she removed her gown and walked into the bathroom. "I can show you things that you never thought were possible to be done in a tub."

Dean dropped the blanket and followed her into the bathroom. The jetted tub was bubbling like a cauldron on a fire, but their interest was elsewhere as they kissed passionately and climbed into the tub. This is where he belonged, with Linda, he thought to himself, forgetting everything that happened last night and the questions he wanted to ask her.

"What a way to start the day off," Linda thought to herself as she finished curling her hair, starring at Dean in the tub, his head resting against the wall with a wash cloth over his eyes. He looked so peaceful. She loved him so much that it hurt. She wondered if things got sticky if she would be able to kill him to protect herself.

"Linda," Dean suddenly spoke. "We need to talk about some things."

"Let me guess you're little friend woke up last night and told you I came out of a space ship and buried her, right?" Linda asked sarcastically.

"That's a good one," Dean laughed as he removed the cloth from his eyes. "Actually, I read in the paper last night that you donated a hundred thousand dollars for the downtown renovations."

"Yes, as a matter of fact, I did," she broke in. "I was wondering when you would hear about that. It's no big deal."

"No big deal! A hundred thousand dollars is more than most of the people here make in ten years! I call that a pretty big deal," he said, sitting up in the tub.

"I wasn't aware that I had to clear it with you before I spent any of my money. I'm so sorry my lord and master," Linda said, getting irritated at him.

"I never said you had to clear it with me, it's your money, and I don't care what you do with it. I just have heard you say a million times how you dislike them and the way they're running the city, and yet you go and do this. Why? Are you trying to buy them off?" He said.

"Buy them off?" She laughed. "Do you think people who have money just run around buying people off? That's like me saying all you hillbillies here pee in outhouses. I'm offended."

"Yeah, I can tell. I just want to know why you made such a large donation to people you hate. It just doesn't make sense," he said to her, watching her closely.

"I happen to like living here, and I think the downtown area is a very beautiful place, and I would like to see it fixed up. Who knows, I might want to put a store of my own in down there? I thought you would be happy. You know it looks good that your girlfriend is so generous. It might help you in the elections. And besides, with all these gruesome things going on around here I thought it would be nice to see something good happen. Good grief, can't anybody do anything nice around here?" Linda yelled as she started to leave the bathroom.

"Linda, where are you going? All I did was ask you a question! It's not like I accused you of espionage!" He yelled after her, getting out of the tub.

"I need a drink, is that okay with you?" She yelled back from the other room.

"That sounds great; would you bring me one too?" He called after her.

"You don't like it, remember? It looked like blood!" she said as she stepped back into the bathroom and threw another towel at him. "Don't get water all over the floor!"

"So, you could bring me something else," he said, smiling at her as he toweled off.

"Fine, I guess I'm also here to wait on you now," she mumbled as she left the room.

Linda had just finished pouring their drinks as he came into the kitchen just wearing his jeans. His bare feet left wet prints on the floor where he walked. She glared with disapproval at his appearance, shaking her head over to Stella, who was busy putting shelf paper in the cabinets. Dean quickly put his shirt on, trying to avoid any further confrontations with her.

"I'm sorry I upset you, I just wish you would tell me things like this. I can't help but get suspicious," he said as he sat down at the table. "It's part of my job to suspect every one of malicious doings."

"It just seems like every time we're together anymore you're asking me questions. I'm sick of it," she told him, taking a long sip of the cold blood.

"I'm sorry! I'll try not to ask so many questions. It's just what I do, that's why I'm a sheriff!" He repeated to her as he picked up his glass of orange juice. "Did you make this?"

"No, Stella did so it's safe to drink. While we're on the subject, I guess I need to tell you that the mayor is about to appoint me a special seat on the city council," Linda said with a smile.

"The city council?" Dean laughed. "Why would he do that?"

"Why not?" She asked her smile fading.

"Well for one thing, you don't live in city limits. If I remember right that would eliminate you from serving and second, I thought that was something that had to be decided on by the voters."

"Then they will just have to amend the rules," she said as she took another sip of her drink.

"That sounds legal," he laughed, but stopped once he realized she was serious. "Why do you want to be on the council? You can't stand those people."

"It's a business decision, one that I wouldn't expect you to understand."

"I'm sorry, I didn't mean to upset you, I didn't think you were that serious about it," he apologized. "I think it's great that you want to get involved and I think you will make a great council woman."

"I forgive you, now go to work and get out of my hair!" She said, taking his glass and putting it in the sink.

"Baby, if I was in all that hair of yours, no one would ever be able to find me!" He said as he got up and kissed her.

"That's very funny. You'll need that sense of humor if you don't get reelected and have to get a real job," she said, turning away from him. "Would you like me to make you some breakfast?"

"No! I still have not paid the doctor bill from the last time you made me toast. Thanks anyway," he winked.

"On second thought, I think you better keep your day job," she said as she watched him leave the room. "Stella, would you order some flowers for me, I need to go see a friend at the hospital. I'll pick them up on my way in."

Linda quickly drank the rest of the blood from the glass and hurried upstairs to get dressed. Today would be a good day to see Samantha, to find out if she really did not remember anything about last night or if she was just faking it. The sun was shining brightly through the large maple trees that lined both sides of the street that took her to the Hagan Cove Memorial hospital. It, like most of the other buildings in the town, was very old and had great architectural features that you could not find in the buildings that were built today. She stepped from her car, grabbed the flowers and rushed into the building, anxious to see Samantha. She never thought in a million years she would be excited to see her!

"Well you look good," Linda said to Samantha as she entered the room and placed the flowers on the nightstand beside her bed, pushing past Valerie, who was sitting in the chair. "These are from Dean and I. We hope you're feeling better."

"What the hell are you doing here?" Samantha demanded.

"Do you want me to call for security?" Valerie asked.

"I was hoping that you and I could put the past behind us. There's no reason for us to keep fighting all the time. It really hurts Dean when we go at it, and I want to call a truce. I can't stand to see him in such pain," Linda said pleasantly.

"I've heard it all now!" Valerie said, getting up from the chair and going to the telephone.

"You are so full of shit!" Samantha said to her. "I can't even stand to look at you, let alone be your friend."

"Such awful language. Here I spend all this time picking out the most cheerful dress I have to brighten your saddened day and this is the thanks I get?" Linda said, pretending to be hurt.

"I'm so sorry; I keep forgetting you have virgin ears, especially the way you get around. Valerie, would you please escort her out, I'm sure there is some kind of health code being violated here. Didn't you just read it to me earlier about no whore's being allowed?" Samantha asked her.

"Um, okay," Valerie said, not really sure how to respond.

"Excuse us, Valerie. Samantha and I have a few things to talk about," Linda said as she pushed Valerie from the room and closed the door. "I would think that after I saved your life last night that you would be more thankful than this!"

"Oh come on! If you had known I was buried there you would have never rescued me and you know it! So just stop playing the hero. For all I know, you put me there!" Samantha said, getting angry. "Don't you have something else to do, like your nails maybe?"

"You just never stop, do you? Well I'm tired of trying to be nice to you. I give up!" Linda said softly.

"If you're so innocent, then answer a few questions for me," Samantha said to her, sitting up in the bed, her head throbbing from pain.

"Ask away. I have nothing to hide," Linda said as she sat in the chair that Valerie was in earlier.

"Why does death seem to follow you around? First in Kansas City, now here. Nothing ever happened here till you moved in. Don't you think people are getting suspicious?" She asked. "I mean you can't expect to keep getting away with it. I used to feel that I had to expose you, but now I realize you're going to do it yourself."

"I think that you have an over active imagination that gets the best of you. Obviously Dean has not told you that Duke is the one that appears to be doing all this and framing me, including your little accident last night. He's a very dangerous man," she replied in her defense.

"Oh please, I've known Duke since grade school. He's a lot of things, but he's not a murderer! And another thing, how would he be getting these men to come with him? That's not his style, if you know what I mean," Samantha said as she reached over for a glass of water.

Linda kept in her laugh as she watched Samantha slowly take a drink and set it on the table. It was a funny thought imagining Duke seducing men and killing them. "And I suppose you are an expert on Duke's sexual escapades?"

"I think I would know if he was interested in men! For God's sake, this is a small town, everybody knows everything about you," she yelled.

"Well wouldn't that work for me also? Wouldn't this same small town know that I was out running around behind their sheriff's back? Wouldn't they have seen me also?" She asked, getting up from the chair and moving away from her, trying desperately to remain friendly.

"You're just better at hiding yourself, except you messed up with the first one, remember Ray Thompson? Just what exactly do you do with their bodies?" Samantha asked.

"You just have it all figured out, don't you!" Linda said, getting irritated with her because she was right as she moved closer to her bed.

"You're slipping up and it's just a matter of time before they catch up with you! Dean's getting suspicious, isn't he? That's why you're here trying to be my friend. You need some brownie points. Well, I hate to break it to you, but it didn't work. They're going figure it out eventually and I'm going to be there watching every step of the way!" Samantha told her, trying to keep herself from jumping off the bed and attacking her.

Linda glared down at her trying to hold back her urge to bludgeon her. She had to stop her before she drew any more attention to herself! She cleared her throat and took a deep breath. "I think that you lost a little too much oxygen in your brain last night."

"Actually, despite what happened, I seem to be thinking very clear," she quickly shot back.

"You think that you have had a rough time lately? You keep messing with me and I guarantee that these last few days will seem like child's play! And when I take you on, you won't end up in a hospital. It will be the morgue! You can thank your lucky stars that Dean showed up last night, because I would have left you to die!" Linda said as she grabbed the flowers she had brought and threw them across the room, smashing them against the wall. "Get my message!"

"Is everything okay in here?" Valerie asked as she rushed into the room.

"I guess Samantha did not like my flowers," Linda said as she started to leave. "Thank you for this stimulating conversation, I know I feel better."

"Get out of here! Get out!" Samantha started screaming. "Get that woman out of here now!

A large lump formed in Samantha's throat as she watched Linda leave the room. It was all coming back to her; everything about the horror last night that her mind had covered up was suddenly exposing its ugly self to her. It was Linda who had drugged her and put her in that grave! The room started spinning fast; her heartbeat was about to explode from her chest as her eyes filled with tears. All she could do was scream!

Linda slammed the car door and started the ignition. "That bitch was going to pay! And soon!" She thought to herself as the car sped off down the road to city hall to see Dean. She did not know exactly what she was going to do to that woman, but it was going to be seriously painful. The car slammed into the spot marked visitor parking and she jumped out, quickly entering the building, almost running. Dean jumped out of his chair as she slammed the door to his office and sat down in a chair by his desk.

"Do you realize you almost gave me a heart attack?" He joked.

Linda said nothing, but the redness in her face and the heavy breathing told him to just be quiet for a few minutes, she would talk when she was ready. He had never seen her so mad. Finally after a few calming breaths she seemed to relax.

"I just left the hospital. I thought you said the deranged bitch had lost her memory?" Linda said, feeling the hostility building back up.

"I said that she had a partial memory loss pertaining to last night. Please tell me you did not go in there and cause blood shed!" He waited for a reply but got none. "Oh Linda! What in the hell were you thinking? You two hate each other! She thinks you're the devil incarnate!"

"I thought maybe we could put the past behind us and move on. Boy was I wrong!" Linda said angrily.

"The only place you two can bury the hatchet is in each others backs! I strongly, no, I want you to stay away from her. Please!" He pleaded.

"Well, you can't say I didn't try," Linda said as she got up from the chair and went to the open window. "I can't believe you don't have air conditioning in here."

"There's a window unit, but it's too early to hook it up yet. Listen, I need to talk to you officially. I know you don't want to, but I really don't have a choice," he said, watching her tense up.

"Great. You know Dean, I thought we had a little discussion about all these questions this morning," she said as she turned around and faced him. "It's really getting annoying. I've already made a statement."

"Just one more time, why was Samantha going to your house last night?" He asked.

"Because I invited her. I was sick and tired of all her accusations, so I called her and told her I wanted to have it out once and for all, with just the two of us. I even paid for her cab, but she never showed up," Linda answered quickly.

"The cab driver said he dropped her off at your house," Dean replied.

"Well something happened between the highway and the house, because she never showed up," she told him, crossing the room and sitting back down.

Linda sighed as she prepared herself for never ending questions once again. It was starting to seem like every time they were together he was quizzing her about why she did this, why she did that, and every time it was all involving Samantha Marshall!

"The cab driver said you specifically told him to drop her off at the highway and let her walk to the house. Is this true?" He waited for her to nod. "Why?"

"Because I felt a little walk would do her good. I had no idea that Duke or whoever was out there waiting for her. Okay! I'm sorry; I probably would have had him drop her off at the house if I had known! Well, probably not!"

"You probably would have dropped her off at the house! Listen to yourself Linda! I can't believe you just said that," Dean said, almost shouting. "She could have been killed last night!"

"There is no love loss between Samantha and I, Dean! You know that so don't act so damn surprised," Linda said, getting louder herself.

"I didn't think you wanted her dead!" He demanded.

"No, really I don't. I love her invading every conversation we have, I love the fact that she blames me for every thing bad that has ever happened to her! Listen, are you done. I've had enough talk about that woman today and I want to go home," she told him as she started to get up.

"I just don't understand why you didn't hear anything. You even had a couple of windows open," he told her, making her sit back down.

"I told you and your little pinheads out there that I had the television on in the bedroom and did not hear them until they took off," she said, getting impatient.

"The cab driver said he dropped Samantha off at six. I called you at eight; I came by your place at a little after eight thirty?" He asked.

Linda decided to herself mentally at that moment if she and Dean did not work out, she would never date another guy in law enforcement. They always ended up being pain in her ass! She loved Dean but all this fighting and questions was really starting to take its toll on her.

"Yes, I guess. Though I have no idea what time the cab dropped her off," she said, looking down at her fingernails. She had to remember to get rid of that color. The two fake ones that replaced the ones Duke broke last night were not easily noticed unless you really looked.

"What happened to her between six and eight?" He asked.

"How the hell should I know? I wasn't exactly sitting on the front porch waiting for her, I had stuff to do," she replied.

"That's not what you said last night," he said, puzzled by her answer.

"What?" she asked getting irritated even more, then forced herself to calm down. "What are you talking about?"

"You said you were out on the porch," he reminded her.

"No I did not," she replied.

"Yes you did! Last night when I called you and let the phone ring and ring. When you finally answered it you told me you were outside on the porch. Remember?" He asked her, giving her his full attention, anxiously awaiting her replay.

"I was only out there for a little while, not for two hours. I had things to do," she said, getting angry.

"What kind of stuff?" he wanted to know.

"I think I might need to call my lawyer before I answer any more questions Sheriff. You see, when you first started asking I thought you were my boyfriend asking me, but now I see differently," she said, reaching for his phone.

"You're free to call a lawyer if you want, but you have to understand that I'm just trying to figure out why you didn't see or hear anything before I showed up at your place," he told her, pulling the receiver from her hand.

"If you really want to know, I was trying to figure out how I wanted the dishes placed in the cabinets that Stella was working on this morning. If you recall, the kitchen is in the back of the house. I can not see the drive way from there. If I had known the little twit was going to be abducted I would have watched for her. Now if you will excuse me, I'm going home. I have answered all the questions I intend to. You are invited to my house tonight for dinner, only if there are no questions or any talk of Samantha Marshall, unless the bitch is dead! If you can't promise me that, then I don't want you near me," she told him, getting up from the chair and opening the office door just as a deputy was about to enter.

"Watch it!" She yelled at him.

"Linda, wait a minute," he called after her.

"Oh, by the way, I'm on my way up to see the Mayor, in case you had to know, since you seem to need to know my every move these days!" She said as she pushed the deputy aside and stormed off.

Linda ignored the stares of everyone in the outer office as she walked passed them and out the door into the hallway of the city hall. She was losing control over Dean. Something had to be done to pull him back before Samantha snatched him away! That stupid bitch. No one in her life had given her the trouble that she had and it had to stop!

"I swear that woman has more lives than a fucking cat!" Linda said as she opened the door top the mayor's office and stepped in.

"May I help you?" The receptionist asked.

"My name is Linda Edwards, I'm here to see the Mayor," she spoke, trying to calm down from the excitement she had just left.

"I don't see an appointment for you," she said as she looked through her book.

"I don't need one," she said as her eyes filled with fury. "Tell that fat bastard I'm here and I want to see him now!"

"I don't think I like your attitude," the woman said, shocked by Linda's outburst.

"Well, I don't particularly like being in the presence of a middle aged sea hag either, so let's compromise and you go tell the Mayor I'm here."

"Uh," the woman sighed, speechless. "He's, he's not here. He went to lunch."

"When will he be back?" Linda demanded.

"Any minute, but he has another appointment."

"Cancel it!" She yelled, as she stepped into his office and slammed the door.

# Chapter 22 - Cleaning up the council.

"Mrs. Edwards," Mayor Arnold Norton said as he entered the office with a scantly dressed woman in his arms. As soon as he saw her, he pushed the woman aside. "What a nice surprise."

"I hope you don't mind the intrusion."

"Not at all," he said, quickly turning to the woman. "Becky dear, why don't you wait out in the lobby for me, I'll only be a few minutes."

"Don't be too long Arnie, I have another appointment," she said as he quickly pushed her out the door and shut it before she could say anything else.

"Sorry about that, my secretary was not at her desk," he said as he crossed the room, sitting down in the chair behind the desk that Linda had just vacated.

"I'm sorry about not having an appointment, but I was in the building and thought maybe we could discuss my appointment to the city council."

Linda could tell by the sudden expression in his face that this meeting wasn't going to go much better than the last two she had with Samantha and Dean. She was beginning to think that maybe she should have just stayed home today and not even bothered getting out of bed!

"Ah, yes that," he said nervously. "You see Mrs. Edwards, I brought that before the council, and they voted the idea down, I'm sorry, I did everything I could."

"I'm sure you did," Linda managed a fake smile. "So what you're telling me is that you guys want my money, but you don't want me, correct?"

"It's nothing like that; it's just that we have no vacancies on the board at this time. Maybe you should try Boonville or New Franklin? Maybe they might be able to do something for you. As for Hagan Cove all our ward seats are full."

"Well then maybe we should create a vacancy," Linda said coldly, not taking her eyes off him.

"I don't think that would be possible," he said, starting to break out in a nervous sweat. "Even if there was a vacancy, you still could not fill it."

"Why not?" She asked, trying to contain her anger.

"You do not live in the city limits of Hagan Cove," he replied. "In order to represent a ward on the council you have to live in that ward, not to mention be voted in by the public."

"I own property here in town!"

"Is it your legal mailing address?" He asked.

"It can be," she said through gritted teeth.

"Then I strongly encourage you to run for election in the fall."

"The fall!" She yelled. "That's too far away! I want that job now!"

"I'm sorry, there is nothing I can do, my hands are tied."

"Then maybe I'll just have to go after your job!" She said as she grabbed her purse off the chair.

"Then I look forward to the competition in the fall," he said as he stood up. "Good luck Mrs. Edwards."

The Mayor had made up his mind and he was not going to let her bully him into anything. No one on the council wanted her in there, including himself. The woman was over powering and too scandalous. That's the last thing this city needed, even if it did cost them the generous donations she had been giving! "Good luck, Mrs. Edwards."

"I don't need luck," she said with an angry smile, "I have money!"

Linda walked out of the office, pulling the door closed. She reached into her purse for her keys. Digging through the clutter, pushing aside a bottle of pills that she had just picked up from Samantha's pharmacist to use on her later, she pulled them out. She had to think for a minute, everything was going wrong. Maybe it was time for a new Mayor and she could not, nor would she wait until fall! Within a couple of seconds it hit her, she had a plan. She looked over at the secretary that was giving her an evil eye.

"Where is the hooker?" She asked her.

"The lady went to the restroom," she replied coldly.

"Down the hall?" Linda asked as she started out the lobby door, then stopped and went over to the woman's desk, opened her purse and pulled out a twenty dollar bill. "Here, go buy yourself a personality."

The woman didn't say anything, just took the twenty dollars and put it in her purse as she watched Linda Edwards leave. The restroom door pushed open just as she reached it. A woman was about to step out, almost bumping into her.

"Excuse me," she said as she started to pass.

"Wait a minute," Linda said as the woman stopped and turned around. "Could you help me for a minute?"

"Sure, what is it?" She asked.

"Is there anyone else in the restroom?"

"No," she said as she followed Linda back into the room.

"Could you stand and watch for me for a minute, I need a fix," Linda said to the woman.

"Alright," she said as she watched the door while Linda went over to the counter with her back turned to the woman, pretending she was snorting coke. "You must need one pretty bad to do it here. There are cops all over the place!"

Linda continued to pretended she was snorting drugs. She cleared her throat and turned back around to the woman smiling at her, wiping her nose with the back of her hand as she introduced herself. "Thanks. Some things just won't wait. You work around here?"

"Yes, I work part time as a waitress," she said as she straightened her hair in the mirror.

"And the rest of the time?" Linda asked with a smile.

"Ain't it obvious?" The woman laughed.

"I just wanted to make sure, I didn't want to offend you," Linda said to her as she watched her closely. "You make pretty good money around here?"

"Think I would still be a waitress if I did?" she said, laughing kind of loud. "Ronnie, he's the guy I work for, says business will get better as soon as July gets here. That's when all the small towns around here have their festivals and shit. Dumb as hell but they bring in the visitors. Horny visitors with money! In the mean time I have too give free bees to fat fucks like the mayor so the cops will look the other way."

Linda's brain went into overdrive as she started devising a plan. She had to figure out a sure fire way to get the hooker to kill the mayor without her realizing she was doing it. Suddenly the plan hit her like a torpedo. She smiled, putting her plan into action.

"I know how it is, I had the same problem in Kansas City," Linda said as she as she started touching up her make up.

"No shit!" the woman said in shock. "You do it too?"

"How do you think I made all my money?" Linda pushed. "I sure as hell didn't work for it."

"You wanting to start back up, I'm sure Ronnie would take you on," Becky told her excitedly. He would probably give her a cut if she brought on someone like her to the group!

"I don't know, I've been thinking about it," Linda said as she purposefully knocked the pills out of her purse and onto the floor, careful to make it look like an accident.

"Here," she said as she picked them up and handed them to Linda. "What are these?"

"Something I picked up in Kansas City, I thought I got rid of them. Since I left the business I haven't needed them anymore."

"What do they do?" She asked curiously.

"Sweetie, they can make even the lousiest john seem like the best lover you ever had. I swear it's the only thing that helped me get through a lot of nights."

"Really?" Becky asked, looking at the pills. "I tried something like this before that Ronnie recommended, but it didn't do much for me."

"Maybe you didn't take enough of them," Linda said as she took the bottle from her. "Last time I used these I took six of them, no maybe it was five."

"So many of them, it's a wonder you didn't overdose."

"You can't overdose on these; they are made of herbs and shit like that."

The woman was hooked on every word Linda told her. She could have said the world would end tomorrow and this flake would have believed her. She continued putting her plan into action as she turned to the mirror and started applying her lipstick.

"Really?" She said as she looked at the bottle closely.

"You want to try them?" Linda asked, looking at her through the mirror.

"You wouldn't mind?" She asked as she held out her hand.

"No, not at all. Like I said, I'm not using them," she told her as she dumped the contents of the bottle in her hand. "I need to keep the bottle though so I can get it refilled again if I need it."

"So I should take six of them at once?" She asked.

"I tell you what I would do if I were you. Since you haven't tried them before I would take only four, at least until you get use to them, then next time take more. Besides, he needs to take them also."

"I don't know if I can get Arnie to take them," she said, sounding a little depressed.

"Just break open the capsules and put them in his drink. He will never know," Linda said smiling to the woman. This chick was so gullible! "Since you will be mixing the drugs with alcohol, I would give him at least seven or eight capsules. The alcohol dilutes it."

"Thanks, this is really nice of you," Becky said as she stuck the capsules in her purse. "If there's anything I can do for you, let me know. Here, let me give you my number."

Linda smiled as she pulled out her cell phone and entered the numbers as Becky gave them to here.

"Got it," Linda said as she returned her cell phone to her purse. If you see the pills aren't working go ahead and give him more. Remember they are all natural so they can't hurt him."

"Thanks, and give me a call sometime, we can hang out."

"I will," Linda said, as she started to leave. "Oh Becky, Don't tell anyone about what I told you, I'm not sure yet if I want to get back into the business. My boyfriend doesn't know and I'm not sure if I'm ready to tell him yet."

"Sure, No problem. Like I said let me know if you do decide to and I'll hook you up with Ronnie, He's pretty cool. You won't make as much here as you did in K. C. But with your body, I think you'll do pretty good."

"Thanks," Linda said smiling as she watched the woman leave. She turned and glanced in the mirror, smiling at her reflection smiled. "Ignorant hillbillies. The Mayor should have known better than to mess with me. One way or the other I'll will get on that damn council."

Linda left City Hall and did some shopping for the next couple of hours, then started feeling guilty about her fight with Dean. After a brief consideration she turned around and headed back to City Hall and stepped into his office. He looked up and smiled

"You still mad at me?" He asked.

"Yes, as a matter of fact I am, but since for some crazy reason I love you, I'll forgive you, but you better be on time for dinner."

"I promise," he said as he got up from his desk and crossed the room to her. "Come on, I'll walk you out."

The door opened, crashing into the wall just as they were about to reach it. A deputy rushed in, almost running into them.

"Dean!" he said, out of breath.

"Shawn! Calm down, you're going to have a stroke!" Dean said, looking at him. What is it?"

"There was a call that just came in that the mayor's just been shot at a rundown motel between here and New Franklin.. He was in there with Becky again. Her pimp caught them two together. Shot the Mayor and severely wounded her," the deputy told him excitedly.

"This whole town is going completely mad! Listen Linda, I will see you tonight, no questions, I promise, but it'll probably be late," he told her as he and the deputy hurried through the office and out the door.

"Shot!" Linda said to herself in surprise, and then laughed. "I could have kept the damn drugs."

Linda sighed and looked around the office. What a crazy world we live in, she laughed to herself as she grabbed her purse and started to leave. She stopped abruptly at the dispatcher's desk and looked at the man sitting there.

"Where's the woman that is usually here?" Linda asked him.

"You mean Kathy, she had to leave, the school called because her son missed the bus again," he said.

"Oh, what ever," Linda said and slowly walked out to her car. "Thank God I don't have children."

"What was she going to do with Dean?" She thought to herself. He was asking way too many questions. Stopping him was going to be a lot harder than the others were. Somehow she would find a way to get his mind on other things, she thought with a smile. And she would start tonight. She unlocked the car door and headed home. It was still early maybe she could take a little nap. She had no plans to get any sleep tonight.

---

Linda took one last look in the hallway mirror before entering the dining room. The table was set with the best dishes. Stella even had fresh flowers and candles topping the beautiful table. Everything was perfect. Her black silk gown fit snugly as she rubbed her hands over her body, smoothing any wrinkles in the fabric.

"Is everything to your liking, Mrs. Edwards?" Stella asked as she was about to leave.

"It's perfect!" Linda smiled to her.

"Everything is in the oven on warm; all you need to do is serve it. Are you sure you don't want me to stay?" She asked.

"No, that won't be necessary; I'll see you in the morning. Good night, Stella," she told her then watched as the woman left. Tonight she wanted Dean all alone.

She quickly thought about her dinner plans, but mainly for the desert afterwards. The phone started ringing, bringing her back to reality.

"I'm sorry hun, but I'm not going to be able to make it. This mess with the mayor's death has me really backed up, and to top it all there has been another man reported missing," Dean spoke into the phone.

"What do you mean another disappearance?" Linda asked, puzzled. She had not been out for a while. This one wasn't her doings.

"I'll come by tomorrow and tell you all the grizzly details. I love you," he said as he hung up.

"Dean!" She yelled into the phone. "Don't hang up on me!"

Linda slammed the receiver down, groaning out as she grabbed the phone and threw it across the room, her temper flaring as she picked up her glass and sipped the white wine. It tasted stale. She threw it too. He had promised her that he would be here tonight! All her plans for a nice romantic evening had now vanished.

"It's that stupid Samantha bitch again! I swear, God as my witness I'm going to rip that woman's skull apart. I'll tear you into so many pieces they will never be able to figure out who you are!" She screamed, then grabbed the tablecloth and pulled it and everything from the table off onto the floor, busting the dishes into tiny pieces.

Linda stepped over the mess and went into the kitchen for some blood. No, this would not do. Tonight she needed fresh blood! She went to the parlor and got her purse. Just the thought of fresh blood excited her. Tonight she might even have two.

The Porsche pulled into the new club in town. It was early but the place was already packed. She stepped from the car and went in. Instantly she noticed she was way over dressed; in her hurry she had forgotten to change clothes. Everyone was starring at her. Maybe this was not such a good idea. She thought as she went to the bar and sat down anyway.

Linda took a sip from her drink and turned around on her stool to face the dance floor. The opening in her dress showed off her long legs. There were several men here that fit her desires. Soon one would move in. They always did.

"I glanced twice, and behold a vision of great beauty developed before my eyes," the young man said as he came up to her.

"You sound like a really bad greeting card. What were you going to say next your prince charming has arrived?" She said, smiling careful so as not to insult him.

"You know me like a book. Have I tried to pick you up before?" He joked.

"Oh no. You would remember if you picked me up," Linda told him, keeping her eyes on the crowd to make sure no one was watching them too closely.

"Well then, I think I'll have a seat," he said as he sat down on the stool beside her.

"Excuse me, Mr. Charming; did it ever cross your mind that someone may be sitting there?" She asked him.

"Well they're not now," he told her as he took her hand and kissed it. "You are way too classy for this joint."

Linda glanced him over and finally decided he would do. He was younger than the guys she would normally go after but tonight the pickings were slim and he was cute. As the bartender passed he ordered both of them another drink.

"What does Mrs. Charming think about you being here making moves on strange women?" She asked as she took a sip from her drink he just delivered.

"No ring here," he said, holding up his bare finger. "I'm a one woman man. Do you honestly think that I'd be here talking to you if I had an old lady at home?"

"Well then, you need to get lost. I only like married men. They don't want any commitments, just one night out. Besides, when I'm done with them there isn't enough for seconds," Linda laughed.

"One night stands work for me. Just a quick good bye when it's over," he told her, moving closer.

"I don't know if you could handle me," she warned.

"I think it's more like can you handle a real man like me," he whispered into her ear.

"Are you sure?" She asked.

"Absolutely."

"All right then, you have been warned. Here's the game. I'm going to smack your face, then get up and leave. You wait ten minutes then meet me around the corner on Fourth Street. I drive a red Porsche. You can't miss me," she said to him.

"Why all the drama?" He asked.

"Because, unlike you, I'm not single. I'm dating the sheriff and I don't want any of these people seeing me with you and blabbing to him," she told him, then slapped his face, threw out a twenty on the bar and left the building.

Just as planned, he showed up ten minutes later and jumped into the car, admiring it as they drove off down the dark street. The same dark street that just a few days ago she had driven from Duke's place after she had killed Mary Pullman.

"How did you get a car like this, rob a bank?" He asked her, rubbing his hand across the dash.

"No darling, car lots," she joked.

"I have to confess, I like it kinda rough," he said as they pulled up to the mansion.

"Good, I like it rough too," she said back to him then threw him against the car and kissed him.

Little was said as she led the way up to the front doors and then into the house. His mouth dropped open as he looked around at the elaborately decorated house.

"What's your real name Mr. Charming?" She asked smiling at him, dropping her keys on the hallway table.

"Rick, Rick Anderson, what's yours?" He replied, looking into her eyes.

"Linda. You know Rick is my husband's name. He's a real ass hole," Linda said as she started upstairs. "Are you coming?"

"You have a husband and you date the sheriff?" He asked as he followed her. "I think you and I are going to get along great. Is your husband out of town?"

"I guess you could say that," she said as she led him down the hall. "And you don't have to worry about the sheriff. He just stood me up."

"His loss, my gain," Rick said closely behind her.

❦

Dean hated it when Linda was mad at him, and he could tell by the tone in her voice on the phone that it would be awhile before she let him live this one down. He looked over the new missing person's report from tonight and closed it. The man had been found with a hooker in the same motel that the mayor had been shot and killed in just four hours earlier. What was this town coming to? There was a knock on his door and then a deputy entered.

"Sheriff, Pastor Peterson's wife is on the phone and says it's urgent that she talk to you. She's on line two," he said, then left the office.

"Mrs. Peterson, this is Sheriff Dean Richards, what can I do for you?" He asked.

"You know me Sheriff; I'm not one to tell stories. I mind my own business, but there is something going on and I'm not sure what to do about it," she began.

"Go on," he replied.

"The night that the Pullman girl was murdered. I saw this fancy red car there about the time it happened, but it wasn't a man driving it. It was a woman with long blond hair. She had on a long dark overcoat. Was only there about five minutes and left very quickly."

"Are you sure it was a woman and not a man dressed like a woman?" He asked, giving her his full attention.

"It's hard to tell anymore, the boys hair is as long as the girls, but no I'm pretty sure. Walked like a woman. Charlie, my husband, told me to mind my own business and not get involved. So I didn't. But tonight I saw that woman again. She was parked in front of my house for about ten minutes. Then this man walked up and got into the car," she told him nervously.

"What kind of car was it, Mrs. Peterson?" He asked.

"I'm not sure, but it was red, one of those fancy expensive cars. You know the ones like those rich people drive on TV."

"Did you get the license number off the car?" He asked, not really needing it.

"No, it was too dark," she replied. "I'm sorry.

"Okay, Mrs. Peterson, let me do some checking on this and I'll call you back for more details. What's your number?" He asked, and then wrote it down as she told him.

"I hope I'm not coming off as some old busy body, but something just didn't seem right about it and I felt I should let you know," she continued.

"No, I'm glad you called, I will look into this, thanks Mrs. Peterson," he said and hung up the telephone before she could continue. One thing about her, once she got started talking she didn't know when to stop!

The woman had all but given him Linda's name. He looked over to the shelf and saw the newspaper with Linda and the mayor's photo on the cover. What was she doing? Was she really involved in the disappearances around town also? A witness just placed her at Duke's house the night of Mary Pullman's murder. And now she was picking up a man on a corner? Dean quickly grabbed his keys and rushed from the office. Maybe if he went to the mansion now, he might just find out. But the question was, did he want to know?

# Chapter 23 - Caught in the act!

"So you don't think I can handle a man like you?" Linda asked as they reached a closed door at the end of the hall.

"I tried to warn you," he replied as he kissed her. "You will be begging for mercy!"

"We'll see who's begging for mercy later. I should warn you, I like to tie my men up. Have you ever been tied up before?" She asked, grabbing his hands and holding them tightly together.

"Once or twice," he said with an evil smile.

"I like it a little bloody also, how about you?" She asked with excitement in her voice.

"You like a little blood, huh!" He said as he reached into his pants pocket, pulled out a knife and cut his palm. He grinned as the blood oozed out.

Linda laughed as she reached down and grabbed his hand, slowly moving to her mouth and started sucking up the blood. Slowly it dripped down her throat, awakening her body, unleashing the animal inside her that was needing desperately to feed.

"Come on in to my guest room," she said as she opened the door, pushing him into the room. He moved close to her but she pushed him away. "Not so fast. I'm going into the restroom to prepare; you get undressed and get into bed. I'll be back in a minute."

Rick watched as she went into the bathroom. He could not believe that this was a guestroom. It was the fanciest room he had ever seen. Quickly he undressed and climbed into the bed. Linda stepped from the bathroom still dressed. She could tell by the look in his eyes that he was disappointed. She crossed over and lit the gas fireplace and flipped off the lights.

"Never seen anyone light a fireplace in June before," he laughed.

"I love the mood it sets. Why do you think I keep the air conditioning on so high?" She smiled as she went over to him.

"You don't waist any time," he told her as she started tying up his hands to the wood bedpost.

"I'm going to promise you a night that you couldn't imagine in your wildest dreams tonight," she said as she tied up his feet.

"Why do I get the feeling you have done this before?" He asked with a smile.

"Practice makes it perfect," she told him, then kissed him on the lips, biting down, drawing blood. The new injury did not seem to bother him as he kissed her passionately.

Linda pulled back, reaching over to the night table where she retrieved the knife that she had used many times before. Rick laughed loudly as she came close to his bare chest. He was really getting into this! He was the first one to ever act like this. Maybe she should keep him around, she thought as she ran the knife back and forth over his chest.

"Hey now remember, when I agreed to blood, I did not mean an arm or leg," he joked.

"Don't be silly; what would I do with your arm or leg?" Linda asked as she slid the blade gently across his wrist.

"Harder, break the skin!" He demanded.

Linda definitely had a live one tonight! She did as she was told and let the blade slice into his wrist, cutting into the artery. Her mouth quickly went down to his wrist and she started drinking the blood.

"Don't take my whole hand off! Shit! Now look, I'm going to need stitches! Man, don't bite so damn deep! Untie me!" He demanded.

"Stop being such a baby!" She told him as she went around the bed and sliced into the other wrist. "You're the one that insisted on coming home with me, remember? I told you I was looking for a married man, but no, you just had to come, so now you have to just shut up and take it."

Rick struggled desperately to break free but was unable. His struggles made the blood flow faster. She loved this part. The more they struggled, the faster the blood would pump. He muttered one last scream before the knife opened his throat and ended his life. Suddenly headlights from an approaching car shown through the lace curtains. Someone was here!

Dean jumped out of the car, ran up to the house and threw opened the front doors. Something was very wrong; he could feel it the minute he stepped over the threshold. He called Linda's name but there was no answer. He looked into the parlor and through the dining room, seeing all the dishes smashed on the floor. He placed his hand on the revolver that was in his holster by his side, ready for any surprises that might pop up. A door slammed on the second floor just as he reentered the foyer and heard sounds of someone running down the hall above him. Quickly he started up the steps.

"Dean, is that you?" Linda yelled over the balcony, and then backed into the darkness as he reached the top of the steps.

"What's going on?" He asked, curious as to why she was backing away from him.

"Nothing, just go downstairs and get a drink and I'll be down in a minute. I need to get cleaned up. I wasn't expecting you," she yelled to him from the end of the dark hall.

"Why were you parked on Fourth Street earlier tonight? Who did you pick up?" He asked, ignoring her request. "What's going on here Linda?"

"We can talk about that downstairs, just go, I'll be there soon!" She demanded.

"I want to know now! Not later! What the hell is going on?" He said as he reached her.

"Nothing, why?" She asked.

Dean reached over to the wall and flipped the switch lighting the chandelier overhead. He gasped at the sight of her. She had blood all over her hands and smeared across her mouth. It took a second for him even be able to talk as fear swept over him.

"My God, what's happened to you? You're bleeding!" He said, touching her mouth. "Did someone hit you?"

"It's... Its red paint, I'm painting you a picture. I picked it up instead of my glass and accidentally drank it," She told him desperately attempting to get him downstairs. "Are you hungry, we can go get something after I get cleaned up?"

"I've never known you to paint, Let me see it," he said as he reached for the doorknob, not believing her.

"No! It's a birthday gift for you, I don't want you to see it until then," she said, grabbing his hand away from the knob.

"My birthday is eight months away; I want to see what's in that room now!" He said, pushing her away and opening the door.

"Dean, stop! No!" She yelled, but it was too late.

The door flew open and the light flipped on. The body of a naked man lay tied to the bed. His wrist and throat were ripped open, the body and sheets were covered with blood. Linda walked into the room and stood by the fireplace, staring down at the flames. Dean crossed over and looked at the body for a second in silence before and running into the bathroom and vomiting.

"My God Linda, what have you been doing?" He asked in a dazed voice as he reentered the room.

Everything was now making sense. She was involved in all the disappearances, even the attacks on Samantha. Linda was doing it all! No wonder it all started just as she moved in. His eyes suddenly focused on the quart jars beside the bed filled with blood. Just like the ones in the refrigerator that she would drink out of on a daily basis. He leaned against the wall for support as his head kept spinning with the revelations of what had been happening.

It was the same thing that he had watched her drink the other day. Oh God! His stomach started turning again, and once again he barely made it to the bathroom. Linda slowly followed, looking at him hunched over the toilet. She started to go to him but stopped herself.

"Dean, I'm sorry, I... I know you don't understand what's happened here. It's not as bad as it seems, really, if you would let me explain I'm sure...," she began.

"Not what it seems!" Dean yelled, cutting her off. "There is a dead man tied to your bed! Just how did he get there? Huh? Oh I bet it was

Duke wasn't it? While you were rearranging dishes he snuck in here and tied this guy up and killed him. You heard a noise and ran up here just in time for a blood vessel to explode and hit you in the mouth, right?" He asked grabbing her arm, stopping her as she turned to leave.

"I'm sorry Dean!" She said as tears rolled down her cheek.

"Save it! The only thing you're sorry about is that I caught you! Did you fuck him too?" He yelled to her.

"I never slept with anyone but you! I swear it on my life!" She pleaded.

Dean let Linda go as he rushed out into the hallway, into the guest bedroom across the hall. The telephone felt like a fifty-pound weight as he picked it up and started dialing his office. Never in a thousand years would he have believed that the woman he loved more than anything was capable of doing this.

"Please put the phone down," Linda whispered as she came up behind him and put her arms around him.

"Don't you even touch me!" He demanded as he shrugged her off and started dialing again. Linda reached over and pulled the cord from the wall.

"You can't turn me in. I can't let you!" She pleaded quietly.

"What are you going to do, kill me? Do you want me to take my clothes off and lie down in the bed so you can butcher me?" He asked as he started unbuttoning his shirt. "I'd go into your room of choice, but it's already taken."

"I would never hurt you! No matter what. My God, Dean, I love you more than anyone in this world! Don't you know that?" She yelled at him.

"You would never hurt me! Don't you think what you're doing is hurting me? I wonder if you even know what love really is. God Linda, how could you do this to me?" He demanded.

"You have to believe me; I never killed anyone for the enjoyment of doing it. I only killed for their blood. I need it or I will die. The others were to protect myself! I'm a predator. I will do what ever it takes to survive," she said, her voice quieting down.

"What do you mean, you need it to survive? What do you think you are some kind of a vampire? Do you have fangs?" He shouted at her.

"If you love me like you say you do, you would not yell at me like that! I'm not a vampire! Yes, I drink blood, and without it my health will deteriorate. I have no choice but to do so. I have no control over it," she told him as she sat on the bed.

"This is the craziest thing I think I've ever heard! You have completely lost your mind!" He yelled as he left the room.

Dean walked quickly down the hall, not sure exactly where he was going. But he knew he had to get away from that room. He could tell by the noise Linda's shoes made on the hard wood floor she was following not to far behind.

"I've been drinking blood since I was old enough to figure out how to do it! Long before I met you! So don't you even say that I don't love you, because falling in love with you was my biggest mistake! My mind clouds over when I think about you and I can't think straight. I started making mistakes," she said as she followed him one of the other guestrooms.

"Don't blame me for your carelessness! Where are the other bodies?" He demanded as started checking the other rooms on the second floor room before starting downstairs.

"Just don't worry about it!" She yelled, following him around. "You're acting like a crazy man!"

"Oh, you have not seen anything yet!" He said as he threw open the kitchen door.

"Dean, just calm down! Screaming at me is not going to solve anything!" She said, following him to the refrigerator that he had just opened.

"Not much left, is there? I guess we'll have to go get some more!" He said, then grabbed the jar and threw it, smashing it into the wall and splattering everywhere!

"Stop it Dean!" She yelled, running to him before he wasted it all.

Dean grabbed her and pushed her away; knocking her to the floor, then reached for the others and smashed them too. The kitchen was now covered in blood and glass. After he had completely thrown everything that was in the refrigerator onto the floor, he sat at the table and ran his hands through his hair. How could she have done this to him? Linda sat on the floor starring off into space, not really believing what was happening. She had lost the only man that she had ever loved.

"For the last time, where are the bodies?" He demanded coldly.

"There's an old freezer down in the basement. The last room," she said, then watched as he jumped from the chair and rushed to the basement.

Linda slowly got up and followed him down. She could hear him yelling and throwing things around in the old locker. It's empty, where are they?" He asked as he came back up to the kitchen. She was drinking a glass of water.

"I put them in Duke's car and made him drive off into the river," she said quietly, setting her glass down in the sink.

"How many?"

"I don't know I lost count," she replied.

"You lost count!" He laughed and grabbed the glass away from her, throwing it across the room. "You lost count!"

"I give up trying to talk to you. You obviously have gone mad! I'm going upstairs to clean up," she told him, leaving the room.

"Linda, get back here, I'm not through with you yet!" He yelled after her. "Do you think I can just let you walk away from all this? My God Linda, I'm the sheriff!

"I'll start going over the state line, out of your jurisdiction, no one will ever know!" She said as she started going up the stairs.

"I don't believe I heard you say that! Did it ever occur to you what you're doing to these guy's families. Their wives? How about their children! You robbed them of their fathers Linda! How do you live with yourself! You are destroying families!" He yelled after her.

"The only way I can live with myself is by killing guys who are destroying their families themselves! These guys are running all over town sleeping with God knows who! Don't you think its better for those kids to be without these unfaithful bastards then grow up to be just like them?" She yelled turning and facing him.

"That's not your decision!" He yelled, then stopped and sat on the steps grabbing his aching head. "I can't handle this anymore! How could you do this? Damn it, Linda! How could you?"

Linda started back down the steps to him where she knelt down and looked into his eyes. What she saw scared her. He looked up and laughed at her. He had completely gone mad and she had caused it!

"How did you do it? Go to bars flaunting your body, and then bring them home? Seduce them a little more, fuck them and then cut their throats? Do it to me Linda! Show me how you did it! I don't want to live any more any way! Fuck me and kill me!" He demanded, grabbing her arm. She broke free and ran down the steps and into the library.

Dean followed her in, dropping down in the chair by the fireplace. He was laughing quietly to himself. His right hand formed into a fist that kept beating on the arm of the chair.

"Where's Duke? Did you kill him like the others?" He asked in between laughs.

"He's in his car in the river like I told you," she said, holding on to her bruised wrist where he had grabbed her a minute ago.

"The others, how many?" He asked, getting angry again.

"I thought we had already been through this!" She yelled.

"How many more bodies? I want to know, damn it!" He yelled, jumping up and knocking the chair over.

"Stop it, Dean! Just stop it! Just once in my life I wish I could find someone who loved me so much that it did not matter what I did. Not my looks, not my money! Just plain me! I thought it was you, but just like before I was wrong," Linda said, starting to cry. Her life was over.

"Linda, my love for you has never been in doubt! Why do you think I'm so angry? It's because I love you and I don't know what to do. I can't pretend I didn't see this! You are a murderer, plain and simple. You take peoples lives. It's my job to arrest people like you!" He said moving closer to her.

Linda backed away from him to the wall and used it for guidance around the room to the door, never taking her eyes off him. When she reached the door she turned and ran. He could hear her running down the hall, and then the master bedroom door slam shut and the house filled with silence.

Dean slowly walked over to the bedroom door off the library and pushed it open. She was standing in front of the large bay window in the dark, just staring off into the night. She was motionless like a statue, except for her occasional sniffling.

"Do you know you are the first person to ever really love me and now you're leaving me. Do you have any idea what it feels like to never have anyone love you?" She asked suddenly.

"No," Dean whispered.

"It's an unexplainable pain. My parents never loved me; they didn't even love each other. After I killed them, my aunt took me in. She never held me in her arms, never said those words that I so desperately wanted to hear. My husband, the night he proposed to me told me he didn't love me, but we looked good together. With me at his side he could climb the social ladder. I was his trophy wife. You were the first person in my life that ever said you loved me and actually meant what you said. I wish I could be different, I've tried, but I can't," she said as the tears rolled down her cheeks.

"When did you start drinking blood?" He asked.

"When I was a small child. It started with animals, and then when I killed my father I found that human blood gave me more strength. It made me stronger. Healthier," she replied. In a way it felt good to be able to talk to someone and hold nothing back.

An eerie silence fell over the room as Dean said nothing. He just leaned against the fireplace mantel trying to collect his thoughts. What was he going to do? How did he ever get in this mess?

"Did you bury Samantha last night?" Dean asked, but he knew what she was going to say.

"I had no choice. She was incapable of minding her own business. She just kept running her mouth all over town. I didn't know what else to do," she said flatly as she continued to look out the window. "I never attacked her before then, I'm not responsible for everything else, she imagined it. I swear, Dean. You have to believe that!"

"I don't know what to believe anymore," he said as he turned and left the room. She heard his heavy steps in the main hall just before he left the house. A moment later she heard his car start and then he was gone.

It was over. Dean was going to turn her in. She went across the hall and cleaned the room like usual. It would be nice for the police to come to a clean house. The kitchen was so badly torn up she did not bother with it. Linda slowly went back downstairs and into her closet to pick out her favorite dress. They would probably be here soon to pick her up.

# Chapter 24 - The new Mayor

Linda suddenly awoke to the noise of glass breaking downstairs. As she dragged herself out of bed she glanced at the clock. It was two in the afternoon! All at once she began to remember the horrific events of the night before.

"Oh God, Stella!" Linda yelled as she ran from the bedroom, through the back hall and into the kitchen. A sigh of relief came over her at the sight of Dean cleaning the mess up instead of her faithful housekeeper. She could not imagine having to explain the mess to her.

"I think you're going to have to replace the wall paper, the blood stains will not come out," he said, throwing the last of the glass into the trash can. "I called Stella and told her to take the day off. I hope you don't mind."

"No, that's fine. I didn't expect to see you here," she said in a daze.

"I didn't expect to be here," he paused. "I covered the Duke angle of your story with a false sighting in Georgia. Everything is taken care of."

"You're not leaving me?" She asked with tears in her eyes.

"Linda, you've made me so angry at what you have done, I don't know really what to do with you. I drove around all last night and this morning trying to decide what was the right thing to do. But I couldn't do it. I'm in love with you. Linda, you need help, and prison could not give it to you. I'm going to search around for a good doctor that will help you get better. I will help, but you have to swear to me that you will never take another life again! If you need blood, take mine. Promise me you will never kill again. We can get over this, I know we can. You have to work with me!" He pleaded as he took her in his arms and held her tightly.

Dean's emergency beeper suddenly sounded. He pulled away from her and went to the phone to call his office. He listened in a state of shock as the deputy told him of the murder of Mrs. Peterson. It couldn't have been Linda, she didn't even know about her. He looked across the room at her drinking a glass of water. She looked so innocent, but as he found out last night, looks could be deceiving!

Hanging the phone up, he informed her of the latest tragedy, told her to get some rest and informed her he would be back later. Quickly he got into his car and drove into town. Just what he needed; someone else was out there murdering people. It was almost more than he could handle. Would he be able to cover up Linda's deadly secret? The biggest question was what to do with Samantha and how to keep her and Linda permanently away from each other.

As he got out of his car a fellow deputy rushed up to him and greeted him, then filled him in on the Deloris Peterson murder investigation. Dean listened patiently as he went through all the findings at the scene. Nothing was making sense anymore.

"Oh, by the way," the deputy added as they walked into the building. "The new Mayor, Lozetta Actonia, is waiting for you in your office."

"They have already sworn in the new mayor?" Dean questioned as they entered the building.

"City council did it first thing this morning. They tried to get a hold of you but you didn't answer, so they swore her in without you."

"Okay, thanks," he told him as he took a deep breath and entered his office, shutting the door behind him.

"I was wondering if you were coming in today," the new Mayor asked as she put down the files and got up from his desk. She was dressed nicely in her obviously new red skirt and jacket. He had never seen her before in anything other than jeans and tee shirts. She had even gotten her hair done.

"You know this is my office and you're going through private files," he told the little woman.

"Come on now Dean, just chill out. We all have to work together now. I'm glad you're here because we really need to talk about a few things," she told him as she had a seat.

Dean sat down in his chair, trying to get comfortable. He did not know how much more he was going to be able to take before he exploded, and something told him that whatever this woman planned to talk about was not going to be good. He could feel a terrible headache coming on.

"It's about Linda Edwards," Lozetta began. "I really don't want to have to tell you this but I really feel like I don't have a choice here. I know you and her have gotten pretty chummy lately and I think that's great, I really do. But I have to tell you there are a lot people out there that don't care much for the idea that you two are seeing each other. You know we have the elections coming up this fall, I think that you need to cool it for a while. I know you're a young man and you have your urges, just go out there at night when no one will see you, just stay out of the public eye. That's all I'm really trying to say."

"I think that I can handle my private life on my own without the help of you or the city, thank you," Dean said, trying not to get angry.

"I'm just doing what I'm told. The people have been coming to me and saying that they feel that she's coming between you and your job. That's why there are so many unsolved murders and these silly disappearances here lately. Now personally, I happen to like the woman, she's very generous. The money she donated to the city was great. And I'm sure when she hears what I've done for her she will keep it coming," she said smiling at him.

Dean could feel all the blood rushing from his head as he took in the last words she had just said. He knew deep down that things were going to get far worse than they already were. He took a deep breath and leaned back in the chair preparing himself for what he was afraid she was going to say.

"What do you mean, with what you have done?" He asked.

"Last night Deloris Peterson called me with this crazy story about a beautiful woman with long blonde hair that drove a shiny red sports car was involved in the murder of Mary Pullman. She was so upset that she did not know what to do, so I told her to call you," she began. "Later I tried to call you but Kathy, your dispatcher, told me you left in a hurry, so I figured you must have put the same connection together that I did."

Dean let out a sigh. "My God, she knows about it," he thought to himself. His head started pounding as his hands got cold and clammy. He wasn't sure what he was going to do? Things were way out of control.

"So I went out to Linda's house," she continued. "I started to knock on the door, but you two were involved in a horrible fight. The windows were open, so naturally I couldn't help but hear you guys arguing about all those disappearances and her involvement. Since you did not arrest her last night, I assume that you're keeping your mouth shut. Well, I think that it's for the best."

"What did you say?" He stuttered.

"I said you made the right decision not to arrest her. All she did was rid this town of a few troublemakers. No one around here liked Duke anyway. And maybe now all the husbands in this town will start staying home with their wives where they belong and not with those tramps humping everything in those damn bars. Look at what happened to our former mayor and that tramp Becky Bagger, their little indiscretion cost both of them their lives. Maybe now with those immoral people gone we can get back to the family oriented town that we used to have," she said as she got up from the chair and stood in front of his desk.

"What did you just say?" He asked in shock. He could not believe what he had just heard.

"You heard me. Now to our other little problems. Mrs. Peterson I took care of, but you need to do something about Samantha Marshall. Maybe you could encourage her to move someplace far away. I would hate for anything else to happen to that poor woman. We have to protect the things that we love. You love Linda, and this town loves her money."

Dean felt like he was in a daze as he recapped her talk about what she was going to do to make the town a better place. Suddenly her last confession sunk in and he looked up. She had killed Deloris Peterson? He felt short of breath.

"You killed Mrs. Peterson?" Dean repeated. What else was this woman going to admit to?

"Now you just separate yourself publicly from Linda Edwards and let the riff raff settle down. We do need to get her under control but there are still a few low lives we can afford get rid of. I'll let you take care of that. And you know, wait! I have an idea! What do you think about a blood drive for her? Every few months the town could get together. Half for charity, the other for her. No one would ever have to know. Just you and me. We can pull this off Dean if we just work together. How does this sound to you?" She asked him pleasantly.

"Sounds like you have lost your mind," Dean said to her.

"No, I just have my priorities straight, which you need to do as well, and I'm sure when this all sinks in and you have come to your senses you, will realize it to. Now, stop seeing her in public. Make everyone think you broke up. We can't protect her if we don't get re-elected. Now can we?" She said with a smile.

"Is that an order?" He asked.

"No," the mayor laughed. "Just a little professional advice, that's all."

With that the Mayor said good bye and left a stunned Dean behind. He could not believe that the new mayor of Hagan Cove had just admitted to murder and she did it to protect Linda. His strong headache was moving in with an even stronger force now. Sitting back in his chair he thought back over the last twenty-four hours and the impact it had on his life. He never dreamed anything like this would ever happen here in Hagan Cove, where he had lived most of his life. He had to make some changes. There was no way he could go on with things the way they were now. He sat behind his computer and typed a letter, printed it out and quickly left the office, turning down the hall just before Linda walked through the front doors of the sheriff's station.

Linda asked for Dean as she came upon his office. The deputy told her to wait in his office, telling her that he would be back soon. Quietly she stepped in and looked around. She had been in here several times, but never really looked carefully at it. On the far wall were several pictures of Dean and his friends at bowling games, baseball tournaments and other sporting events. She thought it was sad that he never did anything with them anymore. Mostly thanks to Samantha. That little bitch was turning everyone against him.

"I wasn't expecting to see you till tonight," Dean said quietly as he walked back into his office with some boxes.

"I was bored sitting at home and thought I would come into town and do some shopping. I didn't know you were such a sportsman," Linda said as she looked back at the pictures.

"Not much any more," he replied as he started taking things off his desk and putting them into the boxes.

"Dean, what are you doing?" Linda asked puzzled.

"I resigned," he said blankly.

"You did what?" Linda asked in shock. "Because of me?"

"That's just a small part of it. I really don't want to talk about it right now," he said as he continued putting things in the boxes.

Linda watched in shock as he quietly filled the box and folded over the lid and put it by the door. He glanced over to her and managed a smile then picked up another box and started loading it with pictures off the wall. "Dean, I can't let you do this. You love this job!"

"I love you more," he replied, not looking at her.

"Arrest me. Let me go to jail. I can't let you do this. I can't live with myself knowing you had to leave your job because of me," she said with tears in her eyes.

"It's too late. Maybe next week we can leave town for a while, I don't know, take a vacation. Just leave everything behind. But right now I would like to be alone, if you don't mind," he said, opening the door for her and walking her out to her car.

"You can still turn me in and save your job," Linda said once they reached the car.

"I don't want to. I need you with me more than I need this job and these people," he said and kissed her good bye.

Dean watched as her car drove off down the road. It was funny; he never thought he would have to give up his job. Until a few months ago he figured he would eventually marry Samantha and that he would be Sheriff until he died. It was funny how a few short weeks could change your life forever. Now Samantha was out of the picture and he had Linda. She would be his new life. Not this job or this town. Maybe they could just pack up and move somewhere else where no one knew them.

The rest of the afternoon he piled all his things into his jeep until all his stuff was out of his former office. He closed the door and looked at the shiny nameplate on the door. "Sheriff Dean Richards," it read. He reached up and pulled it from the wooden door and threw it in the trash. Quickly he left the office without saying good bye to anyone. He just could not deal with good byes right now.

The jeep was unloaded just before dark and all piled into the corner of his living room. Maybe after his and Linda's vacation he would put it up. There was really no since in hurrying, he was hardly here anyway. He picked up the phone and called Linda and told her he was too tired to come over tonight and that he would see her tomorrow. Thankfully she did not ask any questions. He sat quietly for a few minutes thinking to himself and then picked up the phone and dialed his brother's number. It had been ten years since they last talked and it was time to make peace.

Unfortunately he had waited too long and his brother had either gone back to jail or hadn't paid his phone bill. For the first time in his life Dean felt so alone, No family, and no real friends. He sat in the darkness of the room and thought about where his life had gone so wrong. Was it too late to change it?

# Chapter 25 - A time to die.

Linda pulled back the drapes, glancing out the parlor window, waiting for Dean. It had been three hours since he had called this morning. He sounded so depressed. She was really starting to worry about him. Things would have been so much better for them if Samantha Marshall had kept her big mouth shut and left her alone.

Europe was nice this time of year, Linda thought to herself as she continued her watch. Maybe they could go there next week for a month or two. Just put everything that had happened here behind them. Who knows, maybe they would stay there and never come back. Deep down she knew Dean would never leave here. This was his home. He had no desire to leave; he had told her that before.

If only Samantha had just minded her own business! It was definitely time to do something about her. What she did not know, but this time it would have to work, their happiness depended on it. A car pulled up the drive and came to a stop by the front porch. Dean was finally home. She left the window, and threw open the doors and ran to him. He held her so tight she thought he was going to suffocate her.

"I've been so worried about you. Are you okay? I wish you had called and said you were going to be late," she said as they walked into the house.

Dean never answered her, he just walked into the parlor and over to the bar to pour himself a drink. She could tell by the shine in his eyes he had already been drinking. Something was definitely bothering him; he seldom drank much more than a sip of alcohol.

"Dean, please talk to me. Are you going to be okay? You never drink like this," she asked, taking the glass away from him.

"She killed her," he replied quietly.

"Who killed who? What are you talking about?" Linda asked, confused.

"This whole fucking town is going nuts. Every last one of them," he said angrily. "It's my fault."

"What happened Dean, you're scaring me," Linda said to him.

"Do you have any idea what you have caused around here? You now have innocent people killing to protect you," he shouted at her. "I guess I should say protect your money."

"What? I don't know what you're talking about," Linda said, stepping away from him.

"Our new mayor, Lozetta Actonia, do you know her? Well you too should become friends, she thinks the same way as you do. She was here last night. She overheard us yelling at each other. She knows everything!" He told her, picking up the glass she had taken away from him.

"Oh my God!" Linda said, sitting down on the sofa. "What are we going to do?"

"Oh, don't worry, she's going to protect you as long as you keep the checks coming, you can bet on that," he told her as he leaned against the wall. He slid against a picture, knocking it off the wall and exposing the bullet hole that Samantha had made a few nights earlier. "What the hell is this? No, never mind, I don't want to know. The less I know, the better I like it."

"The Mayor killed someone?" Linda asked, looking at him. "Who?"

"Deloris Peterson, know her?" He asked.

Linda shook her head no. Dean was spiraling out of control and she wasn't sure what she could do to help him. He stumbled back to the bar and tried to pour another drink but couldn't get the top off the container. He finally gave up.

"Yeah, I didn't think so. She was the preacher's wife. You may not have known her, but she knew you," he said as he made his way to the chair and sat down. His head was killing him.

"How could she have known me? I've never been to any of the churches here," Linda asked.

"She lived behind Duke and Mary Pullman's house. She saw you leave the scene about the time that the crime was committed. Then the other night she watched you pick up your latest friend in front of her house," he scolded. "That was brilliant. You were really thinking with that one."

"I can't believe this, what was she doing up in the middle of the night?" Linda yelled.

"Well, you'll never know thanks to the Mayor. Why don't you two get together and form your own little cheating husband club. For group outings you could go on a killing spree. Oh, by the way, I think she has a couple more people for you to get rid off," he laughed, getting up and falling, hitting his head on the wooden arm of the chair.

Linda jumped up from the sofa, running to his aid. He had a small gash in his forehead from the fall. She helped him up to the sofa and looked at his injury. He quickly moved his lips to hers, surprising her, but she kissed him back. She needed his touch so desperately. Linda helped him up from the chair and into the bedroom where she got him to the bed just before he passed out. She bent over and kissed him on the forehead, then slowly moved over to his wound and licked the fresh blood. She needed it so badly that she did not know how much longer she could wait.

"I'm going to take care of everything, I promise you," Linda told him as she took off his shoes and covered him up. "Everything is going to be just fine."

⸙

Samantha Marshall looked at the clock on her hospital room wall again for what seemed to be the millionth time in the past two hours. She could not imagine what was taking Brad so long. She had to get out of this place before it was too late. Something bad was about to happen, she could feel it in the air. Linda Edwards was getting more dangerous everyday. Crazy things were happening all over town, and she would bet what few earthly possessions she had left that Linda was behind everything.

The hospital was giving her several different kinds of drugs that she would spit out after the nurse would leave. After what Linda admitted to her the other day she would never trust any medication again. She had not bothered to tell anyone what Linda had done, especially not Dean. No one believed her, so why waste her breath.

If she was ever going to get out of this place she would have to play Linda's game just like Brad had said. And that was exactly what she was doing. Sooner or later people would put things together, and she hoped it was going to be sooner than later. She did not know how much more she could take.

"How are we this afternoon?" The nurse with the nametag "Sammi" entered the room.

"It looks more like evening to me," Samantha snickered.

"Well you're right it's after seven," she giggled as she looked at her watch. "The days just fly by."

"Not when you're in here they don't," Samantha told her as the nurse took her dinner tray and started to leave. It was kind of scary that they would let a woman like that take care of sick people; then again she noticed that most of the time she was just sitting on the patient's beds watching others do her work.

"Can I get you anything before I go?" Sammi asked.

"Could you bring me the TV listings?" She asked.

"Sure thing," she said as she left the room. Thirty minutes later she returned. "Here you go."

"I didn't know you were going to write it yourself," Samantha told her, looking at the nurse's handwritten copy of the selections on television that night.

The nurse told her that the other nurses got angry when the TV listings were loaned out. Samantha started to tell her she could have just used a copy machine and saved herself a lot of trouble but decided it wasn't worth it. She watched as the nurse washed her hands in the sink and started to leave the room just as Brad was about to enter. She rolled her eyes as they flirted with each other for a moment before she finally yelled at Brad to get in there.

"I know I'm late, but I like to never found any clothes for you," Brad said as he entered the room.

"What the hell took so long? I could have made clothes out of the bedspread and been gone by now," she said, snatching the sack from him and going into the bathroom to change. "Where did you get these awful things? This is worse than some of the clothes that Mrs. Ridgecliffe wears."

"What is the emergency?" He asked, looking at the TV selection that Sammi had just dropped off.

"Have you not read today's paper?" She yelled from the bathroom.

"No, some of us have a job and then had to go clothes shopping for the insane. Why?" He asked.

"It's on the table by my bed. Look at the front page," she said as she came out. "I bet you picked these out on purpose."

"I told you I was in a hurry," he said, reaching for the newspaper.

"They don't even match!" She scolded.

"Dean resigned! I can't believe it! He loved that job; it was all he ever wanted to do. Have you talked to him?" He asked.

"I tried his apartment, but there was no answer, so I called Linda, she would not let me talk to him of course. I have to see him, and there's no way I'm going there alone. We're Dean's best friends and we have to get him away from her before it's too late. Let's go," she said, taking his arm and pulling him out of the room.

"How are you going to get out, you're a patient here, remember," he told her, trying to stop.

"Dean is the most important man in the world to me. He needs me and nothing is going to stop me. If something happens to him… I don't know what I would do," she said as they turned down the hall and started walking faster. To Brad's surprise, no one tried to stop them.

"I can't believe I just helped you escape from a mental hospital. Could I do time for that?" He asked as they reached his car and got in.

"It wasn't a mental hospital," Samantha corrected him as they pulled out of the parking lot. "Just shut up and get us there, and hurry, Dean needs us."

Brad quickly drove through town and down through the country roads, careful not to exceed the speed limit over five miles. He had heard that cops usually wouldn't stop you for that, and as a cop passed him he sighed with relief that it must be true.

"Man I hope you're right, because if this is all in your head he'll kill both of us," he told her as they turned up the drive to the mansion.

Brad's car pulled up the circle drive in front of the house and parked behind Dean's jeep. Most of the lights were off except for a few rooms on the first floor, making the house seem less intimidating.

"Are you sure you want to go in there?" Brad asked.

"Positive, are you coming?" She asked as she opened the door and got out.

"I'd rather not be involved. I'll wait here, you yell if you need me," he said, hoping she would not make him come with her.

"Fine you chicken. Just stay here," she said as she walked up on the porch and rang the bell.

It was funny to her that she swore she would never come back to this house again and yet she still kept coming back for more. This time it was different! Dean was involved and she would do anything for Dean, especially if his life was in danger!

"I can't believe this. What the hell are you doing here?" Linda asked as she opened the door.

"I want to talk to Dean, not you, you psycho bitch. Get out of the way, Dean!" She yelled as she pushed Linda aside and entered the house.

"He's not here. He took my car for a ride, so just get out of my house," Linda lied as she held the door open even though she knew Samantha wouldn't buy it.

"Just stop all that yelling and let her in," Dean said, coming in from the dining room.

"God Dean, you look like hell. Are you feeling all right?" Samantha asked, rushing over to him.

"Look who's talking. What on earth are you wearing?" Linda asked her as she looked at her clothes.

"Just don't worry about it. I came to take Dean home, come on let's go," she said, glaring at Linda.

"He is home," Linda smiled. "Would you like a drink Samantha? I'm sure I could find something you would like. A little intoxication might do you some good."

"Not in this lifetime!" Samantha said as she went over to the sofa and sat beside Dean, taking his hand. It was cold to her touch. "I could not believe when I read in the paper that you resigned. Why?"

"Personal reasons that I don't care to talk about with you right now," he said, getting up and starting for the foyer. "I'm going to bed, I've had all I can deal with today and I just don't think I can handle anymore. I need to lie down, I don't feel good. Sam you're here at your own risk."

Samantha watched as Dean left the room and started through the library into the master bedroom. Linda was over by the fireplace giving her an evil look. Tonight she wasn't scared of her or anyone else! She had to save Dean from this horrible woman. She waited patiently until she heard the door close before she spoke.

"What have you done to him? I've never in all the years that I've known him never seen him like this. He's not even Dean anymore! Are you drugging him too? So you can keep him here? I'm begging you; let him go before it's too late! You can have any man you want! Please just let Dean go before you destroy him too!" She demanded. "Please Linda, just let him go!"

"Dean's here because he wants to be here. He likes it here! You just can't get over the fact that he just blew you off. He doesn't even like you anymore, so get over it!" Linda laughed.

"Look what you have done to him! Just a few months ago he was a fun, happy guy, now look at him! He looks like hell, what are you doing to him! Do you like seeing him like this? I thought you loved him!" Samantha yelled.

"Everything that is causing his unhappiness leads directly to you! Every single bit of it. You just keep pushing yourself into everybody's life whether they want you there or not. You're a busy body! Why don't you do everyone a favor and go home and blow your brains out!" Linda said to her. "Oh, I forgot, you burned your house down."

"You are such a bitch! I never thought it would be possible for me to hate another human being as much as I hate you right now! I'm going to get Dean out of here, and I just dare you to try and stop me!" Samantha warned, turning to leave the room.

Linda watched as she walked out. She wanted to scream out, but held it in. Things were bad enough in the house with Dean drunk, she didn't need Samantha's grand standing also. She followed her into the hall and stopped at the sight of Dean who had just come out of the master bedroom. Samantha had been right about one thing, he looked bad.

"I thought you were going to bed." Samantha said surprised as she saw Dean come out of the darkness of the library.

"I was, but when I heard you two going at it I thought I better come back in here before someone got hurt," he said. His breath smelled strongly of alcohol. He had apparently been drinking some more since he left the room. "Besides who could sleep with you two yelling?"

"Why are you letting her do this to you? She's slowly killing you. Can't you see that! You're drunk now! Dean, you never used to drink till she came along. Why can't you wake up and see it! First she took possession of you, now she's made you give up your job! Why don't you just open your eyes?" She screamed at him.

"Stop it, damn it, just fucking stop it!" He yelled, pushing her aside, knocking her down. Linda just stood back silently, very still. Dean was out of control, and both women knew it. "Why can't you just leave me the fuck alone?"

"Dean, you have to leave this place, come with Brad and me, we'll help you. We will get you out! She can't control you if we all stick together," Samantha pleaded.

"You just never stop, do you? You just keep going on and on. I've always hated that about you. You just keep pushing and nagging! It's not Linda that's driving me crazy. It's you! You're the one who won't leave things alone; you have to keep dragging it out night after night! It's you Samantha, not her!" He yelled as he stumbled against the wall.

"I'm just trying to help you! Can't you see that, wake up!" Samantha cried.

"I don't need your fucking help! Can't you get that through your thick skull?" Dean shouted as he stormed from the room and out the front doors.

Samantha followed him to the front door and stopped. She thought about running out there and telling Brad to grab him and both of them take him out of here, like an intervention, but knowing Linda as she did, she would turn it around to the police and call it a kidnapping.

"I hope you're happy with what you have done to him. You have literally destroyed him. Do you like what you see?" Samantha asked turning back to Linda.

"That's funny, the way he talked it was you that made him that way, not me. With my help, he'll be good as new. I'm going to get him away from you and your pathetic lies! You're always telling lies. I don't think you even know what the truth is anymore, do you?" Linda asked as she walked past her to see where Dean went. Unable to see him in the darkness, she went back to the parlor.

"My fault! You're the one who waltzed in here flaunting your body and your money. In just a matter of weeks you managed to single handily manipulate everyone in sight. You're a vile, sick, disgusting person!" Samantha spat. "I hope you burn in hell for what you have done to him!"

"I think it's time you get off your cross and get the hell out of my house!" Linda demanded.

"What if I don't? What are you going to do? Threaten me again; try to bury me alive again? Just like last time. What's next in these sick little games you play?" Samantha yelled at her. In a flash Linda stormed forward at Samantha and knocked both of them over the sofa and to the floor. Samantha reached up and grabbed Linda by the throat, tightening her grip as Linda grabbed her throat and squeezed.

There was a loud crash in the foyer as the front doors slammed shut. Both women looked up as Dean came into the room with a pistol in his hand. There was a deadly look in his eyes that sent shivers down Samantha's spine. She had never seen him like this. What had Linda done to him?

"Dean, what are you doing with that gun?" Linda asked, getting up from the floor, her voice shaky.

"This has to stop! She knows too much! She's never going to leave us alone. I just want us to be left alone!" He said through gritted teeth, breathing heavy as he pointed the gun at Samantha.

"You should have heard the way she was talking about you while you were outside. She said she thinks you were killing people just like I was. She said we're both terrible evil people. It was horrible. I tried to make her stop. But she wouldn't," Linda said, encouraging him.

"She's lying to you Dean, just like she always does. She's sick! Can't you see she's making you that way too! I can help you! Please Dean, let me help you! Put the gun down before you do something you will regret the rest of your life!" Samantha pleaded.

"The only thing you're going to regret sweetheart is if you don't kill her. She's the one that's crazy. Even her doctor will say so. We can say she came out here to cause trouble and you shot her in self-defense. They will believe you. You're their Sheriff, remember," Linda said, getting close to him.

Both women watched as Dean would look at one and the look back over at the other. It was obvious he had a battle going on in his drunken mind and didn't know what to do. He shook his head and screamed out, but the women kept on encouraging him to shoot the other.

"Don't listen to her, Dean. Shoot her. Stop her before she completely destroys you. You know what she's done here. You have to have seen it! Don't let her get away with it anymore! Help me stop her! Think of the people she has hurt. Think of the ones she's going to hurt in the future! You can't let her keep doing this," Samantha pleaded. "Shoot Linda and end all this craziness!"

"Just shoot her and put her out of her misery!" Linda demanded. "Then we can get on with our lives!"

"Shut up, Linda!" Samantha yelled as she started to cry. "You don't want to shoot me Dean, Remember you love me. How many times did you ask me out before Linda got here and messed with your mind, remember. Well I love you too! I've been afraid to admit it, but I'm admitting it now. I always have. From the first day I saw you I loved you. It's killing me to see you like this!"

"No! He doesn't love you! He loves me. You love me Dean, remember?" Linda said as tears filled her eyes and her voice became shaky. "He loves me! Not you! You remember Dean how it feels when we're together, nothing can compare to it. We need each other!"

"You love me?" Dean quietly asked Samantha as he lowered the gun.

"Yes, I always have, I just couldn't tell you," she cried.

"No you don't! She's lying! She would say anything right now to keep you from shooting her," Linda yelled as she moved closer to him. "Dean, she's just playing mind games with you, shoot her!"

"I don't know how you can look yourself in the mirror with all the things that you have done to him! How can you even say you love him after everything that has happened! You don't even know what love is, let alone how to show it. Everyone you love you destroy! You don't love Dean you're just using him the same way you used that police captain in Kansas City. You sleep with them and pump them for information! You're an evil monster that preys on people and you deserve to burn in hell!" Samantha screamed at Linda.

"What captain in Kansas City?" Dean asked, pointing the gun at Linda.

"She's lying to you. She's trying to turn you against me so you will not kill her! Just shoot her!" Linda yelled, grabbing the gun, aiming it at Samantha and firing it just barely missing her. Then she fired again, this time hitting the sofa.

Samantha screamed and hit the floor just as another shot fired. Dean grabbed the gun away from Linda as she backed away from him and grabbing the wall for support. Her body shook with anger as she tried to recompose herself.

"Dean, please help me," Samantha cried from the floor. "Don't shoot me. Please don't kill me!"

"What is going on in here?" Brad yelled as he ran into the house and stopping just in front of Dean. "Dean, give me the gun, please!"

"Brad!" Samantha yelled. "Get the gun away please, hurry!"

"Dean please for God's sake, give me the gun," Brad begged him.

"No! No, I can't. It's too late, it's just too late," Dean said as he wagged the gun around the room. "It's too late!"

"It's not too late, just give me the gun. Don't you recognize me buddy? It's Brad, remember? There's Samantha over there! Remember Samantha? We're going to get you some help, I promise," Brad said as he started moving slowly over to Dean.

"I know who you are Brad, I'm drunk, not stupid! Just get away!" He shouted as he pointed the gun at him.

Dean looked down at Samantha. Tears were falling from her face, the same face that he had known and loved for many years. Then there was Brad, slowly moving close to her to protect her. He had never seen such fear in his eyes. He had caused her tears, and his fear. It was his fault. He then looked over at Linda, his Linda. He had failed her more than any of them. He had told her he would take care of her, that he would help her. All he had done was caused her more trouble. For the first time he noticed she was wearing that same white blouse as the night he first met her, when she kissed him. He loved her so much, but he could not kill for her. The room started spinning around as perspiration formed on his forehead once he realized what he had to do.

Dean aimed the gun over at Linda. His hands shook as tears clouded his eyes. He could see her leaning against the wall; tears were falling from her eyes. He had let her down. There was also fear in those beautiful blue eyes. He had caused the woman he loved to fear him!

"I'm sorry I let you down. Oh God Linda, I love you more than I ever thought I could. I just … I just can't do it," Dean said, gasping for breath. "Please forgive me"

"There's nothing to forgive. You did nothing wrong, it was me! I beg you to forgive me!" She said as more tears ran down her face.

Dean took a deep breath. Quickly he pulled the gun back around to him, aimed at his chest and pulled the trigger. There was a loud boom that echoed through out the silent mansion. The last thing Sheriff Dean Richards heard was Linda's screams.

The shot exploded and stunned everyone. Samantha was the first to move, jumping up and running to Dean's body. Linda just stood frozen against the wall in shock. Brad ran over and checked Dean's pulse before running to the telephone on the bar and dialed for help.

"Get your filthy hands off him, now!" Linda screamed as she picked up a lamp off the table and threw it at Samantha knocking her in the head. Samantha tried to pick herself back up off the floor as Linda stormed from the corner and attacked her.

"Brad! Help me!" Samantha screamed as Linda grabbed her by the throat and started squeezing. She reached up and punched Linda in the face, knocking her off of her.

Brad tried to report Dean's shooting to the emergency operator but the sound of the women fighting in the background made it too hard for her to understand. He quickly hung up and pulled Linda off of Samantha, trying desperately to keep them separated.

"Get out of my house now! All of you get out!" Linda screamed at them as she ran over to Dean and held his head in her arms. "Dean! Wake up please, I need you, don't leave me please!"

"Samantha, no!" Brad said stopping her from going to Dean's body. "Just go outside. There's nothing you can do. Just go out and wait for the ambulance. Please, for the love of God, just do it."

"You killed him, you stupid bitch! You killed him! I promise you

*the Murderess of* RIDGECLIFFE MANOR

that no matter what I have to do, you are going to pay!" Linda screamed at her, then looked back down to Dean and started carrying on a quiet conversation with him like he was alive.

Brad watched as Samantha ran from the room and sighed as he heard the front door slam shut. For once she listened to him. He looked over at Linda, with Dean cradled in her lap. His blood all over her as she rocked back and forth talking to him. Brad now realized that what Samantha had said about Linda Edwards could very well be right, and after what he had seen tonight he was now starting to believe that she was more dangerous than ever! He shook his head in disbelief. His best friend had just killed himself in front of him.

"Dean, please wake up, I'll do anything for you, just don't leave me alone! Please don't leave me here alone, I need you," Linda pleaded and cried.

Brad left the room and stood by the front door waiting for help. He couldn't stand to stay in the room another minute. He had tried to say something to Linda, but she did not even know he was there. Samantha was sitting in Dean's jeep, her head resting on the steering wheel.

Dean was dead! It was so hard to believe. Just what was going on in this house tonight? When he entered the room Dean had a gun pointed at Samantha. He must have been out of his mind! He would have never hurt her!

## Chapter 26 - Letting go

The ambulance turned into the drive, quickly rolled up to the house as its siren blasted. Brad watched in silence as they rushed into the mansion. In the next room he could hear Linda yelling at them. It was just too much. He needed some air.

The paramedics quickly rolled Dean out of the house and into the ambulance slamming the doors. His head was not covered! Was he still alive? Brad ran over to the ambulance and pulled the paramedic aside.

"Is he going to live?" Brad asked him.

"He'll be lucky if he makes it past the driveway. I'm sorry man," the guy told him as he pushed him aside and went on with his work.

Brad watched as the ambulance raced off down the drive as he walked over to Dean's jeep. Taking her hands he pulled Samantha out of the jeep and into his arms. Both looked up as Linda slammed the front door to the house and ran over to her car. In the short time she had been alone she had managed to change out of her blood covered clothes.

"I want you to get that bitch off my property, and if she ever comes within one hundred feet of me again I'll rip her head off!" Linda yelled at Brad as she jumped in her car and raced off after the ambulance.

It was just a matter of seconds before she was behind the ambulance as it pulled into the emergency room entrance. As they came to a halt a team of doctors and nurses ran through the doors and grabbed the stretcher.

"You're going to have to wait here!" The nurse demanded to Linda as she followed close behind, pulling her back into the waiting room.

Through the glass in the door she watched them take Dean around the corner to a place she could not see him anymore. It took every ounce of strength she had to hold herself together. Dean was going to be fine! She was sure of it. He had to be. A nurse came over and sat beside her and asked her a lot of questions about his insurance and his medical history. Most of them she could not answer. She wrote some things down on her forms and started to leave just as she left two deputies strolled over. As they questioned her, Linda wondered what Samantha would tell them. If she were smart she would keep her mouth shut this time.

"Ms. Edwards," the doctor said as he opened the door to the waiting room.

"Yes," Linda said, jumping up just as Brad and Samantha rushed into the room.

"I'm sorry, Dean didn't make it. The damage to the chest cavity was too much. He died before we had time to even attempt to repair the damage. I'm sorry. It's a great loss, to all of us," the doctor said with his head bowed.

"I want to see him," Linda said silently as the tears covered over her eyes.

"Of course. The nurses are finishing up and then they will be out to get you. Take all the time you need. I'll notify the funeral home. I'm sure they will be here shortly," he said then left the room.

Linda looked over at the deputies as they removed their hats, than over to Samantha and Brad standing perfectly still in the doorway. No one said a word as they looked at each other in a daze. A nurse came from the other room and took Linda by the hand, escorting her to Dean's body.

The woman led her down the short hall into a large room with several curtain dividers. Slowly they moved to the last one and she pulled it aside. Dean was lying on the bed, looking as though he were asleep.

"Take all the time you need," the nurse told her, then left her alone.

Quietly as if not to awaken him, Linda moved over to him and touched his check. She almost expected for him to suddenly awake and yell at her for waking him up. He just could not be dead! Her heart felt as though it was going to explode. The only person in this world that ever loved her was now gone. She just sat there for a few minutes quietly watching him, wishing he would wake up.

"I'm so sorry I did this to you, please forgive me," Linda said as the tears flowed from her eyes. "Please forgive me!"

There was some noise behind her as she turned around and saw two orderlies entering the cubical. They notified her that the lady from the funeral home was in the lobby waiting for her. She kissed her fingers then placed them to his lips. She stood back and watched as they pulled the sheet over his head and rolled the bed from the room. She followed them down the hall until a nurse took her by the arm and led her back into the lobby. Brad and Samantha were still there holding hands. The sight of them made her sick to her stomach.

"Hello Ms. Edwards, I'm Laverne from Hagan Cove Funeral Home. I'm so terrible sorry about Dean. He was a wonderful sheriff and this whole town is going to miss him greatly," the nicely dressed older woman said taking Linda's hand.

They quickly discussed a few of the details and set up an appointment for the next day to make all the arrangements. After a couple more minutes, the woman said her good-byes and then quietly walked over to Samantha and Brad and spoke shortly to them before leaving.

"These are Mr. Richards' personal items that he had on him," the nurse said as she brought her a clear bag with Dean's wallet and things. "We'll need for you to sign for them."

Linda followed the nurse over to the large desk and signed it along with some other releases saying she would cover his bills since he was now unemployed and uninsured. She finished and walked back over, sat down and looked at the bag. It contained his wallet and car keys and some change. She just could not make herself get up and leave. She had a crazy feeling that if she stayed just a minute longer the doctor would come back and say that they had made a mistake and he was alive and wanted to go home. But she knew that was not going to happen. Dean, like everyone else in her life, had left her.

"Linda, do you want me to drive you home?" Brad asked as he walked over to her.

"No, I need to be alone," she replied, surprised by his offering but not looking up from the bag. "Thank you anyway."

"I… I could help with funeral arrangements. If you want," he replied softly, his voice shaky.

"That wont be necessary," she said, then looked up to see a tear roll down his cheek.

"Please," he said fighting his emotions. "Let me help bury my friend. Please."

"Okay," She replied softly. "Meet me tomorrow at ten at the funeral home."

"Are you sure you don't want me to drive you home?" He asked again.

"No, just get Samantha out of here," she told him.

Linda watched as he crossed the room back over to Samantha, who had not said a word. He took her hand and led her through the doors marked exit. For the first time since Dean died she noticed that the waiting room was as empty as she felt.

The car engine roared as she started it up and headed home. Just the thought of going back to the mansion brought dread to her heart. A shiny object caught the corner of her eye as she passed under the glow of the orange street light. It was Dean's keys. She quickly turned around and headed to the apartment building. She had never been to his apartment but he had showed her where it was, and now she stood outside his door. She pushed the doorbell, wishing he would answer, but all she got was silence.

The key quietly slipped into the worn lock and unlocked the door. With a push it opened and the darkness from within swallowed her. She reached up the wall and flipped on the light. A small lamp on a table by the sofa came on. It was your typical bachelor pad. None of his furniture matched, but it was clean with the exception of several boxes he had piled in the corner from his office yesterday. She walked over to his television and looked at the picture of him and Samantha, Valerie, and Brad. It had apparently been taken on a camping trip for each of them was holding a fish. She regretted that she had no pictures of her and Dean together. She wiped the tears from her eyes as she picked up the picture, looking at it deeply.

Samantha's smile in the picture sent chills down her spine. It was all that little bitch's fault! If only she had stayed away! She was always where she shouldn't be. If she had minded her own business, Dean would be alive. Her hand trembled as she placed it back on the television.

The phone rang just as she walked into the kitchen. She let it ring again, and then she answered it. She said hello, but who ever it was had hung up. She placed it back in the cradle and glanced at the memos and other things on the bulletin board beside the phone. One in little square paper caught her eye. It was a receipt she noticed as she removed it. It was a lay away receipt for a local jewelry store. She placed it on the counter and went through the apartment to his bedroom. She opened his closet and pulled out a white button down shirt. She took off her clothes and put it on then crossed the small room to his unmade bed. Quickly she pulled back the covers and slipped in. A faint scent of his cologne surrounded her and brought him close even though he was far away.

Everything that had happened tonight started to disappear from Linda's mind as she started remembering everything they had done together these past few months. The love they shared, how he defended her honor with Samantha and the others. They would be together soon. She would see to it. Dean was going to come home and Samantha was going to pay for hurting him. She would make her feel pain beyond anything she could imagine. Samantha was going to wish she had died the other night when she buried her. Linda rolled over and looked at the clock. It was after midnight. She sighed and closed her eyes. Dean was going to come back to her. He had to. A lone tear fell from her eyes as she fell asleep.

---

"Of all the people I know, Dean was the last one I would have ever thought to kill himself," Valerie said as she sat in the oversized chair, stuffing her feet under her and then smoothing out her white bathrobe.

"If I had not seen it with my own eyes I would have not believed it myself," Brad replied. "Don't you think that you should check on Sam, she's been in the bath tub for over thirty minutes."

"She just needs some time alone. She watched the man she loves die in the arms of another woman. I can't even begin to imagine how she feels," Valerie told him as she took another sip of her hot chocolate. "I wish I could have been there.

"There's nothing you could have done," he said quietly. "I wonder what Linda's doing right now?"

"Hopefully pulling the trigger on herself!" Samantha said, coming down the stairs joining in on the conversation.

"I made you some hot chocolate. It's on the counter in the kitchen," Valerie told her, watching her manage a smile and go after it.

"Are you okay?" Brad asked quietly as she returned to the living room and took a seat across from Valerie.

"It's just a lot to deal with. I never dreamed it would have come to this," she replied as she took a sip of her drink.

"Sam, you know you're not to blame for what happened tonight. Dean was really messed up. It's not your fault," Valerie told her sympathetically.

"I'm to blame, and both of you know it! Dean died loving that deranged woman because he thought I didn't love him! You should have seen his face tonight when I told him, he was shocked. If Linda had not kept messing with him he would have put the gun down. I know it. He should have been with me, definitely not dead, and none of this would have happened," she started.

"Sam, that's not true, you had no control over what happened…," Brad interrupted.

"Yes Brad, it is true!" She interrupted. "If I had listened to my heart and not my head, things would be very different right now! Who knows, we might have been married and had children. But one thing is for sure, he would be alive right now, and with me!" she said, unable to control her tears.

"Oh Samantha," Valerie said, getting up and going over to comfort her. "You can't think like that or you'll drive yourself crazy with guilt."

Brad got up and poured himself another scotch and looked out the window into the dark night. Behind him no one said a word. Other than a few sniffles from the women and the clock ticking on the mantel, everything was silent.

"He was out of his mind. He didn't even know who he was. He even tried to kill you Sam. What could have pushed him over the edge?" Brad asked, still looking out the window.

"It was her. She probably drugged him," Valerie said quietly.

"No! I think he knew what she had been doing and couldn't deal with it. Linda is great at manipulating and messing with people's minds. I really don't think he would have shot me," Samantha replied through her tears.

"I heard him shoot at you!" Brad said, turning around. "That's when I came into the house."

"Dean didn't pull the trigger! Linda took it from him when I told him I loved him! She saw the effect it had on him, and realized she was losing her power over him. She's the one that tried to shoot me! Dean grabbed the gun away. He had it back when you came in," Samantha told him, defending Dean.

"Oh my God!" Valerie whispered.

"If he hadn't taken the gun away, she would have killed me," Samantha added.

"I just can't see her being able to push him that far over the edge. Dean was strong," Valerie asked, still holding on to Samantha.

"I can," Samantha said loudly. "Linda has a lot of power over people."

"You think he found out she was involved in some of the things that's been happening around here?" Brad asked, sitting back down and rubbing his hands over his tired eyes.

Valerie cleared her throat as she crossed back over to her own chair now that Samantha had calmed down. Her hot chocolate slowly slid down her throat warming from the chills the nights events were giving her. She tried to think about what it must have been like being there tonight, and then quickly stopped. She didn't want to know!

"Dean was a good Sheriff. He was smart; I think he figured it out that she is behind all these disappearances. I would even bet he caught her in the act of murdering one. He may have even figured out that she was the one that buried me alive the other night. It was something big to mess him up as bad as it did," Samantha said as cold shivers ran through her body as she relived the memories of that night.

"I thought you could not remember that night?" Valerie questioned, looking with horror in her eyes.

"Not at first, but remember when she came to see me in the hospital?" She asked and waited for Valerie's nod. "It all came back. She drugged me. I could not move at all, not even my mouth! She brought Duke up from the basement I think, I'm not sure. He looked like he was half-dead! I don't remember what she said, but she made him leave with her. I was floating in and out of consciousness. I don't even think she knows that I know Duke was even there. They were gone for awhile, then she came back for me and dragged me outside and put me in the hole and started filling it up. All I could do was lie there and watch her. Then everything went black. The next thing I know I was in the hospital listening to everyone say Duke tried to kill me."

"Why didn't you tell me?" Brad demanded.

"Because I knew you would not believe me. Linda has been behind everything that's happened to me. She admitted it that night she drugged me. Those two times at my house, you remember I said I saw her, well she wasn't really there but she paid my pharmacist to slip something else in my pills as a bonus. She may not have been there, but she was the cause if it. I told everyone that, but no one believed me, so why would you believe it if I told you that it was her that tried to kill me and not Duke," she said as she started crying again. It felt so good to tell her friends everything she had been holding inside her.

"I'm sorry we did not believe you, but we do now, don't we Brad?" Valerie asked.

Valerie got back up and gave Samantha a big hug and whispered 'I'm so sorry' into her ear. The two held on to each other for a few seconds and let the tears fall. All the strain that their relationship had been under was now released. It's like it used to be between the old friends.

"We have to go to the police. They have got to find Duke's body," he added.

"If you go to them they will just think you're as crazy as me. Linda has this entire city wrapped around her fingers. They will do anything for her. She keeps pumping money in their wallets. Do you honestly believe they would arrest her and stop that cash flow?" Samantha asked, looking at them.

"She's right Brad. I saw our new mayor driving around in a new shiny car just this morning. You and I know that she can't afford that. And look at all the construction going on downtown. I read in the paper that she was financing that," Valerie added.

"Then what are we going to do?" He asked.

"Nothing," Samantha said.

"Nothing!" both Valerie and Brad asked in surprised.

"That's right. Brad, you saw Linda tonight. She was devastated by Dean's death. Despite her insane ways, she really loved him. His death hit her as hard as it did us and she's not thinking clearly any more. Dean helped her by keeping her informed with all the police activities. But with him gone, she doesn't have that connection anymore. She's completely on her own. She's going to slip up and fall flat on her face. It's a matter of time before she does," Samantha told them.

"Yes, but if Linda Edwards was as devastated as you say she was, doesn't that make her even more dangerous than she was before? I mean, if Dean was the only thing that kept her going and she caused all this trouble, can you imagine what she might do now?" Valerie asked.

"I'm counting on that!" Samantha told her.

"Maybe so, but that woman wanted you dead! I doubt seriously that her mood has changed. Girl, if I were you I would get a ticket out of town and not tell anyone where you were going," Valerie told her, concerned.

"She's right Sam. Maybe you should think about leaving for awhile, just until she's caught," Brad added. "Maybe Valerie could take off and go with you?"

"Sure, it could be fun, maybe we could go to Rome. Remember how you said you would like to go there?" Valerie said, getting excited. "I'm sure Brad would finance it for us!"

Brad started to say something but Valerie gave him the evil eye that said shut up and agree with her if he knew what was good for him. "We'll have to see about that," he quickly added.

"No! I have to make sure that she goes down. Dean saved my life. Now it's my turn to see that the woman who is to blame for his death goes down. Even if I have to die doing it! She's going to pay," Samantha replied with coldness in her voice.

"I think we should all try to get some sleep. I think we can discuss this in the morning," Brad said, getting up from the chair.

"Yeah, you're right. I'm really tired," Samantha said as she stood up, crossed over to the window and looked out. "I know it's only been a couple of hours since he died, but I miss him so bad."

"I know sweetie, we all do," Valerie said, coming up behind her and taking her arm.

"Somewhere out in the night, Linda Edwards is there still breathing and waiting for the next person for her to take control over and destroy their lives just like all the others. God help them!" She said, then looked away from the window and allowed Valerie to help her upstairs.

Brad felt cold chills rip through his body as he listened to what Samantha said. Maybe she was out there watching them right now! One thing was certain. After Dean's funeral, he would never go anywhere near her again.

# Chapter 27 - The homecoming.

The buzzing of Dean's alarm woke Linda. Looking around in a daze it took her a few minutes to figure out where she was. Then suddenly it all poured back into her memory, every painful minute of it. Just yesterday at this time Dean was alive and well. Now he was dead. It just didn't seem possible, but deep down she knew it was. Quickly she put her clothes back on and made the bed, grabbed the layaway receipt and left the apartment.

Outside the clouds had moved in and covered the sky with a dreary gray. It perfectly matched her mood. She went to the funeral home and met Brad. Together they put together a very nice funeral for Dean, but Linda noticed that Brad almost seemed afraid of her. God only knows what garbage Samantha had told him.

When they were finished Linda left quietly and headed for her next destination. The car pulled into the closest available parking spot to the jewelry store, sighing as she entered the store. It was nothing like the ones that she used to shop at in Kansas City, but for this area it wasn't too bad.

"Good morning, my name is Regina; can I help you with something?" The Friendly sales clerk asked.

"I need to pick up this layaway," Linda said and gave her the receipt quickly, wanting to hurry and get out of there.

Regina looked it over carefully and went into the back room. Linda glanced at the jewelry on a rack sitting on the counter, pulling a few pieces off; she placed them by the register. "As long as she was here she might as well buy a few things," she thought to herself. Regina came back into the room and handed Linda the ring box.

"You must be the lucky bride to be. Dean has told me so much about you. Is he outside?" The woman asked. It was apparent she did not know about his death.

"Lucky bride?" Linda asked, opening the ring box and staring at the beautiful engagement ring inside. Linda's heart skipped as her eyes clouded over. Dean was planning to ask her to marry him.

"Isn't it gorgeous? It's the best one we had in the store. He was here over an hour picking it out. You're a very lucky young lady to get a man like Dean Richards," Regina said, watching her as she admired the ring.

"Put the balance and these other things on my card," Linda told her as she handed her the jewelry and her credit card.

Regina took the merchandise and started ringing it up while Linda slipped off her wedding rings that her husband had given her and placed them on her other hand. Then she put Dean's ring in place of them. He had been paying on it every Friday for the last three weeks and still had not paid even a third of it yet. No wonder he never had any money. She really wished he hadn't been spending his hard earned money on her, but it made her feel good that he did.

The clerk gave her the credit card, bagged up her other purchases and said good bye as Linda left the shop. The hot muggy summer wind took her breath away. The summer heat had arrived and definitely was here to stay for awhile. Despite the sickness in her stomach, Linda returned home and took care of cleaning up the mess that had been made the night before. Stella asked no questions and Linda gave no answers. The two just went about getting Ridgecliffe Manor back together. The painters would be there tomorrow to put new wallpaper in the kitchen and parlor. Once finished, all remains of any struggle would no longer be apparent.

The clean up and consistent phone calls from friends she did not know made the day go by fast, but the lonely night dragged by slowly. Several times she reached across the bed expecting to feel his body, but all she felt was the cold empty sheets.

The morning finally broke through, awakening her with the desperate need for blood. Unfortunate for her, she had promised Dean she would not kill another man.. Linda pulled her black pin striped skirt and matching jacket out of the closet and laid them on the bed before crossing over to her dresser to pick out her jewelry for the day. She wanted to get to the funeral home in plenty of time for the visitation before everybody else arrived.

The Porsche pulled in front of the large Victorian house that was now a funeral home. It was hard to believe this was the last time she would see Dean's body. Tomorrow he would be buried. Just thinking about his name brought a stabbing pain to her chest. The director of the home led her in and opened the doors to the large room where his coffin was. She still had three hours before the actual visitation began, but she had to see him, to be near him.

Linda watched as the woman left the room and closed the doors behind her. The coffin was at the end of the room and there were several rows of chairs for people to sit in. Flowers and plants were spread all over the room. The vibrant colors of the flowers seemed to bring the room to life. If only they could do the same for Dean.

Quietly she walked down the aisle and stood just before the closed casket. She ran her perfectly manicured fingers over the lines of the beautiful casket. Her fingers ran from top to the bottom where she placed her purse down and reached into it for a lighter to light the candles around the room. The flickering lights brought her a much needed peace of mind, she thought to herself as she flipped off the overhead lights. The room was so beautiful.

Slowly she lifted the lid and locked it into place. He looked so handsome in the suit she had picked out for him. Linda smiled, as her eyes once again filled with tears. She lowered her mouth and kissed him on the lips. Was it her imagination or had he returned her kiss? Could it be he wasn't really dead? No, he was just pretending. He had told her he had a plan for them and this was it! She sighed with relief. Dean was alive! It was okay, she could keep his secret.

"You look so handsome. I'm so proud of you," she told him, talking to him as if he was alive. "This should have never had to happen."

Linda walked away from the casket and started smelling the flowers and reading the cards people had sent. Some of them she knew of, others she didn't.

"You're so lucky to have so many friends who care about you. They have sent such beautiful flowers. They love you, but you know I love you more. No one will ever love you as much as I do," she said with a smile, glancing down at her new ring. "I love your ring. I'll wear it forever! No one will ever make me take it off."

Once again she walked to the casket and kissed him. She pulled back and with her finger outlined all the features of his handsome face. She loved his face. Stepping back, she walked down the aisle, touching each row of chairs as she passed them. Why doesn't he get up? He doesn't have to pretend with her. Anger started filling her, eating away at her. Her hands piddling with each other as she paced up and down the aisle. Reality began to set in as she realized he was really dead!

"How could you do this to me? Why did you leave me here all alone? You told me you were going to help me, remember? But you left. Why? Tell me!" She yelled, running to him. Suddenly as quick as it had begun, her anger vanished. "I cleaned up your mess last night. You got blood all over the floor when you shot yourself. You know, it's funny I guess we're even now. The other night you cleaned up my bloody mess and last night I cleaned up yours."

Linda started chuckling to herself as she went over to her purse and pulled out her cosmetic mirror to check on her appearance. People would be here in a couple of hours and she needed to look her best. She finished and placed it back in her purse.

"I'm going to send someone over to pack your apartment and move your things to the mansion as soon as possible. That way when you come home you will never have to leave," she said as she reached down and straightened his tie.

Brad had tried his best to get her to have his uniform put on him. He said it was his favorite thing he owned, but she had insisted on a suit. He looked so handsome. Once again Brad was wrong.

"I know how much you like the mansion, you told me so. Oh, I forgot, yesterday I enrolled in a cooking class, so when you get home we can get rid of Stella and I'll do all our cooking. I'll be a regular wife! You are going to be so proud of me," she said as she walked over and sat in one of the chairs. "I do think we are going to have a serious problem with Samantha. You know how she runs off at the mouth every chance she gets, but lately she's been very quiet. I think she's up to something. What do you think? Would you answer me please? You know how mad I get when you ignore me! I hate to be ignored! Dean! I'm talking to you!"

Linda tried again to control her anger, but it was going to burst open no matter how hard she tried to contain it. She jumped up and grabbed the folding chair and threw it across the room, knocking over several other chairs and a few plants.

"How could you do this to me?" She screamed at him as the tears rolled down her cheeks. "You're just like all the rest of them. You screw me and leave me! You used me! Why are people always trying to hurt me? I honestly thought you were different, I really did. You never did love me, did you? You were using me to make Samantha jealous. Didn't you? Answer me, Dean! Didn't you?"

Linda turned and rushed down to the other side of the room, pulling the curtains back to look outside. People in the neighboring houses were going about their business as though her pain didn't matter. Each of them needs to feel pain, she thought to herself.

"How could you do this Dean? You used me! You used me!" She kept repeating as she turned around and went back over to the casket. "I loved you more than I ever loved another living soul. And you betrayed me. Did you sleep with her? I can see it in your face. You did, didn't you? That's why she was always causing me trouble. Because you were trying to make her jealous by using me. Isn't that right? Answer me, damn it! Would you open your eyes and look at me!"

Linda yelled and cried at him as she grabbed his stiff body and shook it violently, trying to get him to open his eyes. She reached with her finger and tried to open them, but they would not open. She let loose and stood back.

"You're not fooling me. I know you're not dead. You just want me to think that so you and that little tramp can run away together. I'm smarter than you think. I'm on to your game, so give it up! Stop playing dead and get up! I hate it when you do this to me!" She yelled then suddenly stopped, putting her ear close to his mouth. "What? You're right, I'm sorry. You were going to kill her. You were going to kill her to save me! Oh! Oh God! I'm so sorry for doubting you, can you forgive me? I'm going to take care of her. You will be so proud of me. I'll take care of all of them. Each and every one. Not one of them will be left when I'm through with them. I love you. Can you forgive me for doubting you?"

"Is everything in here all right?" Laverne, the director, asked as she entered the room. "I thought I heard some yelling in here?"

"No, everything is just fine. I accidentally knocked over some chairs. I'm sorry," Linda said as she went over and blew out the candles. As she passed Dean she leaned in and whispered, "I'll get you out of here tonight. I promise. You will be home before you know it."

Linda grabbed her purse, briefly talked to Laverne then exited the building. Outside the sun was now shining brightly. She felt so much better since her and Dean's little talk that she decided to take a walk. She had a lot of things to think about and the most important was how she was going to get Dean out of that place. There had to be a way. Just when she was about to give up hope a man walked past her in dark dirty clothes. He was a convict if she ever saw one. This was a sign from Dean that he was going to help her. Slowly she followed him into a restaurant and watched him order, then pull out a newspaper from his back pocket.

"Mind if I have a seat?" She asked, sitting down before he could answer. "I see you're looking in the help wanted section. I have a little job. It pays well. Actually very well, are you interested?"

The strange man looked her over with a sinister smile. He eased his hand under the table, placed it on her leg and started moving it forward. Linda instantly jammed her leg upwards, smashing his hand between her knee and the table. Quickly he pulled his hand away.

"Don't flatter yourself," she told him sternly. "That's not the kind of job I was talking about."

"I don't need this shit," he said as he started to get up.

"It is well worth your trouble," Linda said as she threw out a hundred dollar bill on the table.

"Listen lady. If you want me to off your old man, you're going to have to forget it. I just got out of the joint last week and I'm supposed to stay out of trouble or they revoke my parole. I don't think my parole officer would understand my not showing up tomorrow because I had to murder someone, now do you?" He asked as he pulled a toothpick off the table and started picking his teeth in front of her.

"I don't want you to kill anyone. He's already dead. I just want you to break into the funeral home and get him and bring him to my house. That's it," she replied with a friendly smile.

"You want to keep a corpse in your house?" He asked her. "Lady, you're into some freaky shit!"

"I'm sure if you don't think you can handle it I can find someone else," she said as she started to get up from the chair.

"How much?" He asked, grabbing her arm and stopping her.

"Five thousand. Are you interested?" She asked, reaching into her purse and pulled out a wad of money, holding it to where he could see.

"Where do I drop him off at?" He asked, grabbing it away from her.

Linda reached back into her purse for some paper and a pen and wrote directions to the mansion. She tried to contain her excitement at the thought of having Dean back home with her again.

"You will receive the rest when you deliver," she said smiling brightly as she handed him the directions. "If you pull this off, I might have another, larger project for you. A chance to make more money than you ever imagined. If you're caught though, don't come running to me. I don't even know who you are. Be at my house at midnight."

Linda said no more as she got up from the table and left. Dean was coming home tonight and that was all that mattered, she thought to herself as she walked back to her car. She jumped in and raced home. She had a lot to do before Dean came back.

---

"Good evening," Samantha said, greeting Brad as he stepped into the kitchen. "How was work?"

"Fine, thanks. You cooked dinner?" He asked surprised. He could smell the food but saw no evidence that she was cooking.

"It's in the oven. Almost finished, why don't you wash up," she told him as she wiped off the counter top and put the last few dishes away out of the dishwasher.

Brad went to his room and changed from his suit and tie into a pair of sweats and headed back down. Having someone at home cleaning and cooking dinner for him was something he could definitely get used to. He could not remember the last time he had a home cooked meal.

His thoughts of a fine dinner rapidly disappeared as he re-entered the dining room and saw two TV dinners awaiting him. One for him and one for her.

"Thanks again for letting me stay here for awhile. I don't know what I would do without you," she replied as they sat down to eat. "I hope you like meat loaf."

"I told you it was no problem, and yes I love meat loaf," he smiled, taking a bite.

"Valerie was supposed to cook but she had this hot date," Samantha said as she watched him eat. For a moment it seemed like things used to before… before Linda.

"I know. That's all she talked about at work today. Have you given any thought to coming back to work yourself?" He asked.

"Yes, it's just hard. God knows I need the money. The insurance company will not cover my house so now I have to go work out a deal with the mortgage company. Do you think they will take both arms, or just one?" She joked.

"Both, probably a foot too," he added.

Brad watched her smile just before she took another bite. He was debating if he should tell her some of the latest gossip going around town about Linda. He never knew how she would take the news anymore with everything that had happened.

"How's you dinner?" She suddenly spoke interrupting his thoughts.

"Good," he said after he had finished swallowing. "You know I heard something around town today."

"What?" she asked, taking a drink.

"It's about Linda," he said, watching her smile fade at the mention of her name.

"What has that woman done now?" She asked coldly.

"She made another contribution to the city, this one in the sum of a million dollars. Suppose to be in honor of Dean, to buy police vehicles, office computers, and things like that. She plans to give it to them at the city birthday celebration on July fourth," he told her shyly, still shy of her reaction.

"That woman never stops. She uses everything that happens no matter how tragic and twists it to her advantage. It just amazes me. How much did you say she was donating?" She asked.

"I heard a million, but you know how rumors start around here," Brad told her; relieved she was not getting too upset.

"She's getting scared. Afraid people are not going to buy her little miss innocent act anymore. Now she's just buying insurance. She doesn't have Dean now to protect her so she has to buy the city. Brad, we have to get a plan to trap her. If we play our cards right it will just be a matter of time before it's over and she will have hung herself," Samantha said as she picked her plate up and took it to the kitchen.

Brad quickly finished his last bite and followed her, grabbing his own plate as he did. The thought of what might be going on in Samantha's head scared him. He needed to talk her down before she did something stupid and made matters worse.

"It's high time she gets a dose of her own medicine." Samantha said taking his plate.

"I don't know what to think anymore. I will say this; I don't think that she is thinking straight. When we were making the funeral arrangements she would sometimes talk about him like he wasn't dead. I don't know, it kind of gave me the creeps," Brad told her as he watched her load the dishwasher. "Are you sure you don't want to go to Dean's visitation tonight?"

"No, I said good bye this morning. I don't want to be around all those people, you go ahead," she told him as she threw the trash away.

"I think I'll go by earlier myself," he paused. "What do you think she's up to?"

"Knowing her like I do, it's hard telling. Dean was what held her together, now he's been pulled out from under her and she's crumbling down, fast! You know, it's funny. All this time I thought Dean was in danger but she would have never hurt him. In her own sick way she really loves him and that is going to be her downfall," she said as she left the kitchen and went into the living room.

Brad glanced around the recently cleaned kitchen. He really liked having the women around; the house hadn't been this clean since his wife died. He heard Samantha call him from the other room. He grabbed a beer out of the refrigerator, flipped off the light and headed to the living room.

"I still think it might be a good idea for you to leave town for awhile," Brad said, following her.

"I can't afford to leave…," she suddenly stopped. "Oh my God! That's it! She follows a pattern. I know her next step. It's just like in Kansas City. Remember I told you right before she moved here things were starting to heat up with her and all those so called accidents? It's just like here. She's about to leave Hagan Cove. Let's just hope she just leaves peacefully like she did in Kansas City."

"Oh, come on Samantha, if she was planning to leave town she sure as hell would not have donated all that money to the city," Brad replied as he sat on the sofa.

Samantha looked over at Brad and sighed. He was probably right about that, or was he? The money very well could be a diversion for something even bigger. Chills swept through her as she tried to imagine what Linda was thinking.

"Lets face it, a million dollars is a lot of money to donate and then just leave," Brad added.

"I think there is a plan for that money. It might be to buy her a little time before she disappears. We have to make her slip up and get caught before she takes off. What are we going to do? I want her to pay for what she did here!" Samantha said nervously.

"So what do you recommend we do?" Brad asked, afraid of her answer.

"I guess just wait for her to strike. And be ready for anything. I would not put anything past her," Samantha said as she sat down opposite him. "I know she will try to get me one last time before she leaves. I can feel it."

※

Linda glanced at the grandfather clock in the foyer for the thousandth time. Where was that man? He was over an hour late! Dean would be exhausted. Did he get caught? Maybe she should have found someone else. Too bad she killed Duke.

Once Dean got home she would be able to think clearer. She had to take care of Samantha once and for all then they could leave this place. She was flying back to Kansas City tomorrow to withdraw some cash and put it in a safe place for later, just in case things went wrong. Always have a back up plan. This town would be sorry that she ever came through it. It was their fault Dean was dead! Theirs and Samantha's. They would all pay.

Hopefully this man would be able to deliver and prove to be trustworthy for her next task. If he succeeded, both of them would be very happy. Him with a million dollars, her with the town's blood on her hands. She wanted every one of them dead! All of them, especially Samantha Marshall! Linda took another drink from her glass then held it tightly. She wanted to squeeze that woman's head until it exploded, she thought as the glass busted under her pressure. Maybe she would stick a piece of dynamite in her mouth and blow her head off!

"Everyone would say poor Samantha really lost her head this time!" Linda said out loud, and then started laughing hysterically.

There was always acid. That would be a slow and agonizing death. Very painful. Yes, that would work. Acid it would be. She would melt her face off, and this time, if she would happen to live, she would wish she hadn't. In the darkness she noticed a pair of headlights turn up the drive. Finally!

"It's about time! Where in the hell have you been?" Linda said angrily as he stepped from the van.

"Ran into a little problem. Nice pile of bricks you have here," he replied, looking up at the mansion.

"What kind of problem?" She demanded. "Where's Dean?"

"In all the excitement of the job you forgot to tell me which stiff he was," the man replied calmly with a sick smile.

"This is a small town! How many dead people could there be!" she yelled.

"Three to be exact. Pick him out," he said, opening the back door to the van. "You did not say which one, so I just took all three."

Linda smiled. She liked this guy. He would actually use his brain. She directed him to take Dean to the freezer in the basement for now until she got back in town. He would be safe there. Stella would have a cow if she found him while she was gone. He put him inside then followed her back upstairs and watched her pour him a drink.

"So what is your name stranger?" She asked as she handed him his drink and gave him the money she promised.

"I don't think names are important," he replied as he took a drink.

"It is if you want to make a million dollars," she said, smiling and sitting in the wing back chair by the fireplace.

"Call me Alex," he replied, giving her his full attention.

"Well then Alex, let's get down to business. Everything I tell you will only be said this one time and then never spoke of again. I can tell by looking at you that you are a man with connections. Correct?" She asked.

"Smart dame," he said, finishing his drink and getting up to pour another.

"Like all jobs of this nature there are some risks, but I believe that you can handle it. If you get caught, I've never seen you before, and you will never be able to prove anything. I have enough money to see to that. Do you understand?" Linda asked as she accepted the drink he poured for her.

"Completely. You have my undivided attention."

The man sat down and waited for her to tell him what she wanted him to do. It was obvious to him that it was going to be something big and illegal, but for a million dollars he would definitely listen. The woman was definitely off her rocker but if she could deliver the money he would help her out!

"I want you to completely level the city of Hagan Cove. Not one brick should remain standing. There are large utility tunnels that run under most of the main part of town. I have several city maps, thanks to my volunteering to help renovate the area, that will help make your job a lot easier," she said with a wicked smile and an evil deadly look in her eyes.

"You want to blow the whole town up?" He laughed.

"Completely destroyed! You put the explosives under the city and rig it up so that I can push the button from here. There's a parade and celebration downtown on the fourth of July. That's when it should happen. Do you think you can handle it?" She asked, taking a sip of her drink.

"I can handle it. But I will need help. Professionals and they don't come cheap," he said, once again giving her a sinister smile.

"How much?" She asked, getting a little irritated.

"Two million. One when I give you the control device and the other after the bang. Deal?" He asked, getting up and extending his hand to her.

"Deal!" She said without hesitation, taking his hand and shaking it.

"You must be really pissed to want everyone dead. There won't be an empty cemetery for fifty miles," he said as he started for the front doors.

"I don't give a damn if it fills up every cemetery in the state. They all deserve to die! Do you have access to chemicals by any chance?" She asked, stopping him.

"What kind?" He said, turning and looking at her.

"Acid. Face melting kind, not the drug," she said before he spoke. "Something that will melt the skin right off your bones."

"No problem," he replied.

Linda walked into the dark library, over to her desk and grabbed the plans and a folder with the information he needed to complete the job and quickly walked back to him. She was so excited she had found someone that could make this work. Dean would be so proud!

"Good. Here are the plans for the city, courtesy of the town's redevelopment group. Meet me here one week from tonight at midnight with the device and I'll have your money. And Alex, if you pull this off perfectly with no hitches, I might even send you a bonus," she said as she opened the doors for him and followed him to the van.

"You are one crazy broad. Remind me to never piss you off," he said as he got into the van.

"That is very good advice. I must warn you that if you try to screw me over, I'll kill you. There is no place on this earth that I can't find you. You wouldn't want to know how I would do it," she warned.

"You just get me my money. The threats go both ways," he told her, then shut the door, started the engine and pulled off down the drive.

Linda watched as the van disappeared into the night. She wondered what he was going to do with the other two bodies. She smiled to herself as she walked back into the house. Dean was home and she had found the right man to settle the score with that whole damn town. They would pay for making Dean give up his job! Every last one of them!

"In a couple of weeks Hagan Cove will be a memory!" She said to herself as she reached over and dialed the phone.

"Hello," Brad said sleepily.

"Hi Brad, its Linda, I'm sorry if I woke you," she replied, smiling at her reflection in the mirror.

It was now time to start putting her plan into to motion and she decided not to wait another second! Brad would be the first step in helping her to settle the score with this damn town, and he like always would be putty in her hand!

"Brad?" She repeated after a moment of silence.

"Yeah," he said slowly waking up.

"Did I wake you?" She asked, pretending she cared.

"Don't worry about it, is everything alright?" He asked concerned.

"Yes, everything is as fine as it can be. I'm sorry to call so late. I seem to lose track of time now and then. I didn't realize it was so late but, I thought maybe we could go have dinner after the funeral tomorrow, there are some things I have of Dean's you might want," she said.

"I don't know Linda," he paused.

"Please," she begged. "I'm sure he would like for you to have them."

"Alright, I... can probably do dinner, but I can't be gone too long. I'll catch up with you tomorrow and set up a time to meet."

"That's perfect. Good bye Brad," Linda said as she hung up the phone and laughed. "Oh Brad you are so easy to get. You stupid fool!"

Linda got up from the sofa, turned off the lights and went to bed. Soon her plan would be in motion and nothing would come between her and her revenge. Especially not that pesky little bitch Samantha Marshall! She'll be too occupied with Brad's little problem to follow her!

# Chapter 28 - Playing games.

Brad listened; dropping his hamburger in disbelief as Valerie informed him of the robbery. "Who in their right mind would break into a funeral home, destroy it and then steal all the bodies out of it? The world was becoming a sick place," he thought to himself.

"Did you talk to Laverne?" Samantha asked. "How bad was the damage?"

"I didn't talk to her personally. All I know is what was told at city hall this morning," Valerie said as she poured her some tea and closed the refrigerator. "Can you believe that something like this happened here?"

The talk of the funeral home break in had taken up so much of Valerie's meeting this morning with the planning committee that they hardly even talked about the fourth of July parade they were supposed to be planning. The event was coming soon and they still didn't have everything planned out.

"Poor Dean," Samantha managed to say after a moment of silence. "What would someone do with a dead body?"

"God, I don't even want to think about that one. There are so many sickos out there!" Valerie said shaking the thoughts that were popping in her head.

"Three bodies at that!" Brad added. "So I guess the funeral is off?"

"Yes," Valerie said, sitting down. "They said if the bodies weren't found by the end of the week, the city would hold a memorial for him at the park."

"Someone notify Linda?" Samantha asked her.

"I don't know. I'm sure they did."

"I bet that was a fun call to make," Brad said, getting up from the table and throwing away the hamburger. "I'm supposed to go over there this afternoon after the funeral, but since there isn't going to be one, I wonder if she'll still want me to come."

As soon as the words came out of his mouth he knew it was a big mistake. Samantha would bust a blood vessel over this one. He should have just not told her! She had actually been calming down since Dean had died, there had been no out burst, no crazy episodes, until the one that was about to happen now!

"What!" Samantha said jumping up. "Are you crazy? How could you go over there, knowing what that woman is capable of?"

"I didn't really have a choice, she called late last night, and I agreed before I really knew what I was saying."

"What does she want?" Valerie asked, helping Samantha back to her seat, trying to calm her down as she looked suspiciously at him.

"What do you think she wants?" Samantha asked sarcastically.

"She said she had some things of Dean's that she felt like I should have," he said as he picked up the phone and dialed Linda's house, ignoring Samantha's remark.

"What is she doing with them?" Valerie asked Samantha while he dialed. "Shouldn't his family be doing that?"

"There isn't any family, just a long lost brother," Samantha said as she angrily started cleaning up the lunch mess.

Brad just couldn't leave well enough alone. It figured to Samantha that he would be the one that Linda would go after first; after all he was male and easy prey! How could he be so stupid as to agree to go anywhere near her after everything she had done? "Linda," Brad said after she answered. "Hi, it's Brad Dalson. I just heard about what happened at the funeral home, I'm so sorry. I can understand if you don't want to have dinner now."

"No Brad, please could you come over here. I really don't want to be alone. It's been such a horrible day. I think having company would be wonderful," she pleaded.

"Ok, I'll be over," he looked at his watch. "In about half an hour if that's alright with you."

"That will be fine, thank you, Brad, I really appreciate it," she said sadly as she hung up.

"You're really going over there?" Samantha asked in a state of shock. "Are you serious?"

"I didn't know what to say. You should have heard her, she sounded so sad!" He said in his defense.

"Poor thing," Samantha spat out. "Brad, I don't want you over there. It's too dangerous!"

"I'm going to have to agree with her," Valerie said. "We really don't know what that woman is going to do next."

"I'm a grown man. I think that I can take care of myself."

"With anyone else I would agree, but she's not like the other women out there. She is killing grown men bigger than you are. You're no match for her," Samantha warned.

"Besides you horn dog, you've had the hots for her since you met her," Valerie quickly added. "I don't think you should go out there either. If she even bats an eye at you you'll be carrying her up the stairs to the bedroom."

"I better go with you," Samantha spoke up as she started to leave the kitchen and headed for her bedroom to change clothes.

"Yeah right!" Brad hollered after her. "Linda isn't going to let you anywhere near that place!"

"He's right Sam!" Valerie added.

"Alright Valerie, you go," she said as she came back into the kitchen with them. "I don't want him out there alone."

"I can't, I have to show some property in Boonville," Valerie told her. "I'll be gone most of the day, in fact I should already be at the office."

"I don't need a baby sitter," Brad said as he left the kitchen.

"Yes you do. Like Valerie said, you are a walking hormone!"

"That's real cute," he said as he went upstairs and closed the bathroom door.

Samantha groaned loudly after his door had shut. There was no way she was going to let Brad go out there, especially alone. She had to do something to stop him, what exactly she didn't know, but it better be fast or Brad would be Linda's next victim!

"We can't just let him walk out of here and go over there, God only knows what she is planning," Samantha told Valerie.

"There isn't much we could do about it. He's a big boy, if he won't listen to us and he gets into trouble, he'll have no one to blame but himself."

"Getting into trouble is one thing, but getting himself killed is another. Remember my dreams!" Samantha said loudly. "She's going to get him next. She finished off Dean, probably even stole his body, and now she's going after Brad. I've got to stop her."

"Sam, you can't help someone that doesn't want it. Besides, I hate to get you going but there still is no solid proof that she has even killed anyone."

"How much more proof do you need?" Samantha yelled.

"I'm sorry," Valerie said, trying to calm her friend down. "I didn't mean to upset you. I'm just being flat out honest with you. We may know she's doing it but proving it with evidence is a whole other thing!"

"I know, you're right," she sighed, then went over and picked up the phone book.

"What are you doing?" Valerie asked.

"Kelly and Brad are still seeing each other, aren't they?" She asked.

"Yes, I think so. Why?"

Samantha might not be able to stop Brad from going over to Linda's house but she knew someone that would. There was nothing better at stopping a man in his tracks then bringing his girlfriend into play, and that was exactly what she was going to do!

"She was always insanely jealous, when he even talked to another woman, right?" Samantha asked smiling as she remembered the other night with the fight between Linda and Kelly.

"I don't think I like the direction this is taking," Valerie said as she walked over and took the receiver away from her and hung it back up. "Girl, You're gonna cause one hell of a cat fight and we won't even get to see it!"

"What are you two doing?" Brad asked as he walked back down the stairs and picked up his keys.

"Nothing," they answered as Valerie hung up the phone.

"Valerie, if you want I'll give you a ride back to the office so you won't have to walk," he said as he started for the door, then stopped, waiting for her reply.

"That's alright, it's a beautiful day, don't mind walking. I'll see you later," she said, then watched as he gave them a suspicious look and left. She turned back over at Samantha who already had the phone in her hand and was dialing.

"Kelly, hi, it's me Samantha, I'm sorry to bother you, but I was looking for Brad. Is he there by any chance?" she asked politely.

"You are so evil!" Valerie whispered.

"He's not?" She sighed. "That's funny; he was gone all night last night and stopped here for a couple of minutes to clean up and left. I just assumed you two were doing something special. Oh well, if you see him will you tell him I need to talk to him, it's urgent. Thank you… Oh wait, just a minute."

She paused for a couple of seconds.

"Oh, I'm sorry to bother you but Valerie just walked in and said he was over at Linda Edwards's house. I didn't know you two had broken up?" Samantha asked as she quickly jerked the phone away, shielding her ears from the obscenities that Kelly was yelling into the phone. She was trying hard not to burst out laughing.

"Let me hear!" Valerie demanded. She took the phone, listened for a second, and then handed it back. "That girl's using words I never even heard of!"

"Kelly, please calm down, I feel so bad that I had to break the bad news to you," she said, trying to be serious. "I don't know what I would do if I were you. Men are such pigs! Wait just a minute, Valerie wants to tell me some thing."

"What are you doing, are you crazy!" Valerie whispered.

"Kelly, Valerie thinks you should jump in your car and run right out there and settle this mess once and for all! Put that bitch in her place!"

"No, I…," Valerie said, quickly lowered her voice. "You are going to get us in such trouble!"

"I don't think you have enough time to let your hair dry. I'd just jump in the car, rollers and all, and head on out there so you can catch him in the act. And then you give that woman hell for all us women. Women like her are no good!" Samantha said, starting to giggle. "You call us back and let us know what happened. Alright, I'll talk to you later. Bye."

"Brad is going to be pissed, and I'm going to be late," Valerie said as she rushed into the kitchen and put her glass in the sink and then headed for the front door. "You know I'm going to deny knowing anything about this!"

"Go ahead; I'm woman enough to take the blame for both of us!" Samantha laughed and watched her friend leave. Valerie was right; he was going to be mad, furious was more like it. She sure wished she were going to be there see it!

Brad nervously pulled the keys out of the ignition and stepped out of the car. A heavy cloud had temporarily covered the sun, making it eerily dark. He walked up on the porch and rang the bell. He had to admit that the house looked great on the outside. It was amazing what had been done to the place in such a short amount of time.

"Hi," Linda said as she opened the door and let him. "Please come in, I was about to fix myself a drink. May I get you one?"

"No, thank you," he said, remembering how Samantha had told him she had poisoned her.

"Have a seat," Linda said as she walked from the room.

Brad watched her walk out of the room through the darkened dining room. Man was she hot! She was wearing a short form fitting dark blue low cut dress that buttoned down the front. Her long blond hair was pinned up with a few curls left dangling down. She turned around and smiled at him as if she knew what he was thinking, then went on into the kitchen.

"This was not a good idea!" he said to himself after she was gone.

The empty parlor gave him chills as he replayed the scene from the last time he was in this room. Everything had been cleaned up and put back into place. Looking at the room now you would never be able to tell that anyone had even died there.

"I brought you a glass of water just in case you changed your mind," Linda said as she sat the glass down on the end table next to him, and sat opposite him in the chair. "Thanks for coming. I really haven't had many visitors out here. Maybe I'll have a party someday and invite everybody."

"Have you heard anything from the funeral home?" He asked as he picked the glass up, and took a drink and silently prayed that there was nothing in it.

"No," she said, and then paused. "Can you believe this sick world we live in? Even funerals aren't safe any more."

"They have no idea who did it?" He asked, taking another drink.

"No, probably never will. Listen Brad the real reason I asked you to come over isn't because of Dean's things. Actually I haven't gotten around to going through them yet, but if there's anything you want, just let me know."

"Then why did you call?"

"I know we kind of got off to a rocky start, and I know Samantha and I will never be friends, but I hope someday that we'll at least be civil to each other," she began.

"So you're not planning on leaving town?" he asked.

"I'm going to Kansas City for a couple of days to take care of some business, but I plan to return, and when I do I want to have a new start on life. Dean's death has made me realize we only live a short time here on earth and we need to make the most of it, so I was thinking about going into real estate, starting up my own office," she said, taking a deep breath. "And I would like you to run it."

"Me!" Brad said with surprise. "I don't know what to say."

"Yes would be a good reply," she said with a bright smile. "It would be extremely classy all the way."

"I don't know, I've worked for Max for years," he replied.

Brad quickly started processing her words. The thought of getting out from under Max and being in a company that he would be running sounded really good to him, but at the same time he wasn't real sure that Linda could be trusted.

"Max is an old man, who knows how much longer he'll want to stay in the business. Then what will you do?" She asked him bluntly. "Have you really thought about your future? I realize you have some money of your own, but what about when that runs out?"

"What about Valerie and Sam, we've sort of been a team for the last three years."

"Valerie maybe, but I have to draw the line with Samantha," Linda said taking a sip of her drink. She set it on the table and crossed her

*the Murderess of* RIDGECLIFFE MANOR

legs, her skirt slightly sliding up her exposed thigh. "Besides, I seriously doubt that she would come work for my company."

"You're probably right there," he said as he loosened his collar a bit. It was starting to get stuffy in here.

"Is everything alright?" She asked, noticing his discomfort. "I could turn the air conditioning up if you like."

"No, I'm fine, thanks," he said as he took another drink. He could feel the sweat forming on his forehead.

"Brad, you're sweating like crazy," Linda said as she got up from her chair and grabbed a tissue from the table, sat beside him and wiped his forehead. "Why don't you take off your jacket?"

"Maybe I should be going," he said as he got up from the sofa.

"Don't be silly, you just got here," she said as she helped him take off his jacket. "There now, that's more comfortable, isn't it?"

"Yeah," he said as he cleared his throat. "Could I have another glass of water?"

"Of course," Linda said as she picked up his glass. "If you would like something stronger I have a fully stocked bar here in the corner."

"Make it a scotch," he said, changing his mind.

Linda laughed to herself as she watched him from the bar. The poor guy was so nervous he was about to wet himself. He really was cute, cute like a puppy. She poured him his drink and slowly walked back over to him. She watched his eyes never leave her.

"Here you go," she said, handing him the glass, setting the bottle down beside him. He quickly drank the glass and poured another. "Let me loosen your tie for you."

"It's alright," he said, pulling away from her and downing the second glass. "I really should go."

"I don't think you really want to, do you?" She asked, massaging his shoulders.

"This really isn't a good idea," he said, not believing those words slipped from his lips. Any other time he would have been all over her.

"Just relax," she said as she removed his tie and opened his shirt. "Turn around." She said as she pulled his shirt loose from his pants and slid her hands up under the fabric and started massaging his back.

"Oh Linda," Brad sighed as she massaged him. The tension he had been feeling was slipping away as he got into the moment.

Linda's hands slid down his back, then around his stomach and up his chest. He could feel her body pressed up against his as she ran her hands up and down his body over his flat stomach and down the front of his pants.

"Wait!" He said, pulling away from her and ripping his shirt as he did. "I can't do this."

"Come on, Brad! The girl's supposed to be the prude!" Linda said as she pulled his ripped shirt off him. "I know you want to; I can see it… in your eyes."

"Dean was my best friend," he managed to say as he undressed her with his mind. "I can't."

"Dean left me. Now I'm yours if you want me," she said as she seductively looked at him. "Go ahead and do what you're thinking. Trust me, the real thing is far better than you ever imagined!"

Brad slowly reached over and touched the front of her dress. His hand moved around the low collar and slowly started to undo the buttons one by one till it was completely opened. Her white lace bra shown brightly as his hands reached in and grabbed her chest. Pulling himself to her he kissed her on the lips and felt intensity he never imagined. Slowly his hands slid up around her neck and then to her hair where he pulled out the pin that held it and let it drop down over her shoulders.

"Let's go upstairs," she said as she got up from the sofa, taking his hand and leading him into the hallway to the stairs.

"I really don't think," he began as he followed her.

"Don't think," she said, kissing him again. "Just enjoy."

Linda led him down the hallway and into the guestroom and closed the door. She kissed him passionately on the lips, then helped him undress and climb into the bed. She finished unbuttoning her dress and slipped it off, letting it fall to the floor. She crossed the room, opened the drawer next to the night table and pulled out the nylon stockings. Then she climbed into bed and sat on his chest.

"You want to play a game Brad?" She asked as she smiled.

"What kind of game?" He nervously asked as she took his arm, and tied it with the stocking and then tied the stocking around the bed post. "I don't know about this."

"Trust me," she said as she repeated the procedure with the other arm. "This will be a night you will never forget."

"It already has been," he replied, closing his eyes as she tied up his feet.

"I'm glad you think so," she told him as she kissed his chest and then slowly started kissing up to his neck. She stopped with his neck and licked around his Adams apple and started sucking on the skin.

"Careful, I'm a little old for a hickey," he nervously joked as he tried to pull loose.

"Don't fight it Brad!" She ordered as she kissed down his shoulder blade, over to his arm and then slowly moved down his arm to his wrist. She placed her lips around it. She could feel the blood pumping inside his veins.

"Linda, stop! I want you to untie me!" He demanded.

"Just shut up!" She ordered as she pulled her head away from his arm and stared at him. Her eyes were full of fire and her face seemed to be slightly distorted. She looked almost like a predator!

"Get off of me now!" He ordered. Her evil look gave him chills and goose bumps up and down his arms. She smiled and turned away from him, her hand reaching over to the nightstand for the knife.

"Linda, No!" came a familiar scream from the other side of the room. "You promised me!"

Linda turned around and looked at the door. "Dean!" she cried as she jumped up off Brad and moved against the wall.

Brad looked around at the empty room and then over to her. Why did she call out Dean's name? He struggled with the restraints but had no luck. "Please Linda, let me go!"

"You promised me," Dean said, then disappeared.

"No!" Linda said breathing heavily. "I didn't mean to, I'm so hungry. Please don't be mad at me."

Brad looked around for Dean, but saw no one. A cold chill swept through the room. Linda caught her breath, then quickly went to the bed and started untying the stockings.

"Go, get out of my house and don't ever come back here!" She ordered as she picked up the lamp off the table and threw it across the room, smashing it against the wall.

Brad quickly put on his pants, grabbed his shoes and tore out of the room. Slamming the door, he ran down the steps, almost falling a couple of times. He started to stop to get his clothes in the living room but changed his mind. He just wanted to get the hell out of there. He threw open the door and ran smack into Kelly, knocking them both onto the porch floor.

"What the hell is going on in there?" Kelly said as she quickly picked herself up off the floor and watched as Brad quickly got up. "And what happened to your clothes?"

"Come on, we have to get out of here!" He said as he took her hand and practically dragged her off the porch and over to her car.

"Brad!" She said, stopping as they reached the vehicle. "What's wrong with you? You look like you've seen a ghost!"

"Kelly, don't argue with me, just get in your car and get out of here as fast as you can!" He said as he opened her door and pushed her in. "I'll meet you at your place and explain everything."

Brad slammed her door, then ran across the drive and jumped into his car. He reached for his keys, but they were gone. He started to panic. They must have fell out of his pants up in the bedroom. He looked up at the house and saw the shadow of Linda looking out the window, watching his every move. He remembered the spare set he had put in the ashtray.

"Thank you God!" He said as he opened the cover and pulled out the keys. A few seconds later he was down the driveway tailing Kelly, wishing she would speed up.

Linda watched as their cars drove down the drive and disappeared. She wondered how Kelly had known Brad was here, but her curiosity didn't last long. She couldn't believe she let him go. She was sure he'd tell everyone including Samantha, and who he wouldn't tell she would! The pains in Linda's stomach made her double over for a minute. She thought she was going to throw up. She took a deep breath and started out of the room stepping on Brad's keys.

"Ouch!" Linda shouted as she reached down, picked them up and held them in front of her face "Forget something Brad?"

A sinister smile crossed her face as she decided what exactly she was going to do with them. She crossed the room and slammed the door shut as another hunger pain hit her. She quickly went down to the master bedroom and entered the bathroom. Carefully sliced her finger open and drank the juicy red blood that flowed out. Forget what she had promised Dean, she needed blood and she needed it now!

---

"Samantha!" Brad yelled into the cell phone as she answered.

"Brad?" She asked in surprise. "What's wrong, what is it?"

"Call a locksmith and get him over to the house now! Linda has my keys and I don't want her to have access into the house!"

"She has your keys!" She repeated in horror. "What's going on Brad? What happened?"

"I'll tell you when I get home, just call the locksmith. I'm on my way to Kelly's to try to sort this mess out," he said and paused. "I guess I don't have to guess how she found out where I was, do I?"

"I'm sorry Brad, I was just worried," she began.

"You could have gotten her killed tonight," Brad said as he hung up the phone.

"What!" She said into the receiver. "Brad!"

Samantha hung the phone up and quickly looked through the phone book and dialed the locksmith's number. His promise to be there shortly did nothing to calm her nerves. She anxiously slid the chain lock into place before pulling a chair from the dining room table and blocked the door. Quietly she sat in front of the door and waited for him.

# Chapter 29 - Making plans...

Samantha slipped from her bed, put on her robe and went downstairs to the kitchen. This town was really getting to her. Everyone was running around like a bunch of crazy people! Since Dean died burglaries and car theft had risen all through town, and now someone had stolen bodies from the funeral home. She yawned as she entered the kitchen and laughed at Brad standing over the stove making breakfast in his boxer shorts.

"Good morning sexy," she laughed as she poured a glass of orange juice.

"Glad you finally noticed," he joked.

"Trust me Brad, its hard not to notice with you reminding me every day," she said as she got out the cereal.

"You sure have been in a good mood lately," he said, flipping his pancakes over. "Want one?"

"Not your cooking, no thanks! And yes, I have been in a good mood. Linda Edwards has been out of town the last few days. Didn't you notice it had stopped raining and the sun has been shining everyday?" She asked as she opened the refrigerator. "Where's the milk?"

"I just used it all in the pancakes. I thought we were not going to mention her name anymore," he said, not looking at her.

"Brad, when are you going to tell me what happened, it's been almost a week now," she asked leaning on the open refrigerator door.

"I don't want to talk about it. I thought you would be happy that I believe you now."

Samantha smiled and closed the door. It did feel good to finally have someone believe her. Others including Valerie said they believed her but deep down she wasn't so sure. Something happened with Brad at Linda's house the other day that made him a believer; she just wished she could get him to tell her what it was.

"I am glad that you believe me, I just wish you would tell me what convinced you."

"Maybe some other time. How do you know she's still out of town?" He asked.

"I heard Linda's housekeeper telling the girl at the grocery store she's suppose to be back late tonight. I guess I will have some pancakes," she told him as she put her bowl in the sink.

"I knew you could not resist the great chef's world famous pancakes," he said in a bad English accent, changing the topic of conversation.

"Just give me one of the damn things and spare me the theatrics!" She said as she handed him her plate. "Are you still on the decorating team for the fourth?"

"Yep. Want to help?" He asked.

"No! I told Pastor Peterson that I would take some of his wife's clothes over to charity. That's my good deed for the month," she said, wishing she had not volunteered.

"If you didn't want to do it why did you tell him you would?" Brad asked.

Samantha chuckled as Brad poured another pancake into the skillet, spilling most of the batter over the edge and on the stove. "I just felt bad about Mrs. Peterson falling down those basement stairs and dying. I thought it was the least I could do. After all she was my Sunday school teacher when I was a child."

"Don't you two look cute!" Valerie said as she entered the kitchen and put her keys on the table.

"You just getting in or did you leave early?" Samantha questioned, raising her eyebrow.

"I told you I had a breakfast meeting with the Mayor and some other idiots about the upcoming parade this Saturday. It's going to be here in days and we're not going to be ready. All those morons do is fight! I swear, if I wanted to hear all that bitching and belly aching I'd stay here and listen to you two. Brad, where the hell are your clothes? There are ladies in the room," she said, suddenly aware that he was in his underwear.

"You tell it girl!" Samantha said jokingly.

"Excuse me; what did you say you were, oh yes, a lady! I hate to be the one to remind you this, but this is my house! I don't bitch when you two run around in your underwear," he told her as he scooped the pancake up and put it in his plate. Valerie took the plate and sat down at the table by Samantha.

"I made that for me!" Brad exclaimed.

"Don't be such a baby! You can make another one. And when have you seen us running around here in our underwear?" She asked.

"Well you're welcome to start any time you want," he told her then turned back to the stove and started making another pancake and mess.

"You're just so kind," she told him as she used the last of the syrup, and then quickly put it back in the refrigerator before he noticed.

"I just want you two to feel at home," he said with a wicked smile.

The girls started eating their pancakes that Brad had made for them. Both had tasted better but decided not to say anything since he was actually the one cooking instead of them. Valerie continued to fill them in on the morning's events as Brad finished up his own pancakes.

"You know Val; I think it's great that Brad is so proud of his body that he can show it off like this. A lot of guys would be embarrassed to run around with a big hole in their shorts like that," Samantha said, winking at her.

"What are you talking about?" Brad asked, looking over his back.

"You're right, it is kind of romantic having the moon shining by the table," Valerie added.

"Don't be shy now! It's a little late!" Samantha laughed and yelled after him as he left the room.

"You're terrible!" Valerie joked.

"A girl has got to have fun sometimes," she added. "You want to split his pancake?"

*the Murderess of RIDGECLIFFE MANOR*

"No!" She said quickly as she watched Samantha start to take it and then stop.

"Yeah, that would be really mean wouldn't it?" She asked sitting back down. "Besides they weren't that good. How do you screw up boxed pancake batter?"

"Who the hell knows, oh, before I forget, the Brook's house on Third Street went up for sale this week. I know how much you always liked that place," Valerie told her as she jumped up and turned the burner off under Brad's pancakes.

"And just what do you think I would buy it with? The insurance Company didn't pay for my last house. I now own a very expensive vacant lot!" She reminded her.

"Well you might consider going back to work!" Brad said as he came back into the kitchen wearing sweat pants. "You two think you're real funny, don't you? There was no hole."

"We knew that, but you didn't, sugar butt!" Valerie said smiling.

Both women broke out in hard laughter as Brad pretended he didn't hear them. Normally he would have gotten angry at their teasing him but it had been so long since he had heard any laughter around the place that he decided it was best to let it slide. He would get even with them later!

"It was kinda funny," Samantha added.

"Here I give you a roof over your head and treat you like my own sisters and look at the thanks I get," he said, trying to sound hurt.

"We were treating you just like we would a brother, right Val?" she asked as Valerie shook her head.

"Did anything actually get accomplished in your meeting this morning?" Brad asked Valerie, changing the subject.

"Not really. It was so boring; I could have had a better time having a root canal! I don't know why I ever volunteered. They have hired some guy to check out the city's utility lines under the downtown. It seems the ever popular Linda Edwards has donated money to help update and bring the city into the future of technology. We're so lucky," Valerie told them.

"She's so caring, we are really lucky to have her," Samantha interrupted.

"The guy's totally weird! Kinda sexy with his just out of prison look. He looks familiar, but I don't know where I would have seen him before."

"Then why did you hire him?" Brad asked, reaching into the refrigerator and grabbing the empty syrup bottle, then throwing it in the trash. "Thanks a lot for saving me some."

"We didn't, he works for Linda Edwards. She said he was the best. Here, you can have what's left of mine," Valerie said handing him her plate.

"Did you check him out?" Samantha asked, becoming concerned.

"Yeah," Valerie said smiling. He's hot, in a dirty kind of way. Oh Sam, that boy did know how to fill out some jeans."

"Enough!" Brad yelled out. "I'm trying to eat!"

"Did anyone think to check his references?" Samantha asked smiling.

"No. He's not doing anything, just looking things over and making update suggestions, kinda of like an inspection type thing. Why?" She asked.

"Because if Linda is involved, it can't be good! Some one should be with him," Samantha told her.

"I'm not crawling through those nasty tunnels. God only knows what's down there. Besides, what on earth could he be doing in there, molesting sewer rats?" she asked as she put her glass in the sink.

"Knowing her, anything. She's been awfully quiet lately. I think she's up to something," Samantha said, trying to keep her good mood from slipping away.

"That's not what Laverne said at the funeral home," Brad added.

Brad had held in the information about Linda loosing it at the funeral home because just mentioning her name around the house seemed to cause major damage, but since they had brought her up he figured it was safe to tell them what he had heard.

"God Brad, you're like an old gossip lady." Samantha laughed, but eager to hear what he had to say.

"Oh, dish the dirt baby!" Valerie said excitedly.

"She said the day of visitation Linda came a couple hours early and was totally flipping out. She was talking and yelling at Dean's body. Laverne said she could not understand what she was saying, but she was really going at it. Even threw a chair across the room. Then when

Laverne called to tell her Dean's body had been stolen when the funeral home was vandalized she really hit the roof. Told Laverne if she didn't find the body in a week she would take legal action! Laverne said she yelled for half an hour," Brad told them. "And the other day when I went over there she was totally flipping out. It's giving me chills talking about it now."

"Oh Brad baby you're better at spreading gossip than I am," Valerie said winking at him.

"Yes, but that does sound like the Linda Edwards we all know and hate," Samantha said. "Brad, what did she do the other day to you?"

"I don't want to talk about it," he said as he started eating the pancake that Valerie had left him.

"Then stop bringing it up!" She demanded.

"Did they ever find any of the bodies?" Valerie asked.

"Are you kidding, with that new Sheriff we have? That guy doesn't know his butt from a hole in the wall," Samantha added.

"I heard from a good source he was sitting having a bowel movement in the urinal at city hall yesterday! Really, a friend of mine who has jury duty went in and saw it. I swear!" Valerie said laughing.

"Oh Val! Come on!" Samantha said laughing.

"I swear! I could never make anything up that good," Valerie told her.

"I don't know about that," Brad interrupted. "But I do know that Laverne said it would be at least two more weeks before they would get everything replaced from the burglary."

"Why do you think they took the bodies? I mean what on earth are they going to do with them?" Valerie asked.

"Word around town is that it might have something to do with the occult," Brad said.

"We don't have any of that around here, do we?" Valerie asked, getting chills just thinking about it.

"According to the news they're every where!" Brad said as he finished his breakfast.

"Would you two wake up? This has nothing to do with the occult! It has Linda Edwards name written all over it! That crazy bitch is up to something. I don't know what and I'm not sure I want to either," Samantha said as she got up and started doing the dishes.

"I thought you said she was out of town?" Brad asked, bringing her some dishes off the table.

"She didn't leave till a couple of days after the burglary. Besides, she probably hired someone to do it. She wouldn't want to break a nail you know," Samantha said holding up her fingers and waving them around.

Valerie laughed and held hers up, copying Samantha's moves and noticed she had a chip in one of hers. She cussed out, trying to figure out how she had done that. Brad made a joke, only to get hit with her napkin in the face. He made a smart comment as he picked it up and threw it away. Samantha laughed and sighed. Things really did seem normal again, but for how long she didn't know.

"You know, I could understand her taking Dean away. But what would she want with the other two bodies?" Valerie asked she helped clear the table.

"Probably just wanted to add them to her collection," Samantha told them as she wiped off the counter.

"Can we please change the subject?" Brad asked.

"Oh my God! I almost forgot to tell you. Diane Shiane from WDEK news in St. Louis is going to be here covering the parade on the fourth. Isn't that cool?" Valerie said excitedly.

"Diane Shiane? Are you kidding, that woman is about as intelligent as a stack of bricks. I hardly think her arrival here will benefit us that much," Samantha commented from the kitchen.

"That's not very nice. I happen to think she's cute. And no one can tell a story like she can," Brad said smiling.

"You hit it there! All that woman does is tell stories, false ones! She doesn't have a clue what's going on around her! She could be there to report on a fire where several people died and she would be concerned that the fireman's uniforms don't match the fire trucks and that the city should consider a fund raiser for new ones!" Samantha said as they entered the living room. She's obviously sleeping with someone."

"I remember that one!" Valerie said, following them. "I laughed until I cried"

"You two are making that up," Brad laughed.

"My favorite one was when she interviewed the Vice President when he was visiting St. Louis on the reelection campaign. Instead of asking him all the political stuff all the other reporters were asking, she asked him what he thought about making those flushable tissue toilet seat covers mandatory in all public bathrooms! The poor man didn't know what to say. He probably went back to Washington and told the president we were idiots down here," Valerie said, laughing hysterically.

"I remember that one too!" Samantha added. "The poor guy was speechless! And the look he gave her was priceless!"

"You two are terrible. You should be ashamed of yourselves. I think you two are jealous," Brad said, defending the newswoman.

"How did you guess? It's been my life long dream to be a dumb white woman!" Valerie laughed.

"It's just that I have never heard you two say a nice thing about another woman before," he stated.

"Oh Val, you know what we should send her over to interview Linda Edwards! That would be a hoot!" Samantha said laughing so hard she almost fell out of her chair.

Even though she was laughing on the outside, Samantha was terrified on the inside. Linda Edwards was about to strike again; she could feel it in her bones. It would be soon! Maybe even tonight when she returned from Kansas City. That woman was completely on the edge and was capable of doing anything. She wished that Linda would just leave town now! Before it was too late. But deep down she knew that would not happen. All she could do was sit back and wait for it to happen and hope she would be alive after it was over!

"Do you think Linda Edwards will come to the parade?" Samantha asked.

"Probably. She's practically paying for it!" Valerie said, still laughing.

"Why?" Brad asked.

Samantha did not answer; she just turned her head and looked out the window. That's it! Linda was going to do something to her at the parade! But what? She would have to be very careful around her on Saturday and stay far away from her. Linda would not get to her again!

Linda waited patiently on the front porch for Alex's arrival. Just like last time he was late! The cool late night summer breeze blew in off the marshes, helping her to stay calm and relax. These last few days in Kansas City had been a nightmare. She hated going back there and stirring up all the bad memories she had left there, but she had to take precautions and cover herself if this plan did not work. She had hidden a great deal of cash in the Kansas City house, so if she had to run she would have money to live on. In the distance a set of headlights turned in the drive and started up.

"Good evening boss lady," Alex said as he got out of the beat up car.

"You're late again," she told him as he reached the porch.

"I could leave, but then you would never get to use this," he said, holding up a glass jar of liquid.

"Is that what I think it is?" She asked, smiling at the jar like a child with candy held in front of them.

"The one and only. Be very careful; you spill this on your hand and it will eat all the way to the bone," he said handing it to her. "I have something else you might find very interesting."

"What?" She asked, looking at the control device he was now holding. "Is that my little gift for Hagan Cove?"

"Flip this switch on and it activates, then push the green one and kiss Hagan Cove good bye! I rigged up the gas lines under the main street. I would not go near your windows when you pull the switch," he informed her as he leaned on the porch rail.

Alex watched as she looked the device over, smiling like a satisfied customer. She gently ran her manicured fingers over all the buttons. He could tell that she couldn't wait to push the button. "What a psychotic bitch," he thought to himself and continued watching her.

"This place is almost five miles away from Hagan Cove. Will I really be able to feel the blast all the way over here?" she asked with a wicked smile.

"I don't think you understand. There are enough explosives under that place to shatter every window all the way to Fayette, where I will be at the post office picking up my money out of the post office box. Am I correct in thinking so?" He asked.

"Absolutely!" she said laughing. "Box sixty eight. It's under guard until the big bang, so you better not be screwing me over or you will never get the chance to spend it. Do you understand?"

"Listen lady. You are a deranged psychopath. You are blowing up an entire town and killing every body, and you don't even have the slightest touch of remorse. Do you honestly think I would chance screwing you over and having you after me? I just hope that you realize I can be a force to reckon with as well in case you attempt to try to screw me out of my money," he told her.

"Your money will be there. I may be a murderer, but I always keep my promises. Are you sure no one will go down in those tunnels and find the explosives?" She asked.

"I seriously doubt it. Those things are nasty down there. Big old rats and mice. No, I don't think you have to worry your pretty little head about it getting discovered," he informed her.

"Very good. I'm very pleased with your work. Thank you, Alex. I strongly recommend that you disappear and never come around here again. And never tell anyone what you did! That is a sure way to get caught," she said as she led him down off the porch, walking him to his car.

"No my dear, thank you," he said as he got in and shut the door. "Pleasure doing business with you."

Linda watched the car drive off down the drive, then looked down at the device she held in her hand. Something about that man seemed awfully familiar. His posture or maybe his looks, she couldn't tell. She quickly wiped it from her mind. In just a few short days Hagan Cove would be a memory. Nothing will be left, she thought with a smile. She went back into the house and turned off the front porch light. She was tired but she had something else to do before bed, someone she needed desperately to see. She went upstairs to the third floor bedroom where Dean's body was lying in the bed.

"It's almost complete sweetheart," she said as she sat on the corner of the bed and ran her hands through his hair. "Are you warm enough yet? I know you were upset with me for leaving you in the freezer so long, but I could not take a chance of Stella finding you. You know how nutty she is. I just thought I would tell you that everything is all set and ready to go for Saturday. All we have to do is get Samantha to come out here. With the explosion in town, I can't exactly go there. I'm sure I'll find a way to get her here."

Linda kissed him softly on the lips, then got off the bed and crossed the room to the door. He looked so peaceful sleeping there. It was good to have him home again. As she started to turn off the light she heard a noise, or more like a voice. Dean was speaking to her! She quickly turned back to him.

"What?" She asked, walking over to him. "You think I should get Stella out of town? You're right she has been a good and faithful employee. All right, let me think. I'll send her on a trip somewhere. I'm glad you thought about that. Good night, sweetheart," she said as she left the room and started back downstairs to the master bedroom.

---

Samantha stirred in bed as she desperately tried to go to sleep, but something deep inside her would not allow it. The sleeping pill she took thirty minutes ago should have kicked in by now, she thought to herself. Every night since Linda had returned she had not been able to sleep. After lying there another ten minutes she got up and went into the kitchen for a drink of water, careful not to awaken the others. She took her glass and went out on the balcony, leaning over the rail she looked out into the night.

Something was very wrong, but she could not detect what it was. There was a movement in the bushes. A dark figure walked down the driveway below, not noticing her above. Once again she felt the uneasiness that he was familiar. Something about his walk and the way he carried himself. The blood all drained from her face as she gripped the rail to balance herself. It was Dean!

"Dean, stop!" She yelled, but he paid no attention as he continued to move forward.

Samantha ran into her room and threw on some jeans and a tee shirt and quickly pulled on her shoes and was out the door in just a matter of seconds. She could still see the outline of his body ahead. She ran to catch up but could never actually meet up with him.

"Dean, stop! It's me Samantha!" She yelled down the street after him.

She continued to run after him until they were downtown standing by city hall where his office used to be. The downtown was completely deserted this time of night. It was just the two of them. He stopped and sat at the top of the steps by the ornate lamppost. He put his hands over his face covering his eyes. She slowly moved towards him stopping at the foot of the steps.

"I knew you could not be dead. I just knew it!" She said with tears in her eyes. She wanted to run to him, but something deep inside her told her to stay back.

Dean pulled his hands away from his eyes and ran them through his hair and leaned back against the closed doors of the courthouse. His eyes were filled with pain as he stared ahead. Even though she was talking to him he apparently did not hear her. She reached out to touch his hand but her hand went through him. She jumped back, startled and almost fell down the stairs.

"Dean, what happened to you?" She said, her voice shaking.

He just looked out into the street without responding. A single blood filled tear formed in his left eye, then ran down his cheek. She followed his gaze and looked down into the street below. It was now filled with people. Friends and neighbors who lived around town. What were they doing out at this time of night? She walked down the steps into the crowd that had mysteriously formed on both sides of the sidewalk all around the town square. There was dead silence throughout the town even though it was now filled with hundreds of people like someone had put the entire city on mute!

"What's going on here?" She asked herself, her voice echoing throughout the town. She reached over and tapped the deputy officer on the shoulder. "Excuse me!"

Samantha jumped back and screamed as he turned around. His face was decayed. Others turned around upon hearing her screams and they too were in the same state of decay. She turned and ran up the stairs back to Dean, but he was gone. The others had turned away from her and were now watching the street as several silent marching bands and corpses of clowns paraded down the street.

"Oh no!" She said quietly to herself. "It's the birthday bash parade that's supposed to be going on tomorrow! But why is everyone dead?"

Samantha spotted Dean again as he walked through the crowd and into the street. He looked up and stared directly at her. His eyes were filled with so much pain that it broke her heart. Suddenly there was a loud explosion as the streets exploded. She gasped as all the buildings in the town caught on fire! Glass and brick exploding everywhere, covering the townspeople. One by one the buildings collapsed around the town, burying the people and catching them on fire. None of them moved, they just stood there and let it happen. She ran out into the street looking for Dean but could not find him. She screamed his name as loud as she could. Her voice echoed into the silent but deadly night. It was all clear to her now that Linda Edwards was going to destroy the whole town!

"Dean!" She screamed again just as another blast exploded around her, covering her with flames. She screamed in agony.

"Samantha! Wake up!" Brad yelled, shaking her.

"What's wrong?" Valerie yelled, running into the room.

Samantha jumped up from the bed, ran to the window and looked out at the sunny morning outside. She wiped her sweat covered forehead with her palm. Her rapid breathing slowly started to calm down. "We have to stop the parade! We have to get everyone out of town!"

"Samantha, calm down, it was just a dream!" Brad said as he sat on the bed.

"No, you don't understand! Linda's going to blow up the town! We have to get everyone out!" She screamed.

"Oh Sam, You were just having another nightmare. Linda wouldn't do something like that. She's mean, but not that mean!" Valerie said as she went over to comfort her.

"You don't know her like I do!" Samantha said to her in desperation.

"Sam, that's completely crazy. Why would she do something like that?" Brad asked.

"I don't know, Dean came to me last night and led me to the parade! Everyone was dead! He wanted me to know so I could warn people! Don't you see!" she pleaded.

Samantha tried hard to explain every little detail she had seen in her dream to them. She should have known they wouldn't believe her, they hadn't believed anything else she had told them before. She pleaded with them to help her stop the parade before it was too late.

"I think we need to call your doctor. He said to call if any more nightmares happened," Brad said as he went over to the phone and picked it up.

"No! Don't you dare call him! We have to warn everybody!" She yelled.

"Samantha, just think! Linda Edwards is a guest speaker at the ribbon cutting ceremony. She's going to be right in the middle of the parade. She isn't going to blow it up with her there. Come on, use your head," Brad said as he sat back on the bed.

"I don't know, but I do know Dean was here last night to warn me!" She said, looking at Valerie for support.

"Dean is dead! You were there, remember!" Brad reminded her. "What are you seeing ghosts now?"

"Okay Brad, that's enough. Let's give her time to think a bit, and she will realize it was just a dream. Remember, it's just like those ones you had at home when you thought Linda was there when she really wasn't. You've had to deal with a lot of pressure lately. It's no wonder you have all these bad dreams again," Valerie said as she led her back to the bed.

"It was so real," Samantha said, fighting back the tears.

"Why don't you take a shower and get cleaned up and Val and I will make you some breakfast," Brad said as he got up from the bed and started for the door.

"We have to stop the parade! I don't know how, but we have to," Samantha told them.

"Sweetheart, we can't stop the parade, it's going on in less than five hours. You'll see, everything will be fine," Valerie said as she got up. "When did you start sleeping in your clothes?"

"What?" She asked quickly looking down.

Samantha glanced down at what she was wearing. It was not the nightgown she put on before she went to bed, but the clothes she had changed into when she saw Dean. He really had been here! She had to stop Linda! He had come here to warn her. She just smiled at the other two and watched them leave. It was no use telling them anything; they did not believe her. Linda Edwards was going to destroy the town and it was up to her to stop her! Something deep inside her told her that by the end of the day either her or Linda would be dead. Samantha hoped it wasn't her.

# Chapter 30 - Revenge!

The sun glistened through the trees that lined the streets on the way into town, giving it a beautiful post card look. People were working in their yards, all excited about the festivities going on this afternoon. Deep behind their smiling faces were murderers! They had murdered Dean by forcing him to give up his job and now she was going to murder them. Linda pulled the car up in front of the closed bank and got out.

"Good Morning," an elderly woman said as she passed her.

Linda greeted her and went on to her business. The street posts were all decorated with red, white, and blue banners, put up by the town decorating committee. Most of the stores had "Happy Birthday Hagan Cove" plastered all over their windows. The parade was still three hours away and already the crowds were gathering. Linda walked up to the bank and waited for the plump man to unlock the door.

"I really appreciate you opening up for me on such short notice. I decided last night it would be much better to give the mayor and city council a real cashier's check rather than some phony piece of paper," she said as she entered the bank.

"No problem, I'm really worried about you carrying so much money around," he said as he sat behind his desk, and started making out the cashier's check. "All you need to do is put the name of the city at the top and hand it to them."

"This is small change compared to what I carry around with me. I do thank you for your concern though, I'll finish filling it out when I get home, Mayor Actonia told me to label it under a certain name and I forgot what it was," Linda lied. This money was going to Alex, not this stupid city, she thought to herself. Besides, it would be blown away by the time she was supposed to hand it over.

"It's really wonderful that you think so much of our community to make such a large donation. It is something that everyone will be able to enjoy for many years," he commented, smiling to her.

"Well I have to admit it is a little selfish, after all I live here too and I plan to enjoy the benefits that this money is going to bring also. Thank you, Mr. Duncan, for your time. My bank in Kansas City will be making a transfer of funds into my account here on Monday, would you please call when it arrives?" She lied again. This place would not be here Monday.

"No problem, enjoy the parade," he said as he unlocked the door.

"Actually I'm looking forward to the fire works afterwards. Nothing like a little holiday spirit," Linda said as she left the bank and got into her car.

Quickly she glanced around the town one last time then drove off. This would be the last time she would see Hagan Cove, or these miserable back stabbing people again. They took Dean's job away and destroyed him, now she was going to take their town away and destroy them! The red sports car headed towards Fayette to the post office where she promised to leave the money for Alex.

"Good bye Hagan Cove!" she said as the car passed city limits.

---

"Good Morning Saint Louie! This is Diane Shiane reporting to you live from Hagan Cove, Missouri on this beautiful sunny day. We're here to celebrate this great city's some hundredth birthday. I'm not sure which one but I know it in the hundreds. I know it just seems like yesterday that they were using feathers to sign those rolled up papers and making it a city! Though we do dress a lot better today than they did back then. Just imagine folks how much better our society would be today if they had our keen fashion sense way back then!" the perky little blonde newswoman said, smiling into the camera.

"Oh good Lord, she's been sniffing her hair spray again," April complained to Peggy, the camera operator. "Ignorant bitch!"

"Cut!" Peggy yelled as she put the camera down. "Diane sweetie, that was great! Why don't you go take a break and get something to drink and mingle with your fans. Stay away from that blue icy cone stuff though, remember it makes your tongue blue and that doesn't look good on the camera. We don't want to scare our viewers."

The two women watched as the wardrobe lady helped her out of her microphone. Diane mumbled a few things about April that they couldn't hear before she turned and walked off. Peggy figured it was probably for the best, the last thing she needed today was another fight between the two of them!

"That stupid bitch! That should be me in front of the camera not pulling all these damn cords around," April said as she flung one of the large black camera cords into the back of the van. "One of these days, I'm going to take one and wrap it around her skinny little neck!"

"April!" Peggy said, grabbing her by the shoulders and looking wide eyed at her, "How many times have I told you not to talk when I'm rolling. Everything you said went on tape! Now I have to do it again. Do you know how long it took to get her to learn her lines?"

"I can't help it, I'm sick of this shit! Everybody knows she's sleeping with the station owner. I mean, come on, she can barely walk and talk at the same time. That should be my job!" April said in her defense.

"I know she's a little empty on the top but we have to put up with her unless we want to go stand in the unemployment line. And besides the viewers seem to like her," Peggy said, dropping her arms off April's shoulders.

"Oh good lord, look at her now!" April said to Peggy. "You told her not to get the blue snow cone so the dizzy bitch got red. Look at those lips! You'll be able to see them three channels away!"

Diane gave April the best 'drop dead' look she could and went on eating her snow cone. This was one of the things she liked about covering the little town events like this was all the great food. She had already made a mental note about where she wanted to eat lunch.

"Good morning, I'm Mayor Lozetta Actonia and this is my assistant parade coordinator Valerie Fischer," the mayor said as the two women came upon the news team.

"Hi, I'm Peggy and you of course know Diane Shiane," Peggy told them as they shook hands.

"Yes, it nice to finally meet you, I watch your special reports every night. By the way, I love your lipstick," Lozetta told Diane. "We would like you to set up over in the grand stand by the court house, that's where most of today's ceremony will be. We were supposed to get a check donation today but our sponsor is ill, so she will not be here but I'm sure there are plenty of other things to report about," Lozetta said with a smile.

"Linda Edwards isn't going to be here?" Valerie asked suddenly speaking up.

"No, she canceled, said she has the flu," Lozetta said, getting irritated that Valerie interrupted her.

"Oh my God!" Valerie said as she ran from the others to find a phone.

"I'll be ready for my interview shortly," Lozetta said quickly, bringing all the attention back to her.

Valerie ran as fast as she could in her heels, through the courthouse and into the mayor's office. What if Samantha's dream last night had been a premonition of what was to come? It happened on those reality shows on television all the time. Before when Linda Edwards was going to be here she knew there was no way she would blow the town up, but now that she wouldn't be there it was a different story. She picked up the phone and dialed Brad's number.

"Sam, it's me, Val! Listen, I don't have long, but I think you might be on to something. Linda Edwards canceled her appearance at the ceremony today!" Valerie said breathlessly into the phone.

"Oh no! Are you sure! I can't believe this! We have to warn every body," Samantha said in a daze.

"It's too late for that, no one would believe us! I bet that man she hired that worked on the tunnels set it up!" she said, looking around and trying to think of a way to stop it.

"What are we going to do?" Samantha asked.

"Is Brad there?" She asked her, coming up with a plan.

"No! Max called and they had a cash offer on the Kellerman farm, so he had to run all the way out there. He's going to be gone all day. He was furious that he was going to miss everything. Why?" Samantha asked, fear in her voice.

"Okay, let me think," she paused for a minute. "No one will believe us if we run up and down the street yelling at them, so will have to go search the tunnels ourselves."

"I thought you said you wouldn't climb through those things!" Samantha reminded her.

"I know but someone has to stop her!" Valerie said, still out of breath.

"I have a better idea; let's get to her before she does it! Pick me up, I'm getting dressed," Samantha said as she hung up the phone and rushed into her room to change clothes.

Tears glazed over her eyes as she pulled her hair back into a ponytail. She wiped her eyes with the back of her hand and ordered herself to stop. Things like this weren't suppose to happen in real life, especially in her life. How were they going to stop Linda? If only Dean was here. He would know what to do. He had been here last night to warn her. Hopefully it wasn't too late.

Valerie rushed into the house and told Samantha she would be ready in a minute. As told a minute later she came out of her room, no longer in her dress but now in jeans and a tee shirt. Both women said nothing as they rushed toward the front door, but were stopped by the sudden ringing of the phone. Samantha looked at the caller id and saw Linda's name. She nervously reached down and picked it up.

"Oh good, you answered. It's me Linda. I hoped I could find you at this number," Linda said. Her voice sounded strange.

"Why are you calling me? You're the last person I expected to hear from," Samantha said coldly.

"I'm not sure really, I just don't have anyone to talk to anymore. I think we need to talk about what happened the other night. Maybe we can put the past behind us. Who knows, maybe even try to be friends," Linda said without much emotion.

"I seriously doubt that! But you are right about one thing; we need to talk about what happened the other night. Why don't you come over here and we'll talk. We can watch the parade from the balcony," Samantha said trying to bait her.

"No, I can't bare to leave. I don't feel like running into people, why don't you come here?" Linda asked.

"Fine!" Samantha said angrily. "I'll be there shortly."

Linda did not reply, just hung up. Samantha followed. She knew

Linda had no plans to clear the air and be friends. This was part of her plan. Some how they had to stop her before it was too late. If only she could have gotten her into town. There was no way Linda would blow the city up if she was in it.

"What did she want?" Valerie asked as she shut the door and started down the sidewalk to the car.

"She wants me to pay her a visit. We better come up with a plan fast!" Samantha said as she got into the car.

---

Police Captain Steve Willis turned his rented car into the city limits of Hagan Cove. Instantly he smiled and relaxed even though the long drive from Kansas City had worn him out. He definitely saw why Linda had chosen this place. It was so beautiful and nicely decorated for the Fourth of July. It had been several years since he had a vacation, and since Linda was in town last weekend and forgot to visit him, he decided he would just pay her a visit.

There were still some unanswered questions about Michael Williams's accident. And with this real estate agent here in town writing him all these bizarre emails about Linda's possible involvement in a killing spree he decided maybe he should talk to her some more.

The more he thought about the things she wrote the more he began to question the facts surrounding Linda's missing husband and his mistress. It seemed impossible knowing Linda as long as he has that she would do something so sinister, but it could have happened. He felt guilty that he did not call first but she would have just tried to talk him out of coming here like she did a couple of months ago. No, it would be fun to surprise her.

The rental car swiftly pulled into the closest parking spot he could find. Steve tucked his shirt back into his jeans as he walked into the crowd of people standing on the sidewalk watching as the big parade started. It in no way compared to the parades they had in Kansas City, but the people seemed to enjoy it.

The lady standing next to him started carrying on a conversation with him like she had known him all her life. He learned from their conversation that she owned a jewelry store and that her name was Regina. Her twin boys were in the marching band that was coming up at the end of the parade. Finally he interrupted her and asked for directions to Linda's house, only to get several questions asked in return before she told him how to get there. One thing you could count on in a small town is everybody getting into your business.

Judging from what Regina told him, Linda had made quite a name for herself here. Her reputation was about as bad as it had been in Kansas City. The one thing that bothered him the most was this Dean guy that she told him about. Linda had neglected to tell him about him. Since he was dead, he wasn't going to be a problem, but what scared him is what other things she could be hiding.

He let the thought slip away as he smiled and thought about seeing her again, listen to her talk her way out of yet another sticky situation. Linda always had a logical answer for everything. It seemed no matter how far off it was, she could convince you it was true. She should have been a lawyer.

He wrote down the directions Regina gave him, then said good bye and started walking to his car. The birds overhead seemed to be humming in tune with the beat of the band marching in the parade. Nothing like the fresh air of the country, he thought as he got into his car and headed to see Linda. Boy was she going to be surprised to see him!

"Look out Linda, here I come," he said with a smile as he started out towards Ridgecliffe Manor.

---

"Where in the hell are you!" Linda yelled into the empty room as she paced around waiting for Samantha.

Time was running out, the parade was just starting and everyone would be downtown. Wouldn't you know that Samantha would try to screw this up too. Maybe she should have let her die in the explosion also. No! It was going to be fun killing her and watching that miserable bitch die. Outside a car door slammed.

"It's about time; I thought you changed your mind...," Linda started, suddenly stopping when she noticed that Samantha was not alone. "I didn't know you were bringing someone with you. Hi Valerie."

"I hope you don't mind my tagging along. I didn't have anything else to do and when Sam said she was coming out here I just had to come and see what you did with the place. It looks great!" Valerie said, pretending to be impressed.

"I just wish Samantha would have told me she was bringing someone with her. I'm not much in the mood for company," Linda said, trying to hide her anger.

"I'm sorry, I should have called. That way you could have gotten more drugs and had another hole dug, right?" Samantha asked sarcastically. It was amazing that with Valerie here she actually felt like they could take Linda on.

"I see you're still delirious. Everyone knows it was Duke, not me, that tried to kill you," Linda said as she went to the bar and poured herself a drink. "I'd offer you one but as you told me the other day you would die of thirst first. What a pleasant thought."

"I thought you were sick?" Valerie asked, changing the subject.

Linda tried hard to hide the fact that she was furious right now. It figured that Samantha would pull something to make this afternoon difficult! Guess she would just have to handle Valerie personally as well. "I just did not feel like being in front of a lot of people. I assume the parade drew a large crowd?" She asked.

"A few thousand I would say, how about you Sam?" Valerie asked.

"At least. You know something funny though, Valerie and I noticed on the way over here that there were a lot of police coming in and out of those underground cable tunnels under the city," Samantha lied.

The two women watched the color almost drain from Linda's face upon hearing her words. Samantha had hit the nail with the hammer on that one! Maybe they had a chance to actually win this one; she just wished she had some back up coming!

"What!" Linda asked, holding her drink tightly. "The utility tunnels?"

"Yeah, you know the ones that run under the downtown that we were looking at expanding last week. I don't know what was going on but there were cops from the other counties there also. I think that one was the FBI," Valerie added, watching Linda very closely.

"Linda, are you all right?" Samantha asked, trying not laugh at Linda's sudden look of terror. It was working!

"I'm fine, thank you. I just haven't been feeling like myself lately. I have a blood disease and I've had to cut back on my medication," Linda said, opening the drawer behind the bar.

"I do hope there is a cure," Samantha said sarcastically.

"Yes, oddly enough there is. I eliminate everybody that gets in my way," Linda said as she pulled out the gun and fired at Valerie before she had time to get out of the way. Valerie fell instantly to the floor in a pool of her own blood, her blank eyes staring out into space.

"Valerie, oh God, what have I done?" Samantha screamed as she started to run to her friend.

Samantha checked Valerie for a pulse, relieved to find out she still had one! She tried hard to think what her next move would be. There was no room for a mistake now. She had to bring Linda down today!

"Get up, you can't help her now, besides you have already cost me enough time as it is!" Linda shouted and pointed the gun at her. "Recognize this gun? You should, it's the one you left here the other night when I, I mean Duke, buried you alive. Boy, things would have been different if you would have just died like a normal person! But no, you had to just pop up and come back to life!"

"Linda, please put the gun down, Valerie needs my help!" Samantha pleaded.

"That bitch is as good as dead. And so are you. This time you don't have Dean or anyone else to save you!" Linda laughed.

"It's not too late to stop all this. I'll help you, please, just put the gun down," Samantha said, trying to think her way out of this mess.

"You know Samantha; you have to be the stupidest woman I know. After all the things that I have done to you and yet you still come out here? I don't know if you're a glutton for punishment or if you enjoy it. In any case, it's over today. Before I kill you though I want you to witness something. Actually, I want it to be the last thing you remember," Linda said with a wicked laugh.

Samantha's heart was beating so fast she thought it was going to explode out of her chest. She had to agree with Linda, her coming out here after everything that had happened was one of the stupidest things she had done. Unfortunately when she learned her dream was coming true the only thing she thought about was stopping her.

"Call it my last goodbye gift for you."

"What is it?" Samantha asked, afraid she already knew what she was going to show her.

"This," Linda said as she pulled into view a small device and flipped a switch that turned it on.

"What is that?" Samantha asked although she already knew.

"It's my special gift to the city of Hagan Cove. They took Dean's job away, which ultimately ended his life. Now I'm going to take away their city and end their lives," Linda said laughing.

"Oh my God! It was true! Everything Dean showed me last night is really going to happen!" She said to herself but Linda overheard.

"What are you talking about? Dean was not with you. He's dead. You're lying!" Linda laughed.

That's it, Dean! He would be her savior even after death. Linda was so obsessed with him and if she was going to bring her down then she had to attack her with Dean's memory. It was her only chance at stopping this.

"That's what you think. Dean did not die. We just needed you to think he did. We have been lovers for years; he was using you so we could steal your money. The plan was to make you fall in love with him and then we would get your money. And you fell for it! Hook, line and sinker! He'll be here any minute, when we left he was gathering up the others to arrest you!" Samantha said managing a smile.

Samantha was hoping to mess with Linda's mind long enough to make her forget about blowing the town up and give her time to get the switch away. It might not have been the best plan, but it was the only one she could think on such short notice.

"No!" Linda screamed and cocked the gun. "Dean loved me! He never slept with you, he told me. You just can't stand the fact that we made love almost every night that we knew each other, and finally he stopped thinking of you. You're pathetic. All you do is lie! Dean never left the house last night. I would have known it if he did."

"Left the house last night?" Samantha thought. Linda's words skipped around her brain as she tried to make sense of them. "You don't know everything he does. Once after he had been here he came to my house and told me that having to have sex with you made him sick. He said your body repulsed him. You dressed and acted like a big city whore! He also said you were as lousy in bed as you were a cook!"

"No!" Linda said quietly. Her breath grew faster as her eyes filled with tears. The gun in her hand shook. "He would never say that! He told me he loved me!"

"He lied! He despised you!" Samantha continued.

"He was just like the others. He never loved me. He never loved me!" She whispered through the tears.

"I'm sorry, but it's true. You're the type of person no one could love. Not Dean, your husband, even your own family. Why don't you just do yourself a favor and kill yourself. No one will miss you. Just do it," Samantha pushed.

Sweat formed on her forehead as Samantha kept pushing her ever evolving plan to work. She had to convince Linda that she and Dean were after her money; he didn't love her, never did, and make her kill herself. If she killed herself this would all be over!

"You must think I'm as stupid as you are!" Linda said suddenly laughing. "That was a pretty good show you just put on. I thought my performance was better though, did you like the tears? But I happen to know it's all a lie! Dean is dead! You have seen way to many movies if you thought you could mess with my mind and get this device away."

"No, he's not! Don't you think it's funny that his body is missing? We made it look like a burglary. That way he could leave. He's been hiding out at Brad's house, if you don't believe me just come with me. I'll show you," she pleaded.

"That's a good one Samantha, but there's just one small problem. I'm the one that stole the body and two others. Not you. And if you don't believe me, go up to the third floor guest room. You will find him resting peacefully," Linda said trying hard to stay focused. Samantha's game playing was ridiculously funny.

"It's not too late to call this off. We can go back to the way it used to be. I mean, come on, who would believe me that you were going to blow up the town. I could say that Valerie's shooting was an accident. I won't tell a soul! I swear, God as my witness! Let me go and put that device down and we will forget this ever happened. I promise! You know that you will miss fighting with me! You have to admit its kind of fun. Who are you going to argue with when I'm dead?" She pleaded.

It was quite entertaining to Linda watching Samantha come up with her stories and desperate attempts to stop her. This day was actually becoming better after all, but the best was going to be the ending when Hagan Cove was reduced to ruble, and Samantha Marshall was dead!

"Come on Samantha, there are plenty of people out there that I can argue with! Give up the lame excuses! There is nothing worse than when you're about to kill someone and you have to listen to them plead for their life. Die with some dignity! There is nothing in this town worth saving! It's filled with pathetic, ignorant people that are just waiting for someone to put them out of their misery, and I'm going to be the one to do it!" Linda said, and then pushed the green button.

Samantha screamed and hit the floor, expecting an explosion, but nothing happened. Nothing but Silence. Linda cursed and hit the back of the device with her hand. She pushed it again, but once again nothing happened.

"No! You screwed me! I'll rip your heart out Alex!" she screamed as she threw the device at her image in the mirror.

---

Regina watched as the strange man walked off through the crowd. That's all they needed around this town was another city big shot coming here to tell them how to run the city. Linda Edwards was enough. Now with Dean dead she was on the prowl again, and the women in this town were not real comfortable about it either.

Another twenty minutes worth of floats passed down the street. People's cheers continued, their children laughing and playing. It was the perfect summer day. A loud applause roared through the spectators as she looked up and watched the pretty float with the winner of this year's town beauty pageant drive by. She waved and smiled. What a beautiful day, she thought to herself. Then suddenly there was a loud roar and an explosion as buildings blew up all over the town square, bricks and glass flew through the air, hitting and killing people everywhere. The street ripped open as flames and thick black smoke engulfed everything in sight.

The explosion shook and busted windows everywhere. Captain Steve Willis looked in horror in his back mirror at the flames roaring into the skyline behind him just as his vehicle was knocked into the large stone pillar standing along the drive of Ridgecliffe Manor. His head lay on the steering wheel, causing the horn to blast continuously.

Blood from the large gape in his forehead flowed down over his closed eyes. Inside the mangled mess of the mansion there was dead silence.

The explosion was so loud it rung the church bells in Fayette as the eastern sky filled with a black thick smoke. The townspeople all walked around in a daze trying to figure out if there had been an earthquake. All of them except for the man sitting on the park bench outside the post office. He looked at his watch and smiled. The crazy bitch actually went through with it!

Alex got up and went inside of the post office. A large man looked at him as he entered and then looked back out the window at the rising smoke. Alex looked for the designated box as the man came up to him, without saying anything handed him a key and quickly walked out. Just like she promised, there was the cashiers check. He smiled as he went back outside into the now smoke covered day.

"Burn in hell Hagan Cove," he said to himself as he drove off. Everyone in that town deserved to die. They had treated his brother like dirt, ultimately causing him to kill himself. They had never really got along with them being on opposite sides of the law, but family blood has to stick together. Now revenge was his! It just happened to be his luck that he ran into his brother's crazy girlfriend. He glanced down at the cashier's check and smiled. "I would have done it for free. This one was for you Dean! Rest in peace bro."

Alex's old car drove out of town and turned on the highway. Florida was great this time of year, he thought with a smile. Several fire trucks passed on the opposite lane heading to the inferno that was once Hagan Cove. He looked in his mirror at the thick black sky that towered behind him. It almost looked like night. He laughed again and proceeded forward. Revenge on the town that destroyed his family and pushed him out had just made his life complete.

# Chapter 31 - The final battle.

The explosion had shattered several of the windows, cracked the plaster, and knocked pictures off the walls, Samantha noticed as she dizzily got up off the floor and looked around. She stuck her fingers in her ears and shook them about, trying to stop the ringing that the explosion had caused. Linda was getting up at the same time, laughing about what she had just done.

"My God Linda! What did you do?" Samantha yelled at her as she pushed the drapes aside and looked out the window at the black smoke filling the skyline over the trees. She pushed herself away from the window and ran into the hallway and tried to open the front doors.

"Won't open, will they?" Linda smiled, walking into the hallway holding a key in one hand and a glass jar in another. "I have another surprise for you. Good thing it didn't break in the explosion!"

"What ever it is I don't want it!" she screamed out as she ran from the door and started up the stairs, scolding herself as she did. "Why didn't she run through the library and out one of the back doors?" she thought to herself.

"Don't run away from me you bitch! I'm not finished with you yet!" Linda yelled as she threw the glass jar, just barely missing her as it splattered all down the wall.

Samantha did not look back to see what it was, but she could hear it sizzling behind her. She reached the second floor and continued up to the third floor, remembering that there was a window on the third floor hallway that led to a back fire escape off the roof. That is if it was still there. "She hadn't been as dumb as she thought she was," she thought to herself as she ran up the back servants stairs that led to the third floor.

Once into the large third floor hallway she ran to the back escape window only to find it padlocked shut. Unfortunately the glass had not broken out during the explosion. She sighed in frustration as she ran to the closest bedroom door. As soon as she opened it she gasp in horror at what was in the bed before her.

In shock, she slipped across the hard wood floor to the bed, starring off in disbelief. Dean's decaying corpse lie as though he were asleep. Linda had not lied! She really did steal the body. On the floor below she heard Linda ravishing around down there hollering her name, ordering her to come to here. Like she would really just stop fighting for her life and run to her.

"Oh Dean! What has she done to you? I'm so sorry I couldn't stop her. If only you would have listened to me things would have not gone this far. I promise you, I'm going to stop her this time. I don't know how yet, but I will. I promise I won't let you down again. And you will get a proper burial. You have my word," she whispered to him.

Samantha walked quietly back across the room and out into the hall. She opened the door to the ballroom just as Linda stomped up the back stairs. She screamed and ran into the room, slamming the door and locking it. Linda was soon laughing outside the door as Samantha put all her weight against it for extra protection to keep her out.

"So I guess you saw Dean really is here, didn't you," Linda said out in the hallway, noticing that the bedroom door was open. "He does love me more than you. Poor pitiful you. Nobody loves you."

"Give it up Linda; you're never going to be able to lie your way out of this one! You went too far this time!" Samantha yelled at her.

"No you give it up. I'll just say that before you died, you tried to frame me because you blamed me for Dean's death. I know it's missing something, but it will sound much better in court coming from my lawyer. Oh, by the way, if you're going to do what I think you're planning to do forget it!"

Linda started to tell her there is no way out of there but decided to let her find out herself. There was a roof door in there but it had been sealed shut because it was leaking. The only way out was out the door or plunge three stories to the ground. Linda preferred the latter for her.

"You might as well give up Samantha, there is no way out!" Linda screamed as she raised the hatchet she was holding and slammed it into the middle of the door. She heard Samantha scream from inside the ballroom.

Samantha dropped to her knees in pain from the fresh wound in her back where the top corner of the blade had gone through the door and grazed into her shoulder. She could feel warm blood soaking her shirt. The hatchet was pulled out and crashed into the door repeatedly until there was a hole big enough for Linda to slip her hand through it and unlock the lock.

Samantha picked herself up and ran to the set of windows facing the front yard. All the glass had been shattered by the blast as the drapes blew frantically in the wind. She raised the window frame and started to climb out on to the two foot hidden gutter system that ran completely around the house.

"Oh look, the ballroom. One of my favorite rooms in the house. Isn't the wallpaper just beautiful? I picked it out myself," Linda said, looking around the damaged room, and then looking down to the fresh blood on the floor. "Look what you did! You got blood all over my freshly waxed floor! You are going to pay for that! Poor Stella worked for days on this floor!"

"Stay away from me!" Samantha screamed through the broken window as she pulled her legs through, ignoring the terrible pain in her shoulder.

"Samantha damn it! I don't have time for this crap! If I would have known we were going to do all this climbing I would have not worn heels!" Linda yelled out as she ran to the window. "Get in here now!"

"Linda, stop!" A male voice yelled from the hallway. He was leaning against the broken door covered in his own blood. He was breathing very heavy.

"Steve!" Linda said in shock, turning around and seeing him. "What in the hell are you doing here?"

Samantha continued along the ledge around the corner of the house and looked inside the other broken window. She saw Linda halfway out the window and some man named Steve all bloody in the doorway! Oh God! It was that guy from the Kansas City police department. The one she had written to after she received all those clippings from the newspaper!

"Help me! Officer, it's me Samantha! I'm the one who wrote to you! She blew up the town, now she's trying to kill me!" She screamed into the broken window.

"I did not know you two knew each other. Isn't that just great? Any other surprises I need to know about Samantha!" She yelled angrily to her as she got out of the window and climbed back into the room. Slowly she started walking towards him smiling, but his eyesight was distorted from the head wound.

"Linda, what in the hell have you done now?" He asked, his voice quivering.

"Nothing. Why didn't you call me and tell me you were coming, I could have picked you up at the airport," she replied, continuing her slow walk towards him, the hatchet hidden behind her back. "You know I don't like surprises!"

"Look out! She's got a hatchet!" Samantha screamed to him.

The handle of the hatchet smashed upside his head, knocking him to the floor before Samantha's scream could give him enough warning. Linda dropped the hatchet, turned toward the window, and ran fast, exploding through the wood casing and into Samantha's body with a powerful force. Both women crashed down onto the roof of the second floor wing extension on the side of the house.

Linda pulling herself up off Samantha punched her in the face, knocking her back down on the roof before she had time to try to defend herself.

"Not so powerful now, are you Samantha!" Linda yelled grabbing her by the head and dragging her across the roof to the edge. She took a deep breath and started to lift her up over the metal ornate rail that lined the roof.

"Let go of me!" Samantha screamed as she kicked Linda in the stomach, knocking her away.

She put her leg over the rail and started to lower herself down the roof to the gutter ledge, holding on to the roof rail as she did.

"Get off my house!" Linda yelled as she came at her again and started prying her hands off the rail.

Samantha's body slid quickly down the slope of the second floor roof to the hidden gutter and over the edge, leaving her dangling. She tried to push herself up to the ledge but her body was so sore and weak that she didn't have the strength. Overhead she could hear Linda climbing down the roof and landing on the ledge like she had planned to do.

"Give me your hand. I'll pull you up!" Linda ordered. With one hand grabbing Samantha's hand and pulling her forward, she used the other to hold on to the window casing for support so Samantha did not pull her off the ledge.

Samantha, having no other choice, gave it to her and was surprised as Linda started pulling her up and on to the ledge until she was standing beside her, leaning against the roof tiles like Linda was. Both women were out of breath as they looked at the smoke filled skyline that was once Hagan Cove.

"Why did you just do that?" Samantha managed in between breaths. "Why did you pull me up?"

"Because if you fell dangling like that you probably would have landed on your feet like a cat. Might have just broken your leg. But if you were to fall sideways, there is a good chance you would die. Like this!" Linda said, and then pushed Samantha backward off the ledge.

Samantha screamed and grabbed a hold of Linda. Both women fell from the second story landing into one of the overgrown bushes beside the house. The two women struggled and fought inside the bush as the sharp branches tore into their skin. Linda punched her again, this time knocking her out of the bush and on to the hard ground. She then managed to pull herself out and stand up over her, breathing hard. Samantha looked up in terror as Linda bent over and grabbed a large rock, holding it directly over her head.

"Time to meet your maker!" Linda yelled her eyes large and her breathing rapid. "The pleasure is all mine!"

"Put the rock down, you sick bitch!" Valerie yelled as she fired a warning shot from the porch rail that she was slumped over for support, her head bobbing back and forth from dizziness.

"What now!" Linda yelled looking over at the house at Valerie holding on the post. "Don't you people ever die around here?"

"I said drop the rock now. Do not make me repeat myself again bitch!" Valerie ordered.

"No!" Linda screamed and then started to smash the rock on Samantha's face just as another shot was fired from the gun.

The rock fell to the ground, just barely missing Samantha's head before Linda fell beside it. Her eyes were wide and ferocious as her body shook. She had her hand on her side where the bullet hole was oozing blood. Words were pouring out of her mouth, but they were not comprehensible. Samantha crawled as far away from Linda as her body would push her and then collapsed exhausted.

"Kill her!" Samantha screamed to Valerie. "Shoot her again! You have to kill her!"

"No! I want her alive! She has to answer for what she did," Valerie yelled as she collapsed on the porch floor, barely able to hold on to the gun.

"She'll just get away with it like she always does!" Samantha pleaded. "Stop her now!"

"Not this time!" Valerie managed to say. "We got her!"

In the distance sirens could be heard leading down the gravel road towards them. Samantha let out a sigh just as the tears began to roll out uncontrollably. The cars roared up, coming to a screeching halt. Doors opened and cops jumped out.

"Thank you God!" Samantha whispered as she let her head fall to the ground. "It is finally over!"

Samantha awoke, painfully turning her head around looking at the paramedics. They were carrying her on a cot over to a large shade tree on the side of the house away from all the commotion. One of the men washed her bruises and asked her questions about pains in other parts of her body. He told her they only had one ambulance to transport everyone in because most of them were on their way to what was left of Hagan Cove. Since she was hurt she would need to be taken in a cruiser as soon as possible. Valerie was the first to be taken and was now on her way to the Boonville Hospital. Samantha sighed with relief when she was told that her friend who had saved her life was going to be all right.

"How are you doing?" Steve asked as he hobbled over to her. His clothes were covered with dried blood, his head was heavily bandaged.

He looked like he had been in a war. "I don't think we have been formally introduced. I'm Captain Steve Willis."

"I'm Samantha Marshall, and thanks to you I think I'll survive. You on the other hand look like a mummy," she said with a slight painful laugh.

"I feel like one. She got me pretty good in the head," he said, placing his right hand over the bandage and rubbing it gently.

"Where is she?" Samantha asked, looking around in fear to make sure Linda Edwards was no where near her. "Is she still here?"

"Relax; they already took her away to Boonville. She'll never be back. Thanks to you and your friend, she won't be hurting anyone again," he said as he slowly sat beside her, leaning against the trunk of the tree for support.

"Maybe in real life, but I will carry her around in my nightmare for the rest of my life," Samantha said, staring off towards Hagan Cove and the black cloud of smoke that still rose above it. "Is there anything left?"

"I don't know. I had just reached the main gates when it exploded. The blast knocked my car into that stone pillar down there," he said, looking in the direction of his car.

"I can't believe she really did it! Who called the police? Someone had to let them know we were here," she asked, looking at him.

"I think they said your friend did," he replied softly as he watched her eyes fill with tears. "I thought Linda was in trouble and I busted through the front door. I heard you two arguing upstairs so I went directly up there. You know what happened from there. I awoke when these guys showed up and started pulling and tugging on me. Sorry I wasn't much help."

Steve noticed her body suddenly stiffen and her face go completely pale. He looked over and followed her stare to see what had affected her so badly. Two men were carrying a large black body bag out the front doors and off the porch. They placed it into the back of the station wagon and shut the door. It must have been the body of the man that he had seen upstairs.

An officer came over and told him they were ready to transport them to the hospital. Steve slowly got up using the tree trunk for support while the paramedic helped Samantha up off the cot, after refusing to be carried over to the police car.

Samantha got in and watched as Steve climbed in beside her and silently took her hand. As the car took off down the drive she leaned into his arms and cried all the way to the hospital. It suddenly hit her that everyone she knew and loved was most likely dead.

Steve held her tightly but did not speak as he just allowed himself to drift off into his own personal thoughts. Why did he not see it earlier? If he had been doing his job instead of trying to get closer to her, none of this would have ever happened. All those innocent people would still be alive celebrating the holiday. He felt so stupid that he let Linda pull the wool over his eyes. Thinking of all the people she had murdered over the years and some of them were right under his nose.

Why had he not seen it! It was all there right before him in black and white. Not only did she make him look bad, but she made his whole office look like those foolish cops in those silent black and white movies that used to run around like chickens with their heads cut off. She was a master of deception. A real evil genius. At least now she would be going to where no one would ever be hurt by her again. If it hadn't been for Samantha's persistence she may have never been caught. Thanks to her, Linda was going to get what she deserved!

## Chapter 32 - Picking up the pieces.

Samantha glanced with disbelief out the window as she drove into town. The closer she got the more destruction she saw. It had been three weeks since the blast and she finally had gotten the nerve to come back and say good bye. Brad and Valerie had tried to convince her to let them come with her, but she had told them she needed to do this alone. Now she wished she had let them. Maybe this was not such a good idea after all. She could feel her stomach turn to knots as she got closer. Newspapers from all over the world had flooded to the area to tell their version of what they thought really happened. The sad thing was most of them did not even come close.

Linda Edwards, despite all the murders and destruction she had caused, had somehow managed to get the public's sympathy. She was an instant celebrity. Her picture was on the cover of almost every magazine in print. There was even talk of a movie being made about her with top actresses fighting over the chance to play her. It was sad that she lived in a world that made heroes out of cold-blooded killers! "And people wondered why crime was so high in America today," she thought to herself. Unfortunately, crime was glamorized and being honest and sincere was downplayed. The real heroes were the innocent people in that quiet little town that died because of Linda Edwards

Already several people had come to her and Valerie trying to get their story for TV movies and shows. The money they offered was unreal, but despite her financial difficulties she would not break down and sell out. What really happened here was so bad that no movie could ever bring it out well enough. She just hoped that no one would ever have to relive the terror on television or real life.

Samantha pulled the car up to the barricade that was made by the armed forces that had been called in to keep the press, sightseers and looters away. She showed him her driver's license that proved she was a resident and watched as he took it, wrote down her name and address and told her to proceed with caution. Bulldozers had moved most of the debris out of the middle of the road and piled it all along the side of the streets. It looked like a tornado had ripped through town. On this end of the town a lot of the buildings were still standing but had been knocked off the foundations by the blast, making them dangerous. Most of the victim's families were moving the furniture and personal belongings that were left out of them now so they could be demolished. Once everything was out a large orange X was placed on the building, letting them know it was ready for demolition.

A large barricade and armed forces covered the entire street about a block ahead, headed up by a large yellow sign warned people to keep out. From there not only was the destruction too bad to enter, but there were also still people searching for missing bodies that most likely would never be found. Most of the people in town were totally destroyed and nothing was left behind to find. They said in the newspaper that the blast caused a new channel in the Missouri river. It was now running through what was the down town, making the search for bodies even more difficult.. She had no desire to go over there. Just seeing this was bad enough. Samantha sniffed and turned on the road that she had drove on so many times before, and parked in the parking spot where Dean used to park his jeep.

She looked up at the two story building that stood before her. It like all the others around here did not have a single piece of glass left in it. There was a big yellow X on the building with numbers on it, which meant that it had been searched and the survivors and the bodies of those who didn't had been removed. Quietly she walked up the flight of stairs to the apartment and stopped. Half of her wanted to turn and leave, but the other half needed to stay. The door had been kicked in apparently when the building was being searched and was now just pulled closed.

Samantha pushed it open. As she entered she was overwhelmed by the loneliest, emptiest feeling she had ever felt. She looked around at the room of Dean's apartment where they had gathered so many times; Brad, and Val, Dean, and her and watching Sunday football and arguing over which team was better. The ghost of their laughter filled her ears as she looked over at the broken television. She would give anything to be able to do that again.

A slight gust of wind blew in the broken sliding glass door that led to the balcony, causing the blinds to rattle. The apartment was in shambles. It looked like someone had done more than search for survivors in here. She proceeded forward into the apartment looking around and wiping the tears from her eyes.

A quiet crunch ripped under her feet as she walked further into the room. She bent over, and picked up the picture, dropped to her knees and clutched it to her chest as she cried harder than she ever had, everything that had happened the last few months completely caught up with her. Oh God, she missed him. The hole in her heart was bigger than the one downtown. She wiped her tears, took the picture of her and her three best friends and closed the door. She had to leave now while she had the strength. She still had one more stop to make before it got dark. Since the explosion almost the entire county had been without lights and gas. It was an eerie place to be here during the day; she could not imagine what it must look like at night. Not to mention there was a curfew, making it illegal to be in the city limits after dusk.

The car turned with a creak as she made a u turn in the middle of the road and left Hagan Cove. The drive out to Ridgecliffe Manor brought back the memories of that last day before life as she knew it ended. She pulled the car into park as she got out; pushed open the old iron gates, returned to the car and started up the drive.

The mansion looked colder and more sinister than it ever had before. All the windows were boarded up tightly with plywood to keep people out until Linda's estate was settled, which from what she had heard could be years. Several families of the victims were suing her estate, and by the time they all got through Linda Edwards would not have a dime. The once beautiful plants that hung from the porch roof had died after being neglected for the past three weeks. She wondered if they left all the furniture and Linda's jewelry inside before they sealed the place up.

Samantha got out of the car and sat on the hood, looking up at the place that had caused her so much grief. It was time she took the bull by the horns and conquered it. This evil pile of bricks was the cause of all those men dying! Of Dean's death and the end of life in Hagan Cove! This horrible place. This was where it all started! If only it had not existed Linda Edwards would have never come here. If only her company had not advertised in that nation wide homes magazine she would have never known it was here.

"This place should be burnt to the ground, and demolished. Nothing good comes from this here!" She said out loud to herself.

A slight breeze caught her hair and blew it in her face. Would things ever get back to normal? She slid off the car and started to get in but something made her feel like she should turn around. Something or someone was watching her. Quickly she turned around, her mouth dropped open and tears once again filled her eyes.

Dean stood on the front porch leaning on the post smiling at her! He was wearing his usual sheriff's uniform, his shirt had the sleeves rolled up like he always did. She smiled and started towards the house. It was so good to see him. She stopped at the bottom of the steps and looked at him. His brown eyes were no longer sad and empty, but happy. He smiled to her again, showing his perfect white teeth. He held his finger to his lips and blew her a kiss, then turned around and walked back into the house, going through the plywood as though it wasn't there.

"Dean, stop! Please come back, don't leave me, please!" She cried, banging her fists on the wood.

Samantha unsuccessfully pried with her fingers to try to loosen the board. Glancing around she searched desperately for something to pry it open. She beat on it again, begging for Dean to come back out to talk to her, to hold her.

A sudden brisk of wind blew past her and she heard him whisper in her ear, "I love you." She smiled through her tears and sat on the porch. Maybe she should buy this place? Then she would forever be with Dean.

*the Murderess of* RIDGECLIFFE MANOR

Who was she kidding; she didn't have a dime to her name. No, she had to leave. It was time to say good bye.

"Good bye, Dean," she said softly as she got up and started down the steps.

A sudden peaceful feeling swept through her body and she knew that leaving was the right choice. She had to move on and staying here would just hold her back. As she reached the car and opened the door she looked one last time at the boarded up mansion. It no longer looked evil. Dean was there now. It was his home. He had always liked this crazy place. Even when they were kids this place fascinated him. Now it was his forever. She smiled as she got in the car and drove off. This would be the last time she would ever be here again, she thought to herself.

Samantha drove across the river to Boonville where she was staying in a house that Brad had been fortunate enough to find. With all the people who were left homeless, houses for sale or rent were impossible to find no matter what price range. She pulled the car to a halt and jumped out, anxious to see her friends. They were all three very lucky to be alive. They had survived!

"Are you okay?" Brad asked as he greeted her at the front door, giving her a hug.

"Fine," she said as she hugged him tightly. "I'm fine."

"Did you take care of what you needed to do?" He asked with concern.

"Yes, I did," she said smiling. "What's going to happen with Dean's things out of the apartment?"

"Valerie and I are going to get everything out and take care of it this weekend. Was there something you wanted?" He asked as they walked into the living room.

"I have everything I need," she said as she sat down and put the picture on the table.

"It's about time you got here! Brad's been about to drive me crazy! I don't know what I'm going to do after you leave for Kansas City tomorrow. You are still going, aren't you?" Valerie asked as she came in from the kitchen.

"Yes I am, but boy am I going to miss you two," she said laughing.

"Are you sure you really want to go? I mean, Linda's mark will be up there too," he reminded her.

Brad had told himself he would not interfere in her decision but it wasn't going to be easy. Staying here was going to be hard on everyone and they needed each other to get through this. He watched as her and Valerie rambled on. Though he wouldn't show it or admit, a piece of him was dying.

"I'm not leaving to get away from her. I could never get away from her. Unfortunately I will always carry a part of her with me forever. It's just that in the few weeks we were together Steve and I really bonded. I think I want to explore it some more. I let Dean get away, but I think I might try to grab on to this one. See what happens. I somehow have this feeling he would approve," Samantha told them, almost laughing.

During Samantha's recovery captain Steve Willis had been a rock to her, helping her through all her physical therapy and the mental anguish she was going through. She really had to give him credit for her fast recovery. If there was anything good that came from all this tragedy it was to allow love to come in when it comes knocking. You never know if it will come back.

"Well more power to you! Besides, there are no good ones around here left, not that there was much to begin with," Valerie joked, giving Samantha a great big hug.

"What about me?" Brad spoke up loudly.

"Brad, I think Val's saving you for herself!" Samantha joked.

"Bite your tongue! What on God's green earth would I want that sorry excuse for a man," she said as she punched him in the gut. "Look, he even lets me beat him up!"

"Owe that hurt!" He joked.

"Oh baby I'm sorry, did I mess up your sprayed on abs?" She pouted and gave him an air kiss.

"Oh yeah!" Brad said as he wrestled her to the floor and tickled her, careful not to hit her gunshot wound.

The rest of the night the three of them talked, laughed, and cried together into the wee hours of the night. Things were going to get back to normal, Samantha thought to herself as she anxiously tried to go to sleep. She had to get up early to meet Steve. She was going to miss them desperately but she had to go to Kansas City. Just thinking about Steve made her heart skip. No one but Dean had been able to do that before and she was sure he would approve; after all, they were a lot alike. She smiled as a single tear slid out of the corner of her eye.

# The Epilogue

The crisp fallen leaves crunched under her bare feet as she was drug forward into the night, the wind whipping fiercely around her, its iciness hitting her flesh like a wet strap. This could not be happening again! It had been almost a year since the last nightmare. Now it was back and it could only mean that Linda Edwards was back too! The unseen force like so many times before pulled her forward despite her resistance. Through the clearing of brush she was able to see a large brick structure ahead.

"No! It can't be that house again! Please no!" She pleaded.

Instant relief filled her as she got closer and realized it wasn't Ridgecliffe Manor. Curiously she walked up the concrete steps and opened the metal doors and stepped in. The relief feeling she had earlier was now replaced with confusion? Where was she? The building she entered looked like a school hallway with many doors. The walls were painted an ugly shade of light green. She went down the hall to a set of stairs that entered into the basement level.

Subconsciously she knew she should not go down there, but she felt compelled to do so as if she really did not have a choice! Step by step she proceeded down until she entered a short hallway with two double steel doors that read "No Admittance- Psychiatric Ward." She moved closer and touched them; they were very warm.

"What is this?" She asked out loud as she pushed on the doors. To her surprise they opened.

Instantly she was overwhelmed by an odor of rot and decay. She tried to turn and run back up the stairs but her body moved forward, as she did the florescent bulbs overhead flipped on like magic. The sudden light exposed a ghastly sight. Bloody handprints and smears were all over the walls along with two large puddles of blood on the square tiled floor. She quickly moved forward, hoping to find a way out, but it only led her to more stomach turning sights. What looked to be the nurse's station was covered with the corpses of nurses even a few patients. They were so bloody and chopped up it was hard to tell who was who.

Samantha screamed and ran as fast as she could down the rest of the hall turning around the corner and running into a closed door. All the blood rushed from her face as her eyes grew large and her knees started to buckle. On the door was the name of Linda Edwards! She reached with her hand and touched it.

Instantly it exploded into thousands of little pieces, the force sucking her into the room where she was thrown into complete darkness. Linda's sadistic laughter erupted all around her. She flipped her head around, expecting Linda to appear at any minute. Then lost her balance and fell to the floor. On her hands and knees she crawled until she bumped into a wall and used it as a guide to stand up. She felt around the darkness for a door. Slowly she reached for the knob and turned it, scared of what it might reveal.

The door opened allowing a bright light to burst in, blinding her. She could hear soft violin music in the background but could not see anything. The room came into focus just as the door slammed shut behind her and latched. She was in the decayed remains of the dining room at Ridgecliffe Manor. The windows were boarded up so she could not see out, but the large chandelier lit the room, exposing the dining table which was covered with rotten moldy food.

An unseen force slowly moved all the chairs out from the table as ghostly figures appeared and started eating the old food. The more they ate the more real they became. Their features were distorted and decayed like the food they were eating. She suddenly realized that she knew some of them! There was Ray and a couple others. Duke was in the corner playing the screeching violin music that made her head hurt.

"Well, well, you did make it! Gentlemen, doesn't Samantha look good? Still a little chunky though," Linda said as she entered the dining room through the back door.

Linda once again was dressed elegantly in a red evening dress, her hair meticulously done, as were her dark red fingernails. The men all looked up and acknowledged her presence, then went back to gorging themselves on the food.

"How long has it been? My gosh, about a year now huh? Can you believe how fast time flies when your incarcerated? I must say, you are definitely showing your age," Linda said as she went around patting the corpses on the head as if they were her children.

"Why are you doing this to me? Why can't you just leave me alone?" She screamed at her.

"Because I still owe you one, remember? You couldn't possibly think I would let you get away, did you? I always pay a debt. Hello my darling," she told the corpse that had his back to Samantha as she kissed his forehead.

"You do remember everyone here don't you, especially Dean."

Samantha stayed against the wall as she slid around the room to look at the corpse Linda was talking about. Sure enough, it was the remains of Dean! Samantha started to cry.

"Don't look at me like that! You're the one that killed him," Linda said as she crossed the room and ripped the remains of the drapes off the wall. She threw them on the floor and then took her fist and hit the plywood covering the window, sending the wood, splintering out the ground below. "I think there are some more people here to see you, take a look. Remember them?" Linda asked as she moved across the room away from the window knowing Samantha would not look with her standing there.

Slowly she moved towards the window, careful not to get too close to the table and the eating corpses. Outside the people who had died in the explosion was standing, swaying back and forth as far as her eyes could see. There must have been thousands of them.

"This is your destiny. You belong with them and they've come back for you!" Linda said as she picked up the large knife off the table and rushed towards her. Samantha screamed as the knife plunged into her body.

"Samantha, wake up!" She heard someone yell.

Samantha jumped up out of the bed screaming. She was so tangled up in the covers that she lost her balance and fell off the bed. Steve rushed to the other side of the bed and held her as she cried uncontrollably. She took in a deep breath and kissed him, holding onto him tightly. She relaxed as she realized she was back home in her house with her husband of six months.

"Are you all right? Do you want me to call a doctor?" He asked as he caressed her long hair.

"No! I'm fine, just a nightmare, that's all. I'm fine really. Is that breakfast I smell burning?" She asked.

"Awe shit!" He yelled, jumping up and running from the room.

The tension slipped from her body, quickly forgetting the nightmare she had just gone through. She thanked God every day for sending Steve to her. If it hadn't been for him she would have never survived this past year. She put her robe on and looked at her reflection in the mirror. Boy was she a scary sight! Steve must really love her.

Samantha picked up their wedding picture from last spring. If anything good happened from Linda's reign of terror it was her meeting Steve. It took her awhile to get back into it, but she was selling real estate again, this time in Kansas City. She had finally been able to move on from the past.

Unfortunately Hagan Cove had not. A few people had tried to rebuild the town, but they had not succeeded. An island had formed when the explosion caused the river to flood the remains of the town and it had been turned into a wildlife reserve. A monument had gone up to remember the town that was, but everything else was gone. Just a memory and the monument was all that remained. Valerie had met the man of her dreams and was living in Chicago and Brad was still playing the field in Columbia, mostly the ongoing new arrival of college girls every fall, and still selling houses. She decided she would call them tonight. She longed to hear their voices. She put the picture down and went into the kitchen to eat the breakfast her loving husband had made for her.

After a breakfast of burnt eggs and toast she showered and rushed to work. She loved her job and her coworkers were really nice, although they were not as much fun to work with as Brad and Val, but they were respectful and very helpful. She walked by the front desk, picked up her messages and sat in her own private office, a luxury she never had in Hagan Cove

"Samantha, can I ask a favor of you?" Judy asked, standing in the doorway.

"Sure what is it?" She asked her coworker.

"I have a showing at one that I tried to cancel, but the lady would not change it. She just had to see it today! I'm sure she won't buy the place, but you never know. Well anyway, the problem is that my son has a doctor's appointment at noon, and I don't think I'll be done in time, could you possibly show it for me? I would really appreciate it," she asked shyly.

"No problem. I don't have any appointments this afternoon anyway. It will give me something to do," Samantha smiled as she fibbed.

"Great! I owe you one. I'll give you all the information and directions before I leave," Judy said and left the office.

Samantha sighed and looked at her watch, trying to figure out what to do next. She had so much paperwork to do before her meeting with a new listing tomorrow. She liked to do lots of comparables and assist her clients on getting their homes ready for sell. With the market as bad as it was, every home had to be at the top of one's game. As she promised, Judy dropped everything by her office with directions and keys. The house was a pretty white colonial in the exclusive part of the city. She liked looking at those houses and dreaming someday that she and Steve might have one like them, but with Steve's minimal salary and with her still paying on a vacant lot in Hagan Cove along with establishing herself in town, it was doubtful it would happen any time soon. She grabbed her car keys and left.

Samantha sat in the car and waited for the potential buyers to show up. She hated it when people were late. It brought back chills as she remembered that afternoon she was waiting for Linda Edwards to look at Ridgecliffe Manor. She was shaking the thought as a black convertible pulled up the circular drive. Samantha's heart skipped a beat as a woman in a black tight dress with large white pearls stepped out. She had on large dark sunglasses and a large designer hat covering her hair.

"Oh God no! It can't be her!" She whispered to herself, her heart beating faster.

"Hello, you must be Judy," the woman said with a heavy southern accent as she held out her hand. "I'm Laura Lee."

*the Murderess of* RIDGECLIFFE MANOR

Samantha said hello and told her about Judy not being able to make it as she shook hands with her. She sighed as the woman took off her hat and her shoulder length red curls popped out. She almost burst out laughing. She was loosing her mind! Linda Edwards could not be free. She would know it, Steve would have told her. He would have been the first to know.

"It's a beautiful house," Samantha said as she led the woman to the top of the stairs.

"Yes, I know, I looked at it the other day. I just wanted my husband to see it. He should be here shortly. I hope you don't mind waiting," the woman asked.

Samantha gave her a confused look as her words sunk in. She was sure Judy had said this was the first time the lady had seen the place and even suggested it was a waste of time because she doubted she would buy the place.

"Samantha?" the woman spoke up interrupting her thoughts. "It is alright to wait isn't it?"

"Sure, no problem at all, shall we wait inside?" She asked as she unlocked the door and let her in.

The two women laughed and talked for about twenty minutes as they waited for Laura Lee's husband to arrive. Samantha relaxed and enjoyed talking to her. She loved her accent. But was a little suspicious that she never removed her sunglasses, even inside the house.

A small sports car pulled up the drive and a tall man got out.

"There he is. Hi sugar," Laura Lee said as she went over and kissed her husband.

"Sorry I'm late, got held up getting our plane tickets. I'm Dr. Edwin Addams, pleasure to meet you," he said, extending his hand to Samantha, and put the other hand around his wife's narrow waist.

"I'm Samantha Willis; it's a real pleasure to meet you. Are you going on a trip?" She asked casually as they started walking through the first floor of the house.

"Yes, Barbados, I really hate the Kansas City winters," Laura Lee said as she went upstairs.

Dr. Addams stayed downstairs and asked the usual questions, leaving his wife to investigate the second floor alone. He, like his wife, was very friendly.

"Darling, can you come here for a minute? I'd like to talk to you alone please," Laura Lee called out from the balcony.

"Excuse me," he said as he went upstairs and followed her into the master bedroom.

Samantha looked out the large picture window in the living room at the fall colors on the trees in the front yard. She had a real good feeling that these people were going to buy. She would have to split the commission with Judy, but as much as this place was going for it would still be a hefty check.

Laura Lee started coming down the steps with a very large suite case. She headed for the front door and then noticed the newspaper on the porch. Picking it up, she went into the living room and joined Samantha.

"Where did you get the suit case?" Samantha asked, puzzled.

"Just something I left behind," she said smiling. "I always loved the fall lighting in this room. Those red leaves from the maple trees always gave this room a spectacular coloring."

"Something you left behind the last time you looked at the house?" Samantha asked, confused.

"No silly, when I lived here," the woman said, taking off her sunglasses and loosing her accent as she opened the newspaper and looked at the front page. "You really didn't know it was me, did you?" She asked with a smile.

"It can't be! There's no way you could get out!" Samantha whispered.

"It is, and I did get out. Nothing or no one gets in my way. I must say though I was shocked to see you here today. I thought you would still be cleaning up the mess. What a nice surprise. And what's with this Samantha Willis crap? Don't tell me you and Steve got together. I thought he had better taste than that!" She said laughing.

"No! It can't be, it can't be, this is just another dream," Samantha kept saying over and over.

"Take a look," Linda said as she handed her the paper.

Samantha reached out and looked at the newspaper. The headline read "Convicted Murderess at Large after Institute Blood Bath." She dropped the paper and stared at Linda, her flaming red curls outlined her face as her piercing green eyes stared back at her.

"Amazing what hair color, contacts, and an accent can do, isn't it?" Linda laughed.

"Why did you come back here?" Samantha asked.

"Remember when I came back here the week before the big bang?" Linda asked as Samantha shook her head yes. "Well I withdrew a lot of cash and stashed it in the house here in case something failed and I needed money. No one asked questions because I had made it known that I was giving it to the city."

Linda smiled as she thought back to the days back in Hagan Cove. All the fun times she had there with Dean and the mansion. She had wiped all the bad stuff out of her mind. Life was too short to allow the past bring her down. She had a bright new future planned now, and no one was going to stop her.

"Poor Edwin upstairs," Linda continued. "He was dumb enough to believe me that I loved him. You should have seen me. My performance was grand, and he was a big help in getting me out of that awful hospital. The good doctor of course didn't stand a chance against me. Last week he liquidated his assets and if he did as he was told the money should be in the back of his car. We're off to a foreign country somewhere, or so he thought. Men! They will do anything for you. Don't you just love them?"

"Where are you going now?" Samantha asked in a daze.

"It's a beautiful little town that I saw it in a magazine. They have this large beautiful house there: I have an appointment to see it the day after tomorrow. You know, it's funny, the agent I talked to on the phone reminded me of you," Linda said as she smiled.

"You will never get away with killing me," Samantha said, trying to keep her knees from giving way and dropping her to the floor.

"Oh I think I would, but I'm not here to kill you. Besides, you would probably come back from the dead and haunt me. I'm going to leave, and if you value your life and everyone you ever knew, you will never mention that I was here. If you tell anyone, and trust me I will know if you did, I'll come back here and get you when you least expect it. I'll have nothing to loose but my freedom. Is that worth your life?" Linda said as she started towards the front door.

"You leave here and never get in contact with me or anyone I know again, or I swear, God as my witness, I will kill you!" Samantha told her through gritted teeth.

"I'm so scared," she laughed as she picked up the suitcase. "Tell my darling husband when he wakes up thanks for everything. Good bye Samantha. It's been a real pain in the ass knowing you."

Samantha watched as Linda put the suitcase in the trunk and opened the door to the car Dr. Addams had been driving. Linda pulled out another suitcase and put it in her car. She turned back towards the house and waved to Samantha, then started to walk around the car.

"Dr. Addams," Samantha called as she started up the stairs.

When he found out Linda walked off with all the money she would not have to worry about turning her in. Samantha was sure a man like Dr. Addams would never let Linda Edwards beat him out of money. She went into the master bedroom and expected to see him lying on the floor, but there was no sign of him.

"Dr. Addams!" She called out again as she walked into the room.

There was a noise behind a closed door in the master bath. She walked briskly over to it and threw it open. The doctor's body fell on her, splashing his fresh blood all over her face and body. Despite trying not to, she swallowed the blood in her mouth. Instantly she felt a soothing feeling pour through her body. She felt more alive than she had ever felt. She moved her lips over to the slit in his throat and drank. It took every once of strength she had to pull away as she let out a blood curling scream.

Outside by the car Linda could hear Samantha screaming. She laughed as she put her hat and glasses back on, climbed in the car and started the ignition.

"What a beautiful life!" Linda shouted as she laughed and pulled down the drive and out on to the street. "Look out South Carolina, here I come!"

## *The* END